TALES OF PANNITHOR: CLAWS ON THE PLAIN

James Dunbar

For Mairead and Martin.

TALES OF PANNITHOR: CLAWS ON THE PLAIN
By James Dunbar
Cover image by Mantic Games
Map created by Ciaran Morris
This edition published in 2025

Zmok Books is an imprint of

Winged Hussar Publishing, LLC
1525 Hulse Rd, Unit 1
Point Pleasant, NJ 08742

ISBN PB 978-1-950423-13-2
ISBN EB 978-1-958872-80-2
LCN 2025932971

Bibliographical References and Index
1. Fantasy. 2. Military. 3. Action & Adventure

For more information
visit us at www.whpsupplyroom.com
Twitter: WingHusPubLLC
Facebook: Winged Hussar Publishing LLC

An Introduction to Pannithor

The world of Pannithor is a place of magic and adventure, but it is also beset by danger in this, the Age of Conflict. Legions of evil cast their shadow across the lands while the forces of good strive to hold back the darkness. Between both, the armies of nature fight to maintain the balance of the world, led by a demi-god from another time.

Humanity is split into numerous provinces and kingdoms, each with their own allegiances and vendettas. Amongst the most powerful of all is the Hegemony of Basilea, with its devout army that marches to war with hymns in their hearts and the blessings of the Shining Ones, ready to smite those they deem as followers of the Wicked Ones.

Meanwhile, the Wicked Ones themselves toil endlessly in the depths of the Abyss to bring the lands of men to their knees. Demons, monsters, and other unspeakable creatures spill forth from its fiery pits to wreak havoc throughout Pannithor.

To the north of the Abyss, the Northern Alliance holds back the forces of evil in the icy depths of the Winterlands. Led by the mysterious Talannar, this alliance of races guards a great power to stop it from being grasped by the followers of the Wicked Ones. For if it ever did, Pannithor would fall under into darkness.

In the south, the secretive Ophidians remain neutral in the battles against the Abyss but work toward their own shadowy agenda. Their agents are always on-hand to make sure they whisper into the right ear or slit the right throat.

Amongst all this chaos, the other noble races – dwarfs, elves, salamanders and other ancient peoples – fight their own pitched battles against goblins, orcs and chittering hordes of rat-men, while the terrifying Nightstalkers flit in and out of existence, preying on the nightmares of any foolish enough to face them.

The world shakes as the armies of Pannithor march to war…

Pannithor Timeline

-1100: First contact with the Celestians

Rise of the Celestians

-170: The God War

0: Creation of the Abyss

2676: Birth of modern Basilea, and what is known as the Common Era.

3001: Free Dwarfs declare their independence

3558: Golloch comes to power

3850: The expansion of the Abyss

Ascent of the Goblin King

Tales of Pannithor: Edge of the Abyss

3854: The flooding of the Abyss, the splintering of the Brotherhood, and Lord Darvled completing part of the wall on the Ardovikian Plains.

Drowned Secrets

Nature's Knight

Claws on the Plain

Free Dwarfs expelled from their lands.

3865: Free Dwarfs begin the campaign to free Halpi – the opening of Halpi's Rift.

3865: The Battle of Andro; *Steps to Deliverance*

Pious takes place six months before the events in *Steps to Deliverance.*

Hero Falling and *Faith Aligned* take place several weeks after the events of *Steps to Deliverance.*

Honor's Price begins in early spring and ends in late August.

Pride of a King starts in the winter of 3865, but most of the events take place in 3866.

3866: Halflings leave the League of Rhordia.

Broken Alliance

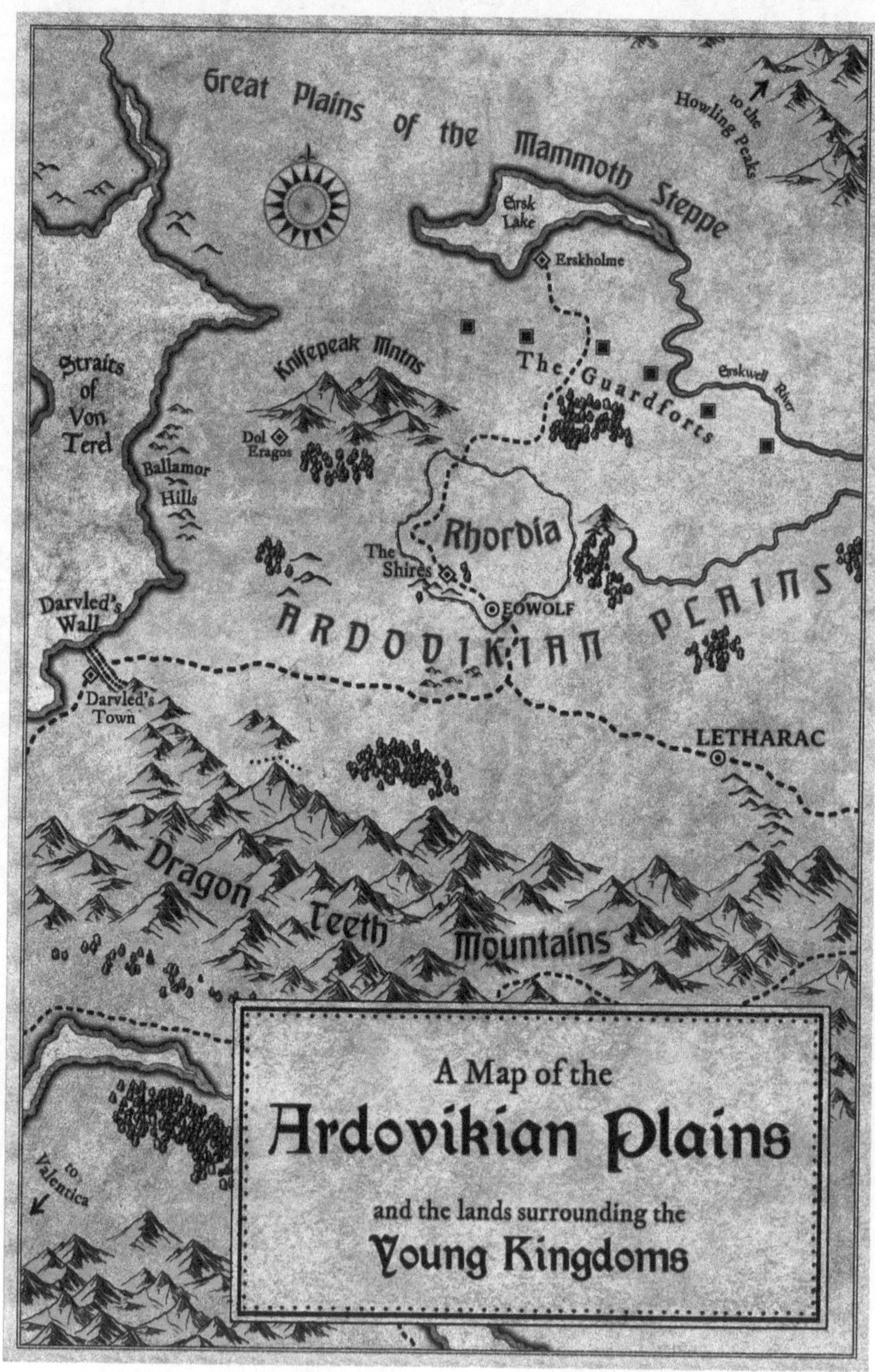
Great Plains of the Mammoth Steppe
to the Howling Peaks
Ersk Lake
Erskholme
Straits of Von Terel
Knifepeak Mntns
The Guardforts
Erskwell River
Dol Eragos
Ballamor Hills
Rhordia
The Shires
EOWOLF
Darvled's Wall
ARDOVIKIAN PLAINS
Darvled's Town
LETHARAC
Dragon Teeth Mountains
to Valentica
A Map of the
Ardovikian Plains
and the lands surrounding the
Young Kingdoms

Sleep, sweet child,
make full your nightly dream,
lest the dark be empty,
its void to stalk and teem.

Taken from a lullaby of the Southern Kindred elves, translated to the common by Drusus Messor

Prologue

Darkness had long since fallen, and the town of Keatairn lay still. Silence nestled over the slopes of the surrounding valley, drowning out the trickling of its many streams. The near cloudless sky above left little for the wind to hassle, and so it weaved listlessly among the houses, drifting along narrow streets and narrower back alleys. Its journey produced no sound, not even the rattle of a loose shutter. Light from the still waxing moon glittered softly on slated roofs, and it was enough to impart the illusion of shimmering motion to tired eyes. Such eyes may nevertheless have discerned a hint of Keatairn's usual vibrancy, the unexpectedly grand houses these roofs sheltered leading the onlooker to wonder at the lavish materials used in their construction, at the scale of the town's entrance square, at the splendor of its high-spired temple. But Keatairn was still. If it was not the stillness of death, it was, at the very least, the absence of life.

From far away, a roll of thunder buffeted the outer edge of this peaceful void, spilling over the hills and echoing dully through the valley. Its presence was a mystery, a riddle to which the sky offered no answer, and to which the valley paid no interest. Silence resumed, and the valley remembered nothing. Some time later – perhaps minutes, perhaps hours – the thunder returned, bursting across the landscape with a resounding boom, its presence sustaining stubbornly. The enduring waves of sound were punctuated by unnatural cadences, roars and shouts and wails. To this cacophony was added a steady rhythm, a regimented pounding that grew louder with each pulse. Lights began to appear over the northern hills, flickering like fireflies glimpsed through long grass. In the space of minutes, a dozen lights became a hundred, became a thousand, and the roaring sound was raised to a level unthinkable only moments past. With ravenous speed, the army poured down into the valley, making straight for Keatairn.

To the southwest, in the twisted mouth of a cave set into the valley's tallest hillside – for there are no mountains among the Ballamor Hills, far-flung range on the Ardovikian Plain – something stirred. The shape of the opening was small and awkward, a full head shorter than the average man, and narrow. One after another, two figures emerged from its gloom. The darkness of their cowled robes gave the brief impression of ethereal apparitions, as if shadows had formed in mockery of man. They moved slowly to the top of the narrow stone steps that wove their way down the hillside. Hands emerged, hands of flesh and blood, and reached up to pull back their owners' hoods, revealing harrowed faces beneath. Their heads were clean-shaven, and their beards were long. Neither could be younger than forty. They took one quick look at each other before embracing the panorama before them. From here, one could see the whole valley and the dominating sprawl of Keatairn at its southern end. At the foot of the hill, a short distance from the southern gate, the stone steps joined the old road – although in truth, such a joining was barely acknowledged by the thoroughfare, artery of wealth and flagstone, plunging southward with self-importance and utter disdain for the cautious trail of stone steps. It was a trail the pair had walked many times.

They looked to the north. The advance of the lights had slowed somewhat, no doubt as the invaders poured over the empty farmlands that clung to the web of waterways on their way to join the river. It would not be long till the horde reached the unattended north palisade, breaching its scant resistance and laying waste to their childhood home, eventually discovering the steps and the cave. But there was enough time, should they go now. They could descend the ancient steps, mount the old road, and evade their doom. For a while, at least. But as they looked out upon the tide of destruction that approached, no such thoughts crossed their minds.

The first to have emerged turned to face the other.

*****

"It is time," said Urien. He began walking back to the cave, expecting his companion to follow. He glanced back after several steps and stopped.

"Sevan?"

Sevan turned with a start. "Hm? Yes?"

"I said that it is time." Sevan's eyes showed him to be far away, and it took some moments before the meaning of the words reached him.

"Ah. Of course. My apologies, Urien. It's just..." He looked back to the valley, took it all in one last time, before turning to follow. Urien watched him approach, sympathy weighing on his heart for his friend of many years. And, he admitted, for himself. Theirs was a duty that few would envy, and fewer still would understand.

He waited for Sevan to catch up before continuing to the cave, leading the way. "I feel the same," he said. "You know I do."

He was just about to duck into the opening when he felt a hand on his shoulder. He stopped again, and turned to face Sevan. His companion had his eyes on the ground and a strained look on his face.

"What is it?"

"This is a mistake." Sevan blurted the words out clumsily, as if they had to fight their way free. Urien blinked. It was among the last things he would have expected from the mouth of a Keeper, and for a moment, he could not comprehend. Then Sevan raised his eyes, and Urien saw fear. Irritation flared in his chest and leapt for his tongue.

"This again? Now?! Sevan, we all agreed, *you* agreed. The vote was unanimous!" Sevan looked away, his face flush with shame. He pressed on, however, despite Urien's reaction.

"If we were to use it instead, it might give us a chance... and not just us, perhaps all of Pannithor..."

"What *are* you talking about?"

"I mean, we've all heard the stories. The Abyss expanding, goblins swarming over Galahir, and now the greatest orc invasion the Plains have ever seen!" As he spoke, his voice grew in confidence, each word adding a new layer of assuredness. Perspiration glistened on his face despite the cool night air. "Perhaps Lucol was right? Perhaps this is the end?"

Concern now replaced irritation. Sevan was clearly panicking, and Urien needed him calm.

"Look at me." His friend's gaze seemed to pass through him, locked on the cave entrance. "Look at me!" Urien grasped him by the shoulders, and Sevan's eyes finally settled on his own. There it was again. The fear.

"Sevan, our home is lost. The world will go on. Or it won't." He gave him a small shake. "*None of that matters*. We are Keepers of the Gate, the last of them. Our task is set. We *must* prevent it from being found."

Sevan looked at him pleadingly. "But... perhaps–"

"Perhaps, what? Use it?! Think, Sevan! It's ancient! Not a one of us understands its secrets, they've been lost for millennia. For all you know, we'd as likely doom Pannithor as save it!"

The fear continued to swirl in Sevan's eyes, primal and dark, but through its distortion, Urien was sure he saw a glimmer of reason.

"And besides," he continued, releasing his grip to place one hand reassuringly on his friend's cheek. "It has been decided."

Fear's swirl began to disperse, its distortion to clear. They looked at one another, and Urien knew his friend had returned.

The moment was broken by a roar of triumph from the valley below. They turned to look and saw pillars of smoke rising from the north. The fields were burning, and from the loud, echoing thumps, the enemy had reached the north gate.

"The orcs work quickly," said Urien, patting Sevan on the back. "Let's go."

They entered the cave. For several yards the passage was dark and cramped, and they were enveloped by the familiar smell of damp earth. Jagged rocks jutted awkwardly from the walls, threatening to gouge the incautious or the ignorant. The pair knew their formation well, however, and slipped by with intimate ease. Rounding a sharp right turn, a soft light came into view at the tunnel's end about a dozen yards further. As they approached its source, the passage walls smoothed off and widened slightly, and their artifice gradually became clear – rather than a haphazard molding of nature, the cave had been crafted with intent.

Urien and Sevan entered a small, square antechamber, a lamp casting barest illumination on its stone. As his eyes swept over the familiar space, Urien's gaze came to rest on the door directly ahead of them. Iron and plain. But it was special. Behind it stood that to which he had dedicated his life. To which he would now give his life.

Urien glanced over at Sevan. He was standing to the left of the entrance, his eyes focused on a small wooden box mounted on the wall. Urien stepped toward an identical box to the entrance's right. Urien recalled when, as a young man, he had watched Brother Lucol replacing the older, worn out boxes with these ones. That day he had glimpsed the ancient levers encased behind them, and not in his darkest dreams had he expected to do so again.

On the front of each box was a keyhole, for which the only keys were held by Urien and Sevan. One for each box. Urien reached into his robes and produced his key. It felt cold in his palm.

Sensing Sevan's approach, Urien turned to face him, blinking back tears.

"And so the circle closes, friend," said Sevan. His voice was calm. Urien's vision had become hazy, and he reached out and embraced him.

"Soon our duty shall be done," he said, his throat tight, fighting to hold back the tide, "and we shall know–"

Urien gasped as the wind left his lungs. He tried to draw breath and did so with difficulty, something that first left him confused, then panicked. The weight of his robes was suddenly intolerable, and his stomach felt sodden. He raised his head to look at Sevan, but his waterlogged eyes found only a passive blur.

Pain. Overwhelming pain exploded from his midriff, and Urien groaned. Sevan, whose robes Urien had grasped by the fistful, stood rigid and unmoving. He began to slide down as the strength rapidly left his legs, all while his eyes were locked on Sevan's blurred visage. He tried to speak, but his mouth hung loose, imploring.

"I'm sorry," said Sevan flatly.

As he slid further down, he saw something glint out of the corner of his eye. He blinked as he turned, and the dagger rushed into focus, bloody to the hilt. Anger surged, and he clawed desperately at Sevan's robes before collapsing to the ground, his head facing toward the iron door. Urien's vision dimmed. He heard the clatter of the warm blade hitting the cold stone floor.

*****

Sevan looked at his shaking hands, feeling as though he were in a dream. His right hand was covered in blood, the imprint of the dagger's rough handle still visible, so tightly had he gripped it. He could smell the blood, could practically taste it. Set against this horror, his left hand was clean. Innocent, even.

He hadn't wanted this. But what choice did he have? Urien was inflexible, had always been so. This was the only way. He looked down at his friend's immobile body, at the gathering pool of dark red. He would prepare Urien to join their brothers in the crypts below. It was the least he could do, and more than he would have received were they to have enacted that folly.

But it would have to wait. Pannithor needed help, and it was clear that only he had the nerve to deliver it.

He looked at the iron door, his mind's eye piercing beyond it to the object within.

"I can save them all."

He strode across the antechamber to the lamp and lifted it from the wall, noting with satisfaction that his hands had stopped shaking. He crossed the remainder of the room, grasped the iron handle and, after a brief pause, pulled the door wide.

The darkness shrank reluctantly before the lamp's glow, revealing scant more than a short passageway and several feet of the room beyond. Sevan stepped forward and set the lamp down. Reaching into an alcove in the passage wall, he retrieved an even larger lamp, better suited to the room ahead, and began to ignite it. After a minute or two of difficulty, its flame leapt into life. Scooping up the first, he raised them one in each hand as he entered the chamber.

The room was large. Far larger than the humble antechamber would imply. Its shape also differed markedly. Rather than a stone box, the chamber walls rolled away smoothly, outward and upward, to form a perfect dome radiating twenty feet. Along the base of the wall to his right, a stairway opened in the floor, beginning a broad, spiraling descent into the ancient tunnels below. Sevan paid it no mind. After all, the priests of Keatairn's temple had sealed their entrance before they fled with the rest of the town, and the stairs offered neither threat nor escape. Stepping across the threshold, Sevan's attention was held solely by the room's central feature.

A slender lancet archway, some seventeen-feet high and six across, dominated the chamber. It appeared to have been carved from a single cut of dark marble and was perfectly smooth save for an upward point at its crown, thrusting toward the ceiling's center. Though he had seen it many times in his life, Sevan could not help but gaze in wonder. Usually he came in here for study, in particular when scribing new copies of decaying archives. Occasionally he came just to look. This time was different, however, and knowing this provoked in him something akin to religious fervor.

Or terror.

He shifted his gaze to look directly through the arch and immediately regretted it. Even in its inert state, one could not see through its span without a sudden sense of disequilibrium taking hold. He closed his eyes and breathed deeply, waiting for it to pass. Secure on his feet once more, he began to cross the chamber, maintaining careful focus on the ground before him. He quickly reached the opposing side and stood before the object he had attempted to glimpse through the arch. It was as tall as he was, stone and cylindrical. Rather than the minute and mysterious mechanisms built into the chamber's walls, it was covered top to bottom in symbols. Setting the smaller lamp down, Sevan ran his hand over the pillar, detecting the near imperceptible divisions around each symbol, and drew back when he saw the trail of blood that followed his fingers. He began to circle it, allowing his knowledge of the object to come to the surface.

There wasn't much. After hundreds of years of study, the Circle had deciphered very little of the significance behind the symbols. They were from a time before the highest days of Primovantor, or at least assumed as such. But they were not entirely distinct from that era. Many of the symbols had found their way into Primovantian iconography, some being immediately recognizable, others having greatly mutated. In attempting to discern their meaning, the scholars of the Keepers had one great advantage that, as it turned out, was also their greatest stumbling block – they knew the archway's purpose and, by extension, the pillar's role in it. This, combined with the enduring use of the Primovantian calendar throughout Upper Mantica, which appeared to borrow heavily from this ancient script, meant that they had identified the range of symbols relating to the days and months of the year. As for the rest, there were many theories, and no answers. There could never be any, thanks to the Keepers' first and most ancient rule: *it must never be used*. Without the possibility of testing their theories, the Keepers of the Gate lost interest in the active study of the chamber.

Sevan stopped his circling. There they were. He crouched down to examine four symbols, spaced in pairs one column and three rows apart. Exactly as he'd dreamed them. Sevan's nights had been tormented for many weeks now, even before word of the orc invasion reached their secluded community. Always the same terrifying image roared through his mind, of orcs swarming through Keatairn's streets, hacking up and devouring the inhabitants, malevolent eyes glowing red in the dark. Those eyes turning on him... It was then, when the fear reached its zenith, that these symbols would appear before his mind's eye, their promise of the dream's end bringing relief. Offering salvation.

Hands shaking once more, Sevan reached out and touched all four symbols at the same time. He pressed the symbols. They slid smoothly into the pillar, stopping after half an inch, and remained there when he released them. That was it. In that small act, he had violated his oath. There was nothing left to do but see this through. Before he could recover himself, all four of the symbols clicked out together, causing him to flinch away in surprise.

Sevan's jaw dropped. The four symbols were glowing. Their light was weak, a blue luminescence that wrestled with that of the lamps. But they were *glowing*. And not only them, he realized, but the top of the pillar as well. He moved closer, craning his neck and standing on the balls of his feet to see. The source was a thin blue line, which formed a perfect circle. The moment he saw it, he knew exactly what to do. With a laugh of pure joy he reached up, placed his bloodstained hand inside the circle, and pushed.

The walls burst into life, launching a thin shower of dust into the air. It was as if they had become liquid, ripples tumbling and colliding, dividing and uniting in a swarm of activity. The mechanisms, stationary for gods knew how long, were working.

Overwhelmed, Sevan spun on the spot, trying to see everything at once, his eyes burning from the dust. The noise was incredible, a tremendous buzzing of overlapping rhythms that seemed to throw his insides to and fro. Amidst this flood of motion, the ground remained still, and the mismatch of sensory input caused him to stumble to the chamber floor. A low rumble joined the ensemble, and then the grinding of stone on stone. He looked around for the source, but it seemed to be coming from everywhere. Something above caught his eye, and he looked up. The top of the dome was spiraling, the movement becoming faster as it closed in on the center. In the space of moments, a hole appeared in the middle of the swirl. There was an echoing snap, and all motion ceased.

The silence was deafening. Sevan sat perfectly still, gazing up at the hole. A beam of moonlight floated gracefully through the small aperture, landing gently on the archway's topmost point. He realized that he was holding his breath and hurriedly exhaled. In his stumbling, he had come to a position side-on to the archway. Not wanting to miss a thing, Sevan scampered to his feet, circled quickly around toward the entrance side of the chamber, and looked on in awe.

At the top of the arch, under its crown, tiny droplets were forming. The substance was luminous, casting white light in all directions. Sevan watched as a droplet grew heavy and fell, his eyes following its rapid descent, and marveled as it disappeared on contact with the ground, without sound and without trace.

Moonlight, he thought. *Liquid moonlight! Or perhaps even starlight?*

More droplets were falling now, their pace steadily growing. As the frequency built, trickles began to appear, erratic at first but quickly forming into thin streams of light. At the edge of his perception, Sevan realized that the silence was being replaced with a humming sound, harmonious and pleasant, like a crystal choir. He fell to his knees, rapture radiant in his features. The streams expanded and merged, becoming a torrent, a cascading waterfall of moonlight. Its growth ceased, the flow became constant. It was open.

Sevan knelt immobile, waiting. Light from the archway danced playfully on the chamber walls, its pattern recalling the rippling motion of the mechanisms, resonating with the continuous sound of the pacific chorus. But the chamber was still.

A minute passed. And another. Sevan had no idea what would come next, or what might be expected of him.

I've opened it, he thought. *Wasn't that enough?*

A third minute passed. Evidently he had to try something. He cleared his throat.

"To any being, mortal or divine, who hears my words," he called, projecting his voice at the curtain of light, "Aid us! Pannithor suffers!"

The gateway appeared to react to his voice, the intensity of the light increasing sharply, and Sevan shielded his eyes. His heart leapt.

They had heard! His prayer would be answered!

But… something was wrong.

It was the humming. Still quiet, still at the borders of perception, but where once there was harmony, it now sounded… not right. Discordant. A jarring tone that grated on his senses, grinding his elation into a state of disquiet. The light too had changed, its color taking on a bruised and sickly hue. Its intensity diminished somewhat, and he lowered his hands. He could see it clearly now, a blotch of deep purple that was expanding at the gate's center, gradually contaminating the stream of light. Behind the spreading stain, a shadow began to take shape.

"Hello?" he breathed, little more than a whisper.

Giggling laughter echoed throughout the chamber. It sounded like a child, but unnatural, like a mocking emulation of mirth. It bounced around the room, and he had the sensation of something whizzing past his ear. He stumbled backward, eyes darting. The laughing voice was rejoined by another, a woman's, its sound at once melodious and malevolent, rich and hollow. Their rhythm was perfectly matched, and yet the voices moved independently of each other in a disorienting weave of resonance. Inside the gateway, all white light had now been consumed, the temperate stream replaced with a raging flood of violet, at once polluting the room with its glow and elevating the darkest shadows. The smell of ozone scorched the air and, beyond the arch, the outline of a figure grew firmer, the torrent contorting as it began to pass through…

Sevan fled. The laughing woman shrieked as he scrambled to his feet, the childish voice began to monotonously shout its laugh, "*HA! HA! HA! HA!*" He lurched into the short passageway, heart racing, mind reeling. Just as he was about to cross into the antechamber, he stopped dead, leaning against the threshold. The light from the gateway behind caused his shadow to loom large, blotting out half the room. He stared, transfixed, unable to believe his eyes.

Where Urien had lain, there was nothing more than a pool of blood. Above the pool, Urien's box was open, its lever in the downward position. A dagger – his dagger – had been jammed into the mechanism, holding it in place. Dumbfounded, Sevan looked again at the pool and realized that its shape was wrong, that it trailed across the room and into his shadow – toward the other box.

He quickly stepped to one side, making way for the light. A huddled figure was revealed, leaning weakly against the stone wall. It was Urien. He had his hand on the other lever. Sevan's box was wide open.

"No!" yelled Sevan, hands diving into his robes, already knowing it was in vain, that his key was gone. Without once looking back, Urien pulled the lever.

There was a brief buzzing from the ceiling as the mechanisms did their work, and the entire antechamber collapsed in on itself. Masses of solid rock buried Urien instantly. The cave was sealed.

Sevan stumbled backward into the passage, managing to maintain his footing. The sound of the impact left his ears ringing. Dust exploded over him, rushing into the chamber beyond. Struggling to breathe, he turned and blundered after it, coughing and blinking away tears. His stomach churned, convulsing sharply, causing him to retch. Foul taste flooded his mouth, and he spat before squinting into the gloom.

The fog of particles rendered the purple light hazy, further compounding his blindness. Rubbing at his eyes once more, he sensed something approach. His hands fell away, but he kept his eyes tightly shut. The chamber's cold crept along his sweat-soaked skin. He began to shake all over. The laughter had come back, but this time its source was focused. And getting closer.

What semblance of will he still possessed was bound to one, single thought – *I must not look*. He felt its shadow gradually engulf him–

I must not look.

–saw the light go dark from behind his eyelids–

I must not look.

–heard a third layer of laughter emerge, deep and ancient.

I must not look!

Sevan looked. His mind broke. He began to laugh, tears of horror forging gullies across his dust-caked cheeks. Darkness fell, and he was still.

1

For those who to history's honorable cause would themselves commit, and with particular attention to the cataloging of artifacts from the age of our Primovantian forebears, this warning is herein proffered…

Vespilo A., *On the Location and Identification of Primovantian Antiquity,* Appendix IX *'From the Gatekeepers' - The Mystery of Keatairn*

Toward the western end of Lord Darvled's Wall, on its southern side and in a questionable looking tavern, Xavire Almenara shifted in his chair. Thin sheets of light, a parting gift from the evening sun, gave spare illumination to the otherwise dingy establishment. Slipping through pervious walls, they streaked across the table around which he and three others sat, and alighted on the small pile of coins which lay there, twinkling mischievously.

Xavire shifted again. One of the beams had drifted onto his face, blinding him through his glasses, and he tried to escape its glare. Uslo frowned at him impatiently. It was Xavire's turn. Vision cleared, he looked again at the cards. He had a chance, no doubt about it. It was a good hand. He glanced around at the others.

To his left and across from him sat two men. Their rich auburn hair, pale skin, and high cheekbones revealed them as hailing from the Dragon Teeth Mountains. They were from a mercenary outfit named, not coincidentally, 'The Dragon's Teeth', which drew recruits from among the denizens of their mountainous homeland. Brawand and Ryser had been stationed at Darvled's Wall for as long as Xavire and Uslo. In that time, the four of them had done little else but play cards. While the rest of the continent burned in a war unlike any other for centuries, they had passed their modest wages back and forth in their games, more or less evenly matched in ability, and therefore largely held hostage to fortune's whims. Ostensibly, they had been stationed here to protect the wall's construction and had accepted the work with the expectation of fighting the orc hordes that were then surging south across the Ardovikian Plains. As it happened, the combined armies of the Successor Kingdoms, marching north to meet them, dealt with the threat so roundly that only pockets of combat had made it to the wall itself, and none at all to where they were stationed. To Xavire's mind, it was without doubt the easiest job he had yet had in his mercenary career.

He looked to his right. Uslo Dargent, general of the mercenary company Dargent's Claws and Xavire's commander, was staring intently at his cards. Fortune had favored neither of them that day, and Uslo's frustration was palpable. He was sure, however, that his friend would be frustrated regardless of how his luck ran. For unlike Xavire, Uslo bored easily. He'd been fine when the prospect of combat hung in the air like a welcome scent, happy enough to pass the time playing cards until what he saw as the true games began. Xavire, conversely, had looked to the cards as a distraction from the impending conflict.

When word reached them of attacks on the wall's eastern stretch, Uslo had marched straight to Lord Darvled's nearest representative and demanded that the Claws be redeployed to assist. The answer had been a firm no. When told that ogre mercenaries were to be sent instead, Uslo had come within a hair's breadth of going anyway, charges of desertion be damned. In the end, he relented for his men's sakes, but the incident had nevertheless given Uslo a reputation among the locals for either insanity or unbelievable naiveté. Why else, they wondered, would someone demand to enter the nightmare of the east stretch? For the soldiers of Dargent's Claws, however, they knew that neither was true. Well, perhaps a little of the former. Like Xavire, many of them preferred to be far from the fighting. But if their many campaigns across the north of the continent had taught them anything, it was that Uslo Dargent was not a man to hold in the back line – you unleashed him into the thick of it.

It was now eight months since the end of the war, five since the wall's completion here in the area surrounding the west gate, if nowhere else. The mercenaries' camp had become a barracks, and a hastily assembled settlement had been erected by enterprising civilians to service the stationed troops. This burgeoning community was not yet officially named, but the locals had taken to calling it Darvled's Town. This tavern, the Lucky Orcling, was among the first of its developments; and although superior, cleaner establishments had appeared since, it remained the group's drinking and gambling hole of choice. All threat of combat had disappeared, and in the absence of its looming specter, Xavire and Uslo found their moods reversed.

"Fight or flight, Mister Almenara." Captain Brawand was openly smiling now. Confidence gleamed in his eyes. Xavire felt certain that this was not a bluff, that the Dragon's Tooth had let his anticipation of victory get the better of him. He should retreat, he knew that. Play the long game, don't sweat the small loss. Concede the battle to win the war.

"I'll fight." Xavire dropped the necessary coins onto the pile. "Let's see them."

Uslo revealed first. Triple blade. A fair hand. But not enough. Xavire revealed next, a King's Cohort. Out of the corner of his eye he saw Uslo sit back in his chair, defeated. Xavire's focus, however, was on Brawand. For a moment, he was impassive, staring at the Cohort, and Xavire felt the thrill of victory bubbling up through him. Just as he went to reach for the pile, he saw the smile begin to unfold on Brawand's face. The thrill wavered, and he held his breath as the Dragon's Tooth revealed his hand. Xavire sank back, deflated.

"Golloch's bollocks, another Royal Drakon?!" Uslo's voice, made musical by its Genezan lilt, conveyed utter exasperation.

"Must be my lucky day, gentlemen," said Brawand, dragging the coins toward him noisily. Ryser said something in their harsh dialect, and the mountain men laughed. Between the two of them, only Brawand spoke the common tongue well. Ryser understood, however; Xavire felt sure of that. Scratching an itch through his long beard, Xavire looked again at Uslo. The general was staring off into the distance, the fingers of his left hand tapping restlessly against the table in a display of bored agitation. Not for the first time, Xavire noticed hints of gray in the deep brown of his long hair and mustache. When gray eventually turned the tide, some might mistake that for the source of his nickname, the 'Silver Cat' being so-called after the feline emblem that adorned his crest and armor.

Ryser rapidly shuffled the deck and dealt the next round. Xavire ran his hands over his now meager pile of coins as the cards came to him. Uslo's pile was looking no more healthy.

"At the rate you're clearing us out tonight, Brawand, you'll have to find new opponents," remarked Xavire.

"It certainly seems that way," responded Brawand.

At that moment, the tavern door creaked open. They turned to look. The shift change would not be until sundown, and since most activity at the wall corresponded to the shifts, this irregular entrance piqued their curiosity.

The two young men wore tattered furs and worn cloth. They were thin, hair bedraggled, their movements steeped in caution. The shorter of the two led the way, sharp brow beneath a red fringe, top lip shaded by adolescent fluff. As they stepped over the tavern's threshold, their eyes darted back and forth, quickly taking in the occupants. They smelled of hunger. Not the despairing kind, but rather the tight, focussed hunger of survivors. Spotting the tavern keeper, they walked toward where he stood at the bar, leaving the door open behind them.

The taverner stiffened at their approach, his lips tight.

As one, the card players turned away, interest lost. More Plainsmen, no doubt begging for work or food. They were a common sight at the wall, although they were normally too timid to enter any of the establishments.

"Perhaps I should invite them to play," said Brawand as he dealt out the cards, a smile twisting his lips.

"I doubt there's a coin among the whole sorry lot of them," said Xavire, somewhat absent-minded as he examined his hand. Damn. If the spear didn't favor him early, he would have to disengage. "Heck, even before the war drove them south, I doubt they could've mustered more than a few goats to gamble with."

The tavern keeper's voice, which had been steadily rising in volume, now broke into a shout. "I said I ain't got nothin' for you damn Viks! Your debt is with Lord Darvled! If you don't like it, then you can go back home! Now, get out! Out!"

The two Plainsmen got the message. As they left, the redhead turned, barked some unintelligible insult, spat, and then slammed the door.

Xavire sighed as he flicked his opening bet into the middle of the table. He had no doubt that the 'Viks' would like nothing more than to 'go home.' But they couldn't. No one went north of the wall who didn't wear Lord Darvled's colors, and as a result, many who'd fled the orc hordes were now trapped in serfdom, forced to repay a debt they hadn't knowingly incurred. Few would live long enough to see their homeland again.

"You are wrong, you know," said Brawand.

Xavire was snapped from his thoughts. "What?"

The mountain man turned back to the table, reaching out and flipping the first card of the spear. "About Ardovikia. About the Plainsmen. Escalate."

He tossed some coins on the pile. Ryser matched the bet, as did Uslo. Neither appeared to be paying much attention to the exchange. For his part, Xavire hadn't even looked at the revealed card. His eyes were locked on Brawand as his mind re-ran their conversation. Then the pieces clicked into place. Xavire barked a laugh.

"What, about their wealth? You mean they don't even have goats up north? Oh, I disengage," he added in response to Uslo's clear impatience, expressed by the increased pace of his table-tapping. Xavire had lost concentration this round and thought it best to bow out early.

"Quite the opposite," responded Brawand as he flipped the next card. "They have plenty of goats. *Had* plenty of goats, I should say. Escalate." He pushed a small pile of coins forward, and both Ryser and Uslo quickly disengaged, Uslo with an audible sigh of frustration. Brawand grinned as he leaned forward to collect his prize. "And perhaps much greater riches, besides."

The image of the young men, huddled in their ragged furs, drifted through Xavire's mind, and he was skeptical. He said nothing, but the thought must have shown on his face.

"Xavire! Such dubiety! Look, I understand." Brawand sat forward, leaving the deck of cards to one side. Ryser picked it up and began to shuffle. "Your attitude makes perfect sense. You are from a big, southern city, after all. Both of you are," he said, gesturing to Uslo. "Cities that stood tall during the age of Primovantor."

Xavire glanced at Uslo. He was looking off into space, seemingly lost in his own thoughts. His hand had stopped tapping, however, and Xavire suspected that he was listening closely.

"Let me ask you something," began Brawand, addressing Xavire. "Where was the most opulent region of that lost age? Do you know?"

Xavire thought for a moment, somewhat wrong-footed by the question. "Well, I'd guess Basilea, or whatever it was called back then."

Brawand was nodding as he spoke, his smile giving away nothing. "Good. A worthy acknowledgement of your people's eastern rivals, Valentican. And you, Genezan? What do they teach in the island city?"

"Ardovikia," said Uslo.

Brawand let out a laugh. "Exactly!"

Ryser stood up as they talked and walked to the bar. The mood had changed at the table, and it was clear that the game playing was finished for tonight. It was time to drink.

"I'm sorry," said Xavire, leaning in. "I must have misheard. Ardovikia was opulent? But it's just miles of plainsland. And the kingdoms there are, well, young! Hence the name!"

Uslo sat forward in his chair, abandoning all pretense at disinterest. "What are you saying, Brawand? The Plainsmen had wealth in Ardovikia? Is that it?"

Brawand shrugged. "In the sense you know it? No. No cities, no towns. The Young Kingdoms had towns aplenty on the Plain, and some survived the orc invasion. But the Ardovikian Plainsmen are nomadic."

"So what *are* you saying?" The determination was plain on Uslo's face.

Brawand appeared to consider Uslo for a moment. Although he was a captain and Uslo a general, the scale of their respective organizations made the ranks near meaningless since Brawand commanded at least twice as many men. That, and the fact that Uslo's position was about as 'self-styled' as they come. All the same, Brawand still had to follow someone else's orders.

Ryser returned, bringing four tankards of ale. When he sat down, they each took one, made their usual toast to fortune ("That lady least fair!"), and drank deeply. The ale wasn't exactly high quality, but its bitter taste was always welcome. After wiping away the foam, Brawand continued.

"I am simply suggesting, Uslo Dargent, that the things I have heard about the Plains, about their secrets, I would not be searching for towns at all!"

"You're talking about the lost treasures," said Uslo after a moment.

"Lost treasures?" repeated Xavire.

"Yes, Xavire!" said Brawand. "It is said there were many ancient cities in Ardovikia, all of them buried by Winter's ice, laying undiscovered for centuries beneath the Plains!"

"Exactly," said Uslo. "*Undiscovered.* People have been exploring the Plains ever since the floods receded, and save for a few trinkets and the spoils of failed settlements, nothing has been found."

"Nothing that you know of," countered Brawand. "And I would wager that it is not a matter of *if* they are found, but *when*. I would wager my right foot."

Uslo sat back in his chair with a laugh. "Well, you'll forgive me, Captain Brawand, if I leave the wagering to you tonight."

Xavire breathed a sigh of relief. For the briefest moment, something had hovered in Uslo's eyes. A look Xavire knew meant trouble.

"Why Lord Darvled not let people go north."

Xavire and Uslo sat up straight, the unknown voice taking them by surprise. With a start, Xavire realized that the words had emerged from Ryser, who was looking at them both expectantly.

"Did you say something?" Xavire asked.

Ryser cleared his throat and tried again. "Why Lord Darvled not let people go north." Although spoken in a dull monotone, the man was attempting to ask a question.

Xavire pondered. "Well, I think it's pretty clear why Darvled doesn't want the Plainsmen going north, Ryser." But the man was shaking his head.

"No. Why Lord Darvled not let *you* go north."

"Well, I haven't asked to go, for one."

Uslo was looking away again, apparently straining to hide his amusement. *He'd better contain himself*, thought Xavire, fearing if his friend and commander started to laugh now that he too would be swept into idiotic mirth.

Brawand asked Ryser something in their tongue, and they had a quick exchange. Nodding his understanding, he turned back to Xavire. "My man refers to the fact that none are permitted to go north – not the Viks, not free citizens, and not us mercenaries. Even the ogres have to threaten trouble if they want through."

"But some *yes* go north," added Ryser. "Some *yes*."

"Lord Darvled's army..." The words slid from Xavire's mouth as Ryser's meaning became clear, and the mountain man nodded. It was true, the only reason there was work for the mercenary companies on the wall was because the lord's own forces were deployed north of it. Such an arrangement had more or less made sense during the war, but now... now the refugees continued to be 'escorted' south, and supplies for Darvled's personal forces continued to flow north. Why? What were they still doing up there?

"Scavengers," said Uslo softly.

Quickly draining the last of his ale, Xavire thumped the tankard down. He forced a grin.

"Above our pay grade to think about that stuff anyway, eh lads? Drink up, next round's on me."

Both Brawand and Ryser laughed and set themselves to emptying their tankards. Uslo was staring off into space again.

Standing up, Xavire glanced at Uslo's face, and what he saw there caused his forced grin to vanish.

The Silver Cat had that look in his eyes.

*****

It was sundown at the wall, and there was a spate of activity in Darvled's Town. The sound of grumpy complaints meeting with good-natured joshing formed a familiar refrain in the lives of the town inhabitants, as throughout the barracks soldiers made ready to relieve their comrades-in-arms, patting them on the back as they passed them on the wall's steps. Three stories high and running as far as the eye could see, the wall was functional in build, absent of ornamentation, and made from varied stone. Its gateway was straddled by a stern barbican, beginning just east of the town. It was the only gateway through the wall for close to five leagues, every mile of which was marked by a square tower. To the west, light formed fading columns of pink and orange against the clouds as the last of the sun slipped over the horizon. In a few minutes, it would be dark.

Uslo Dargent walked alone along the rampart, hands clasped at his back, thoughts swirling. He had no will to drunkenness this night, having left his fellow gamblers only once safely beyond sobriety's grasp. Xavire in particular had seemed determined to put away the ales at pace – Uslo couldn't think why, but he was welcome to it.

"Vestra Ardovikia…" Uslo mumbled to himself. "The Plains of Ardovikia…"

He looked north over the battlements. Save for the obvious absences that way – of people, of tents and rickety constructions – there was nothing to distinguish the two landscapes divided by Darvled's Wall. Miles of grassland, somewhat parched by an overlong summer. And yet, the wall's very placement meant there was *everything* to distinguish them.

"Lost cities… lost treasures…"

His thoughts began to coalesce. *Could it be possible? Could they know? If so, would they* know *they knew?*

Uslo turned south, quickly spying his goal a short way beyond Darvled's Town. A light, perched in growing dark. He ran forefinger and thumb out and down along his mustache. It couldn't hurt to investigate. He just needed to get something from his stash, and then…

With a feline and heedless grace, Uslo set off down the wall's steps.

*****

While Darvled's Town roused itself for the shift change, the activities of a few beyond its hasty architecture had long since died down. Already they sat around a mature campfire, stoking its flames as it stoked their spirits, listening to the bustle from afar. There were eight of them, five men and three women, clad in rough cloth and furs that had seen better days. They were thin. Skinny, even, but wiry, their bodies accustomed to hard living – although from their diminished postures, they were struggling under yet harder conditions. The only youth to be found was in the most recent arrivals, two boys of thirteen years apiece, empty-handed after their wanderings through the town.

Cauhin pushed a lock of red hair from his eyes, stewing in his anger. The tavern keeper's face, framed by disgusting ear hair, sneered before his mind's eye. The way he had looked at them both, like they were less than animals, made Cauhin want to hit something. It made him want to bite.

"Did you eat today?" the man to his left asked. He spoke low so as not to disturb the flow of conversation, and Cauhin had to concentrate to understand his east-plain accent. His stony features would make most folk wary, but Cauhin knew him to be a good man by the name of Riuen. He shook his head.

"Not a bite," added Fillam, to Cauhin's right, his voice high and unbroken.

Riuen's features remained passive, but his eyes showed kindness. He produced two small pieces of bread, somewhat squashed from safe keeping. The boys gladly accepted the offer, but Cauhin felt a sting of guilt as he wolfed down the stale morsel. According to the customs of their people, they were full-grown now. Neither of them should have to live off the charity of others. Nor would they have had to, were it not for last week's incident with the foreman. The humiliation of it all had become too much, and the southerner had been asking for a fight. While in truth the pair were lucky to still be alive, at the time their expulsion from serfdom had felt like a vindication, like freedom. Now, as they desperately scavenged an existence at the margins, untouchable to the southerners and a burden to their kin, they realized why they had been spared – as a warning.

"Seems we're popular tonight."

The elder's voice cut the conversation dead and stirred Cauhin from his thoughts. The group looked around and immediately tensed. While still indistinct, it was obvious that the approaching figure was not one of them.

"Good evening!"

It was a man's voice, colored by an unfamiliar accent. He strode briskly into the light, and Cauhin recognized him as one of the gamblers from the tavern. Wearing high leather boots, dark pantaloons and only a loose shirt, the man seemed strangely untroubled by the cold. From the way he walked, however, Cauhin suspected drink might be involved. His features became visible, shoulder length brown hair and a long mustache set against pale skin. He was approaching quickly but without threat, and the Plainsmen were unsure how to respond. Cauhin noticed a sling bag hanging at his side.

"Good evening," answered the elder, Ottrid.

The newcomer's lively brown eyes sought out the elder, and he smiled broadly, his head nodding in appreciation. Cauhin was impressed to note that the man seemed unfazed by the smell, an inescapable consequence of the group's labor. Without slowing down, he circled around to Fillam and Cauhin, his clear intention to sit between them. The group had little choice but to quickly shuffle along as he casually settled himself. The stink of cheap ale confirmed Cauhin's suspicions, but when the man spoke, his voice was clear.

"I hope you'll all forgive me, I happened to spot these lads heading up this way, and I thought I'd come say hello."

Cauhin frowned. They hadn't hung around the tavern after being booted. In fact, they'd pretty much left Darvled's Town straight away, and they would never go anywhere near the barracks. But he couldn't puzzle it further – the man was still talking.

"Haven't come out this way before," he said, looking around. There wasn't much of interest on the outcrop beyond a smattering of wild shrubs. "These days the only sights I see are from the top of the wall."

The Plainsmen cast worried glances among themselves. Contact with southern soldiers rarely boded well.

The man noticed their response and quickly added, "No, no, don't worry. I'm not a soldier. Well, that's not true. Not entirely." He looked at them meaningfully. "I'm a mercenary. Which may not mean much, I'll grant. Let's just say, you don't have to worry about me. I take no pleasure in the plight of your people, nor do I harbor any love for Lord Darvled. Nor his eyesore, for that matter." He looked back at the wall. In the darkness and at this distance, all they could see was the light from the braziers along the ramparts, warming the soldiers on the night watch. There was a moment of silent consideration, and then the newcomer turned back, a playful smile on his lips. He reached into his sling bag and produced a large brown bottle.

"Wouldn't do to come empty handed," he said, prising the stopper with a dull pop. The rich scent of refined spirit flowed out. Cauhin's mouth watered.

"Dragon Teeth brandy. Six years old, finest quality. Won it last week from one of the mountain men. Gods, luck was with me that day. I think he hoped to win it back, but I'd wager my aunt before letting go of good drink this far west. Not that there'd be many takers," he added, seemingly to himself. "Cheers." The man raised the bottle before taking a hearty swig. He closed his eyes, face blissful. "That's the stuff," he said quietly. He looked around at the group and placed his left hand on his chest. "Uslo Dargent. At your service." He handed the bottle to Fillam on his right, gesturing to him meaningfully.

Cauhin sensed hesitation among the Plainsmen. It was hard to say how much of the southerner's speech they had understood. It wasn't words that divided them but the manner of *talking* – accent, phrasing, expressions, the fundamental culture that lay behind the words were all so stark in difference that the two peoples could often find each other unintelligible. Fortunately, the ears of the younger Plainsmen found it less troublesome to adjust, with their tongues quick to follow, resulting in them regularly acting as interpreters for what was, at its core, the same language. Fillam took a drink, his eyes wide as it seared his tongue, before pointing to himself, coughing "Fillam, son of Amrik."

Understanding dawned on the rest of the group, and they continued to pass the brandy, savoring its flavor, gladly introducing themselves. By the time it reached Cauhin, less than half the bottle remained. He drank, and it was like a taste of the gods, flooding the furthest recesses of his being with warmth, causing his stress and mistrust to recede before it.

"Cauhin, son of Hunlo."

Uslo nodded gratefully as he took the bottle and gulped down another measure. He looked down at it for a moment before passing it on to Fillam.

"It's always a shame to deprive a man of a taste of home, but when it tastes that good..." He smiled, aware perhaps of the rapt attention hanging on his every word. He picked up a twig and absently poked the fire as he spoke.

"Home. It's been so long since I've thought about it, let alone said it." His manner remained casual, but he was speaking more slowly now, each word distinct over the crackling of the flames. "You probably can't tell, but I'm not from here. My home is far to the east, a city in the Infant Sea, if you'll believe it. Two hundred thousand people, living together on an island piled high with buildings, far higher than that barricade over there." He jerked his thumb lazily toward the wall.

Cauhin had never seen any sea, and Darvled's Town was the nearest thing to a city he could imagine. The scale of what Uslo described was so far beyond him as to be meaningless. Yet, for some reason, he found himself enthralled.

"It's called Geneza, and it is beautiful. When you sail to her, she seems to rise up from the water, towers resplendent in the sun. As you come closer, the wind carries the smell of the fish market – not exactly a pleasant smell, let me tell you." He laughed, amusing himself. "But you know what that smell means? It means that you've arrived. And that you will soon taste that very same fish, but prepared in ways that will make the chefs in the arboreal halls of Ileuthar seem like Basilean military slop-cooks. And then, you come into the harbor, the largest west of the Golden Horn, at least until you reach Therennia Adar, that is. And you hear our people's song from every street corner, from every open window. Music is in our souls, you see. To be Genezan, one must know how to sing." He closed his eyes and hummed a gentle melody, his expression dreamy.

"What's he saying?" asked Riuen, the thick dialect of his whisper carrying for all to hear. Uslo continued to hum, seemingly unperturbed.

"He's talking about his home," said Cauhin.

"Why?"

No one had an answer. The bottle continued to make its way around, with those drinking being more frugal than before so as to make it last. Uslo stopped humming and opened his eyes.

"It's been more than ten years since I last saw the city. Sometimes I worry that I'll forget what she looks like, and I suppose that one day I just might." Seeing the question on Cauhin's face, he explained, "I can never return."

"Why?" asked Fillam. Uslo's gaze turned to him, tight brow lending sadness to his smile.

"Ahh, but that's a long story. And not one I'm inclined to share. Not yet." The bottle had reached Cauhin again, and there was just enough left for one more drink. He hesitated and then offered it to Uslo. The Genezan smiled and waved him off. "No, no. That's for you."

"Thanks," he said, and drained the bottle. It was divine to the last.

"Sir Dargent," began Ottrid.

"Uslo, please. And I am no knight, Elder Ottrid."

"Uslo. Why are you telling us all this?"

"It's hard to be in a foreign land. Especially when you can't go home. Not many folk understand it, not really. Not like us. I sometimes find talking about it helps, and that nothing quite helps talking like good company." Uslo took the empty bottle from Cauhin and held it up. "And nothing makes for good company quite like good drink!" He threw the bottle over his shoulder and reached into his bag again, this time producing a leather flask.

"Cheap wine, I'm afraid, but better than nothing." He passed it to Fillam.

An air of discomfort settled on the group. In the early days, when they had first fled beyond the wall, they had spoken of home and little else. However, as their situation revealed itself, discussion of what was lost became too painful. Since then, talk and thought were kept shallow, like a thin bandage over deep wounds. To talk of home was to rip the bandage away, and therefore considered taboo.

In spite of this, Cauhin was intrigued. Few southerners had ever shown any interest in them. He could only think of one other.

"You want us to tell you about the Plains? Is that it?" he asked. Uslo smiled kindly.

"I'd like you to tell me about home."

*****

The sun had yet to reappear, but the sky had already begun to brighten by the time Cauhin returned to the refuge, and the world was cast in blue-gray monochrome. One and a half miles south of Darvled's Town, the motley collection of tents and shacks was barely adequate to the needs of its near three thousand inhabitants. The land was stony and hard, the terrain exposed to the winds, and the nearest stream that they were permitted to use was hours away. No sane soul would choose to live there, and yet it was full to the brim. Many more Ardovikians had crossed into the south by the west gate, but their numbers had been spread across other such 'refuges,' the locations of which none among the Plainsmen knew. Cauhin was among the last to be placed here, and most of those with whom he traveled south had been taken elsewhere. He bore little expectation of seeing them again. But, as he often reflected, it could have been worse. At least they hadn't separated him from his family.

The orcs had already taken care of that.

What a night, he thought happily. He could still feel the alcohol's effects, and the combination of bodily tiredness and mental stimulation left him in something of a stupor. Tonight was special. Not just because of Uslo Dargent and his questions. Not just because they had been finally able to speak of life on the Plains, of home. To speak of it not in mourning, but as if they were back there, as if they were sharing tales around the fire during a hunt.

Tonight was special because he would see her.

His destination came into view as he rounded a cluster of tilting shacks. The two-story building stood at the center of the refuge and was its only stable construction. Built onto the ruins of an old barn and storehouse, the needs of the sick and the infirm for decent shelter quickly saw it converted into a makeshift clinic, a truer refuge than the shambles that lay around it. Cauhin was relieved to see the glimmer of moving lamplight through the shutters. He didn't want to wake anyone. He slipped inside, gently eased the door shut, and looked around.

Four cots, two on each side, rested end to end along the walls of the small room, the only room left over from the original stone storehouse. A fire glowed gently at its center, the light made soft by the large black pot which hung over it. Cauhin smelled stew, and his stomach rumbled audibly.

"Long night, Cauhin?"

He jumped. The voice had come from his right, and he realized it was her. She was crouched in the corner, giving water to one of the bedridden. The hood on her heavy brown robe was up. It seemed she had known it was him without looking.

"Long *and* productive, my lady."

She rose up slowly and turned to face him. Cauhin may not have been tall, but nor was he particularly short. Standing more than a full head higher than he did, she would tower over all but the greatest of Plainsmen. Though the thick garb hid it well, Cauhin was certain that hers was a body of iron, tempered and potent.

"Indeed?"

He nodded. "I think... I think we might have a way."

She pulled back her hood, revealing an oval face with sharp eyes, short dark hair on sun-kissed skin. Cauhin felt his heart give a thump. Shadows from the fire filled the dimples in her cheeks and in her chin, deepening a slight smile.

"Tell me."

2

...On many occasions in the course of one's searchings, be they at the grand markets of the Royal Quarter in our Golden Horn, or perhaps in distant Teiardon of the West, and when inquiring with regards to the provenience of some alleged relic or another being there auctioned, one will oft hear a peculiar response: 'Tis from the trove of Keatairn'...

Vespilo A., *On the Location and Identification of Primovantian Antiquity,* Appendix IX *'From the Gatekeepers' - The Mystery of Keatairn*

Torchlight drew back the moonless night, and Orod cast his gaze over what it had unveiled. Hundreds of pairs of eyes, both curious and hateful, followed his own as they passed over the goblin captives. They had been gathered after several days of hunts, and their numbers were now such that an uprising could prove difficult for his orcs to suppress. Assessing their twisted faces, Orod felt sure that the chances of revolt were slim. He could sense the new order, his order, inexorably binding their collective will. If anyone knew how to bind slaves, it was Orod. He knew it intimately.

Orod puffed out his chest. His armor, fashioned from a length of black-iron chain wound repeatedly around his torso, lent the movement a bright run of clinks. Resting his forearms on the twin Tragarian axes slung at each hip, the orc turned his gaze away from the scree enclosure, peering out beyond campfires into the surrounding black.

"Can they march?" he asked.

"March?" Bolirm, Orod's head skulk, spoke in a ragged hiss, his voice permanently scarred by the fumes of the obsidian mines. "Then we're leavin'?"

"Answer me."

Bolirm grunted. "They can. We might have t'take it slow the first couple days, but they can march."

Orod nodded. It would have to do.

He set off toward of the orc encampment, the light from Bolirm's torch causing his shadow to contort before him.

"The last haul were a pathetic lot," continued Bolirm, their steps accompanied by the clunks of Orod's armor and the squelch of wet earth. "Three hundred goblins in the mob, biggest group we found, and only a hundred or so made it here alive. Hardly worth the effort, you ask me, since 'nother forty were so weak we had to chop them up for the pots. Kept the rest going, at least."

"I don't need them strong, I need them moving." They crossed into the orc camp, and the guards nodded as they passed. "S'long as they're ready by dawn, I don't care. Can you manage that? Or do I need to put someone else in charge of them?"

"I already said they'll be ready to march," repeated Bolirm, his words edged with insolence.

"They'd better be."

They weaved their way between the campfires. Bolirm, his torch dying, tossed it over the heads of a few orcs, and it landed neatly atop a pyre. There were a little over two hundred orcs in Orod's mob, and it seemed that most of them were here. The rest must have gone on a hunt. It was an excellent camp for hunts. Sheltered from the northern winds and with a view for miles, it sat right in the path of the displaced herds. Events to the east had cast many a beast far from its natural home, and the orcs had taken full advantage, fabricating thick furs and equipment from the gargantuan game.

Orod breathed deeply, savoring the clean air in spite of his frustration. They'd stayed too long already. He needed to go west. To destroy. Every fiber of his being demanded it.

They came to the far edge of camp. Light flickered on a ridge a short distance beyond, fire illuminating the shape of a hut from the inside. Waiting outside the entrance stood a figure, hunched on its staff. A still smaller figure peered out from between the legs of the first, its large, mad eyes fixed on their approach. Orod stopped and turned to Bolirm.

"Spread the order. We break camp at dawn."

"Don't you have to check with the shaman, first?"

The words were barely out of Bolirm's mouth when Orod slammed his fist into it. The orc went down hard into the trampled snow. Rolling his shoulders, but otherwise unmoving, Orod fixed him with a firm look.

"Never question me." He crouched over Bolirm. "*I* give the orders. No one else. If you suggest different again, I'll stick you in the pots myself."

Bolirm grunted. Turning his head, he hawked a globule of black blood onto the snow. Though they had their backs to camp, both felt the eyes of the other orcs upon them. Had the moment come when Bolirm would finally challenge Orod for leadership? Bolirm's face was in shadow, but Orod sensed the fury in his gaze. He waited.

"Fine," hissed Bolirm, massaging his jaw. He glanced back at the watching orcs, and as his face moved into the light, Orod saw Bolirm's brand shine white between his fingers. "You're the overmaster."

Bolirm raised himself to sit, but Orod held out a fist in warning.

"Krudger," he said. "I am the *krudger*. We don't use the masters' words."

"Right..." said Bolirm.

"Say it."

Bolirm's teeth were bared. "Krudger."

Orod's anger flashed. He wanted to hit him again. His fists were tight as rocks.

"Get out of my sight."

Bolirm pulled himself up more slowly than Orod would have liked, but he kept his head down, avoiding the krudger's gaze as he sloped off. Orod took a deep breath through his nose, forcing his fists to fall loose. It wouldn't do to show his anger in front of the others. Anger demanded action, and much as he'd have enjoyed caving in Bolirm's face, the skulk still had his uses. The day would come when he'd have to be replaced, that much was certain. But Orod wouldn't just be replacing one orc for another – he'd be setting himself a new rival for leadership. Orod had enough to deal with.

His anger in check, Orod turned to continue toward the hut. As he did so, his eyes passed over the dwarf pillar that stood tall over the camp. He paused, raising his view up to its fifteen-foot tip, smooth and sharp as a spearhead. Bile gathered in his throat, and he gritted his teeth. The orcs had done their best to topple the pillar, but it seemed the ancient dwarfs had hewn it from the cliff itself. Though its intricate carvings were now mercifully defaced by the orcs, the sight of the unbowed monument still caused something to twist in their guts. To give them pain. Save for spitting at it as they passed, most tried to pretend it wasn't there. Orod swallowed and turned away.

The wizened figure of Arlok bowed low as he approached, the goblin between his legs imitating its master. Arlok was a Godspeaker, a rare runt-orc attuned both to the orcish gods and to the arcane mysteries of the world. His body was hunched and thin, all but naked beneath a worn cloak, his low stature mitigated by a headdress of bone and ram horns. His staff too was horned, the gnarled wood topped with the blackened skull of an Abyssal. Before the orcs found Arlok, Orod and his mob had never heard of Godspeakers. Magic was a tool of their oppressors, gods a concern of higher races. His orcs feared Arlok, and shunned him. Only Orod spent time in his presence.

For his part, Arlok was unfazed by how the mob treated him. If anything, he seemed to expect it, choosing to live away from the rest of camp, only moving among them when fighting loomed, burning foul-scented grasses and muttering blessings for the warriors. It was a behavior that put the orcs on edge, though none objected. If Arlok really did have the ear of gods, they reckoned, better he put a word in for them than not.

The Godspeaker pulled back the entrance flap, standing aside for Orod to enter first.

"This will have to be quick," said Orod, ducking to crawl into the hut. The air inside was hot against his face, with the low, circular space warmed by a small and well-tended fire pit at its center. The only item to draw his attention hung on the inner stone wall, a flag made from thick, dark cloth, displaying a broken tooth. Arlok had taken it from the captured goblins. Orod crawled around the fire to sit next to it, eyes tracing the crude design. "We leave soon. I will not tolerate delay."

"Of course, Krudger Orod," said Arlok, groaning slightly in his wispy voice as he crawled in to sit across from him. Arlok's pet let out a giggle as it sat down next to him. The Godspeaker flicked its nose, silencing the little creature, but its eyes remained wide with mirth, rolling back and forth in its head. Until he met Arlok, Orod had never even heard of orcs keeping goblins as pets. It was an amusing idea, though he couldn't for the life of him understand the appeal of this runtish imp.

What had Arlok called it? Yip?

The little git flopped on its back, tongue lolling, and Orod dismissed it from his mind.

"How may I serve, Krudger?"

"It happened again."

"Tonight?"

"Yes. I was sleeping."

"And this is why the horde will march at dawn?"

"Yes."

Arlok leaned forward. The light of the fire pit cast deep shadows across the Godspeaker's face, capturing every crease and submerging his sockets in darkness. "What did you see?"

Turning his gaze away from the Godspeaker, Orod settled on the rough floor, hands folding across his chest as he lay down. His chain armor dug into his back, but he paid little mind. It was a familiar pain.

"I was standing on a flat land. There were no trees, or animals. Just grass. It was empty. Silent."

The images seemed to float up onto his tongue, formed by the same blackness from which they emerged.

"I was naked, and covered in blood. It was dripping from me, black and red. I… I am alone. I look up from the blood, and there are hills on the horizon, stretching as far as I can see. They're far away... but I can hear them."

Orod closed his eyes, willing the memories to form clearly in his mind. Their murkiness remained solid.

"There's... a battle. I can hear orc voices... they're chanting..."

"Yes..." whispered Arlok.

"I feel... a power before me. It's a power that breaks the world. I know it's mine, if I can claim it. If I'm strong. I step forward, and the sun begins to fall. It moves fast. The sky is dark before I reach the hills. I see... I see them burning. Then... I woke," he finished, opening his eyes.

Arlok let out a sigh. Orod looked at him. The Godspeaker was smiling.

"This is good, Krudger. This is the clearest yet."

"Yes," agreed Orod. "The sights are still... strange. They aren't my eyes that see. But the feeling... the feeling is strong. "

"The gods have spoken to you. They have shown you their will. The destiny of orcs, revealed by the gods, to bring an end to all civilization, Wicked or Shining. To free ourselves both from the torment of the lash and the pain of our creation. To bring the Age of Orcs."

The fire hummed gently beneath Arlok's words, delivered in a venerable voice that slithered through the air. The Godspeaker spoke with a grandiosity that seemed to strain at the limits of the orc language. Many words were unknown to the krudger, and even those he did understand formed sentences beyond his comprehension. But none of that mattered. Only the feeling mattered. The pull.

"I must go west."

Arlok nodded. "It is as I said, Krudger Orod. You are called to prophecy. It will begin on what the humans call the Plains of Ardovikia."

Yip the goblin, still laying on its back, made a sound that was somewhere between a laugh and a hiccup. Arlok ignored it. He drew a long breath. All at once, Orod knew what the Godspeaker was about to say next.

"No," he growled. "Don't say it, Godspeaker."

"The gods bid you go west, but that doesn't mean you need to cross the human lands. You can follow the Steppe around them, avoid–"

Orod sat up sharply. The Godspeaker shrank back against the hut wall.

"What did I say?!" he barked.

"Please, Krudger!" gasped Arlok, hands clasped before him in deference. "I only suggest—!"

In a quick movement, Orod drew a section of chain from his armor and flicked it across the hut. Its hooked end flew to within an inch of the shaman's face before going taught, snapping back to loop around his clasped hands, binding them. Orod pulled. Arlok lurched forward, toppling toward the fire pit. His shriek was cut short as Orod grabbed him by the neck, holding him over the flames.

"I won't run from the humans!" Orod hissed through bared teeth, spittle seeping down his chin. He felt his anger take hold. It felt good. "I will meet my destiny, and I will do what the others could not! *I will bathe in red blood*!"

Arlok nodded desperately, eyes shut tight. This close, Orod could see the scab on the shaman's brow, product of when last the krudger had unleashed his ire. He raised his fist to add another mark.

In the corner of his vision, Orod saw Yip sit up. The goblin wore an expression of open anticipation, lips curled high in glee. Orod met its eye. Its face disturbed him. The feeling was like a breach in his red haze, through which slipped a single thought.

Arlok saved my life.

Orod turned his gaze back to the Godspeaker. It was true. Without Arlok, Orod and his orcs would have eventually died on that mountain, stranded by the surrounding floodwaters. By the time the shaman arrived, they had already been forced to eat the weakest of the mob. Arlok said he was sent by the gods, a claim that seemed to be confirmed when he led them across a hidden path in the waters – what's more, from the moment they met, the Godspeaker had known about Orod's dreams.

As Orod considered the scrunched-up face, lit from below by the fire's light, it wasn't gratitude that stayed his fist. Arlok was useful. Better not to risk damaging him too much.

With a disappointed sigh, Orod released him, shoving the Godspeaker away from the flames. He fixed his chain back in place.

"But first, I need more orcs. Goblin slaves are not enough."

Arlok nodded, using both hands to rub his neck. "You will find many of our kind east of the humans, scattered by their humiliation. But… they won't follow you. Not until you prove yourself." He flinched at Orod's movement, but the krudger was only preparing to leave the hut.

"I know. Orcs follow strength." He drew back the entrance flap. Outside, the darkness was already beginning to diminish. The new day was not far off, and his hunters had returned. Orod glanced back into the fire, absently stroking the brand on his chin with his thumb. His eyes wandered up to the banner. It hung lifelessly against the stones of the far wall. "Leave that here when we go," he grunted. Without waiting for the Godspeaker's response, Orod stepped out.

The krudger's mind worked restlessly as he made his way back to the orc camp.

Destiny. Prophecy. The Age of Orcs.

The words seemed to hum in his ear, a trinity of power, setting his teeth on edge. Why should such words hold value for an orc like him? An orc who had known nothing of his gods. An orc who was born in an age of slaves, destined to be raised a slave, prophesied to die a slave. But they were *everything*.

Destiny. Prophecy. The Age of Orcs.

Under the low light of dawn, the words continued to whisper. Orodren'val, whose name in the hated masters' tongue meant 'doomed one,' listened.

3

...Should the matter be pressed, one will be met with the following description, curiously consistent across all accounts: Keatairn is a remote community, a town, nestled in a valley, the base of which by a river is cleft, and beneath which lies the scarcely disturbed abundance of a bygone era...

Vespilo A., *On the Location and Identification of Primovantian Antiquity,* Appendix IX *'From the Gatekeepers'* - *The Mystery of Keatairn*

His heart thumped again, louder, and it kept on thumping, faster and faster. His head hurt. He could feel it growing behind him, a yawning hole of darkness that seemed to twitch and squirm. He knew he mustn't look back. It wasn't empty, it was looking at him, it was–

"Xavire Almenara! Wake up, sir!"

Xavire woke in a haze, caught between dream and reality. In one, he was a boy, pursued by something unseen, its steps thundering behind him – in the other, he was a man, someone pounding on his door. The sound sent pain shooting through his molars.

"I'm up," he grumbled, struggling to evict the words through gritted teeth. The pounding continued without pause. Dragging his mind out of the fog, he shouted "I'm up, damn it!"

The pounding stopped. Xavire sat up and rubbed his eyes groggily. His head ached with a vengeance, his mouth tasted foul. Every inch of his skin was soaked in sweat. He reached for his glasses on the small bedside table, and his hand knocked something. He heard the clatter of an empty tankard hitting the wooden floor. Finding his glasses, he put them on clumsily and looked around. Sunlight poured in through the wide window. He had forgotten to close the shutters last night, and the air was stiflingly hot inside his small room at the barracks. It was poorly-ventilated, but at least he didn't have to share it.

Slipping off the bed, he moved to let in new air. From the angle of the light, it looked close to noon already. He never woke this late in the day, had risen at dawn for as long as he could remember. When he reached the window, the glare of the sun on his face caused his stomach to churn. He closed his eyes, breathing deeply to hold back the nausea. His hand found the latch with blind familiarity, and the window swung open. Cool breeze rushed in, enveloping him in its soothing embrace. He felt relief.

Then the smell hit.

Xavire snapped the window shut. Exhaling slowly, he opened his eyes to assess himself. Still dressed in his uniform. That saved him some time, at least. Then he noticed his right pant leg was caked in brown, and he had the sudden recollection of stumbling into wet mud on his way back from the Lucky Orcling.

What in the Seventh Circle, man? he thought. *How long since you last drank like that?*

It had been... His head throbbed at the effort. Well, it had been a long time. Bits and pieces of the bout were coming back, tumbling uninvited into his mind. He had been trying to forget something. What, exactly, he couldn't remember.

Not a total waste then, he thought, recalling the speed with which his remaining coin had seen itself exchanged for booze.

"Sir?"

Xavire recognized the voice. "Come in, Sergeant."

"Door's locked. Sir."

Willing steadiness in his legs, Xavire crossed the room and turned the key. "There," he said, and stepped away, letting himself fall back to sit on the bed.

The door opened with barely disguised impatience. Sergeant Peris hesitated in the doorway, eyes scanning the ill-kempt room, before taking one short step over the threshold. Xavire tried to resist a smile. He knew the sergeant would like nothing more than to whip this room and its owner into shape. The sergeant's men were the most ordered in the Claws, a legacy of his many years serving in the Valentican military. Peris himself was the picture of precision. His uniform coat was neat and straight, and not a single hair strayed from his gray crop or sharp goatee. Although perhaps a little long in the tooth, he was as fit as one could hope for at his age, and his eyes were keen. Not for nothing did he head the company's crossbowmen, and his score remained undefeated at the butts. Those eyes were now fixed on Xavire. They maintained a diplomatic distance from the mud on his breeches.

"My apologies for having to wake you in such a manner, sir."

Xavire waved his hand, ignoring the poorly disguised jab. "I should be thanking you, Sergeant. I was..." he paused, scratching an itch through his long beard. "...never mind. Who knows how long I would've slept."

Peris's lips tightened in disapproval. "The general wishes to see you, sir. Urgently."

Xavire laughed. "What could possibly be so urgent..." All at once, Xavire remembered. The look on Uslo's face. The look that meant trouble. He groaned. "Fine. I'll change out of these and head on over there."

"I'd... advise you go now, sir. No time." Xavire's mouth fell open slightly. It *must* be serious if Peris was recommending he go out like this. Although it was equally possible that the sergeant would enjoy seeing Xavire march around while covered in mud.

Gods, I hope it's mud, he thought.

"Well alright, but I'm going to have to empty my bladder first," Xavire grumbled as he pulled on his boots. "The amount of ale I had last night, not even a visit from the Shining Ones themselves will come between me and my morning piss."

Peris nodded and quickly stepped out of the room. After pulling on his coat and grabbing his wide-brimmed leather cap, Xavire followed the sergeant outside, veering toward the outhouses.

The smell hit him again. It was as if the sun were intent on spurring the settlement's already lousy stink to even greater heights. Taking a deep breath, Xavire set about relieving himself. When he emerged, he was surprised to find that the sergeant was waiting for him.

"I know the way to the general, Sergeant," he said, fixing his cap.

Peris was as straight-backed as ever, but the hesitancy in his voice betrayed discomfort. "If it's all the same to you, sir, I'll go with you. He asked me to fetch you, see..."

Xavire shrugged. They set off.

Their route took them past the training grounds where the men of the Claws were engaged in the last of their morning drills. Xavire slowed slightly as he passed, his tired mind wandering as he watched the familiar movements. In total, the Claws currently numbered some two hundred men, drawn from throughout the Successor Kingdoms and beyond. Most served as pikemen, and the ongoing drill involved two groups of thirty pushing against each other with training staffs, both arranged in a shield-wall formation, each group attempting to pry open the other. The exercise was being overseen by Sergeant Eumenes, a bronze-faced Sparthan in his middle years. His coat was open and his chest exposed, doubtless to keep cool after the morning's exertions. Xavire could feel the disapproval radiate from Peris, and he had to suppress a laugh. Peris's fastidiousness with regard to the Claws' uniform never failed to amuse him, mainly because its only mandatory element – a heavy coat of dark tan with cardinal-red hems along high collar and sleeves – made it just about the laxest he'd known.

Eumenes flashed a salute as they passed, and Xavire nodded in acknowledgement. He knew most of the men by name, as well as many of their stories, their reasons for joining this eclectic band. He did not, as it happened, know Eumenes's story, but he was sure that Uslo did. Uslo Dargent knew them all.

Once past the drills, the path brought them close to the butts, where they were greeted by the intermittent thumping of crossbow bolts piercing straw targets. There were fifty-one crossbowmen in the Claws, but only about ten were currently in the camp. The rest were spread along the Wall to the west of the gateway. They were the obvious choice for posting during daylight hours, their keen eyes set on the northern horizon. Xavire thought it the easier job. Not only did nothing of import ever happen along the western stretch, they actually got to sleep at night. The pikemen covered night shift, and although their greater numbers meant the task could be spread, Xavire didn't envy them in the slightest. He had worked night shifts during his time in the Valentican City Guard. It had not agreed with him. The memory produced a yawn, and he rubbed his eyes under his glasses.

"Ahoy there, Almenara! Long night?" The shout came from up ahead, and Xavire squinted to make out the figure coming toward them. Bursts of sunlight danced across plate armor, and a smile flashed almost as brightly.

"One of the many burdens of command, Sir Guilliver," replied Xavire, somewhat lamely. "How goes it with our adventurers?"

Sir Guilliver gave a little chortle. "They're with us for now. Although rumors of dragons grow more persistent with every week." They were slowing to meet each other, Xavire ignoring Peris's non-verbal hints that they keep moving. "Fortunately for you, I'm here to remind them of just how useless they all are."

Xavire grinned. "Truly, we are blessed."

And they were. 'Adventurers' was the nickname given to the Claws' cavalry. It derived from the fact that the horsemen were, almost to a man, third or lesser sons of minor nobility, or occasionally of the more successful merchant families. As such, they possessed the necessary wealth for a horse and a set of full-plate armor, but little to no actual experience. Add to that their sheltered upbringing, a great deal of which was spent reading about grand acts of heroism, of valiant feats carried out by the paladins of Basilea or the orders of the Brotherhood, and you had the perfect recipe for a bunch of hotheads who could prove worse than useless on the battlefield. Uslo once told Xavire that he wouldn't even consider them for the Claws, were it not for Sir Guilliver.

Originally from the Vale of Imlar, Sir Guilliver was a hedge knight, a wandering warrior and an expert horseman. Blond and broad shouldered, one could not help but warm to his upbeat nature and jovial smile. After a while, however, Xavire had come to note a certain hardness in his eyes. He didn't know the circumstances of Guilliver's past, whether it was dismissal from service or voluntary exile that brought him to the Claws. He knew only that when Uslo and Guilliver met, each man recognized something in the other, and that was enough for Xavire. Since that fateful meeting, it had been Sir Guilliver's job to whip the adventurers into shape. Under his tutelage, the Claws could boast around a forty-strong contingent of heavy cavalry, in many ways a greater psychological threat than an actual one, and extremely useful for securing more lucrative contracts.

"Look, Xavire." Sir Guilliver glanced around quickly as they drew close and lowered his voice. "Is there something I should know?"

They stopped walking. Sir Guilliver was looking at him seriously.

"What do you mean?" asked Xavire.

"About the general. Is something happening?"

Xavire weighed his words. "Not that I'm aware of." *Yet*, he thought. "Why do you ask?"

Sir Guilliver shrugged. "Could be nothing. Only he missed our morning ride, and that's a first."

Xavire nodded. That certainly was unusual.

"Also, when I was returning my gelding to the stables, I saw that they were readying Volonto. For a journey, by the looks of it."

The throbbing in Xavire's head grew more pronounced. He sighed. Volonto was Uslo's horse, a fine palomino charger. "Whatever it is, Sir Guilliver, I have a feeling we'll be finding out soon enough."

The horseman nodded, satisfied. He gave Xavire a quick pat on the shoulder and a wink before continuing on his way. After a minute, they heard him call out something to Sergeant Eumenes, his voice brimming once more with its usual jocularity.

They rounded the last block of dormitories and stepped into Darvled's Town. Since the settlement had developed only in response to the martial presence at the Wall, the wider complex of the barracks formed an uncomfortable heart to the town. Xavire found it incredible to think of the speed with which it had all appeared. He could remember when the Claws first arrived, could picture it vividly. At that time, the wall was still under construction, but further developed along this stretch than any other, he had later learned. Despite this good progress, the barracks had remained an encampment, for so long in fact that he occasionally still thought of it as such. The first non-military buildings, including the Lucky Orcling, had actually been erected before a single stone was lain for the barracks. The decision to finally upgrade the camp to something more permanent may have been overdue, but it was welcomed by all – save perhaps for the Plainsmen, by whose labor it was built.

Them, and one other besides, thought Xavire as their destination came into view.

Squatting between Darvled's Town and the barracks in stubborn defiance of its surroundings was a single, large tent. Red banners hung on either side of the entrance flap, each emblazoned with a silver battle cat rearing in profile. The guards appeared to have been dismissed. Xavire caught himself shaking his head as they approached. Uslo had simply refused to take it down, as if doing so would in some way be tantamount to a defeat in this dull posting. But the settlement had since accommodated his presence, building around the tent as closely as possible. The result of a commander's pavilion being nestled, however obstinately, between wooden constructions was a decidedly odd sight to say the least.

Peris stopped a little way from the entrance. Xavire waited a moment before asking if he was coming in. The sergeant shook his head.

"No, sir. I'd best get back to the men. I just..." Peris sounded uncomfortable. "I just wanted to say... that he listens to you, sir."

Xavire raised an eyebrow. *News to me*, he thought. "I'm sorry, Sergeant?"

"The general, sir. He listens to you. I don't know what's going on, but I do know that."

Xavire looked at the man carefully, searching for clues among his passive features. Peris had been with Uslo for longer than he had, longer than any man he knew. Uslo trusted Peris, and Peris trusted Uslo, or so Xavire had always believed. Gods, his head hurt.

"Could you speak plainly, Sergeant? I'm not in the mood for riddles."

The hint of a smile touched Peris's lips and was gone. "It's nothing. My apologies. Sir." He gave a quick salute and departed. Xavire watched him go before turning back to the tent.

I'm not going to like this.

Xavire shook his head, casting out the thought, and entered the tent.

Once inside, he removed his cap and turned to hang it on the stand. "Alright, Uslo," he began, affecting an exasperated tone that was only half in jest. "What could possibly be so urgent at this hour..." but it wasn't Uslo. An old man sat at the small table toward the right of the tent, his eyes locked on Xavire. The table was laden with a small feast, and the man was almost comically immobile, a chicken leg halfway to his mouth.

For a moment, Xavire wondered if he was still asleep and this some bizarre dream. Then he took in the man's clothes, his aspect. His smell. A Vik. Alarm purged the tiredness from his mind, and he saw that the man was not alone. Sitting across from him was a younger man, also Ardovikian it seemed. The youth turned in his chair to see who'd entered, and Xavire realized that it was one of the two lads who had come begging last night. The redhead. The one who'd spat.

"Good day, Xavire."

Xavire turned to the voice. Uslo stood further into the tent, his back to Xavire as he leaned over a high table. The Plainsman youth turned to the old man and said something quietly. Whatever it was seemed to reassure him, and they returned to eating.

"Good day... to you all."

This isn't good, he thought. Although Lord Darvled had shown tolerance to many of Uslo's eccentricities, a flagrant violation of decrees regarding the Ardovikian Plainsmen was pushing it. He said nothing, however, and waited for an explanation. Uslo continued to have his back to him and was muttering quietly. The Plainsmen didn't look up. Xavire suppressed a sigh.

"You wished to see me, sir? Urgently?"

The general turned around. From the deep shadows under his eyes, Xavire could surmise that he had been up all night. A mischievous grin unfurled beneath his mustache. He appeared quite mad.

"Yes. Yes!" He strode toward Xavire and clapped both hands on his shoulders, eyes gleaming. Xavire's stomach dropped. He felt certain now, certain that Sir Guilliver and Sergeant Peris had been right to worry. A scheme was coming.

"Allow me to introduce you." He put his arm around Xavire's shoulders, sweeping the other across the space of the tent. Xavire felt a quick sting of surprise when Uslo stepped aside.

There was yet another figure present, standing on the other side of the table that Uslo had been examining a moment ago. It was a woman. She was tall and dressed in thick, brown robes. A tanned and oval face sat upon the bundled folds of her lowered cowl, topped with short, dark hair. Not an Ardovikian nomad, clearly. Xavire's first impression was of a religious order, perhaps one of the southern temples. She stepped around the table toward them, and Xavire noted the way her hazel eyes assessed him. A warrior's eyes, sharp and fierce.

"This is Elder Ottrid," said Uslo, gesturing to the old man. "I met him last night. Knows all the stories of his people and their land."

The Elder Ottrid inclined his head to Xavire, who returned the motion.

"And here we have Cauhin, son of Hunlo. Fine young lad. Truly a bright spark."

The youth, Cauhin, smiled awkwardly, shooting a quick nod in Xavire's direction. He barely noticed. Xavire was looking at the woman, and she back at him, each attempting to solve the other.

"And this," said Uslo, turning to her, "is Lady Alea." She nodded lightly, an amused smile tracing her lips. She looked satisfied.

"Everyone, this is the good friend that I've been telling you about, my second-in-command, Xavire Almenara."

"A pleasure," he said, absently. "I'm sorry, your name is Alea…?"

"Yes."

"Alea, what?"

"Just Alea, for now."

Xavire felt his eyebrows rise. Her accent was unmistakably from the east of the continent. He glanced at Uslo. The general quickly flashed the whites of his eyes, expressing amused solidarity with Xavire's question. He released his shoulders and waved him over to the high table. Xavire followed, and Alea stepped back to give them room. As he approached, he saw that the majority of the table was taken up by a map of Western Upper Mantica, a good few decades out of date by the looks of it. Next to it sat a square of parchment, as well as an ink bottle and quill. The parchment was dotted in scribblings, dominated in its center by an outline of Ardovikia. Xavire picked it up. The sketched map made note of the wall, Darvled's Town, and the three main gates. A line was dashed a little way into Ardovikia, running parallel to the Wall. The various scribblings seemed to be estimates of distance and other figures. Most were scratched out. Xavire had no idea what any of it meant. He looked up at Uslo, but before he could open his mouth, the general spoke.

"Do you remember last night's conversation with the mountain men, Xavire? The stories about Ardovikia? About what is hidden there?"

Xavire nodded. "Yes, sir. Brawand said that Ardovikia was once a prosperous part of Primovantor, but that after the war with Winter, the collapse of her glaciers removed almost all trace."

The general nodded again. "Yes, but only on the surface. The floodwaters didn't destroy what lay beneath. Just buried it."

"So say the stories."

"So say the stories," Uslo repeated, his eyes bright.

"I also recall a lot more skepticism from you last night, sir."

"Skepticism is healthy. But I was curious as well. And since you seemed to be enjoying yourself..."

Memory flashed into Xavire's mind of Uslo excusing himself early while he continued to drink with the mountain men long into the night. His head throbbed.

"...I decided to indulge that curiosity." Uslo lowered his voice. "I heard many more stories last night, Xavire, from the people who know Ardovikia best."

"Sir?"

Uslo smiled widely, his excitement palpable. "And we're going to go get some."

"Some what, sir?"

"Some treasure, of course!"

There it was. A scheme. Xavire looked again at the sketched map. Apart from the dashed line, Ardovikia was blank.

"Forgive me, sir, but I don't see any treasures here." He glanced at Alea. She had been slowly moving around the tent, examining Uslo's possessions. She was now by his armor stand, where the general's full plate hung. It was an unusual set, made from a reddish bronze in a style that hearkened back to a bygone era a thousand years past. A steel working of Uslo's silver cat motif was mounted on the cuirass, and Alea was softly tracing its shape with her fingers. Behind the suit hung the company standard, its cardinal-red fabric displaying the same rampant battle cat as the cuirass, its border lined with off-white tassels.

"Well, naturally they haven't told us exactly where. We've got to hold up our end of the deal, first." Uslo spoke like this was the most obvious thing in the world. Looking around quickly, he leaned in and spoke more quietly still. "I suspect they wouldn't be able to mark it on the map, anyway. They don't use them. But that's beside the point." He straightened up, his expression expectant.

Xavire leaned toward him, his voice only fractionally above a whisper. "And what's our end of the deal, Uslo? What did you promise them?!"

Uslo spread his hands. "It's simple," he began, no longer speaking quietly. "We need them to guide us to the treasure, and they want to get home. Two birds with one arrow. We're going to smuggle the Ardovikians north of the wall."

Xavire took off his glasses and rubbed his eyes.

Okay. Slowly, he thought. *Just need to think this through*.

As far as schemes went, it could have been a lot worse. It was still lunacy, of course, and his immediate instinct was to try to talk Uslo out of it, but that was rarely an achievable task, regardless of what Sergeant Peris might believe. No, best to first run through it all step by step. Give it a chance.

Putting on his glasses, he turned to the table once more and looked at the map that lay there. In all likelihood, their contract at the wall would soon be ending anyway. The war was over, the threat gone. There was simply no need to maintain such a large force spread along the length. The mercenaries would be the first to go. Too expensive, better to extract a militia from the local populace. Cheaper. That's how he'd do it, at any rate.

Xavire glanced over at the two Ardovikians. The old man had his back to him and was pouring himself another cup of wine. The lad had stopped eating. He was looking at Xavire. Waiting.

Getting north of the wall would be a challenge, but not an insurmountable one. The Claws were an efficient bunch, they would be ready to go within moments of receiving the order. This stint at the wall had hardly challenged them, it was true, so there was a chance they'd be a little rough around the edges. But they would manage. With good planning, and better execution, they might even be able to pull it off without anyone realizing, to go north but leave Lord Darvled assuming they'd gone south. Compared to that challenge, smuggling a couple of Ardovikians was no problem at all. They were hardly likely to be missed. Although…

He began to pace. If they were caught with the two Ardovikians – caught trying to take them north, at that – the punishment would be far more severe than for being found simply trying to get themselves across. Also…

Xavire stopped pacing. "Why smuggle them? Why don't we just pay their debt so they can cross the wall legally?"

Uslo looked puzzled. "I think that goes a little beyond our funds, Xavire. But it is fine, I have already decided that the necessary coin to free them will be paid when we return south. Taken from our spoils, just to avoid any… hard feelings with Lord Darvled." From his grin, it was clear that Uslo was hoping for *some* hard feelings.

Xavire frowned. "The debt of two Plainsmen may lighten our collective purse some, but it's hardly an exorbitant sum for avoiding our arrest." There was a confused pause, punctured only by a sigh of pleasure from the old man, Ottrid, as he sat back in his chair. It seemed he'd had his fill.

"I fear you have misunderstood the terms of the proposed arrangement, Mister Almenara," said Alea, her words measured in both tone and volume. It occurred to Xavire that someone curious might easily listen in to their conversation from outside the tent canvas.

Sloppy of me not to think of that sooner, he thought.

"Perhaps someone would care to enlighten me?" Xavire asked, keeping his voice low.

"We're not going to take just these two Ardovikians north of the wall," explained Uslo.

"Sir? Their families as well, is that it?" Xavire felt the alarm pressing against his precariously constructed calm. His head throbbed.

"A few more than that..."

"All of them," finished Alea. "If you want to find your treasure, you'll have to get all of them across the wall."

Xavire stared at her, and she at him, her face displaying a cool determination. After a few moments, he became aware that his mouth was hanging open. He snapped it shut.

"Us– General Dargent, sir... could I perhaps have a word with you? In private."

The general nodded, seemingly unperturbed. He approached the Ardovikians and placed a hand on Ottrid's shoulder.

"If you'll excuse me, friends, I must converse with my right-hand man. I will update you in due course regarding the progress of our plan."

The Elder Ottrid stood up awkwardly and beamed at Uslo. He took the general's hand and shook it with enthusiasm.

"Thank you," he said, the words thick with genuine meaning. He then walked over to Xavire, hand extended. Xavire took it. "Thank you."

"You're welcome," mumbled Xavire, a little taken aback by the tears that were shimmering in the old man's eyes. When the elder turned to leave, Cauhin stepped forward. The youth stood stiffly a moment before extending his hand, his expression ambiguous. It was clear he had yet to make up his mind about him. Xavire shook it. Cauhin then moved quickly to the entrance, poking his head outside. Satisfied by what he saw, he held open the flap for Ottrid and waited for Alea. She was looking at Xavire as if to examine him one last time. Then she gave a quick nod to Uslo and left the tent. Cauhin stepped out behind her, glancing back as he went.

"You have mud on you," he said, and was gone.

Like you can talk, thought Xavire petulantly. He caught himself brushing at the dried patch on his leg and quickly stopped. Glancing at Uslo, he saw that the general was avoiding his eye, apparently in an attempt to contain his amusement.

"Yes, yes, very good," said Xavire, the exasperation completely genuine now. "I hope you realize that if it wasn't for your damned insistence on living out here, and the fact that anyone might overhear us, I'd be yelling right now." His head throbbed, as if in punishment for this lie. Shouting about any of this would be very stupid. "You'd hear me tell you, *explicitly*, just why this is such an Abyss-damned and foolish idea."

"Oh, don't be so dramatic," said Uslo, scooping up an apple from the table. There was still plenty of food left, and Xavire was suddenly aware of how hungry he was. Uslo gestured to it before biting in. "Want anything?" he asked through the mouthful.

Xavire's stomach rumbled in response, but he shook his head. Despite how tempting it all smelled, the thought of eating only made him feel more ill.

"Just water."

Uslo pointed to a set of clay cups and a jug which were sitting on a chest in the corner. Xavire moved to it and set about pouring himself one.

"I know what you're wondering," said Uslo in-between bites.

"Is that so?" Xavire drained his cup and began pouring another.

Uslo nodded. "You're wondering how we'll supply ourselves for such a large expedition without drawing attention."

"A good question. But not quite what I had in mind."

Uslo waved a hand. "You'd have got there eventually. You see, what I'm thinking is–"

"Hold on. Before we get there, let me say what I was *actually* wondering."

"Of course."

Xavire finished the second cupful and refilled it again. "Everyone knows the stories about lost treasures in Ardovikia. But no one has ever found any."

"That we know of."

Xavire shook his head. Uslo was certainly singing a different tune today. Still, he couldn't help but smile. This was definitely the Uslo he knew.

"Fine. That we know of. So, why not? Why, after hundreds of years of adventurers, expeditions, and petty kingdoms, do the treasure hunters only ever find the carcass of whatever Young Kingdom of the Plains has fallen to ruin that year? Why has no grand discovery been made? That we know of," he added quickly.

Uslo shrugged. "Ardovikia is vast, and until recently, turbulent. No one who came searching knew anything about the land, or they had to deal with rivals, or any number of reasons. The Ardovikians, the nomadic Plainsmen I mean, they have no interest in treasures. Everyone so looks down on them that nobody even thought to ask!"

"Really? Nobody else asked them but you?"

"Well, if they did, they probably asked the wrong questions." Uslo was beginning to sound irritated. "It's their *stories*, Xavire, their myths and legends. They didn't know they knew, but if you ask the right questions, and listen..."

"Okay, fine." Xavire moved to the table, seating himself where the Ardovikian youth had been a minute before and setting the water jug among the plates. He gestured to the chair opposite. "So tell me the story."

Grinning with a showman's delight, Uslo sat. After an exaggerated throat clearing, he began to speak.

Over the next five minutes or so, Uslo recounted the story of a legendary huntress among the Plainsmen, a tale that had apparently been imparted to him the night before. It was a patchy affair, with the general on numerous occasions being forced to make a quick leap over narrative gaps – he confessed to being quite drunk when he'd heard it.

The huntress was named Eranie, and was apparently so respected for her skills that she bore a bow gifted by Kyron, the fabled Thornbow. Led far from her usual hunting ground by strange game, she came to a range of hills surrounding a pleasant river valley, its banks strewn with ruins from a time before Winter's War. There she discovered a large group of humans, migrants from the south, who were in distress. It appeared their children were lost in sleep, though it was a sleep more akin to death than not, their skin cold and joints stiff. They said that a creature haunted them, a phantasmic being that plagued their dreams and had carried away their souls underground.

It was this next part of the story which shone clearest, burnished bright in the most fastidious corner of Uslo's memory. Eranie agreed to hunt the creature and lift this strange curse, and so was pointed to a cave leading underground. When she entered, she emerged in a realm of 'marvels,' room after room brimming with unimaginable treasures.

Eventually, after much to and fro, Eranie cornered the creature and forced its retreat into an arch, something the Plainsmen described as 'a cascade of starlight.' When the huntress loosed an arrow after it, the cascade abated, the god-given weapon seeming to break its flow. This, it seemed, was sufficient to free the children from their ill slumber.

When the tale reached its end, Xavire was perfectly still, expression flat as he stared into the bottom of his empty cup. Inside, however, contrary emotions wrestled.

As stories went, it left much to be desired; as evidence for an expedition, doubly so. That said, it was not without promise. If it had merely been crafted to play on men's greed, Xavire would have expected far greater focus be placed on the treasure itself – it seems that when the Plainsmen gave Uslo their rendition, the hoard of underground wealth was almost incidental to the struggle between huntress and shade. A thin promise for so daring an act as defying Lord Darvled. All the same, a smile began to form at the corners of Xavire's mouth. Even in his rotten state, he felt the old tingling awaken in him, the alluring prospect of wealth. Fame. Adventure. No one joined the Claws to live a safe and humble life. Even if he was enjoying the relative tranquility of this posting, Xavire had to admit that a part of him was going a little stir-crazy, a part that would only grow more insistent as time went on. His smile was fully formed now.

"And they know where it is, this cave leading to 'marvels'?"

"They claim so, though they also assert that they will only communicate their guidance through the Lady Alea."

Xavire's eyebrows rose. "Just who is she, Uslo?"

The general shrugged. "A mystery. Clearly from lands east of Galahir, as I'm sure you gathered. It appears she has taken on something of a guardian role for the Plainsmen. She either skirted the lines of Lord Darvled's decrees or else remained beneath notice. I believe the Plainsmen trust her not to be hoodwinked by our fickle southern promises, our cultures being all the same to their eyes."

Xavire shook his head. It was a lot to process. "Alright. Go ahead and tell me about this answer to the riddle of supplies."

Uslo grinned, appearing momentarily like a delighted child. A full-grown, sleep-deprived, mustachioed child.

There was a cough from outside the tent. Xavire immediately tensed, but relaxed when he heard the cautious voice.

"General Dargent?"

"Enter."

A young man stepped through the flap. Xavire recognized him as one of the stablehands.

"Your horse is ready, sir."

"Excellent. I'll be right along."

The lad gave a nod and left. Uslo got up and went to the far end of the tent. He put on the his red-hemmed overcoat and produced a travel bag from somewhere, which he then slung over his shoulder as he made for the entrance.

"Hold on, you still haven't–"

"We'll walk and talk," he said, grinning as he disappeared through the flap.

"Oh, yes," mumbled Xavire as he got up to follow. "Yes. Let's move the conspiring to the streets. And at midday, no less! Why ever not?" He grabbed his cap as he exited after him.

The hot sun beat against Xavire's face, blinding him momentarily. Fixing the hat in place, he saw that the general was moving quickly. He caught up to him and locked step, keeping as close as possible while he spoke.

"So? The supplies?" Xavire kept his voice low as he scanned the disinterested faces of passers by.

"The supplies *and* how to get them across the wall. These puzzles are one and the same, and so is our answer, Xavire!"

They reached the stables. The young stablehand stood waiting, holding Volonto's reins, and the palomino warhorse was laden with travel gear. A long object wrapped in white linen protruded from among the satchels, and Xavire didn't need to see the glimmering hint of a gilded pommel to recognize Uslo's bastard sword.

"I have an idea for how to solve it, but it will require a quick foray east. Try not to let the suspense get to you, my friend!" Uslo mounted his horse.

"Sir, please wait a moment! Where are you going?!"

The general settled himself into the saddle. He tossed a coin to the stablehand. "To retrieve the most valuable weapon in any commander's armory – information!"

This was all happening too fast. "But sir, we still haven't discussed the biggest problem with…" Xavire glanced at the stablehand, but he had already moved away. "…with all of this."

"Which is?"

Xavire motioned for Uslo to lean down, and he did.

"How in the world do you plan on us getting three-thousand Ardovikians over the wall?" whispered Xavire.

Uslo's eyes shone with genuine amusement.

"That part," he said, whispering back, "I leave in your most capable hands." He winked and straightened up. "It's going to take all of your experience in these matters, but I have faith in you."

Xavire was speechless, and he could only stand there as Uslo twisted around to check his gear. The general glanced up at the sky.

"Some weather, eh? Won't be sorry to leave that smell."

Xavire glanced up. He was right. The summer had refused to abate.

"Yep. Looks like I forgot it," Uslo was saying, closing the buckle on his travel pack. "I will simply have to borrow yours." With that, he scooped the cap off Xavire's head and set off at a canter. "I'll expect to see a detailed plan when I return, Xavire!" he called over his shoulder.

"And when will that be, sir?" replied Xavire, watching him fix the pilfered garment in place.

"Tomorrow! Or a week! No more than eight days, I should think!" Then Uslo rounded a corner and was gone.

Xavire sighed, a tired smile forming amidst the exasperation. *And so ends the easiest job of my life*, he thought.

4

...Only speculation can be offered as to where one might find such a place, being absent on any atlas known to your humble servant; and it is here the accounts diverge, with suggestions including an unknown isle among the Ruins of Vantoria, or a hidden community in the Ogre Lands, and other possibilities yet more preposterous...

Vespilo A., *On the Location and Identification of Primovantian Antiquity,* Appendix IX *'From the Gatekeepers' - The Mystery of Keatairn*

He's a big one, thought Orod. Squinting in spite of the overcast sky, he tried and failed to recall the name of the approaching brute. No matter. He wouldn't go down easy, that much was clear.

Neither Orod nor Bolirm spoke as they watched the party making its way toward them. Straddling a huge breed of tusked swine known as 'gores,' the three figures plodded steadily through the rough grass. Mount and rider alike wore heavy plate armor, and the clinking of assorted metals grew more pronounced with every step. Above the heads of the incomers flew a tawny hide banner, sputtering in the uneven winds. The coarse hewing of its fanion cut matched the crude pattern it displayed, a series of overlapping axe heads and gore tusks stitched in faded red. The wind's ripples lent a cleaving motion to the design, a minor curiosity that registered only in the furthest corners of Orod's mind.

That the two did not speak was not to say it was silent. The Godspeaker Arlok, hunched over his staff behind Orod and to his left, had been talking non-stop for several minutes, wittering on in a low voice. The krudger had long since stopped paying attention, but the occasional line or two still managed to slip between his thoughts.

"...Tharg may offer to make you a krusher, but that will be a trick. A test. He will want to kill you no matter what, for otherwise he can never trust your warriors. That is his way..."

Tharg. That was it. Tharg Bloodtusk. Orod thought the name more appropriate for the gore than the orc atop it, but what did he know?

"It's like they aren't even movin'," wheezed Bolirm, the hiss of his scarred voice dislodging Arlok's babble and finally breaking the reverie. "Just... growin'."

Orod could see it too. A strange effect of a strange land. He turned his head, taking in the surrounding landscape. Open and flat. A horizon without mountains.

It was eight days since his forces had departed the Howling Peaks. After a cautious start, they'd upped the pace, stopping for no more than four hours rest each night. By the end of the second day, the snow cover was minimal, and the imposing Peaks had been reduced to a gray smudge in the distant northwest. By the end of the third, they had disappeared entirely; and by the fourth, the hills were growing gentler, rolling ever more lazily until, at some point on the journey's sixth day, Orod realized that they were gone. In their place was an endless green, stretching out in every direction, the sporadic patches of scrub at once random and unchanging.

Out here it would be easy for an orc of Orod's rearing to become lost. He and his orcs had only ever known mountains and mines, spaces defined by the countless ways each spot differed from the next – the shape of an outcrop from south versus west; how the air would change taste when a tunnel descends; the intensity of the sulfurous stink to the north. But Orod was not lost. He could feel the western lands calling to him, pulling him toward the promise of violence. Even in the blinding sameness of the grasslands, he would find his way.

"He's huge," said Bolirm.

Orod turned his attention back toward the oncoming trial. The krudger knew what his companions were thinking. Could Orod really topple this brute? It was understandable that they should be concerned – if Tharg were to win, there was no telling how many of Orod's underlings would likewise be killed to set an example. Orod certainly planned to off a few of Tharg's. But Orod would not lose.

As if hearing his thoughts, the Godspeaker began the lecture anew. "Remember, Tharg must be utterly defeated. You must humiliate him. Word of this will spread, and many orcs will want to follow you. You will soon amass them to your horde."

Tharg Bloodtusk and his retinue had stopped some fifty feet away, expressionless faces assessing Orod's group with only the barest of interest. Orod caressed the heads of his twin axes.

"Let's go."

They began to cross the field, electing to push through the thick patches of needle grass rather than work around them. Orod's eyes never left Tharg. He weighed his rival.

With the exception of his face and hands, the huge orc was clad entirely in thick plate. As Orod neared, he saw that the individual parts were drawn from a variety of sources – his greaves looked like refashioned dwarf chest plates, while his bronze rerebraces could only have come from an ogre – and had been strung together with obvious skill, resulting in a truly intimidating set. Three stacked rows of spikes emerged from either side of his conical helm, vaguely reminding Orod of the command crowns worn by the overmasters of Tragar, although the tuft of yellow-dyed hair emerging as a topknot marked the limits of the comparison. In his right hand, Tharg hefted an enormous cleaver almost twice the length of Orod's arm. The surface along the weapon's heel was dull, a corroded brown produced by countless layers of unwashed blood, yet the edge shone with the virgin white of freshly sharpened steel. The left meanwhile held his shield, forged in the four-pronged style typical of orcs, and a weapon in its own right. Tharg carried it somewhat slackly at his side, and Orod wondered if his opponent had judged him below its use. Whatever his thinking, he had certainly come equipped for a fight.

As for Tharg himself, he was old. Perhaps too old. The green of what little skin could be seen was pale, drained of vigor. Though he held his cleaver firmly, Tharg's body appeared to sag beneath the weight of his armor. Until he met Arlok, Orod had never heard of an orc living longer than forty years. The Bloodtusk looked at least half that again. Not as ancient as the Godspeaker, no doubt, but a krudger's status came from strength alone, not arcane gifts. That he should remain in command for so long suggested a warrior of remarkable prowess, one the youths hadn't dared challenge for leadership. Orod was under no illusions about how he himself would be judged. An upstart, unadorned and unworthy. Tharg would feel confident of victory.

But maybe not. They stopped and were now only fifteen feet away. Orod could finally look his foe in the eye. He saw that the expression which from greater distance had appeared impassive was in fact… stiff. Uncertain.

Arlok stepped forward. "Krudger Tharg, the Bloodtusk," he began, head bowed, one arm sweeping toward Orod, "I present Krudger Orodren'val, the–"

"What's that, Godspeaker? You mean there's an orc in there?" asked the flagger, raising a hand to shade his eyes in mock examination of Orod. "And there was me thinking you'd brought us a pair of snow troll runts. What's with all the fur, eh?"

While they no longer wore the hoods, Orod's orcs were still wrapped in their mammoth-hide suits. The Plains were not nearly as cold as the Peaks, but the hunters had been bred on the edges of the Abyss, and brisk winds were as unfamiliar to them as the flatness of the land. Tharg made no sound but drew back his lips in a snide grin. Although several of his top-row teeth were missing, the lower fangs were bright and sharp.

The left-most orc gave a low chortle. "Never mind the furs, that one's all bound in chains! Reckon he can't figure how to get them off!"

Arlok tried to continue. "Hold on, let's not–"

"Do they do all the talking, or can the Bloodtusk speak?" Orod's gaze hadn't once left his adversary.

"He can," hummed Tharg, the voice deep and smooth, projecting a power not shared by his weary features. "Unlike you. I barely understood a word of that wretched accent, never mind recalling your name." The retinue sniggered.

"So he has a tongue. Good. Shame about his ax warriors. Only six hundred? I expected more from a legendary krudger." Bolirm and his skulks had scouted them that morning. The Bloodtusk was camped around half a mile to the southwest, on the banks of a river that divided the Steppe from the human lands.

Tharg's eyes narrowed. "Your skulks can't have gotten very close, if that's what you think. I have eight hundred. Far more than the two hundred wretches you've got following you, though I s'pose you count the goblins as well."

"Yes, we both lead mighty hordes," laughed Orod. He began to pace in front of them, glancing quickly back at Bolirm. The skulk was fixedly observing Tharg's retinue, hands conspicuously close to his weapon.

"Although," he continued, turning back to Tharg, "I wouldn't take much pride, if I was you. Hundreds of thousands of ax go into the human lands, and only six– no, that's right, *eight* hundred come back?"

"There are more," Tharg replied stiffly, "spread along the river."

"I see! You hear that, Bolirm? There are others along the river? What do you make of that?"

"Sounds like the Bloodtusk is weak," hissed Bolirm, his eyes gleaming with malice. "Sounds like he's got no fight left in him."

"Could be that. Could be something else. The largest horde in an age was broken by the humans. Could be all those other orcs are weak, eh, Tharg? Or they are led by runts. Why else would the Bloodtusk want nothing to do with the rest of them? He's not like them!"

Orod stopped pacing.

"He wouldn't make his ax stay put for so long, scavenging from the land, cowering behind the river. He wouldn't *settle*."

Orod's tone had grown more scathing with every word, until finally it seethed with barely contained fury. Tharg looked equally livid, the deep lines in his face converging into a knot of rage. His warriors, however, appeared curious, and they eyed their krudger with eager expectation. Orod guessed that it had been some time since the last challenge to his rule.

Orod pointed at his foe. "I challenge you, Tharg Bloodtusk, to a krudge! I, Orod, will take your ax, and remind them what it means to live as orcs!"

The three gore riders stared at him in silence. Then, from deep in Tharg's throat, there sounded a rumbling laugh like distant thunder. "You are a runt," declared the Bloodtusk. "Amusing, yes, but nothing more than a chain-bound, fur-clad, shum-brained runt." He laughed again, and this time his orcs joined him.

In that moment, it took all he had not to draw his weapons and launch a berserk attack. But Orod held, and waited. When the laughter finally dried up, Tharg let out an exaggerated sigh.

"I refuse your challenge, whoever you are."

Orod blinked. His eyes scanned the Bloodtusk's retinue. They were hiding their disapproval behind false grins that teetered on grimaces. Yet they said nothing.

"I am Orod!" With his left hand he drew one of his axes. "You will say my name!"

"You are nothing!" shouted Tharg, leaning forward in his saddle. "Less than nothing! You come here from far away, trailing the most pitiful looking ax I have ever seen, talking about things you don't understand, and then dare to challenge me? You have no flagger, no status, no name other than the one your masters gave you! Yes, I know what you are. I know what the brand on your jaw means. A *slave*!"

Orod's blood boiled at these words. Yet he was at a loss. No krudger could refuse a challenge, not while his warriors looked on. Still, Tharg's retinue said nothing.

Tharg straightened up and gave a nod to his flagger before turning to Orod once more. "Go away, and take your 'horde' with you. If they are not gone by nightfall, then I'll set my ax on them. It wouldn't be much of a fight, but they'd enjoy the sport." The riders began to turn their mounts.

Orod knew he had to do something. But what? Panic began to mingle with anger. He couldn't afford a battle between their orcs. He had to kill him now, had to–

Laughter, high and mad, sounded from the Godspeaker. Only it wasn't the Godspeaker – it was his pet. Yip the goblin rolled in the grass, face contorted in mirth, one long finger raised to point at Tharg.

"Scared!" squealed the goblin, tears running the great length of its nose. "Scaredy-scared-scared-scared!"

That did it. Tharg looked to his warriors and saw the predatory threat laid bare in their expressions. If he did not fight now, if word spread among his ax that he had allowed such an insult to pass unanswered, the krudger would lose everything.

"Yes," hissed Orod, feeling the anticipation snake along his bones. "Run away, Tharg. Run back to your *settlement*."

The Bloodtusk glared at him. Then he smiled.

"Alright, slave. I accept the krudge. I will give you death."

He dismounted. The gore grunted at the shift in weight, and there was a heavy *thunk* as the armored orc hit the ground. After handing his shield to one of the retinue, Tharg stepped forward. The huge cleaver was pointed at Orod, held lazily in one hand.

"But when I win, I won't accept your warriors. They will be slaughtered, food for my ax. But not you." He raised his blade to a fighting posture, gripping the long hilt in two massive hands. "You will be food for the crows."

Orod said nothing, heard nothing save the war-drum pounding of his heart reverberate in his chest. He did not raise his weapon, the crescent head of his Tragarian axe resting against his thigh, its twin still slung at his waist. They began to circle.

"What's the matter, slave?" growled the Bloodtusk. "Axe too heavy?"

Orod smiled. The sour fury had turned sweet, a euphoria that both gripped and caressed him.

With an indignant snarl, Tharg swung for his head. Orod saw the attack coming and slipped beyond its reach. He laughed. Orod had experienced the rush of battle many times in his short existence. He had even come to know the thrill of the hunt. This was something else. Or was it more like both at once?

Sidestepping a downward strike, he reflected that he'd never before had to face so deadly a foe for his authority. His speed and strength had always assured dominance over those who challenged him. Only now, however, did he realize just how empty it had felt. How lacking. He ducked under a weighty swing, looping left to prepare for the next attack. Despite his confidence, there was real danger here; one wrong move could end him. Never before had Orod felt so alive.

Tharg stepped forward and brought his weapon back around, this time going low. Again Orod dodged away, finally raising his weapon to deliver a quick and dismissive tap to the cleaver. The metallic *clink* was short lived, but its mockery stung the air. The Bloodtusk let out a roar of frustration and lurched closer.

Too close.

Feinting to the right, Orod suddenly shifted left before moving into striking distance, skirting the cleaver's spine. Reaching outward and upward with his free hand, he dragged his nails across the narrow line of exposed brow beneath the rim of Tharg's helmet before quickly stepping away.

Blood, thick and black, seeped insistently into Tharg's eyes. The huge orc stumbled backward, large fingers struggling to clear his vision as he flailed blindly with the cleaver, warding off an attack Orod had no intention of making. If he had wanted to end things quickly, this would have been the time to do it. But there were other considerations.

Orod glanced over at the gore riders. The savage spectacle held them utterly enthralled, and they all but salivated as they looked on, their loyalties surrendered to the vagaries of violence. Orod knew that the more brutal he made the show, the more absolute his eventual dominion. So he waited, watching with satisfaction as the Bloodtusk ripped the spiked helm from his head and threw it aside.

Wiping away the rapidly congealing liquid, Tharg cast about for his foe, face awash with undisguised panic. After a momentary confusion, the old orc finally found Orod, stood some ten feet distant, weapon held casually at his side. His eyes narrowed.

"You're going to regret wasting that. It was the only chance you'll get."

He charged, readying a horizontal sweep of his cleaver. Orod ducked, anticipating the obvious attack – and immediately realized his mistake. In an unforeseen surge of speed, the Bloodtusk leapt forward, bringing an armored knee into Orod's face. The crunch of contact was deafening. His body whipped up. Pain exploded from his nose, but he barely had time to register before the blurred form of his adversary delivered a back-hand punch to the side of his head. Orod felt himself leave the ground as he went sprawling, tumbling twice over, coming to stop several inches from Tharg's gore.

The animal grunted threateningly as he sat up. Tasting blood, Orod spat at it, propelling a broken tooth at its snout. He forced himself to his feet. Through the dizzy fog of pain, Orod suddenly became aware that the axe had disappeared from his hand. He spun around, scanning the surrounding grass. Nothing.

"Looking for this?"

Tharg dangled the Tragarian axe, pommel held between two fingers, its crescent head swinging back and forth. It looked tiny. Tharg's cleaver was resting on one shoulder in a stance that echoed Orod's previous mockery.

"You need to take better care of your things, slave."

He tossed it away, the dismissive throw sending the weapon far from reach, and then lunged. Orod had just enough time to unhook his second axe before the storm crashed over him. It was all he could do to avoid the torrent of heavy strikes, shaken as he was from the twin blows to his head. With the superior speed of his weapon, Orod managed to repeatedly knock the cleaver off course, all while dragging his body out of harm's way. Tharg roared. In spite of his armor, his cumbersome weapon, his age, the Bloodtusk moved with a ferocious speed, his face screaming urgent fury as he drove into his prey.

A waist-high slice forced Orod backward to the ground, the tip of the cleaver raking across his chains. Predicting the follow-up, he immediately rolled sideways, narrowly avoiding the downward hack. There was a muffled *thump* as the heavy cleaver bit into soil, and he scrambled to his feet, managing to put some distance between himself and his foe. Tharg was coming at him again, and this time he would be ready.

Orod closed to meet the attack head on. Faced with a countercharge, Tharg gave a hurling sweep of his blade, fending off the attempt to get within striking distance. The cleaver moved with frightening dexterity, and Orod's momentum faltered, once again forcing him onto the back foot. He stepped away briefly, and then threw himself forward, searching for an opening, only to be repulsed once more.

Compared with his encumbered foe, Orod could better dictate the flow of the fight, better choose when to attack and to retreat. But the surprising speed with which Tharg brandished his weapon diminished such an advantage, preventing Orod from getting close enough with his solitary handaxe to land a killing blow. He had hoped to exhaust his opponent, as a humiliation more than as a means to victory. But, incredibly, there was now a possibility that Orod would be the first to tire.

As he backed away from yet another rebuff, Orod's heel caught on a thick tuft of needle grass. He stumbled. Spotting a chance, Tharg stepped in with a low swing. Orod steadied his footing in a desperate lurch and prepared to parry the strike, his free hand grasping the butt of his axe. The weapon's body absorbed the hit, but Orod's arms buckled, and the cleaver dug into at least two inches of his thigh before coming to a stop. He let out a groan through gritted teeth and looked Tharg in the eye.

The Bloodtusk was grinning.

"No more running, slave."

Tharg pulled the cleaver toward him. The inconsistent length of metal sawed through Orod's flesh. Blood gushed in its wake, the dark spill quickly lost in the grassy underfoot. Orod limped back, wincing at the jagged pain. Tharg watched him lazily, weapon lowered, savoring imminent victory.

This is it, thought Orod. Tharg gripped the cleaver in two hands once more, raising it with the deliberate calm of the executioner. *The moment. The hunt.*

Destiny.

Surrendering to his instincts, Orod hurled his axe. The weapon, while not built for throwing, soared menacingly all the same, completing a single rotation before biting into its prey.

Prophecy.

Two fingers were cleanly severed at the second knuckle, the hand that owned them slipping from the hilt in surprise. Orod launched the length of chain before the axe had time to reach the ground, his torso twisting back from the axe throw to force maximum momentum. The hook looped dizzyingly around the exposed hilt and caught.

The Age of Orcs.

Orod pulled hard and wrenched the cleaver free. The Bloodtusk, shock blaring in his features, flailed after it, neither of the grasping hands coming close. Orod lunged, pushing off from his good leg into a shoulder bash. Despite his size, Tharg's panicked pursuit of the cleaver made the tackle irresistible.

With a feeble crash of plate armor on the grass, Tharg collapsed.

Ignoring the pain in his thigh, Orod scooped up his Tragarian axe. Tharg had rolled onto his side and was halfway up before Orod got to him. A swift whack across the face with the cheek of the axehead returned him to the dirt.

Orod had to work fast. Placing one foot on Tharg's chest, he aimed a blow in the exposed space between the Bloodtusk's breastplate and left rerebrace, sinking the head deep. The orc roared in outrage, his right hand shooting up to grab the embedded weapon, but Orod's left caught it tight. The axe was withdrawn, only to immediately return, doubling down on the first blow and disabling the limb. Then he jerked Tharg's right arm outward, lifted the axe, and repeated the operation with brutal efficiency.

For the briefest moment – no doubt the moment when he became certain of his fate – Tharg's roar was plaintive. Defiance quickly rose to burn in its place, however, and it was with distant curiosity that Orod observed the tears in his opponent's eyes. They did not move him. They couldn't move any orc, pitiless a species as they were. Yet an orc's tears would often appear, unbidden and useless, in moments of true helplessness. A clumsy oversight from an indifferent creator.

The roaring stopped. Orod removed his foot from Tharg and

turned to face the Bloodtusk's retinue. The two riders looked at their ex-leader with palpable yearning, the spectacle of blood having awoken their hunger. Tharg's gore seemed indifferent. Then the orcs' eyes shifted to Orod, and they shrank back, an instinctual caution telling them to submit. The euphoria of victory surged through every part of him, obliterating the pain in his slashed leg and broken nose. He spat out blood and addressed his newest warriors.

"Listen up! I'm your krudger now! The Bloodtusk failed you, made you wait – for what? For men to chase you further east? Enough! I will gather the ax, remake the great horde, and drive the humans from all lands from here to the sea! It is time! Time for the Age of Orcs!"

Laughter, low and gurgling, bubbled up from the ground. Orod looked over at the sprawled form of Tharg, feeling a sting of irritation. Hefting his axe, he moved to deliver the mortal blow.

"You are a shum-brain, slave."

He pulled back Tharg's head, exposing his neck, and lined up the chop.

"You think it was the humans that drove us from their lands?"

Orod paused. Tharg's eyes widened with spiteful delight.

"You've... no idea! No clue what waits there!" Tharg laughed. "It'll kill you!"

"And, what? I'll spare your life because you'll tell me? Your ax are mine, now. They can tell. You have no worth." Orod raised his axe.

"Their memories are short. They'll follow you because you promise victory. But you'll fail, and when you do, you'll remember what I said here!" He smirked. "You will remember!"

Tharg Bloodtusk choked out one last laugh before the axe fell.

5

...Any skepticism that is expressed toward these traveling merchants is likely to yield little more than firm asseverations of authenticity, with accompanying claims of the good money given to the traveling merchants of Keatairn (who curiously fail to appear whenever such scholars as your humble servant be present)...

Vespilo A., *On the Location and Identification of Primovantian Antiquity,* Appendix IX *'From the Gatekeepers' - The Mystery of Keatairn*

One week to the day after Uslo's departure, a rider was sighted in the late evening traveling in the direction of Darvled's Town. Word passed between the wall's towers by way of semaphore flags, an efficiently deployed system if somewhat minimal in its descriptive range. Today, for Xavire's purposes, it was enough.

"Evening, Mattis," Xavire called as Uslo's pavilion came into view.

The stocky figure on guard stood up straight. "Good evening, sir!" The Claw snapped off a salute. Xavire returned it casually.

"I believe our Silver Cat will be returning at any moment. Be so good as to make sure the stables are ready to receive him, then along and fetch some refreshments."

"Sir!"

The Claw hurried off. Xavire stepped inside, whipping the tent flap back in a vigorous motion.

He felt slightly crazed. His nights were restless, disturbed by dreams he couldn't recall. Wakefulness was no better. All this past week there had been little to distract him from his thoughts, and all thoughts ended in Uslo's riddle: how would they supply two hundred Claws and three thousand Plainsmen for a journey across the Plains? The solution to his own puzzle, physically getting the Ardovikian Plainsmen over the wall, came to him quickly enough. It was pretty straightforward really, when the Claws themselves manned the wall for a significant stretch. Walls were good at many things – repelling armies, for one – but if he had learned anything from his stint in the Valentican City Watch, it was that they were only as good as those who guarded them. Too few eyes and unburdened trespassers could come and go with no more than a little difficulty; should any of those eyes turn crooked, well, it wouldn't matter if the rest remained loyal – the wall may as well have ceased to exist. But to Uslo's question, he could muster no reply. He'd told Xavire he was getting information. Assuming he'd found it, then perhaps tonight Xavire would finally get the answer.

It was stuffy inside the tent, the heavy fabric trapping the day's heat. Without pause, Xavire moved to ignite the hanging oil lamp, dragging a chair over to set beneath it. Only as its saffron glow swept out into the space did he suddenly register her presence.

"We meet again, Mister Almenara."

Xavire's heart leapt into his throat. It took everything he had not to fall flat as he staggered back off the chair.

"Wha–! How–!"

Sitting in the tent's corner, cowled robes drawn up about her face, was the Plainsmen's mysterious eastern advocate, the woman named Alea. She drew the cowl down as she stood, barely restrained amusement on her oval face.

"I am glad you are here," she said. "I think it worth us having a talk before the general arrives."

For several seconds, Xavire stared at her in slack-jawed silence. Then he pulled himself together.

"Very impressive, Lady Alea. Mattis is one of my best sentries."

"I have no doubt."

If she had any reaction to his use of the honorific title, she hid it well. Her hazel eyes felt heavy on him – Xavire knew he was being assessed once more. Pushing his glasses back up his nose, he forced a broad smile before picking up the chair and returning it to the small round table.

"Shall we sit?" he said, gesturing to the one opposite. He waited until she was settled before seating himself. "How did you know the general was returning today?"

"'Knowing' is the province of the Shining Ones, Mister Almenara. I simply made a guess."

Xavire offered an amused frown. "Okay…" He picked up a squat clay jug from the table, thumb against the stopper. "Wine? Can't promise it hasn't spoiled."

Alea smiled diplomatically, apparently unfazed. Her greater height was, if anything, more pronounced while they were seated. "No, thank you. I wish to discuss your plan."

Xavire popped the jug's stopper free with a flick of his thumb, sending it bouncing off the table. "And what plan would this be?"

"The one your general tasked you with."

Xavire finished pouring himself a cup before sitting back in his chair, one arm slung over the top rail. "Told you about that, did he?"

Alea said nothing. Her eyes continued to weigh him.

"As far as I can see," he said finally, "I'm under no obligation to tell you anything, Lady 'just-Alea-for-now.'"

She nodded, as if she had expected as much. "All right, then let us trade questions. What do you want to know?"

"Well, I'd ask your full name, but somehow I'm not sure I'd believe you."

"And what would you believe?"

He sighed. "I don't know. Let's start with why you're here. Darvled's Town is a long way from Basilea."

Alea appeared to grimace slightly at his pronunciation of the Grand Hegemony, though he spoke it as all westerners did.

"I may be from the east, Mister Almenara–"

"Xavire, please."

"Xavire. I may be from the east, but that doesn't mean I'm from Basi-**lay**-uh," she said, pointedly. Then she paused. Xavire was balancing on the hind legs of his chair, but he was listening, and motioned for her to continue.

"I came here some time ago from a land farther east and north of Basilea, a land that is no more. Have you ever heard of the Brotherhood?"

Xavire flailed as his balance tottered, and there was a dull thud when his chair lurched back onto four legs. Wine sloshed over his hand. The Brotherhood! He quickly composed himself. "I, er, yes. I have. A land of knightly orders, sworn to hold back the Abyss? For all the good that did."

Alea gave a half nod, her expression neutral as Xavire continued.

"I saw a group of them during the war. They passed through the west gate, heading north. They looked a bit worse for wear, actually. Are you saying that you're one of them?"

"I am. Or at least I was."

"So you're a..."

"Knight? No. Women were not knights. But all in the realm were soldiers when needed."

"I see. Please, go on." Almost in spite of himself, Xavire was fascinated. This far west, the Brotherhood bordered on myth.

"What you know of us is essentially correct. For a thousand years – since the end of the war with Winter – we in the Brotherhood had dedicated ourselves to containing the Wicked Ones in their prison.

While other peoples bickered over trivial rivalries, we leveraged every member of our society to the cause. And for a thousand years, we held the line. That is, until the line was swallowed by the Abyss, and much of the Brotherhood along with it."

"Many of us didn't believe it at the time," said Xavire, casting his mind back a little over four years. "That the Abyss was expanding, I mean. Hells, I used to wonder if the Abyss even existed at all. But Uslo... the general has seen it."

Alea nodded. "It is not an easy sight to forget. And the smell..." She made a small gesture with her hand, as if sweeping the memories away. "Most of what remained of my people stayed to fight the encroaching corruption as part of the Green Lady's Alliance. But not all. Some lost faith and went in search of new causes. No doubt those whom you saw were one such group. More have joined them since the war's end."

"Yourself included?"

"Yes. I was one of the Devoted. We had... many roles in the Brotherhood. Roles that sometimes took us far from home. By the time I heard what had happened, the war was almost at its end. I returned home in any case and did what I could, but..." She shrugged. "It was over. Both the war, and the Brotherhood."

Xavire looked at her, thoughts swirling. *So she really is a lady.* He leaned forward, resting his arms on the table. "Then I take it you're here in search of a cause?"

"I came west in search, but I am here because I have *found* my cause," she corrected.

"The Plainsmen?"

Alea nodded. "I will get them north of the wall. The Abyss may be far away, cowed by the Green Lady and drowned by trident magic. But there *is* evil here, and I will see it undone."

They sat in silence, their eyes locked. Xavire nodded.

"I believe you."

"I'm glad to hear it." She leaned back, folding her arms in an apparent mirror of his earlier nonchalance. "Your turn."

"What? My story?"

"Your *plan*, Xavire."

"Oh, right." He forced a laugh. "Of course, the plan. Very well. You know the third tower west of the gate? The one they call Lydon's Head?"

"I believe so. What of it?"

Xavire told her. Shorn of all but the necessary details, it did not take long. She looked at him pensively throughout, at one point leaning forward to rest her chin on two fingers. There was no denying it to himself – she was pleasant to behold.

"I see," she said finally. "Yes. It would have to be at night, of course. Too many of the towers are not manned by your general's men, and even a distant lookout would spot us in the daylight hours."

Xavire nodded but could respond no further, for at that moment, Uslo returned.

"My friends!"

He entered with flourish, his arms and smile spread alike, the smell of the road about him. Xavire stood quickly to attention.

"Sir!"

"At ease, Xavire, no need for all that. Please, my lady, do not stand on my account. Here, Xavire, have your hat back – is that wine? Excellent!"

"Xavire just told me of his plan for getting us across the wall," said Alea once they were all seated, Uslo and Xavire with full cups in hand.

"A masterstroke, I have no doubt!" said Uslo, punctuating the statement with a thump on Xavire's back.

"It'll do the job, sir."

"Perhaps," said Alea. "Although there is still the matter of supplying our journey across the Plains. You found what we need, General."

Xavire raised an eyebrow, noting that Uslo appeared likewise taken aback by this declaration.

"I, er..." Uslo recovered, grin flashing. He reached into his satchel, quickly producing a small roll of vellum and setting it down before them. "See for yourselves!"

Xavire unrolled it against the table and turned it so both he and Alea could read by the lamplight. Written in the curt language of military bureaucracy, the document was dominated by a list which related various numbers and abbreviations.

"A schedule?" Alea asked.

Xavire nodded, running a hand down his beard. Some of the figures were clearly dates, covering a period of around six months.

"It's for the supply lines," explained Uslo, his satisfaction evident. "Lord Darvled relies heavily on support from the south, both for the wall itself and for his forces on the Ardovikian Plains. Most of the latter passes through the central gate, but soon enough..."

Xavire, whose eyes had not left the page, was skimming the listed dates. The schedule only accounted for two more months. Recalling that today was the fourteenth, he came to the proximate listing.

Realization dawned. He looked up.

"The next caravan will go through our gate."

"Yes."

"And you mean to steal it," said Alea.

"*Yes!*" Uslo's eyes shone with heady excitement.

"There's still lots to work out," said Xavire. "After all, such a plan presents its own set of problems..."

"But solves many others," Alea finished, a measure of enthusiasm entering her voice. "It lets us use the wall's mechanisms to our purpose."

"Exactly!" said Uslo. He sat back in his chair, running thumb and forefinger down his mustache. "I cannot wait to rob that bastard Darvled!"

"You won't have to wait long, sir. The train will be here in three days." Xavire looked again at the vellum. His foot began to tap as the weight of their impending transgressions settled on him. "It doesn't give us much time."

"I often find," said Alea, "that when a cause is just, as ours undoubtedly is, the Shining Ones will offer you a chance. This is our chance."

"Well said, Lady Alea!" Uslo poured the last of the wine into a third cup, offering it to her. "Let us drink to our chance!"

For reasons he could not entirely explain, Xavire was pleased to see that, this time, she accepted the cup.

They toasted. They drank. They were quiet. It had gone dark outside, leaving the three of them in nought but the lamp's glow. Sitting in the finite space of the general's tent, Xavire thought their undertaking took on a dreamlike quality. Outside, only a short distance away, it seemed that the wall was like a slumbering beast, and they like insects conspiring in its shadow. He noticed Alea was looking off to the side and followed her gaze. The general's curious armor reflected the lamplight in its red-bronze, casting a flickering shadow across the cardinal-red fabric of the standard behind it.

Uslo stood up. They rose with him. The general looked at them in turn, all trace of joviality gone from his dark eyes. Now there was only a hunter's calm. A gur panther in the grass.

"We have much to do. Let's begin."

6

...Most chroniclers treat this matter as an irrelevant oddity, unworthy of mention. While your humble servant finds himself in agreement with the former, to the latter he must demur: it should be mentioned at least once, if only so as to explain exactly why it need not be again. Accordingly is presented the following investigation of 'Keatairn'...

Vespilo A., *On the Location and Identification of Primovantian Antiquity,* Appendix IX *'From the Gatekeepers'* - *The Mystery of Keatairn*

Orod could feel the drums. He was rolling on them, on their pulses that throbbed across skin in time with the afterglow of his loins. Sprawled on the earth, he felt the cold wind blowing from the north, watched it buffet the reeds of the riverbank, making them dance in the corners of his vision. Like claws, sharp and careless. Around him, a semicircle of greatax extended for some thirty feet in every direction, their perimeter set against an outward bend in the great river. No tent had been assembled, nor hut, nor shelter of any kind. *What need was there for such things*, he thought, *out here in the fierce and open wilds?* The very idea repulsed him. He had all the warmth he needed. It was within, radiating from his stomach, where the last vestiges of Tharg Bloodtusk fueled his naked flesh.

The krudger heard a trill of splashes and raised his head. An orc female stood a little way into the river, half-submerged as she washed herself in the slow-flowing waters. Moonlight glistened on her muscular form, once more sending fire along his nerves. Lashka was his mate. She won that right after slaying all challengers, including Tharg's last. The contest had occurred earlier that evening, and as the krudger watched the all-consuming spectacle, Arlok had whispered in his ear, warning Orod not to show the slightest favor. The outcome, he was told, had nothing to do with him. Spying on her from the grassy shore, Orod found no faults in such an arrangement. She was the strongest. She deserved to possess the strongest. Lashka looked back, catching his eye.

Orod was strongest.

"Godspeaker." Orod sat up slowly. His eyes remained fixed on Lashka as he spoke. "How goes the goblins' work?"

"As well as can be expected with the materials available. They are simple, but they won't sink."

"And the other thing?"

"Both it and the rafts will be ready in no more than two days, Krudger."

Orod nodded. "See that they are. More ax are coming to my horde, Arlok. It will take many journeys to bring them all across. I will not accept delay."

"Of course." There was a pause, then the Godspeaker asked, "Krudger Orod, why do you want to cross here? This is the broadest part of the river."

"That's exactly why, Godspeaker." Arlok flinched as Orod turned his gaze to him, meeting his confused expression with a toothy smirk. "The humans won't expect it."

Arlok bowed his head. Orod dismissed him with a gesture. Something had changed in the drums. Their sound was wider. He looked behind him. There was an opening in the wall of greatax, a passage through which two figures approached.

About time.

Pain bit at his thigh as Orod got to his feet. He resisted the urge to rub it, not even glancing at it. Not that there'd be anything to see. The Godspeaker's magic had removed all sign of the wound inflicted by Tharg's cleaver, a process far more painful than the injury itself. His leg twinged again as he turned, dimly echoing the memory of a limb on fire.

The greatax resumed formation. Bolirm stepped forward quickly, seemingly eager to put some distance between himself and the orc sent to fetch him.

"I'm here, like you wanted."

Orod frowned. Bolirm was having to push hard for his voice to overcome the din of surrounding drums, and its scarred hiss ran coarse in his ears, dragging iron.

"Took you long enough," said Orod.

Bolirm grunted. "I had to push my way through. You know they're killin' each other?"

"Course they are. It's a krush."

"...Krush?"

"It's what free-orcs do when a new krudger takes charge. The weak die, the strong rise, and the orcs are united as one horde."

"Right..."

"Looks like you've come through, so far," said Orod. He gestured at Bolirm's face, where a long gash shone under the moonlight, narrowly missing an eye. "What about the rest of the crew?"

Bolirm's brow rose briefly. "We aren't takin' part. I've put 'em on watch, away from... the krush."

Orod met Bolirm's eye. "I see." Anger stirred in his chest. He wanted to kill him. "Yes... I should've known." He took a breath, holding his anger in check. "I've got a job for them."

"What is it?"

Orod stepped away, turning to look across the broad waters of the river, its far side barely visible under the starlight.

"Those're the human lands. Do you know what happened to them, one year ago?"

"I remember you talkin' to the Bloodtusk. His orcs attacked them."

"Not just his orcs. The biggest horde ever gathered."

"...What happened?"

Orod looked back at him. "They failed."

Bolirm's expression was blank. He said nothing.

"A hundred thousand of us went over just two day's march upriver. These orcs say it's shallow there. Narrow."

Orod looked to the river once more, his gaze pausing briefly on Lashka's floating form before returning to the western horizon.

"I want you to take the crew there and go across, then come back downriver and begin skulking. The humans have forts all along the border of their lands. Find the nearest one to this part of the river. Surround it." He turned to look Bolirm in the eye. "Don't let them see you."

"So you're goin' to attack the humans?"

Orod felt his anger spike. Pinning it flat, he drew back his lips, baring his canines in a predator's grin.

"Why else would we come here?"

To his credit, Bolirm held the krudger's gaze. Only the brief flinch of facial muscle gave away his unease. "You said a horde of one hundred thousand orcs failed to beat 'em. Your horde is jus' over a thousand."

"More are coming."

"A hundred thousand more?"

Orod turned his growl into laughter. "Tharg Bloodtusk and the other krudgers couldn't have beat the humans with three times as many. Numbers won't win."

"And what will?"

This time Orod's grin was real. The imagery of his dreams swam before his mind, clearer every night. A power, locked away, straining at its chains. Hills on fire.

"Destiny."

There was a splash from the river, and both orcs turned to watch Lashka step out onto the bank. Even in the dark, Orod felt her meet his eye.

"Go," said Orod firmly. "Do not fail."

If there's ever a moment for Bolirm to try and kill me, it's now, thought Orod. Bolirm had an axe at his belt and was garbed in the thick pelts from the east. Orod was naked.

He waited, watching Lashka as she lay down among the reeds, her muscles flexing suggestively. When eventually he glanced back, it was to see Bolirm turning to leave.

To think that he had once been like Bolirm. That there was once a time when he too would have looked upon so natural a thing as the krush with incomprehension. The idea filled him with disgust. All at once, Orod realized the ex-slaves would have no place in the world to come, the world he was set to bring. They would have to die. But not yet. They had skills the free-orcs lacked. They still had their uses.

"Stop. Wait there."

Bolirm stopped. He looked back, an odd mix of hesitation and defiance in his stance.

"That's a nasty wound, Bolirm." Orod gestured for the God-speaker. "We must see to it."

"What're you doin'? It's not a problem, I don't need– oi!"

Bolirm yelped in surprise. Orcs had appeared to either side of him, locking his arms in their grasp.

"Don't struggle," said Orod, ignoring the stream of curses now pouring from Bolirm. "It'll be over soon."

Even if the pain makes it feel like a lifetime, he thought, but already the skulk was vanishing from his mind. Lashka was gesturing to him, coaxing his undivided attention.

With Bolirm's ragged screams filling the night, Orod went to her.

7

...When engaged with peddlers of antiquity, the primary suspicion in the mind of any seeker should always lean toward the fraudulent; that being the case for any item, regardless of claimed provenience...

Vespilo A., *On the Location and Identification of Primovantian Antiquity,* Appendix IX *'From the Gatekeepers' - The Mystery of Keatairn*

"Well," declared Uslo, both hands raised to shield against the mid-morning sun. "That's..."

"...unexpected," finished Peris.

The general shared a quick glance with the master marksman, nodding in agreement before turning back toward the remarkable sight.

Across the sun-beaten grassland south of the wall, a caravan of canvas-wrapped wagons crested the range of hillocks which skirted the horizon. The wagons – around thirty so far, with more continuing to emerge – were escorted by an orderly procession of spearmen, dressed in the unmistakable drab of Lord Darvled. The narrow dirt road had forced the troop into single files on either side of the train, while at the head rode a trio of mounted officers, banners soaring behind them. Light sparked on breastplates and spearheads, a pure shine suggestive of newly forged steel. The supply train had arrived.

They had been expecting the supplies today, though the hour of arrival was far earlier than any would have imagined. What they had not expected – what had caused an alarmed Sergeant Peris to fetch Uslo – was the ogres.

Emerging behind the caravan along a mile-wide stretch of the low lying hills, their piecemeal grouping in stark contrast to the regimented formation of men, was a tribe. Not an army. A *tribe.* Uslo couldn't believe it. He'd worked contracts alongside ogres before and knew them only as wandering warriors, hiring out their enviable skills on the battlefield to whomever paid the most. But he had never seen ogre children before. He thought he could see them now, carried on open-topped carts and wagons pulled by a variety of long-haired boars and other, equally tusked steppe-beasts. The adult ogres strode alongside, guiding the carts through the off-road terrain with ease. Armed to the last, their weapons were held loosely, slung lazily over enormous shoulders, as if to mock the stiff march of the humans.

"There must be more than a thousand of them!" said Uslo, incredulity tugging at the pitch of his voice.

"Must be," agreed Peris.

Uslo shook his head. Standing on the battlements that ran between the gate and the first lookout tower, they watched the ogres make their way toward Darvled's Town for almost a half hour. More of them continued to appear throughout, until finally all the southern hills were covered in their oversized, oddly graceful forms.

"Two thousand," Peris muttered. "At least."

Uslo said nothing, smiling in spite of himself. He turned west, looking toward the clumsy settlement only a short distance away. He had no idea what the ogres' arrival meant beyond the obvious – that their plan to cross the wall was about to get a lot more complicated. He ran a thumb and forefinger out and down his mustache, feeling the anticipation snake along his limbs. Plans were always the first casualties of battle. They would have to improvise.

"Come along, my good Peris," he said, setting off toward the stone steps. "Doubtless they will want me for the welcoming committee. You, on the other hand, have much work to do!"

"Yes, sir," said Peris flatly, moving to follow.

*****

Xavire felt like death. His head was still gripped in the smothering embrace of the Lucky Orcling's finest, and his eyes felt ready to fall from their sockets. Any sound louder than an insect's buzz produced piercing pain in his left temple. The sun made him dizzy.

One night of indulgence, one last evening of drink and cards to chase away the nerves. To beat back the nightmares. After all the planning, briefings, constant mental run-throughs, not to mention the restless nights, wasn't he owed at least that? And what should greet him come morning, beside the hangover to end all hangovers, but ogres. A tribe of them. *Abyss-damned fool.*

"Gods, Xavire! You look terrible!" Sir Guilliver, resplendent in his full plate armor, golden hair shining like a knight of legend, gave a sympathetic smile, patting him on the shoulder. Even his sweat looked knightly, as if born from courageous deeds.

"Yes, well, you're one to talk."

Darvled's Town was abuzz with activity, its broad streets increasingly full as the supply train drew closer. In spite of the already merciless heat, Xavire guessed there wasn't a single person left indoors, and the air was rich with the scent of dust kicked up by many feet. He and Sir Guilliver were making their way from the barracks to the west gate to join Uslo and the rest of the welcoming committee. In a settlement as spontaneous as Darvled's Town, the gatehouse was the closest thing available to an official building, something no one seemed inclined to change.

"I take it Peris fetched you during drills?" Xavire asked.

The Imlarian knight nodded, moving away from Xavire as they passed a fruit merchant's cart, his stride unbroken as he rejoined him.

"Indeed. The adventurers require a dawn drill every so often. Keeps them from going any softer. Besides," he leaned toward Xavire conspiratorially, lowering his voice as far as the busy street would permit, "you never know when they might get the call to mount up!"

Xavire managed a grunt of acknowledgement, uncertain as to whether it was talk of their imminent journey over Lord Darvled's Wall that sent his stomach spinning or simply the act of talking at all. The plan's first stages were to take place that night, and while the early arrival of the supply train was unusual – such things usually went the other way – he couldn't see any reason why it should change their schedule. What impact the ogres might have was an entirely different question.

Xavire turned side-on, passing a mother who was dragging her protesting young daughter in the opposite direction, and caught a snippet as he passed.

"–not fair! I wanna see the org-ers more!"

"You saw 'em plenty! C'mon!" The mother's voice was firm, but she looked frightened. Xavire could hardly blame her.

They passed the last of the town's shanties and reached the west gate. Uslo was already there, dressed in his riding gear under the barbican's shade. He looked toward their coming, eyes bright.

He was drinking last night too, yet you'd think he'd slept in the lap of the gods, thought Xavire petulantly.

"Good morning!" called the general.

They returned the greeting with quick salutes. "Are we the first?" asked Xavire.

Uslo shook his head, smiling lightly, and jerked a thumb behind him. "The lord magistrate and his man bested us all."

Xavire followed his gesture further into the gateway's shade. Two figures huddled against the closed portcullis. Magistrate Lydon, Darvled's chief representative at the west gate, was short and portly, dressed in a fine set of blue silk with silver buttons and buckles. The other man was similarly well-fed but taller, his dark leather attire striving for ostentation: a puffed out collar of white lace; a thinly-gilded chain necklace; wide-brimmed cap with a long blue feather pinned to its left side.

"Not like Magistrate Lydon to be early," observed Sir Guilliver. They reached the general and stepped into the shade, a sigh of relief escaping Xavire's lips.

Uslo nodded. "I believe he rode in yesterday. Probably wanted to avoid a repeat of the last time."

Xavire murmured his agreement, watching the magistrate while trying to avoid being obvious. He needn't have bothered. The pair were deep in conversation, Lydon speaking behind a matching blue-silk handkerchief, the taller man listening closely, his sycophantic expression no doubt a mask for impatience. Xavire always thought Lydon had something of a sickly aspect. Today it seemed worse than ever – his skin was flushed and sweat-laden, his brow lined with a self-concerned furrow. Opinions differed as to where he was originally from. Though it was not a question that particularly interested Xavire, Lydon's apparent inability to cope with strong smells led him to agree with those who suggested Arcantor, or somewhere near Vantoria. He had heard tell that there were towns and cities along those coasts that had survived from the days of Primovantor, and as such, boasted elaborate subterranean systems that kept the water clean and the air clear. Darvled's Town had nothing of the sort.

The taller man began to speak, shaking his head lightly as he murmured reassurance. He was Drom, the gatemaster, second among Lord Darvled's representatives. Calculating eyes peered from a rectangular face, sharp nose set above the thin lips of an uncommonly wide mouth. Xavire had known many like Drom, particularly during his time in the Valentican City Watch. A climber, smart and ambitious, as corrupt as the day was long. No doubt Drom had once thought the chance for authority at the west gate to be his most lucrative move yet. But Darvled's Town was a dead end, and Drom was as stuck as the rest of them.

Lydon said something else to Drom, and then the two of them stepped away from the portcullis, moving to stand near the Claws. Xavire was suddenly struck with an overpowering floral aroma, a scent so strong that it seemed to coat the back of his throat. He guessed that Lydon's clothes had been infused with it as part of some new attempt to ward against the smells of the commons. The handkerchief suggested it had failed.

"Well met, General, Sir Guilliver." Drom made a curt nod to each in turn, the controlled neutrality of his accent seeping over into his tone. The untitled Xavire was apparently beneath greeting.

"Well met, indeed, my lord magistrate," answered Uslo, addressing Lydon directly. "I'm glad to see you looking so well this morning!"

Lydon didn't respond, nor acknowledge their presence in any way.

"Tell me, General Dargent," said Drom, evidently displeased, "do all mercenary companies permit their men to appear so disheveled, or is that just another one of your famed eccentricities?"

Xavire followed Drom's condemnatory gaze and saw that his undershirt was protruding. He tucked it away absently.

Uslo laughed. "Believe me, Gatemaster, I wish I could afford to dress all my men half as well as you. Why, I can hardly imagine what that outfit cost." He tilted his head, his expression thoughtful as he ran thumb and forefinger over his mustache. "Your dignity, at the very least."

Drom's eyes narrowed, but a voice reached them before he could attempt a riposte.

"Gentlemen! I hope we have not missed too much of the fun?"

Xavire recognized Brawand's voice and squinted as he looked out to the approaching pair. They were wearing scale-mail armor and carried the company's famed dragon-maw helmets under their arms. While each of them was in a better state than Xavire, neither looked nearly as alert as Uslo.

"Lord Lydon is glad to know the Dragon's Teeth have seen fit to join us," said Drom as the mountain men crossed into the shade.

Brawand ignored both the comment and Drom, offering Lydon a perfunctory bow before turning to the Claws.

"What do we think? Any ideas about what a tribe of ogres is doing this far south?"

"What makes you think it's a tribe?" asked Sir Guilliver. "Couldn't Lord Darvled have simply hired another warlord to bring warriors to the Plains?"

"I am not saying that is not a possibility, but I am telling you it is a tribe. Correct, General?"

Uslo nodded. "It's a tribe. At least two thousand strong."

Brawand nodded. "We counted the same."

A stunned silence followed. Though both Drom and Lord Lydon had been trying to appear disinterested in the mercenaries' conversation, Xavire saw they'd each turned a shade paler.

"We know soon, I think," said Ryser finally, nodding toward the road.

Three mounted soldiers were approaching, bouncing smoothly in time to their horses' canter. From posture alone, it was clear that they were officers. In the crowd, Xavire could see no more than a scattering of curious faces turn to follow the passing men. There was no waving or cheering – that was being saved for the wagons, the last of which was just now reaching the end of the south-east hillocks, while the first continued to make its way along the flatter terrain that led up to the settlement.

Or perhaps, considered Xavire, it wasn't the wagons they were waiting for. He could see several children raised on parents' shoulders, their excited pointing reminding him of the girl and her mother. Perhaps it was the ogres they wished to greet.

For their part, the officers showed as little interest in the crowd as was shown in them, their heads remaining tracked to the welcoming party as their horses followed the gradual curve of the road.

Drom stepped forward, hesitating only fractionally at the frontier of shade before stepping out into sunlight. Savoring a final cool breath, the mercenaries followed. Lydon stayed where he was.

"Gentlemen," began the gatemaster loudly, waiting for the riders to slow before he continued. "Lord Magistrate Lydon bids you welcome to the west gate, and hopes–"

"We thank the magistrate for his welcome."

The central figure spoke with dismissive dryness, as if the words were hardly worth their effort. Xavire recognized a fellow Valentican, though one who spoke with the crisp diction of the noble class, likely educated at the Grand Academy. He must have graduated recently – Xavire guessed the man to be in his early twenties. Somewhat long-faced, a neat and dark goatee clashed awkwardly with features that had yet to fully settle from adolescence. Brown eyes assessed them coolly, set high in a head which rolled back into a short bowl of hair, and dispensed swift judgment from beneath thin, sharply tilted eyebrows. The three men brought their horses to a stop.

"I am Commander Vopiscus Chantrille. This is Captain Olvar and Commander Pesayn."

Xavire felt his body jump at the speaker's name. Uniquely among the onlookers – a quick glance showed no recognition on the surrounding faces – he understood the reason for the power dynamic before him. Despite being outranked by one of his fellows, there could be no question that Vopiscus was in charge. The Chantrilles were one of Valentica's most important and influential families. For young Vopiscus to have joined Lord Darvled's army, even as an officer, suggested to Xavire that the commander was a third or lesser son of some branch, a cousin to the true line. Nevertheless, his name held power that went beyond rank, particularly if Lord Darvled sought the support of the family's patriarch. It was likely only a matter of time before the commander was promoted to Darvled's council. Olvar and Pesayn had no doubt concluded the same.

"Captain, Commanders," Drom bowed lightly, his voice containing no evidence of having been interrupted. "I am Drom of Cenia, Gatemaster for the west gate. Allow me to offer pardon for the rather bare reception. Gladdened though we are by your arrival, I confess we had not been expecting it until tonight at the earliest."

"It would have been even earlier, were it not for the road." Chantrille turned as he spoke, opening a wide, flat saddlebag. Olvar and Pesayn were looking up at the wall, their eyes following the battlements east and west. None of them had made any move toward dismounting, and Xavire now realized that not a single hand between them had been raised in greeting.

"I am sorry to hear that, Commander. The southeast road has usually proven adequate, but if there is degradation I'm sure"

"Not the southeast road, you cretin! Southwest!" the commander barked, not looking round until he'd found whatever he was looking for. When he did, Xavire saw that the coolness in Chantrille's eyes was gone, replaced with a searing anger that spread red across his face.

"The– the southwest, Commander?" Drom's voice faltered, his confusion plain.

"Yes, the southwest! The paved road that was to follow freshwater sources along the coast! The highway which was to form the very basis for building the west gate here in the GODS DAMNED FIRST PLACE!"

Drom recoiled visibly under the barrage of these last four words, but Xavire could see they weren't directed at him. He glanced back at Lydon. The nobleman was frozen stiff, his skin paling until it matched the great whites of his eyes. A southwest road along the coast? Xavire had never heard anything about that, and from the looks of them, nor had the other mercenaries. But Lydon knew, and so did Drom.

"B-b-but the war ended before the work began! We… my lord and I simply assumed that–"

"You were given enough resources to build at least twenty-five miles, more if you used them wisely." The anger had disappeared as quickly as it arrived. "Masonry and manpower. Where are they all now?"

This one, Xavire thought he could guess. Though he had never seen it for himself, it was common knowledge that Lydon lived on a manor estate around six miles southwest of Darvled's Town. Building it had been the Ardovikians' first task, and a small number of them continued to make the daily trek from the refuge in order to labor on its grounds.

"They are… I mean to say… they are unavailable." Drom spoke in a monotone, as if hypnotized.

"Unavailable? Even the Viks?"

"No… The Viks are being used for… for waste disposal. In the town."

"Ahh, so the rumors were true. Lord Magistrate Lydon not only permitted the formation of a new settlement, but had the audacity to direct Lord Darvled's resources to it."

A semblance of life returned to the gatemaster, and he straightened up.

"How dare you speak of the lord magistrate in such a manner! What business it is of yours I…"

His words tapered into an incomprehensible murmur as Chantrille heeled his warhorse forward, his eyes still on Lydon as he came toward them. He stopped next to Drom and, gaze still unmoving, handed him a sealed missive.

"This should explain, Gatekeeper."

Flinching at the incorrect title, Drom took the missive, staring at its wax seal. Then his long fingers snapped it open and he began to read. Chantrille meanwhile had finally broken his stare, turning his horse and looking out at the first buildings of the settlement. Not one person in the crowd seemed to be paying attention to the meeting.

"*Pssst*!"

Xavire looked over his shoulder, following the sound. Lord Lydon, handkerchief still in place, was trying to get Drom to bring him the missive.

"*Pssst*!"

Drom didn't so much as glance at the lord, continuing to read the note for what must have been the third time.

"How many are there in this 'town'?" asked Chantrille, his pronunciation of the word halfway to a laugh.

Drom looked up from the missive, his demeanor transformed. "Around one thousand, my… Commander."

Chantrille nodded. "Of which half are stationed on the wall?"

"That would be–"

Drom was interrupted as Lydon strode out of the shaded gateway and snatched the missive from his hand. The gatemaster stared at Lydon as if he'd never seen him before in his life. Then he bowed his head, mumbling, "Apologies, Lord," before turning his attention back to Chantrille. It seemed Drom had found a new path to climb. Vile as it was to behold, Xavire couldn't help but smile at the shamelessness.

"That would be correct, Commander. Aside from the mercenaries, there are some camp followers from the initial deployment, but most are citizens of the region whose prior homes were seized under the Requirement."

"Yes... I see." He continued to examine the settlement, looking over the heads of the crowd whose chatter could be heard growing steadily more excited. "But what I don't understand is why so small a settlement was given priority for the labor of three-and-a-half thousand Viks."

"Those are old figures, my– Commander. There will be fewer Viks now. But to your question, Lord Lydon has a..." Drom's eyes went briefly to Lydon, a flicker of disgust appearing on his lips, "delicate constitution, Commander. He wanted the settlement made sanitary as quickly as possible, with this heat especially, you understand."

Chantrille sighed. "Ridiculous. I want–"

"Who gives a damn what you want! I am the lord magistrate here!"

The yell had come from Lydon, who looked at Chantrille with a combination of indignation and terror. Xavire had never heard Lydon's voice before and was surprised by its strength.

"The Viks are mine! The mercenaries are mine! This town is mine! The west gate–"

"Careful, my lord." Chantrille's expression remained cool, but Xavire sensed the anger simmering. "We don't want you to say something you may regret. Was Lord Darvled's message unclear? Would you like me to explain it to you?"

"I– I can't– you–" Lydon blustered, the handkerchief bouncing with each attempt at protest.

"You are of course correct," Chantrille began, his tone suggesting nothing of the sort. "You are the administrator of this land, and we enter it at your pleasure. What's more, you are an ally of Lord Darvled. His most *trusted* ally."

Chantrille forced a smile that only seemed to move his upper lip, revealing sharp canines.

"As such, you more than anyone will understand Lord Darvled's vision for his wall, to make it more than mere masonry and lumber; to make it the furnace of destiny, the place where we will forge a new age in the Kingdoms!"

The dry indifference was gone from Chantrille's tone. His words burned in the air, fired with the fervor of a fanatic. Lydon nodded, the movement only barely perceptible. Somehow his skin had found an even paler shade.

"It is a vision that requires *cohesion*, Lord. *That* is my purpose!" In a swift move, Chantrille dismounted from his horse and stepped toward Lydon, his torso lurching ahead of him.

Keeping very still, Xavire's eyes sought out Lydon's men. None of the magistrate's guards seemed to have noticed the way Chantrille was bearing down on their liege. Rather, it seemed their focus was on the crowd, and understandably so, since the excitement had reached the point where those at the back were jostling for a better view, with the resulting pressure compelling those at the front to move forward. Xavire risked a glance at Uslo, expecting to find his own feeling of alarm mirrored in the general's face. But Uslo looked amused. He spotted Xavire's glance and gave a quick shrug.

Lydon shrank before the approaching officer, his feet locked.

"Lord Darvled himself has given me this task!" Chantrille placed his hands on Lydon's shoulders, leaning in close. "Will you help me, Lord? Will you permit me to assume your responsibilities? For destiny's sake, I humbly beg of you."

The handkerchief fell away. Lydon's mouth was open. He said nothing for several seconds, during which time, the commander's hands moved further along his shoulders toward his neck.

"Yes..." Lydon managed, finally.

Xavire let out a breath he hadn't realized he was holding. He felt sure that any other answer would have resulted in Commander Chantrille throttling all life from Lydon's frail body. Perhaps Lydon thought so, too.

"Good. Thank you." The commander's tone was calm once more, his posture returning to martial erectness. His hands stayed on Lydon's shoulders, however. "Lord Darvled will be pleased. Now, if you don't mind, perhaps you should go home, Lord? I have much work to do, and I hear your wife has not long given birth to a son? Lord Darvled asked me to pass on his sincerest felicitations." He began to lead the lord away, nodding to Commander Pesayn, who turned his horse and went to fetch some of Lydon's men.

"Well," said Sir Guilliver, looking round to meet the wide eyes of his fellow mercenaries. "That was..."

"...unexpected?" offered Uslo.

It took less than half a minute for the lord's escort of gate guards to disappear from sight, the crowd opening and closing seemingly without so much as a glance at the dejected nobleman.

A bellowed order reached their ears from the head of the caravan, the sergeant calling a halt. The first of the wagons stopped where the southeast road split one way for Darvled's Town and another for the west gate, the order sweeping quickly back down the line. Some fifty wagons in total ceased their rumbling approach, the dust settling on their spoked wheels while the five hundred strong guard of spearmen stood to attention and awaited further orders. Lord Darvled's banner hung limply in the still air at the head of the caravan, the white wall and gatehouse design contorted like snakeskin along the folds of black cloth.

"As I was saying, Gatekeeper," said Chantrille, turning to face Drom. The gatemaster looked at the commander expectantly, and this time, Xavire could detect no reaction to the mistaken title. It seemed he had made his peace with it. "I want rid of this settlement. It just won't do. Why, sections of the wall around the east gate have had what little stonework we put there plundered by local peasantry!" He shook his head. "I won't have such desecrations here."

The commander cast his eyes along the crowd. A hush was falling over the gathered citizens as their excitement was slowly diluted with trepidation.

"If Lydon would rather see the town relocated," Chantrille continued, "he can do so away from the wall. Eight miles at least."

"I'll see it done, Commander."

Chantrille gave a nod which suggested that much was obvious. "Our first priority, however, is the southwest road. Work on sewage must stop at once. There will only be soldiers at the wall, and soldiers can dig latrines." He looked back at Drom. "Get the Viks working on the road immediately. Double shifts, including overnight rotations."

Xavire cast a panicked glance at Uslo. The general's expression was impassive, but Xavire knew he was thinking fast.

"Of course, Commander, I'll make the necessary–"

"Commander Chantrille!" Uslo stepped forward. "If I might offer a suggestion?"

Chantrille turned slowly, thin eyebrows raised as he faced the general.

"This is Uslo Dargent, Commander," supplied Drom. "His mercenaries have been guarding the west stretch."

"Ah, yes. 'General' Dargent." Chantrille clasped his hands behind his back. "I imagine few have heard of the 'Silver Cat' this far north."

Uslo's smile didn't quite reach his eyes. "Commander, the Ardovikians are overworked as it is. They will not survive the schedule you are proposing." These last words were overlaid with a gasp from the crowd, and as one, their eyes went to the source.

Three ogres were striding past the stationary wagons. The one in front was huge even for his species, clad in great sheets of plate, an enormous battleaxe held in one hand. A braid of gray beard hung beneath his wide jaw, and an assortment of tribal tattoos criss-crossed the red-brown skin of his bald head and face. On either side were what appeared to be two guards, dressed in identical ring-mail cuirasses, the long handles of greatswords projecting behind their shaven heads. They were following the plated ogre directly toward the welcoming committee.

"Gods above!" exclaimed Sir Guilliver, barely audible over the now-gabbling crowd. "I'd bet there's more steel in that breastplate than my entire suit!"

"Why's he even wearing it?" responded Xavire. "Is he expecting a fight?"

"It is just their way," said Uslo, shaking his head as he leaned toward them. "They..." and the rest was lost as the plated ogre turned on the spot and shouted something in the face of a fourth, smaller companion. The sudden yell cracked through the air like a cannon shot. Screams leapt from the crowd, with many peeling off and running back into Darvled's Town. The revealed ogre – a female – gave as good as she got, bellowing a reply that bounced along the distant stonework of the wall and made Xavire's stomach clench. Aside from being perhaps an ogre-head shorter, the female had a narrower build, and the features of her otherwise characteristically ogrish face were rounder, the eyes larger. Her pitch-black hair was tied back in a long bind, and on every part save for arms and head she wore a combination of blue-gray wolf furs and tough, bronze studded leathers. The faces of the ogre guards remained impassive, but Xavire thought there was something awkward about the way their heads were turned away from the argument.

Throwing up his arms in exasperation the male turned away. The female hadn't been following him like the others, realized Xavire. She'd been pursuing him.

She continued to yell as the plated male, and his cohort stomped up the dirt road, a sight which caused the last of the onlookers to rapidly disperse, many dragging children whose responses ranged from uncooperative to inconsolable.

Commander Chantrille turned back to Uslo. He was smiling that upper-lipped smile.

"I'm not sure why the Viks are any interest of yours, Dargent, but I'd suggest you have more pressing concerns."

Behind him, the female finished making her point with a final, derisive bark before turning to march back the way she came. Xavire saw the male's eyes roll as they closed, the ogre shaking its head.

"Allow me to introduce Rnmogyr, Warlord and Chieftain of the Urshal tribe. His warriors will be taking your place on the wall."

Rnmogyr reached them in time to hear his introduction and gave a single nod. Uslo returned the gesture, saying nothing.

"From tomorrow, there will be no more human mercenaries manning the western stretch – nor the eastern, for that matter. The great tribes can be relied on in a way sellswords cannot, are *feared* in a way sellswords are not. And with the situation in the ogre homelands being as it is... well. You just aren't a competitive choice, 'General.'"

"It seems not," said Uslo.

Chantrille nodded, satisfied. "I'm glad you understand." He turned and stepped toward his mount. "I want the Claws and the Dragon's Teeth gone by tonight."

"I take it you are aware of our termination clause?" asked Brawand. Chantrille mounted his horse smoothly and made a dismissive wave of his hand.

"The money is with your superiors, Dragon's Tooth."

Xavire strongly suspected that Uslo had stipulated no such clause.

Turning his horse to face Rnmogyr, his head level with the ogre warlord, Chantrille spoke slowly and clearly. Everything about his manner suggested the human mercenaries were forgotten.

"This is Gatekeeper Drom! He will provide you with whatever you need!"

Warlord Rnmogyr peered at Drom through narrowed eyes, as if suspicious that such a man could offer anything of worth. For his part, the gatemaster did an admirable job of keeping his back straight, notwithstanding the odd tremble in his legs.

After casting a last glance at the settlement, now unobstructed by crowds, Chantrille began to ride away. Olvar and Pesayn moved to follow.

"Commander!" said Drom, bowing quickly to the ogre before turning to the departing trio. "What about the caravan? Will the soldiers set camp or would you prefer I find them beds in Darv– in the settlement?"

"That's a question for Captain Olvar," answered Chantrille disinterestedly, not bothering to look back. "He and Commander Pesayn will be leading the train north to supply our forces. Those of us staying you'll find in the barracks."

"Captain?"

Olvar stopped, twisting in his saddle. His voice was deep.

"No need, Gatekeeper. The schedule has changed. We rest, water the horses, let the men eat, but the wagons will be on the Plains before the sun is down."

Then he followed the other officers back toward the caravan, where an order to fall out had seen the stiff lines of infantry break up into clusters of relieved men. Most had gone in search of a spot to lie down and rest their road-weary feet, with only a few ambling toward Darvled's Town in search of other comforts.

"So," began Brawand. "That is the end of that."

The mercenaries stood in a circle, the sun's heat pressing on their exposed faces. It didn't occur to any of them that they move into the shade. Xavire tried to meet Uslo's gaze, but the general seemed to be looking beyond him, lost in thought.

"I suppose I must prepare the Dragon's Teeth for the march east," Brawand continued. "What about the Claws? What will they do now?"

"I'm not sure," murmured Uslo. Then his eyes finally met Xavire's, and he knew. Uslo was thinking the same. They were in trouble. The plan was in trouble.

What in the Seven Circles were they going to do now?

*****

Mind racing, Uslo waved absently to the Dragon's Teeth mercenaries as they left to prepare their men for departure. As soon as they were out of earshot, he began to give orders. The play was a risky one, but it was all the circumstances offered. If he thought Xavire looked sick before, it was nothing compared to when Uslo finished. But only Sir Guilliver had anything to say.

"And the ogres?"

"Leave them to me."

They nodded, and the three parted ways.

With a deep breath, Uslo stepped toward Drom and the Warlord Rnmogyr.

"Forgive me, Warlord," Drom was saying, imploring. "I don't understand!"

The ogre closed its eyes, breathing deeply. If anything, it was the looks on the two guards' faces that were more concerning, although Uslo did note the chieftain's hand flexing on his axe. Smells of untamed mountains reached him as he drew closer, the meaty musk of wild goat and the fresh scent of topsoil as it resisted the runoff from icy peaks. It was eleven years since Uslo last stood this close to an ogre, and he was pleased to find that the experiences he'd accumulated in that time had strengthened his nerve, although he supposed he shouldn't completely discount the possibility that some of last night's wine still lingered in his system. He had, in truth, no idea what he was going to do. But sometimes all one could do was charge in and offer prayer to lady luck, so long as one's nerve held true.

"Hail, warriors!"

The ogres' eyes went wide at the sound of their language in Uslo's throat. Drom's protests stopped dead, his oddly wide mouth falling open as he turned to see who had produced the incomprehensible sounds. Filling his lungs, the general set a firm expression on his face and projected from the chest.

"May the gods favor your blades, and curse those who betray their debts!"

For several seconds – just long enough for Uslo to wonder if he'd committed a grave error – the ogres stared at him in stunned silence. Then as one, they were overrun with mirth, their laughter bursting forth for all to hear. Uslo thought he could feel his bones rattling with the force of it, but he waited, holding his expression tight. Somehow, Drom's mouth had opened wider still, and he gawked stupidly at the tearful ogres.

"Hail, little ogre-tongue!" answered Rnmogyr, his voice smooth as the surface of a slow-moving river and running just as deep. The warlord fought back another bout of laughter, managing to say, "You speak like a son of Waulek!"

His greeting acknowledged, Uslo allowed himself a grin.

"I was with them only a short time, but I learned many things from the warriors of Waulek." At least, he hoped that's what he said. As much as he enjoyed the feel of ogrish in his mouth – it demanded the speaker wield consonants like a weapon – Uslo only knew the barest amount and was forced to intersperse the odd word of common in hope that the chieftain's knowledge of that tongue would see them through.

It seemed to work, Rnmogyr nodding his understanding. "Then I suppose it is forgivable, for a human." The warlord laughed. Though he presumed it was a joke of some sort, Uslo thought it wisest not to join in, opting instead for a nod. Humor between races was riddled with pitfalls.

"Yes. I am General Uslo Dargent," he tapped his chest, making clear use of the ogre word for his rank of choice. He made a short sweep of his hand, indicating the ogre's troubled conversation with Drom. "I saw there were difficulties. Can I help?" His offer caused Rnmogyr to glance at Drom, and the warlord rolled his eyes at the sight of the perplexed gatemaster.

"I asked this human where we can find fresh water, and–"

"What did you say to him about me, Dargent?!" Drom's voice was shot through with panic. Uslo waved him away with an irritable gesture. It took all his focus to understand Rnmogyr, and by the time he regained it, the ogre was already concluding.

"–a word I'm saying!" Recounting his grievance had brought Rnmogyr's ire back to the burn, and he eyed the gatemaster menacingly.

"I understand," said Uslo, shooting a meaningful look at Drom. *Shut up.* When he turned back, he saw that Rnmogyr was watching him expectantly. "I must leave today, but I am happy to answer any questions before I go. Shall we stroll along the wall?"

Not knowing the ogre word for 'wall' nor if one even existed, he turned and pointed to the eastern stretch.

The warlord's consideration only lasted a moment, a final glance at Drom being all it took to settle matters.

"I accept your offer, General." Though the ogres were rightly known as an inscrutable people, Uslo thought he understood the look on Rnmogyr's face: *get me away from this odd little man in his feathered hat.*

Fighting back a laugh, Uslo stepped to one side and bowed low, indicating the stone steps which led up and onto the wall. "After you, Warlord."

"How–?! What–?!" stammered Drom. Uslo ignored him, turning to follow the heavy strides of Rnmogyr and his escort.

So far, so good, thought Uslo, heart rebounding with the thrill of the game. Mounting the steps up to Lord Darvled's Wall, he savored the feeling, the anticipation of seeing the next card be revealed. Perhaps today would be the day when fortune gave him his due.

*****

The Viks' refuge was silent as Xavire and a dozen of Peris's marksmen passed between its shabby tents. Only those unable to work the pits would be there now, likely sheltering from the day's heat. Someone must have seen them coming however, as they found Alea standing expectantly outside the stone storehouse at the refuge's center.

"What's wrong?" she asked, waiting as Xavire took a long drink from his water flask. Gods, it was hot.

"We're leaving," he answered finally. "The supply train arrived early, and it's departing much earlier than planned. We have to go now."

She frowned. "The plan was that we wait until nightfall. If we go now, we'll be seen from the towers on the eastern stretch."

"Possibly."

"Possibly?"

"We're being replaced," he explained, taking off his glasses and wiping them on his shirt. "The Dragon's Teeth, too. By ogres."

Alea looked alarmed. "*Ogres*? But I did not foresee..."

Xavire waited, but she kept the rest of the thought to herself. "There was no way to have predicted it," he continued. "We're to clear out before sundown. Everyone's packing up for the switch over. The sooner we go, the more likely it is no one will be on the towers to see us."

"And if someone does see us?"

He put his glasses back on and met her eye. She knew. He could see she knew even as she asked.

Alea sighed. "All right. I will put the word out and start getting everyone together."

Xavire nodded.

"Of course," she added, "almost everyone is at the pits, where Lydon's guards will be watching. The foreman and his enforcers will see you coming. If any of them get back to the wall and warn the others, we're finished."

Xavire took a deep breath through his nose and looked around at the Claws' marksmen. Determination was set hard in their faces. Peris met his eye, gave him the flicker of a nod. They were ready. Releasing the breath, he turned back to Alea.

"Then we'll make certain they don't."

*****

It was the furthest Uslo ever walked along the Wall. He and the three ogres ranged over three miles east of the gatehouse, after which the battlements ran empty and only the towers held guards. Never mind the fact that Rnmogyr and his tribe had just that day finished a gods-knew-how-long trek to reach Darvled's Town. Ogres, Uslo learned, did not stroll. They roamed. And they asked questions, or at least the warlord did. Throughout the journey, Uslo was denied the oft-overlooked luxury of a wasted breath, his mind, lungs, and outmatched legs scrabbling over what little stamina remained in his hungover, sleep-deprived, still-to-be-fed body.

Uslo loved it. As the traveling performers of Letharac liked to say, each audience was an honor bestowed but once, and he could imagine no better example of this self-congratulating truth than a one-to-one with an ogre warlord. He told Rnmogyr everything he knew about the surrounding area, where the rivers and streams flowed, what wildlife was likely to appear and when, how far it was before the wall stopped being made of stone and instead became an unmanned palisade (not far at all, in truth), running all the way out to the central gate and beyond, where the ogres' kin had been employed since the earliest days of the war. What interested the warlord most, however – what interested the bodyguards, too, who otherwise had been content to follow at a distance – was that before the wall, most of the land around the West Gate had been covered in forest. This seemingly minor detail provoked intense discussion among the ogres, too rapid for the general to understand. They asked him to confirm that, even here, east of the gatehouse, it had been a forest? He answered yes, he believed so, and they seemed to gaze out at the landscape with new eyes, their otherwise impassive faces becoming almost childlike with astonishment.

Thinking perhaps that the topic could provide more entertainment, he began to explain what he knew of the operation. The wall's true army, after all, hadn't been soldiers, but builders, with the hardest labor reserved for the first wave of nomadic Plainsmen to flee south. Mountains of masonry were moved, foundations were laid and built upon without pause, the land was scoured for every scrap of usable material, including, of course, the forests. An unprecedented feat, coordinated by a veritable legion of bureaucrats and engineers. But none of this garnered anything like the same reaction from the ogres. Indeed, they'd looked bored. Uslo quickly realized that they were not interested in how or why the woodland had so completely disappeared. Only in that it had.

Still, for the most part, Uslo was able to hold the attention of his audience of one, his grasp of ogrish growing more assured even as his legs began to falter. For falter they did, and, between the fourth and fifth towers, vision blurring and tongue still trying to wrap itself around his last coherent thought, Uslo felt the world spin. The next thing he knew, he was flat on his back, the hot stonework burning through his clothes, a large hand behind his head and the funnel of a leather flask pressed to his lips. Drawing deep on what he assumed to be water, it took until the second mouthful was making its way down for him to realize that the warm liquid was in fact a strong, syrupy alcohol. It was bitter. It was *disgusting*.

Uslo sat up sharply, his attempts to both cough and gag at the same time resulting in a choked spluttering that sent the third mouthful over his front. Deep laughter, unsympathetic but not unkind, burst around him, and he blinked tears from his eyes to gawk up at the ogres, demanding to know what in the Abyss he'd just drunk. Rnmogyr told him it was called 'Steppe Root,' explaining it was brewed from a flower that grew around the hills of their homeland and was credited with great medicinal power.

"From taste alone, I imagine it is the ugliest flower on the face of Pannithor," the general opined, momentarily forgetting the potential pitfalls of humor. But the ogres only laughed harder.

"Be grateful you've never smelled it being made!" quipped one of the bodyguards, and they howled, thumping each other on the arms and wiping tears from their eyes. Uslo laughed too, although he didn't know what was so funny. He felt better. His body was energized, and while the alcohol was loosening his inhibitions, his mind was somehow all the clearer for it.

"Well then!" he said, springing to his feet. "Shall we continue?"

The ogres laughed again, shaking their heads. The effects wouldn't last, they explained. It was time to head back.

With the Steppe Root in his system – *Steppe Rot, more like*, he thought, spitting in an attempt to clear the taste – and his amusing collapse behind them, all notions of pitfalls were quickly forgotten. Matching the ogres' pace with enthusiastic strides as they returned the way they'd come, Uslo no longer spoke of the surrounding land, but instead proceeded to share as much of his repertoire of amusing anecdotes as he could workably translate. Their mingled laughter spilled from the battlements, seeming to shake the patches of bone-dry grass on either side of the wall. Recalling Captain Brawand's hilarious story of a tryst that saw him hiding in a river from a furious dwarf husband, Uslo began to set the scene – only to find the ogres reacting with hysterics long before he had reached the punchline. It seemed the idea of seducing a dwarf was more than enough to set them off.

At this point, Warlord Rnmogyr shared some stories of his own. While Uslo often missed the humor in his tales, the atmosphere nevertheless reached a level of such abandon that he roared as if he had. Which, Uslo supposed, may well have been the case for the ogres and his stories as well.

By the time they passed through the second tower east of the gatehouse, the noon sun had moved beyond its peak. The west gate was in view, the wall's gradual north-westerly curve allowing them to glimpse it beyond the final tower.

"Do you have a family, General?" Rnmogyr asked as they dropped back onto the walkway.

"The company is my family."

Rnmogyr looked at him blankly.

"My warriors," he explained.

"Ah." They resumed walking. "I understand. But I meant the other kind of family. Do you have children?"

Unbidden and unwelcome, an image rose into Uslo's mind. A grave, hidden away at the back of a cemetery. Two names recorded on the headstone.

"No," he answered, more firmly than intended. Uslo had thought that memory contained, but the Steppe Root must have loosened more than he knew.

Rnmogyr said nothing.

"No, sirs, I have no family waiting for me," he continued, fearful that silence might take hold and leave him at the mercy of his mind. "No home to which I shall return."

The warlord stopped, as did his guard.

Uslo's stomach plummeted. He suppressed a groan.

Although rumors varied wildly about what force was behind the resolution of the crisis in the east, the accounts of its end were all the same – the Frozen Sea had melted, and the resulting flood waters halted the expansion of the Abyss. Before the waters reached that great tear in the world, however, they had surged across the intervening ranges of the eastern Steppe, which were also known as the Ogre Lands. The ogres' *home*.

That's why they're here, he thought. What was it Chantrille had said? Something about the human mercenaries not being 'a competitive choice'? Where before only the warriors had left the homeland to hire themselves out in foreign wars, including those who had come to fight the orcs, now entire tribes were cast across the north of the continent, forced to take whatever work they could get.

Before Uslo could think of a way to recover from his idiotic utterance, Rnmogyr spoke. He was looking north.

"Children change us, but they don't know it. How could they? How could they know there was a time when we were just like them? We understand, and they cannot."

Rnmogyr started walking again, turning his gaze back to the walkway without so much as a glance at Uslo. A little lost, the general followed. Something in the warlord's tone had left him feeling at once wary and with the vague sense that he had been forgotten, that Rnmogyr was in fact engaged in a profound and private dialogue with himself. Or maybe not. Maybe it was the subject matter itself that put Uslo in a state of unease.

Although the warlord's last words had left the expectation of more to follow, they walked in silence for some time. Clouds had appeared in the distant western sky, gray and laden, not the thin white wisps that had skirted the sun this past week or so. On the south side of the wall, the cicada song was dethroned by the sounds of the Urshal tribe setting camp, the padded stomps of many ogre feet flattening down the grassland without much in the way of resistance from the parched scrub. In the grass's wake, conical tents had sprung up like a new and vigorous species of flora, and between their yellow-brown canvas ran the darting shapes of ogre children, bursting with energy after having sat in the carts for so long. Shorter, skinnier, and far less graceful, Uslo reflected that they looked exactly how he might have imagined ogre children to look. Supposing he'd ever thought to do so, which he hadn't.

"But they change, too," Rnmogyr continued, his resonant voice breaking the silence so abruptly that Uslo thought he felt his heart rebound against his ribs. "They show us the changes we could never see. For the longest time, so long you think it might last forever, they listen. They listen and they obey. Then one day–" the warlord snapped his fingers, producing an echoing *crack* with the force of a flintlock, "–no more! They know everything, and the ones who raised them, who guided and protected them," he turned to Uslo, meeting his eye as he banged the face of his battleaxe against his breastplate, "we know *nothing*!"

Ears ringing, Uslo nodded, hoping the gesture didn't look as helpless as it felt. There were only a few topics on which he believed he had nothing to offer, and parenthood was first among them. Certainly, the ogre's contention seemed reasonable enough. He'd heard similar screeds from other parents, in his time, although Uslo had never found it to be a sound analysis of his own youth. Not that he was going to share that, of course.

Rnmogyr sighed. "Maybe it's my fault," he said in a low voice. "Maybe I held on for too long, and now her will cannot bend. That's what my heart-joined tells me, whenever she gets the chance."

Silence resumed. They were almost at the final tower, and Uslo had yet to see an opportunity, any way to declaw the threat the ogres posed to their plan. His efforts at bonding with the warlord had appeared to be going well, but now floundered on the rocks. Uslo scoured his mind, but his efforts returned nothing. A note of panic began to sound in his thoughts.

Just as they were about to step inside the tower, Rnmogyr stopped again.

"No."

He rounded on the general. Uslo felt the last of the Steppe Root's fortifying looseness vanish, chased from his system by the fearsome presence of the righteous warlord. All at once he could imagine what it must be like to face such a thing in combat, the nerve that must be required to hold ranks against an army of such warriors.

Have I just been talking to this? his weak and dazed mind wondered. *This walking weapon?*

"You listen to me, General! Never, ever let your children tell you what is and what is not! Only when they realize that they don't know can they begin to understand the burden of our choices! Remember that, General!"

Aware that his mouth was hanging open, Uslo snapped it shut, willing some moisture onto his tongue.

"Yes," he croaked. "I will, of course."

If he were to have predicted any effect his words might have had on Rnmogyr, this was not it. The ogre warlord's eyes went wide with surprise, his lips turning out in what might have been dismay. Then the look was gone, and Rnmogyr was laughing.

"No, you won't. And why should you?" He laughed again, and Uslo smiled in spite of himself, longing for the company of humankind.

Rnmogyr's laughs subsided as he looked down at Uslo with a half-smile, his eyes serious. "Are you alright? You look pale. More Steppe Root?"

Uslo held up a hand in what he hoped would be seen as polite refusal, swallowing whatever was attempting to climb up his throat. In truth, he would have welcomed another hit of the Root, but he suspected there was little chance of him keeping it down.

"I apologize, General." The warlord shook his head, pre-empting Uslo's protest. "I mean it. We in the Urshal have a rule: we do not give advice where it is not sought."

"Except to children," said Uslo before he could stop himself. The ogre laughed again, but less enthusiastically.

"Yes. You are small, but you are not a child. When this rule is broken, it is our way that the balance be restored. You must give me advice, whether I want it or not."

He's embarrassed, realized Uslo. Warlord Rnmogyr, chieftain of an ogre tribe, was deeply ashamed of his outburst. Uslo glanced at the guards and saw that they were keeping back, their eyes averted from the exchange.

Instinct roared in Uslo's chest. *This is it.* He knew he must be careful, that he must choose his words with utmost care. The game turned on them.

"Not being a parent myself, I cannot offer much on the problems of children, Warlord Rnmogyr."

The ogre chieftain said nothing, made no move at all. He was waiting.

Pausing, Uslo glanced back across the novel sprawl of the ogre camp. A traveling camp, now set indefinitely.

"But as one mercenary to another, I will offer this. In the Kingdoms, when a lord gives someone money, they believe they own that person."

Uslo met the ogre's eye.

"They do not own you. They have contracted you. You and I understand the difference. They do not. I advise you to instruct them on their error at the first opportunity, so they never forget it. So they are reminded just how much they *need* you."

Rnmogyr was silent for a moment, free hand stroking his braid of gray beard. Then he nodded.

"Worthy advice, General. May we each carry the other's words, and share them only with those who seek."

"Agreed," said Uslo, feeling immense relief. He indicated that Rnmogyr lead the way, and together they passed through the final tower and on toward the west gate.

That was it. Fortune had offered a chance, and he'd done all he could. He hoped it was enough. Now there was nothing else but for him to rejoin Sir Guilliver and wait.

Looking across the top of Darvled's Town toward the distant pits, the Silver Cat turned his thoughts to Xavire and his dozen or so Claws, absently running thumb and forefinger along his mustache. The next step in the plan would be happening about now. Its fate – all their fates – was in their hands.

*****

Heat lashed Cauhin's back while he worked the pit, his head down to avoid notice as he pulled stone from soil with bare hands. For the last two days, both he and Fillam had labored alongside their people: hauling earth, shifting rocks, carting foulness beneath the foreman's eye and a sun that seemed to grow more pitiless by the hour. Knowing that they were all set to escape that night made no odds – neither lad could stomach being a burden any longer. Even so, if the foreman found out that either had returned from their exile, a public whipping would be the least they could expect.

Working his fingers around a stubborn patch in the pit wall, Cauhin saw a pair of dark boots approach, walking the perimeter. Cauhin recognized them as belonging to Derraz, a bald and sour-faced enforcer. Derraz stopped, and as he scanned the Plainsmen digging in the ten-foot wide pit, his eyes came to Cauhin. The southerner gave a smirk from beneath a straw hat. Cauhin glared back. He knew Derraz noticed them sneaking onto the site that morning, but it appeared he hadn't seen fit to tell the foreman. Cauhin guessed he enjoyed holding that particular power more than using it.

Just as Cauhin was about to return to his labor, something changed. Derraz's forehead creased into a frown, his eyes narrowing. He was looking past Cauhin, looking at Fillam. Cauhin turned, following the enforcer's gaze. Fillam was standing perfectly straight, his chin up and one dirt-stained hand raised against the sun. He seemed confused. For a moment, Cauhin thought his friend was looking back at Derraz. But then Fillam's eyes went wide, quickly shifting to meet Cauhin's. Somehow, with neither a word being spoken nor any possible explanation, Cauhin understood what was happening.

He turned in the exact same instant as Derraz and they both squinted up at the wooden watchtower on the site's perimeter. The foreman's body, once so imposing, hung limply over the railing, the bloody tip of a bolt projecting from the top of his head. Three Plainsmen were climbing the watchtower's ladder, crossbows slung across their chests. No, not Plainsmen…

Cauhin could have sworn he heard the air rushing into Derraz's lungs. Diving forward, he wrapped his arms around the lackey's spit-shined boots, pushing his legs against the pit wall. He heaved. The southerner's half-primed cry emerged as a yelp, his body toppling face-down with a hefty *thump*. Grabbing his left leg above the boot, Cauhin continued to pull, trying to drag Derraz into the pit, teeth clamped down hard on the yell that was burning in his throat. Too heavy. He managed perhaps six inches before his catch realized what was happening. Rolling onto his side, Derraz kicked out with his free leg, catching Cauhin on the arm. His grip slipped, and suddenly Derraz was sitting upright, hands set at his sides to push himself up. Torn between fury and despair, Cauhin reached out again, catching hold of the right leg. He met Derraz's eye. The southerner must have broken his nose in the fall, and blood seemed to rush along every rage-induced line around his snarling mouth. His straw hat had come off. Cauhin felt the muscles tighten in the enforcer's leg, and knew instinctively that the next kick, this time from his left boot, would be aimed straight at his head.

Cauhin closed his eyes. The leg continued to writhe in his arms. But the kick never came.

"Get off, you shits!"

He opened his eyes and saw Fillam. His friend had leapt half-way out of the pit, and he had Derraz's left leg pinned beneath his torso.

"Quick!" hissed Fillam. "Pull!"

Cauhin pulled. Fillam pulled. Derraz was pulled.

The two youths threw themselves backward, and the lackey landed rear-first onto the pit floor, the sharp impact followed by a pained whine. The sound morphed as Derraz attempted to call the alarm.

"Help–!"

Cauhin drove his knuckles into the Southerner's broken nose, but if anything, the yell only grew louder, and he snapped his now aching hand over Derraz's mouth.

"We've got to shut him up!"

"Get on top of him!"

The two of them climbed onto Derraz, pressing his torso flat and holding his arms beneath their knees. The lackey's teeth clicked. He was trying to bite. Cauhin withdrew his hand in surprise, a disgusted grimace contorting his lips. Derraz stopped struggling.

For an inexplicably long moment, the two young Plainsmen stared at the southerner, and he at them. It had happened so fast. Ten seconds, if that, from him looming over them, to they over him. In that moment, all understood. This could only end one of two ways. Either Derraz died, or they did.

Derraz spat a curse, and the moment was broken. Cauhin's hands reached his neck just as the southerner finished drawing breath for another yell. He began to writhe beneath them.

"Hold him!"

Fillam pressed down, trying unsuccessfully to stop Derraz's legs from flailing and pushing along the ground. But Derraz's arms remained locked beneath them, and Cauhin's fingers held fast. The anger. So much anger, a noxious cocktail of rage and sorrow. His hands seemed to burn with it, squeezing until they hurt. Derraz's neck muscles strained in resistance. Meeting the man's eyes, Cauhin found he relished their impotent wrath, watching as his lips began to change color, first to purple, then blue.

"Down! Get down!"

Warning shouts, dozens of them in Ardovikian voices, rang out across the pits. From somewhere beyond the red fog that engulfed his mind, Cauhin heard a roll of *thumps* as Plainsmen dropped to the ground to take cover. Confused and commanding yells sprang up from the foreman's men, but their voices quickly became panicked as the *snap* of discharging crossbows cut through the air. Bolts whistled overhead, their flights unerring and inevitable, ending with the cries of the stricken. Cauhin heard it all, but he did not listen to anything save the straining of Derraz's limbs, the galloping beats of the dying man's heart. The eyelids began to flutter, the pupils lost focus.

A shadow loomed over them. Cauhin looked up in time to see another of the lackeys stumbling toward their pit, a bolt lodged in his back. Helpless to prevent it, the youths watched as the limp form collapsed over the edge, crashing into Fillam and sending him sprawling. Cauhin felt rather than saw the movement of Derraz's liberated arm, and then whiteness exploded across his vision, followed swiftly by blackness and pain.

Sight returned slowly, to his left eye first, and he saw the blue and cloudless sky. Derraz stepped over him, his form faintly doubled by Cauhin's straggling right eye. The pain in his head was horrifying, radiating nausea throughout his being; but such a feeling could not compare even remotely to that induced by the southerner's face. By its hate.

Derraz transferred the cudgel from his left hand to his right. Cauhin wondered why he hadn't seen it before and realized it must have been hanging on his belt. Leaning forward, the lackey grabbed Cauhin by the front of his tattered shirt and lifted him up. It seemed that his head weighed a tonne, but the well of anger had turned to defiance, and Cauhin forced strength into his neck, allowing Derraz to bring his eternally sour face close to his. His smile was cruel. Blood from the broken nose fell around his lips, dripping from the corners of his mouth.

"Never should've left the Plains, Vik."

Cauhin tried to spit at him, but the effort of holding his head up was too much, the throbs of pain from his clubbed skull too obliterating. His eyes rolled back, and he felt Derraz's face move away, pictured the cudgel being raised to deliver a killing blow.

The hand let go of Cauhin's front. He slumped to the ground.

"What...? Who... no..." Derraz's voice sounded weak. He heard him cough.

Cauhin's eyes flew open, and through their blur he saw the southerner staring down at the bloody steel that ran through his chest, face as sour as ever. The sword withdrew, and a hand appeared at Derraz's shoulder, shunting him dismissively to one side.

For several seconds, Cauhin gazed up at his savior, unsure if it was his eyes or his stunned mind that rendered the sight so incomprehensible. Then he heard the voice–

"Cauhin?"

–and everything rushed into focus. The general's man, the long-bearded one called Xavire, knelt over him. He was dressed in a Plainsman's tunic.

The sounds of fighting had ceased. Cauhin tried to sit up and was rewarded with another wave of pain. He groaned.

"Hold on, son, let me wrap your head. Rest while you can, we'll be moving soon. Take a breath."

Cauhin saw concern in the deep brown of Xavire's eyes, saw in spite of the strange glass circles through which they peered. Anger flared in him. All at once, Cauhin wished he had the courage to tell Xavire what a fool he was. To tell him he was being conned, that there was no treasure, that... that...

All that emerged was, "...Thank you."

*****

They called it 'Lydon's Head,' but that wasn't its official name. It didn't have one. Nor did any of the other towers, for that matter. Still, that was what they called it.

There was nothing cranial in the tower's shape, nor did it stand on any topographical outcrop. Three miles west along the wall from Darvled's Town, it was a plain, rectangular construction with an open top, built using the same varied stone as the wall itself. There were close to a dozen such towers dotted along the stonework stretch, each as unremarkable and unremarked upon as the last. It differed in one, sole regard: it was short. More than a level shorter than its peers, in fact.

Such unfortunate stature resulted from, of all things, bureaucracy. The strict guidelines provided for the wall's construction stipulated that, where there were to be towers, they be built at an absolute interval of one mile separation, no more, no less. Materials were likewise allocated, so that when the builders arrived at the spot Lydon's Head would come to occupy – a sheer gully some fifteen feet deep and fifty across – they were pedantically obliged to commence with the construction and forbidden from relocating to an ideal site only a short distance away. In the end, to mitigate an unseemly dip, many of the allotted materials were directed into the wall itself, a decision which only served to exacerbate the tower's zenithal woes.

All of which suited Xavire perfectly. The tower itself was simply an oddity, for it was still plenty tall enough to hide their activities on its western side from those further east along the wall. But when combined with the gully, well! Then it was a *weakness*.

"Steady! Go!"

Xavire fed a few more feet of rope through, the friction on his hands a welcome distraction from the sun's heat.

"Good! One more! Steady! Go!"

The rope fed through and went slack as the Plainswoman at the other end touched down north of the wall.

"She's down, get ready to bring it back up!"

For the last twenty minutes or so, Claws and Plainsmen together had been helping lower those who, for whatever reason, were unable to do it themselves. Fortunately, there weren't many, with most of the Plainsmen managing to climb down one of the dozen rope ladders placed along the battlements.

Stepping away to let the others secure the next in line, Xavire looked over the north side. His throat stung for lack of moisture. He was drenched in sweat. A closeness had crept into the air, a whisper of humidity that he knew well and yet barely recognized under the scorching heat. Leaning forward until he was looking straight down the wall, he let his eyes wander over the long line of movement below.

It was going well. With the Plainsmen freed and no one in Darvled's Town yet the wiser, they were now gathering up the gear which the Claws had spent the last couple days smuggling over the wall, hidden in the broad gully whose overgrown banks had covered their southern approach and would mask their initial movement north. Not as well as they would in the dark, of course. Xavire had no choice but to hope the disorder on the rest of the wall would serve in its stead. While some of the Claws had gone on ahead, more stood watching the passing Plainsmen from the wall's shaded base, shields wrapped in cloth and slung over their backs, their pikes bundled tightly. Each mercenary wore the company's red-hemmed coat, having shed their Plains-garb disguises.

Xavire lifted his eyes up, tracing the long, thin line of people that was making its way north. Three abreast at the very most, the column extended the two hundred or so yards of the gully, up onto the flat grassland and far into the distance. Alea would be at the front, he knew, and he willed himself to make out her tall form, no doubt looking back to check no one had fallen behind. As much as he wanted to, he couldn't see her.

His gaze shifted back to the gully. Nearly everyone had gone over. He waited for the last of the infirm to be lowered.

"That's it, sir!" called Peris. "That's the lot!"

Xavire nodded, looking across the group. "Good. The rest of you start making your way–"

He cut short as his gaze fell on Cauhin. The young Plainsman's head was bound, a coin-sized stain in the cloth marking a nasty wound.

"Come on, lad," said one of the older Plainsmen, leading Cauhin toward one of the rope ladders. "Time to go."

"Hold on!" said Xavire, stepping toward them. "You can't climb down with that head wound. We'll lower you down." He went to place a guiding hand on Cauhin's shoulder, but the Plainsman moved into his path, fixing a closed fist against Xavire's chest.

"Oi!" yelled Peris, hand on his hilt as he moved to intervene. Xavire signaled for him to stop, his eyes fixed on the Plainsman's stony features.

"I'm trying to help," he said, calmly as he could manage. The Plainsman didn't budge.

"I don't need help," said Cauhin. "I'm fine..." The boy's eyes fluttered. He swayed.

In a quick movement, Xavire pushed past the Plainsman, catching Cauhin before his knees could buckle.

"Easy there. Take a breath."

For several seconds, Cauhin's eyes remained vague. Then clarity returned, and with them...

"Let me go."

Xavire's blinked. Cauhin's expression was hard, but for an instant, it had burned. Frowning, he withdrew his support. Cauhin's legs hovered on the edge of betrayal, but he held them straight. Xavire shrugged.

"Suit yourself." He stepped away. "We're packing up the ropes in five minutes. Anyone who isn't over the wall by then can jump, as far as I'm concerned."

"Come on, lad," he heard the Plainsman say. "Maybe we should lower you down–"

"I'm fine."

Xavire clambered over onto one of the rope ladders, still within earshot.

"I'll see you on the other side," said Cauhin, and when the older Plainsman responded, Xavire was surprised to find himself moved by the emotion in his voice.

"I'll see you on the Plains, lad. I'll see you on the Plains."

*****

Outside the Darvled's Town barracks, Sir Guilliver waited. For about an hour he watched as the Dragon's Teeth readied themselves to leave, loading their carts and vacating the barracks with an efficiency that stood in stark contrast to the Claws and their deliberate delay. Watched, and waited. Over the next hour he watched as Chantrille's soldiers moved in, knowing that it'd only take one expressing a little curiosity to jeopardize their plan, so precarious had it become. Watched, and waited. For two hours more he eyed every corner, knowing that Xavire was likely crossing the wall at that moment, and, assuming the *other* matter had gone well, that all it would take was one of the foreman's men showing up late to work for everything to be undone.

It must have gone well, he had thought. *If not, we'd already be in chains.*

Watched, and... his stomach rumbled.

Breaking for lunch, Sir Guilliver set off alone through Darvled's Town, as much to clear his head as in search of his favorite pie vendor. What he found was at once unsettling and, in a peculiar sense, reassuring. The townspeople lined the wide streets, organizing themselves and their belongings for the road. Darvled's Town was leaving. Word of Chantrille's order had reached them and, while no one was yet forcing them out, most had assumed it to be only a matter of time. The ex-subjects of the Young Kingdoms knew from experience that it was best to get it over with. Amidst all this spontaneous activity, it was little wonder that none had yet noticed the disappearance of so many of the Claws. Or of the Ardovikian Plainsmen, for that matter. Still, being surrounded by such forlorn faces robbed him of his appetite, and he quickly made his way back to the barracks.

Sometime later, Uslo appeared from gods-knew where to give an update.

"The supply train has left. I just watched the last wagon pass through the gate."

"How many?"

"Thirty."

"Fewer than we were expecting, no?"

"It'll have to suffice." Uslo wore his elaborate red-bronze chestplate, white-plumed helmet under one arm. He looked over at the adventurers. They were yet to don armor, instead placing their suits where they were most accessible on the carts in readiness for when the order came.

"Get them suited up in about an hour," said Uslo. "And bard the horses."

"Won't that look suspicious?"

"To some. But I know men like Chantrille. He won't ask why. There will be other matters to occupy his mind."

Sir Guilliver nodded. "Did Xavire have any problems?"

"None that I could discern. I watched them pass out of sight from atop the wall. They're beyond the horizon, and the towers are all empty. I think we can be confident they were not seen."

And then he was gone again.

Yet more hours passed. Sir Guilliver took a swig from his flask, grimacing as he swallowed the warm water. In what felt like the blink of an eye, the dry heat had turned humid. He'd only just put it back on, but already the inside of his suit of armor felt alive with rivulets of sweat, moisture gathered from his sodden clothes beneath. Overhead, the once endlessly clear skies were awash with rolling gray, pressing down closely, making every breath feel as though he were pulling steam through cloth. Despite the seeming lack of winds to drive them, the clouds had moved in quickly from the west, heavy with harvest from the Straits of Von Terel. The rains would come at any moment. He could smell it. Drinking again, he forced the water down and looked around the drill square.

With no squires to do it for them, the adventurers helped each other into their armor. They had long since finished their slow loading of the Claws' five baggage carts, mostly with empty crates and whatever items the company had no choice but to leave behind, the general's tent among them. The carts and their contents were all for show – the plan would give neither pretext nor opportunity to bring them north of the wall. Their horses were saddled and barded, standing beneath a large awning which extended out from the stables. Sir Guilliver had held off ordering the horses barded until he felt he could wait no more – no point making the men or their mounts bear weight any longer than they had to. Other than that, the barracks were silent. Those of the newly arrived soldiers who were staying with Chantrille had taken up their bunks in the quarters and were presumably sleeping off the night march. In the end, none had shown the slightest interest in the Claws' protracted departure.

Taking another swig, his eye was drawn to movement on the wall. The ogres were taking up their posts, hundreds of them spreading out along the eastern and western stretches, most hefting their enormous crossbows the size of ballistas. The Imlarian knight-turned-mercenary supposed that no amount of armor would stop a hit from one of those. He hoped to never find out.

He raised the flask again. Empty. With a sigh, he stepped across to the stable trough, dunking it under while keeping his bracers above the surface, all the while casting his gaze across his band of adventurers. The Imlarian smiled. They really did look an odd bunch. No two sets of knightly armor were ever the same, but this was something else. The styles ranged across the length and breadth of the Kingdoms, and the quality varied almost as greatly. Some wore the full plate like Sir Guilliver, while others had the more modern suits, which tended to forgo joint pieces altogether, sacrificing protection for greater freedom of movement. As unsightly a combination as it was, Sir Guilliver felt his heart swell with pride. For many of the adventurers, this would be their first outing, and so far they'd taken to it with all the headstrong gusto merited by such a name. He had worked hard turning them from a bunch of spoiled and starry-eyed boys into an effective troop of warriors. Still a little spoiled, still a little starry-eyed. But they were cavalrymen for Dargent's Claws, and it should be no other way.

Sir Guilliver turned at the sound of approaching footsteps, fixing the stopper in his flask. Uslo was back.

"That's it," said the general. Uslo was grinning wildly. "They've spotted the soldiers coming back. No wagons. Captain Olvar and the other one were riding ahead. They'll be reporting to Chantrille any minute now."

Sir Guilliver's laugh was at once triumphant and relieved. "So, Xavire pulled it off! Every step!"

Uslo's grin grew wilder. He nodded. "It seems so. Now comes ours. The very last step." The general placed a gloved hand on Sir Guilliver's shoulder. "Are you ready?"

Sir Guilliver reciprocated the motion. "You know, when we talked about accomplishing glorious deeds across Pannithor, this wasn't exactly what I had in mind, my friend."

Uslo laughed. "Nor I! But why should the glories of thieves be denied to men of noble hearts?"

Sir Guilliver grinned. "Couldn't have put it better myself!" He patted Uslo's shoulder. "Let's get on with this madness."

They parted. "Claws, mount up!"

The men settled into their saddles. Uslo was quickest to mount up, quicker even than Sir Guilliver. The general's bronze-barded palomino, Volonto, danced back and forth beneath him, a perfect mirror of the Genezan's excitement. When all were ready, Uslo left a generous bag of coin with the stable hands, and the adventurers arranged themselves in a three-wide formation.

"Forward!"

The column set off through the streets of a settlement without settlers, a place once called Darveld's Town, a place officially nameless. When they emerged, it was to a road which that morning had bustled with a nervous crowd, spectators to the ogres' arrival. Now empty.

Sir Guilliver looked toward the gatehouse as it came into view. The portcullis was up, and the trio of Lord Darvled's officers stood under it. Two horses were being led away by soldiers, the steeds coated in sweat from a hard gallop, sides bouncing with the pumps of their lungs. Through the gateway's open passage, Sir Guilliver was able to glimpse the infantry escort making their way back toward the wall. Their wagons were gone.

Sir Guilliver looked forward in time to see Uslo raise a hand, signaling halt. He called the order and positioned his horse next to the general.

"So, how do we play this? Do we wait?"

Although Chantrille's words couldn't be heard at this distance, their inchoate anger rang clear. They watched as he stormed away from the officers, barking something at one of the gatehouse guards. The soldier stepped away the moment the commander finished, moving with the focus of a man under orders. Running toward the ogre camp.

Sir Guilliver twisted around in his saddle, looking up at the western sky. He could have sworn he'd heard the beginnings of thunder, however distant. But there were no lights in the clouds nor the hazy shadow of rainfall beneath them.

"Now comes the test of it," said Uslo.

Turning back, Sir Guilliver followed the general's gaze toward the west gate. Warlord Rnmogyr and his twin guards were arriving from the ogre camp. The soldier who'd gone to fetch them was far behind, outstripped by the ogres' rapid strides.

"I'm going to see what that's about," said Uslo, his tone matter-of-fact even as he cast Sir Guilliver a wink. "Care to join me?"

Before the knight could answer, Uslo turned Volonto and heeled toward the gatehouse. Sir Guilliver quickly caught up.

They arrived only seconds after the ogre warlord.

Chantrille turned to the mounted men, his mask of dignified nobility straining to contain his fury.

"Dargent?! Whatever it is, take it up with the gatekeeper! Why are you still here?!"

"The sun might finally be hidden, but it is not down yet, Commander."

Chantrille was waving his hand the moment Uslo began to speak.

"Yes, yes! Very observant, although you fail to notice that I am busy, Dargent! Get out of my sight!"

The commander was yelling, his pitch leaping hysterically, and

Sir Guilliver found himself struggling not to laugh. He pressed it down. Laughing at a man like Commander Chantrille could be just the thing to ruin their chances.

"You wanted to speak to me?" Rnmogyr's arms were folded. "Or you call me here to listen to squealing?"

The warlord spoke softly enough, for an ogre. Nevertheless, the commander jumped at his words as if physically struck. Straightening up, he cleared his throat.

"Y-yes." Chantrille shot a glare at Uslo and then pointedly turned his back on the Claws. "My apologies, Warlord." His pitch was steady, but if the commander's tone was anything to go by, it was at the cost of considerable effort. "I… I want a report."

"On what?"

"The supply train! I want to know if your lookouts saw what happened to the supply train!" He took a breath and added through what sounded like clenched teeth, "I would be most grateful, Warlord."

Rnmogyr looked unimpressed. He shrugged. "Soldiers take wagons beyond sight, then soldiers come back without wagons."

"And before that? Did they see anything on the Plains?"

Rnmogyr shook his head.

"If something has happened," said Uslo, "then surely either Captain Olvar or Commander Pesayn will be able to tell us about it."

Olvar and Pesayn stood apart from them but within earshot, faces petulant, bodies shaking slightly with adrenal aftereffects. Sir Guilliver noticed for the first time how young they were. Not one of Darvled's three officers could be over twenty-five.

The general raised his voice and addressed them. "Gentlemen! Would one of you be so kind?"

Olvar looked to Chantrille. Though the Valentican high-born still had his back to the mercenaries, something in his face must have commanded silence, and Olvar's eyes fell in submission. Pesayn, however, stepped forward.

"It was an ambush! They'd blocked the road with stakes, and then voices came from everywhere, thousands of them, hiding in the grass and behind the hills! They told us to leave the wagons or perish!"

Pesayn's voice was charged with something like righteous self-pity. He opened his mouth to continue, but Chantrille's anger would not wait.

"Who?!" he shouted, hands raised as if trying to throttle Pesayn across the space between them. "Who said it?! What did they look like?! How many were there?!"

"I– we didn't see!" Pesayn looked flustered, his straight posture straining against the condescension in Chantrille's outburst. Olvar was hunched next to him, humiliated. "There were so many! The roaring…" his eyes turned north, gazing through the west gate, "…we thought… I thought they were orcs! But then they spoke to us in common tongue, making their demand, and… and… it was over so quickly!"

"Perhaps they *were* orcs?" said Sir Guilliver. He looked at Uslo as he spoke, attempting to sound thoughtful as he fought back a smile.

"Perhaps," said Uslo. "Although I cannot imagine orcs offering surrender."

"Don't be cretins!" sneered Chantrille, casting a glance back at them. "Of course it wasn't orcs! When have you ever heard of an orc who spoke anything but its own barbarous tongue?!"

"Ah, but a goblin could have taught them!" said Sir Guilliver, failing to keep mischief from his tone. Chantrille ignored him.

"We came to get reinforcements," said Olvar, his deep voice just a hair from plaintive. "Our men are still returning across the Plain. With reinforcements, we can take the wagons back."

"By the time your men get there, whoever they are will have looted everything and scattered!" spat Chantrille.

Olvar didn't meet his eyes, his courage apparently spent.

Thunder. Still only a distant grumble in the west, but there was no mistaking it now. None spoke for several seconds as they listened, heads turned up to the sky. A second burst reached them, closer. Much closer.

Uslo glanced quickly at Sir Guilliver. It was time.

"Commander, if you require assistance, the Claws stand ready. One look at my heavy cavalry bearing down upon them, and the bandits will–"

"Are you mad, Dargent? I mean, I know that's what they say, and with armor like that, I can see why. It looks like a damned collector's piece!"

The commander took a step toward Volonto. Uslo seemed unable to restrain a smile as he met the Valentican's contemptuous glare.

"I already have all the assistance I could ever require," Chantrille hissed. Then he turned to Rnmogyr. "How soon can your warriors be ready, Warlord?"

The warlord gave a level look. "They are always ready."

The commander nodded. "Very well. Assemble a force and recover those wagons." Chantrille turned to the mercenaries. "Show's over. I suggest you get a move on if you want to stay ahead of the rain." Although still visibly shaken, the opportunity to put others in their place seemed to have restored a measure of the commander's calm. He began to walk away.

Sir Guilliver felt his heart racing. The ogres were almost as fast on foot as heavy cavalry. Of *course* the commander would use them. Xavire's plan had never accounted for them being here. He glanced over his shoulder at the adventurers. They were watching, trying vainly to look casual as they awaited the order. The only contingency was to charge the gate and hope to get as many through before it closed, and they'd be doing it with ogres in pursuit. It would be ugly.

"How much?" said the warlord.

Chantrille paused. "However many warriors you deem necessary. Preferably as many as possible." The commander resumed his departure, but the warlord's next word stopped him dead.

"No."

Wide-eyed, Chantrille turned. Muted thunder rolled overhead, a deep-throated purr. Sir Guilliver held his breath.

"'No'? What do you mean, 'no'?"

"No, not how many – how *much*. How much you pay us."

"We– we are already paying you. We have a contract!"

"Contract for guarding wall, not wagons. Need new deal. New deal means gold."

Lightning flashed high above, reduced to a flicker in the cloudy light of late afternoon. Sir Guilliver thought he saw it reflected in the sweaty sheen of the commander's skin. By the time the thunder arrived, all color had fled Chantrille's face.

"But we already have a deal! This is extortion!" he cried once the rumbling had abated.

"How much?" repeated the ogre. He looked bored.

Chantrille stared, open-mouthed. Then his anger took hold. "You will do this, or you will have nothing! Is that what you want?! If Lord Darvled hears you have refused this order, your people will be back on the road, begging for work, and– wait!"

Rnmogyr and his guard turned around and were walking away.

"Wait! All right! Two hundred! How's that?"

The warlord stopped, looking back. "Five hundred."

"Five?! I can't– WAIT!" Desperation hung on the commander's every word, his upright stance collapsing as the ogres began to move again. "Fine! Five hundred!"

The ogres walked back. "Deal."

Chantrille's body sagged with relief.

"Half up-front."

"What?! I don't have that kind of money here!"

"No deal without gold up-front. Half is fair."

"I– I can't! But I swear you'll receive it at the soonest opportunity! What do you say?"

Fresh thunder swallowed the warlord's words, but his answer was clear to all. The ogres began to leave again. Uslo glanced at Sir Guilliver, and there were no winks this time, just a bright smile and brighter eyes. He wanted to laugh, a nervous, excited, mad laugh.

"Eight hundred! I can't give you anything now, but I can promise eight hundred!"

The warlord looked back one last time, his eyes going not to the squealing commander, but to Uslo Dargent. The general gave a nod, and it seemed to Sir Guilliver that the briefest of smiles appeared at the corners of Rnmogyr's great mouth. Then the ogre turned and strode back to his people.

"Well, Commander," said Uslo, his voice edged with amusement. "It seems you may require the Claws' assistance after all."

"No…" said Chantrille, apparently to himself. His neat goatee seemed to wobble as his mouth worked loosely. "No, there must–"

Thunder boomed overhead.

"The rain is coming, Commander. My horses won't be able to move as quickly once it starts. Two hundred gold upon retrieval of Lord Darvled's wagons, nothing up-front. You can't say fairer than that."

The commander met Uslo's eye, finally seeming to consider the offer. If Chantrille were thinking clearly, thought Sir Guilliver, he should be suspicious of such a vast drop in wage. But he wasn't. Besides, they had no time to waste. The iron was hot, and Uslo was striking it hard.

Chantrille straightened up. "Agreed!"

Uslo nodded as Volonto pranced beneath him. "Get everyone clear!"

As Chantrille ordered his men to clear the gateway, Sir Guilliver turned his horse and called out to the adventurers. Thunder snatched his words, and so he waved an arm, motioning them over. They were ready.

"Hurry, Dargent!" It was Chantrille's voice, coming from above. The commander had run to the battlements atop the gatehouse. "Get after them!"

"STOP!"

The new voice came from behind them. Sir Guilliver twisted around, standing in his saddle and craning over the heads of the adventurers. It was Drom. He was running toward them from Darvled's Town. Instantly Sir Guilliver knew – Xavire's work at the pits had finally been discovered.

"STOP! THEY–" thunder blared, decimating the gatemaster's alarm, "–VIKS! CLOSE–"

"WHAT?!" called Chantrille.

"Uslo!" shouted Sir Guilliver. He needn't have bothered. The general was fixing his helm in place, heeling Volonto to a gallop.

The Imlarian grinned. This was his favorite part.

"Adventurers!" Sir Guilliver cried. "Ho!"

He heeled his gray gelding, and the Claws set off with a great pounding of accelerating hooves, the sound quickly lost in another wave of thunder. Yelps and whoops leapt unbound from the men, echoing in the stone passageway, and then he was out, charging across the open plain, following the wind-splayed plume of Uslo's helm.

Sir Guilliver looked back over his shoulder. Over half the men were through. He saw lightning arc over the wall. Two-thirds. Chantrille appeared at the north battlement, face incandescent, eyebrows nearly at his hairline, mouth wide and screaming after them. Sir Guilliver couldn't hear a word, but he could guess.

The last of the Claws rode onto the Plains. The portcullis slammed down a second later.

Galloping north, Sir Guilliver the ex-knight, the mercenary, and now the outlaw, sent joyous laughter into the angry sky.

*****

The cheer as the cavalrymen came into view was loud enough to provoke a wince in Xavire's relieved grin. He shouldn't have been surprised. If anything was established during the last hour, it was that not even the storm clouds overhead could challenge such an outpouring of noise, their booms reduced to resentful grumbling. They had done it. It had worked. Every gods-damned step.

The ambush was a miracle. Xavire had chosen the spot for it that first night after Uslo returned; himself, Peris, and Sir Guilliver sneaking over the wall under cover of darkness and scouting the north road. Options had been slim, with the flat grassland offering nothing of promise, a testament to the sound strategy of the wall's location. Naturally, the ambush had to take place beyond the furthest sight of the towers. The less they knew at the wall about what was to happen, the better.

In the end, further north than was ideal, an adequate site was found. The unkempt road passed by a mess of boggy ground – retaining its slickness despite the sun – before curving behind a great outcropping of shale. Around the site, the land began to roll with hillocks and knolls, the grass giving way to thin, semi-solitary trees, interspersed with bush.

After planting stakes behind the outcropping such that they wouldn't be seen until the wagons were almost on top of them, almost three thousand Plainsmen and their Claws escort had lain in wait for the supply train to arrive. The return to the Plains seemed to have breathed new life into the Ardovikians, and Xavire had watched with genuine amazement as they all but disappeared into the land itself, laughing at the dull southerners and their endless prevarication. To be fair, the Claws had a trickier task, having to not only hide themselves from view of the road, but also hold an advantageous position should they be left with no option but direct attack. In terms of soldiers, such a scenario would have seen them outnumbered more than two to one, and they therefore needed to leverage every iota of the land in their favor.

It hadn't come to that. Hadn't come close. Thirty wagons had arrived in single file, moving up the narrow road made narrower by encroaching vegetation. From where he was, peering through bushes that were uncomfortably close to the road, Xavire had been able to see the two officers' faces as they passed at the front of the train. Without Chantrille there to draw focus, he noticed that the two men were at least as young as the Valentican commander. Lord Darvled's banner came behind them, flying high.

The train had rounded the outcropping, and as soon as the order to halt reached the farthest wagon, the Claws had begun to shout their furious demand from all around – *Leave the wagons, or perish!* Whether or not they would have complied, Xavire would never know. For what he hadn't counted on – could never have imagined – was the roar that suddenly exploded from the hidden Ardovikians. Only it wasn't just a roar. It was a wail, a howl, a bray, and a bawl all rolled into one broiling, unceasing drone. It was as if all the pain, all the fear and indignity endured over the past year or so of their lives were being unleashed upon the southern soldiers. It was terrifying. Xavire felt sure he wasn't the only member of the Claws whose bowels were perilously loosened by the sound. He certainly hoped not.

For Lord Darvled's men, there was no question. They ran, Olvar and Pesayn practically trampling their way past the fleeing spearmen, many of whom threw down their arms. They didn't stop. They didn't look back. The Claws had stood up, astonishment plain on every face as they stepped onto the road. It was over.

Since then, Claws and Ardovikians had milled ambiguously around the caravans for anywhere between a half hour and an hour, the desire to examine their catch held in check by the knowledge that they could be moving at a moment's notice. Anxiety hung heavy in the humid air. All knew that if any force save the general's were to appear on the southern horizon, they would be hard pressed to outrun it. More than once, Xavire observed members of the Ardovikians make what sounded like an appeal to Alea. Though he couldn't be sure – and didn't ask – Xavire suspected they wanted to start moving. If that was the case, they had a point. They couldn't wait forever.

But none of that mattered now. Not with the adventurers bearing down the road toward them, long gallops kicking up dust to either side. Still grinning, Xavire shook his head and fixed his hat in place.

"Alright, I want us moving as soon as possible after they get here! Claws! Get ready to help remove the armor and barding! Alea?"

"We're ready." Her voice came from next to him, making him jump. He hadn't heard her approach. He looked round, meeting the amused, sharp eyes under her hood.

Xavire nodded. "Good."

Alea was still wearing the thick, brown robes, but she now held an ornate staff of a kind he'd never seen before – not that he'd seen many staffs. Made predominantly from a bright and mysteriously blue metal, gold was worked along its length in thin, delicate bands, weaving a pattern which reminded him of flowing water. At its head was an egg-shaped hollow of red glass. When Xavire looked at it, it seemed as if light was shimmering within. He tried not to look at it.

With the staff at her side, Alea seemed different. Or rather, she seemed the same, but more. As if a part of her had returned from wherever she had been forced to hide it.

Minutes later, the general and his cavalrymen drew up to yet more cheering. Xavire went to meet them. Swinging smoothly from Volonto, Uslo pulled off his helmet, revealing a grin so wild Xavire could only laugh.

"It's done?"

"It's done!"

Uslo dropped his helm. They each clasped the others' shoulders and laughed.

"It worked, sir!" cried Xavire. "How did it *all* work?!"

"Don't ask me, it was your plan!"

Activity bustled around them, the Claws helping get the cavalry ready for the long march. Sir Guilliver had dismounted his gelding and was coming toward them, blond hair soaked with sweat, still as dashing as ever.

"But the ogres!" managed Xavire after more laughing. "Aren't they coming after us? We have to move!"

Uslo was shaking his head. "The ogres won't be coming. Not unless Commander Chantrille finds a lot of coin very fast."

"Tell me, gentlemen," said Sir Guilliver, thumping them both on the backs. "Are you always this lucky when you gamble? If so, I might have to take up the habit after all!"

"Gods, if only our luck at the tables were as rich as today!"

"If there's one thing I learned from the good Captain Brawand," said Uslo, mustache twitching with mischief, "it's that the best way to win at Sparthan Spearwall is…" he looked at Xavire expectantly.

"Not to play at all?" he guessed.

"No! You play a Royal Drakon!"

"Golloch's bollocks!" they yelled together and howled with laughter. Sir Guilliver smiled, visibly mystified.

Overhead, thunder gave its final warning. Then it started to rain.

8

...Given the obvious doubtfulness of Keatairn's existence, it is therefore surprising that, in the experience of your humble servant, the items are indeed Primovantian relics...

Vespilo A., On the Location and Identification of Primovantian Antiquity, Appendix IX 'From the Gatekeepers' - The Mystery of Keatairn

Dusk crept over the Plains, and the creature stirred. Its head poked out from its shallow hollow, ears back, eyes bright, nose twitching to test the air. With a confidence it had gradually cultivated over the past three days, it inched its way forward, spry fore followed by powerful hind. Rearing back, it stretched itself tall, ears rising to twist to and fro.

Bolirm's stomach growled. Prone among the bracken, he watched the rabbit as it began to munch away on the scrub. His grip on his axe tightened. Compared with previous sightings, the animal had grown careless. If Bolirm were to try now, chances were that he could hurl his weapon into its spine. Teeth grinding, he forced his grip to loosen. Bolirm's crew had bigger prey in sight.

Straddling the surrounding flatland, the fortress caught the last light of day against its ramparts. While not as imposing as even the smallest strongholds of Tragar, the humans had built it strong, stone walls surrounding a square keep, a watchtower rising from one corner. Three days ago, as his skulks encircled the fort under dead of night, Bolirm had delighted in Orod's stupidity. There was a far more vulnerable target than this, one that didn't need goblin boats to reach it. His orcs passed it only hours after crossing the upriver shallows, a fortress of similar size but which had sustained significant damage, he guessed from the last invasion. However, as he lay there with his crew out of sight near the westerly dirt road, hunger compelling him to chew strips of his mammoth-hide gear, Bolirm realized the cunning behind the krudger's plan. Even at a distance, Bolirm had seen that the other fort was brimming with activity, workers repairing the damage to its gatehouse, carts and riders coming and going. An easier prospect for direct assault, but also one which guaranteed that word of their invasion would be borne to every corner of the human lands. This fort, on the other hand... minimal garrison, no patrols along the nearby roads. Like the rabbit, it had grown careless.

Bolirm glanced back at his crew. Many had their eyes on the long-eared rodent, desire plain upon their branded faces. This was the longest they had ever had to wait in ambush. The hunger was unbearable, its void pressing against their minds. Most orcs would have given in, revealing themselves in the process – but not Bolirm's lot. They had long ago learned the patience of hunters. It had been a necessity at first, a means of avoiding the fate of the other escaped slaves, those who mindlessly attacked their master's armies. Of the many thousands that broke from their bonds, only those who followed Orod survived past the first few weeks. Later, after escaping the floodwaters, patience had become a pleasure. The orcs discovered that the more challenging the prey, the more it *demanded* of them, the greater the exhilaration that followed. That was their true hunger, now. They craved the hunter's reward.

The fact that they had Orod to thank for all of it meant nothing to Bolirm. The krudger's ambitions were his own. The time to kill him had passed; instead, Bolirm planned to simply take the crew and leave. Already he sensed the other ex-slaves would gladly follow him in ditching Orod's horde, and this would undoubtedly have been an excellent moment to do just that. But the hunt called to them. The moment Orod had nothing left to offer, they would set out on their own.

The rabbit looked up. Its body went rigid, its tall ears swung toward the fort. In a flash, it scurried to its hollow. Bolirm watched with bated breath, anticipation firing along his nerves.

They were here.

A bell rang furiously in the watchtower. Alarmed voices began calling out, rousing the other humans from their indolence. The orcs didn't need to see it to know the source of their panic. The horde was coming.

Bolirm shifted around, stretching his muscles as he looked back at the crew.

"Remember, spread fast."

Those close enough to hear gave a nod. Most were already busying themselves, variously unrolling slave-hooks or stringing their bows. If any of the humans were to look now, there was a chance they might have noticed the strange rustling of the distant fern or grassy patches that surrounded the western roadways. But all eyes would be facing east, ranged along the battlements as they waited to spy for themselves what the tower had glimpsed over the horizon.

Lifting his head above the frond, Bolirm chanced a look at where the other groups were hiding. The road running out of the fort's west gate split in a fork at around two hundred yards, with branches curving north and south. Both had orcs laying in wait along their length. Among the southern long grass, Bolirm spotted a couple of hooded faces peering back at him. He sent them a nod, and he lay back down. Just a little more patience…

The humans did not make them wait long. Minutes after the bell began its frantic ringing, the doors of the outer gateway were drawn inward, the iron portcullis slowly rising. Four riders emerged before it was halfway open, ducking low in their saddles as they mounted the dirt road. Their cloaks whipped in the air behind them, revealing small, unarmored men – messengers. One each took the north and south road, leaving two bearing heedlessly toward Bolirm. He gripped his axe purposefully, sensing the eyes of the others upon him. They would move only on his signal. He lifted his free hand, fingers counting down from five, four, three–

A horse's whine cut through the air. The two riders pulled on their reins, twisting to look back along the south road. Bolirm hissed a curse.

"Now!" he yelled.

Rising quickly from the bracken, he took one step forward before hurling his axe. The weapon soared toward its mark, edge whistling with menace. Turning back, the human had enough time to glimpse the impending threat before it bit deep into his chest, knocking him clean from the saddle. The unburdened horse reared in panic; a slew of arrows punched into its flesh.

More screams were let out, this time from the north road where mount and rider were being set upon, dragged to the ground beneath nets and slave-hooks. Bolirm barely noticed. He was charging at the remaining horseman, eager to tear him apart with his bare hands. To bite him. In a nimble motion, the human drew his steed around to slip beyond the orc's grasp.

"Spread!" shouted Bolirm, spinning to face the others. "Don't let 'im pass!"

The ex-slaves had already fanned their formation, and now they leapt outward still further, expanding the net. Those armed with bows continued to train them on the remaining rider, maintaining an onslaught of missiles. At the north and south roads, the panicked cries of horse and men had been replaced by the wails of the dying. The sound was soon joined by an explosion of hog-like grunting as the orcs devoured their prize.

Bolirm turned to watch the last messenger come to a halt some fifty feet away. The human's hood had fallen back. His skin was deathly white, his eyes wide. As orc arrows fell around him, his gaze flitted back and forth between his fellows on the north and south roads, helpless to do anything save witness their plight.

An arrowhead grazed the rider's shoulder. It seemed to snap him from his horror. Low in the saddle and gripping his horse's reins, he began to scan the line of orcs which now extended far to either side of the west road, searching for a path through.

Keeping his eyes on the rider, Bolirm strode over to where the man's companion lay. His axe was still lodged in his ribs. Dying, the human choked for breath, his hands hovering uselessly to either side of the weapon.

As Bolirm crouched over him, the remaining rider met his eye.

Bolirm grinned.

Reaching past the haft of his axe, he clamped his fist around the man's throat and *pulled*. There was a familiar and sickly-sweet rip of distressed flesh. Standing tall, Bolirm held the gullet aloft, savoring the warm, red mist that fell across his face, the taste of iron.

The messenger fled. Heaving his horse back around, terror spurred him toward the rapidly closing portcullis. With yells of triumph, the orcs charged forward to fall upon the dead human at Bolirm's feet. Still holding the organ over his head, Bolirm surveyed the western battlements of the fort and spied the soft tones of human faces. He could sense their despair.

Bolirm dropped the gullet into the feeding frenzy. His stomach would wait. For now, the hunt had sated him.

The failed messenger disappeared into the gateway, its portcullis slamming shut behind him. Not a minute later, the first of Orod's horde appeared on the horizon.

*****

"Steady... Launch it!"

The catapult leapt, its tension releasing with a *crack*. Four rocks the size of Orod's fist soared through the air, catching the moonlight as they cleared the quarter-mile distance to the fort's walls. Or rather, most of it. The projectiles gave a roll of *thumps* as they hit the earth, thirty paces from the base of the stonework.

Laughter echoed distantly from within the human defenses. The anxious silence which had greeted the orcs' arrival was long gone. Several of the soldiers mockingly loosed crossbows from atop the ramparts. Their bolts landed some way short of the goblin war engine.

Standing at the head of his horde, Orod fought to keep anger in check. They had been at this for nearly an hour now. He didn't have to look in order to discern the mood of the near ten-thousand ax arrayed behind him. It was fouling fast.

"Wind it again! Move it, you scum!" Six goblins hurled themselves against the levers, the little gits wheezing desperately as they worked to draw back the arm.

"Grimmik."

The head goblin stopped bellowing insults and turned to the krudger. "Yes, boss?"

"You said it would reach from here. What's taking so long?"

"It's a delicate business, boss! Gotta get the ropes just tight enough – can't risk 'em snapping on us!" Grimmik grinned, the light from his torch shining on yellow teeth. "'Course, we could always move a bit closer..."

"No." Any closer and the crossbows would start finding their marks, and he only had the one catapult. Too much depended on it.

"Right, then," said Grimmik. He turned back to the contraption and set about directing a further tightening of the rope bundle. From a safe distance, of course. If anything were to break, the stresses involved would fling cord ends with enough force to gouge flesh. Both the catapult's arm and its torsion bind had been built on the east side of the river and were only brought over behind the rest of the horde. The crossing had been tense. According to the goblins, the slightest moisture could ruin the ropes, rendering the entire mechanism useless. Bolstered by Orod's threat to personally drown each and every goblin if that should happen, Grimmik first of all, the gits got the job done. Their three boats had been disassembled, after which the strongest parts were used to build the weapon's frame. It gave the whole thing the look of an overturned raft.

"They laugh! Oh, yes, they laugh!" Arlok's thin voice was charged with fire. Orod glanced back. The Godspeaker was moving jerkily down the orc line, variously hopping on one leg and leaping back and forth, bone headdress rattling as he swung his Abyssal-skulled staff about him. His pet goblin was close behind, imitating every step.

"They think they are safe behind their stones! But hear me, forsaken children of Garkhan! They are not!" Arlok laughed maniacally, a slithering sound. "The gods are speaking! They say men are doomed!"

"Launch it!" cried Grimmik.

The catapult leapt again, and again the rocks fell short.

Orod ground his teeth, fingering the brand on his jaw. Patience. It was what had got him this far, seen him rise from the obsidian mines to become a krudger of thousands. Just a little more...

He turned to face his horde. Greatax looked back at him from neat ranks; beyond, the ax thronged restlessly. Hundreds of jagged banners twitched and fretted as they caught the fierce winds from the north, a rippling barely visible under the stars. The orcs wanted to attack. But even if they were to possess the necessary gear, taking the fortress in a direct assault would prove costly and with scant reward. Orod had no problem sending his warriors to their death should need arise. Here, however, his victory over the humans must be one-sided. Crushingly so.

His destiny demanded it.

Orod's eyes came to Lashka. His mate was standing before the greatax ranks. Clad in iron scale mail, she gripped a viciously pronged glaive in both hands. She was looking at him, lips drawn back in disapproval.

"Steady!" called Grimmik.

"Wait!" barked the krudger. Orod strode across to the catapult. Enough patience. Leaning over the weapon's frame, he took hold of the torsion lever and twisted it a full rotation. The rope bundle creaked in protest at the sudden addition of strain.

"Stop! She won't take it!" screeched Grimmik. Orod ignored the biggit, circling around the catapult to repeat the turn on the opposing lever. The ropes groaned. Orod stepped back.

"Do it!" he ordered.

The catapult lurched forward, arm slamming into the crossbar and discharging its payload. The projectile quartet surged rapidly to the height of their arc, slowly drifting apart from one another as they fell toward their target. Orod grinned. That had done it. With a burst of piercing *cracks*, the rocks shattered against the fortress wall.

The humans on the ramparts gave a derisive cheer. Orod knew why. The catapult had done little more than chip the stonework. Even with a hundred years of unceasing volleys, they hadn't the slightest chance of penetrating the fort. Not with rocks.

Orod looked at Grimmik. The goblin smiled back awkwardly, a failing effort to hide his irritation at the krudger's maltreatment of the weapon.

"It's ready. Bring them."

In the yellow torchlight, Grimmik turned a shade paler. He nodded. "Right, boss."

The biggit began to spit orders in a string of profane goblinish. There was a brief commotion among the mob as each git attempted to avoid selection, until finally two emerged carrying a long, narrow chest between them. The pair of goblins moved slowly, wide eyes fixed on the container's darkened wood, as if fearing that its lid might fling open and bite them. They carefully set it down before the krudger and scampered off.

Orod's chains jangled lightly as he crouched over the chest. He unhooked the latch and opened it. There was a sigh of hinges, and a familiar smell flooded the krudger with memory. Sulfur and smog.

When Orod had led his orcs out of the flooded Abyssal lands, he'd brought only three things: the chains of his armor, which had bound him from birth; the twin axes of his dwarf master, dead by Orod's hand; and this chest. They had come across it while raiding an isolated Tragarian foundry, between snatching whatever gear they could carry and butchering every worker they came across. At the time, there had been no apparent reason to take the chest. He had once seen from afar the devastating effect of its contents, but he hadn't the means of employing them for himself. Still, something had told the krudger that the chest would prove useful, that he *must* take it.

The gods were guiding me even then, he thought.

Four dome-topped cylinders lay inside, wedged into padded and form-fitting recesses. Orod lifted one out delicately. The metal was cool to the touch, black-iron casing with a bright red circle painted on the domed tip. Its head was solid and weighted – the same weight as the fist-sized rocks. Orod's heart pounded. To think such power could be held by something so small, that it could be locked away. Caged.

He set the shell down and stood up.

"Load them."

The goblins once more lowered the catapult's arm to position. As they painstakingly set the new payload, Orod drew one of his axes.

"Look, now, warriors!" Arlok cried, pushing his lungs to their shrillest limits. "Behold the fate of men!"

"It's ready, boss!"

The moment the words left the goblin's mouth, Orod swung, unleashing his fury in a roar. The axe swept through the restraining rope, severing it clean. Noise retreated from the world, and the krudger watched raptly as the four shells took to the air. Their flight was graceless at first, seemingly confounded by the irregular launch. But with the fundamental assuredness of well-made things, they recalled their purpose, the weighted heads turning to face their goal. They struck stone.

Explosions tore into the fortress like an axe parting flesh. Their light flared blindingly in the dark, and around the resulting spots on his vision, Orod saw great masses of masonry fly inward. Thunder shook the earth, pounding his ears and rattling his chains. The wave of sound passed. Orod drew breath. He hadn't stopped bellowing throughout.

Silence followed. Awed, disbelieving silence. The silence of fear.

The krudger turned to his orcs. Looking across their ravenous faces, illuminated by torches and starlight, he heard the first wails of despair begin to seep from the fortress.

He raised his axe, and the horde bayed for red blood.

*****

The sun rose pale, its light smearing a sallow pink throughout the eastern sky. Birds amassed between heavy clouds, lured across untold distance by the promise of fresh carrion, their presence a blight on the dawn. Atop the broken wall of the human fort, Orod's gaze lingered on them. Blood-slick fingers pulsed against the axes in their grip, muscles burned with fervent heat. Every breath coated his throat in dust, in the scent of iron. His mind was blank.

Despite the wretchedness of the humans' situation, they had put up a good fight. Many orcs had fallen, hindered by the treacherous debris, held off as the defenders plugged the breach in their wall. But the horde would not be stopped, and the humans were soon overwhelmed. The last hundred or so had made a desperate bid to flee through the west gateway, running headlong into Bolirm's nets. Food for the march.

"Krudger."

Orod looked round. Lashka stood a short distance away along the wall. Her glaive and maw alike were thick with scarlet gore. The Godspeaker was with her. Behind them stood the rows of greatax, restrained even now, knowing that the best spoils would be theirs by right.

"Is it done?" he asked.

"Their stores are emptied, Krudger. Every weapon, every scrap of meat – s'all yours."

"How many ax did I lose?"

"Six hundred, at most," said Arlok.

"Good."

Turning away, Orod stepped up to the broken edge of the wall. A sea of orcs churned below, spread through the breach and over the fortress grounds, spilling out of every building and across every surface. The humans' monuments were defaced, their parchments flung onto inchoate pyres. Their corpses were consumed. Orod smiled. The birds would find nothing.

Lashka moved to his side. She looked at him questioningly. The krudger nodded.

Three sharp *cracks* echoed throughout the fort as Orod's mate pounded the battlement with the butt of her glaive. Movement petered out. The orcs turned their heads to look up at the krudger. Those inside the keep gathered at its windows. A quiet fell across the horde. The quiet of expectation. Orod filled his lungs.

"One year ago, thousands of you marched across the human lands. Your krudgers said they were fulfilling a god-given destiny, that they were prophesied to bring the Age of Orcs. One year ago, they failed. *You* failed."

He paused, letting anger burn in his stare. The orcs met his gaze in silence.

"You let the humans gather against you, let them bring allies from across the world. Worst of all, you let them build walls! Is this what defeated you?!" Orod held out his axe, sweeping it across the v-shaped rent in the fortress. "The humans thought it made them safe, but they'd only built a cage!

"None of you knows what it means to live in iron! None of you understands what it means to be free! Our race was forged in shackles, just as I was born in these chains!" He slammed the crescent heads of his axes against his chest. "As our ancestors broke their bonds, so am I chosen to deliver our destiny! And you! You are the horde that will shatter all realms, that will destroy the civilized world!"

In a quick movement, Orod plunged his axes between the links of his chains and yanked outward with their shafts. There was a brief whine of straining metal, and then a *snap*. Broken, the chains tumbled from his torso, piling at his feet before slipping off the edge of the wall.

Roaring cheers burst over him, spilling out and over the desolate plain. Chest bare, Orod lifted his axes as he raised his voice over the clamoring throng.

"My masters named me *Orodren'val* – doomed one! Follow me west, my ax warriors, and I will become *Orodrazk* – the Doom!"

"*DOOM! DOOM! DOOM! DOOM!*"

The orc drums began to pound, driving the word along the krudger's bones. Orod grinned, his satisfaction raw and primal. Victory would be his.

"*DOOM! DOOM! DOOM! DOOM!*"

It was destiny.

9

...(with a measure of hesitancy, it can be revealed that the examples recorded on pages [...] were sold with the insistence that Keatairn was their origin)...

Vespilo A., *On the Location and Identification of Primovantian Antiquity,* Appendix IX *'From the Gatekeepers' - The Mystery of Keatairn*

She was in the house. He could hear the hurried slink of her paws on the floorboards, could catch her shadow disappearing around corners. How she'd managed to get inside only dimly occurred to the boy, the question glimpsed and lost like a figure in the mist. The fact that she'd never come inside before didn't occur to him at all. Such thought was overridden by an urgent and narrow certainty – a cat was in the house, a huntress, and he had to find her. If he didn't, something bad would happen. Something desperate.

Who? Where?

The boy couldn't comprehend the voice that spurred him on. In a sense, he wasn't really aware of it at all. Yet even without his knowing, it pressed on him, weighed him down, breathing its demand against the back of his neck in a voice both rich and hollow.

Who is it? Can you see?

He could. She stood at the end of the hall, a thread of light dancing on tabby fur, her sharp eyes peering at him from the shadows. But as soon as he opened his mouth to call her, she slipped through the half-opened door, tail high and wild.

Got her, *he thought with relief. There was only one way in and out of that room.*

Only, it wasn't the room he'd expected. Having dashed silently down the short hallway, the boy was greeted by the intimately familiar sight of the common room, warmed by the noon sun, smelling faintly of lemon and vinegar. Empty. The cat was nowhere to be seen. The double doors leading out to the lobby were shut tight.

He stepped forward, bending to look under the furniture.

"Here, kitty kitty," he whispered, but that was wrong. She was more than a cat, if the other felines of Valentica were anything to go by. It wasn't just that she was larger. She was fiercer. Nobler and smarter.

"Lady?" he breathed.

The word felt closer, almost right.

What, then? What is it?

The boy straightened up, turning to the door. She wasn't under the furniture. She must have gone past him while–

Tell me the name!

"I– I d-don't know!" he stammered, clueless as to why he was responding to a command he hadn't heard. "Sh-she's just… the huntress!"

For several seconds, he stood perfectly still, mind clouded with fear, heart pounding in his ears. Then a soft meow floated through the air, and he forgot all about the voiceless command. He looked up, following its source, and the boy had to clap his hands over his mouth to stifle a laugh. A bushy tail hung from the east-facing alcove, swaying back and forth as the cat looked out the window.

"Here, huntress, come down," he whispered once the laugh subsided, filling his voice with the sweetness of his relief. He felt strangely liberated. "Come and I'll give you something to eat. I swear."

She meowed again, not looking round. He sighed through a smile. Nothing else for it.

Placing a chair against the wall, he prepared to mount the support pillar. The chair creaked, but he ignored it, shifting his weight onto the familiar grooves in the wood. The huntress seemed to be meowing continuously now, a low and close-mouthed sound. He watched her as he climbed, willing her to show any awareness of his approach. Leaning hesitantly toward the alcove, he tried to woo her again.

"Here, huntress. Come down from up there."

Other than the constant swishing of her tail, she didn't move. The angry meow seemed to be getting stuck in her throat, splitting it into staccato garbles. It was an ugly sound.

"Come on," he tried again, caution spoiling the sweetness of the words, "I promise I can give you something nice… what're you looking at, anyway?"

Her face was pressed against the bottom right of the window, looking down.

The boy's heart began to shudder against his ribs as fear bloomed, holding him in its cloying, heavy fog. All at once, he knew what she was looking at.

"WhO? WheRe?"

The words had come from the huntress, forced through the animal's vocal chords to emerge as a petulant, bubbling rasp. Hearing it sent a sickness throughout his body. But he wasn't surprised. Because it wasn't the huntress. It was the emptiness, the thing that chased him through the night. His mouth worked to scream, to shout something, open and shut, over and over, producing no sound save the slight pops of his dry lips pulling apart.

"WhO iS It? CaN yoU seE?"

"No," he whispered, pleading. The thing turned, and the boy beheld its face with horror. A negative space, smooth as the unseen void, constant as the corners of perception. Eyeless, its mouth a tear.

"YoU seE! We kNow yOu sEe!"

It leapt at him, and the boy let go, falling back toward the floor. The alcove fell with him. Images, incomprehensible sights, sounds, and smells began to tumble through his mind: heavy mists, a dark cloud over open plains, a shadow with the face of nothing.

"TELL US!" it boomed. "WE MUST KNOW!"

"Ow!"

Xavire's body gave a jump. His forehead throbbed, contorting his face into a grimace. He raised a sluggish hand to it.

You banged it off something, his mind grumped at him.

Laying still, he let the nightmare fade away and waited for his senses to regain purchase. A cool, moist breeze caressed his face, blowing freshness through his unwashed odor. There was a tickling on the back of his neck. The hand on his head shifted to the ground, touching grass. Reaching the other out, his fingers traced cold metal not far above. It felt like a bar, although his eyes showed only a dark blur.

He felt around for his glasses, quickly finding them tucked under his cap. Blinking hard, his eyes began adjusting to the dawn light. Broad wooden planks filled his vision, a single iron bar set into their surface. The perfect height to connect with his head. The sight left him hopelessly stumped for a good five seconds. Then a man grunted sleepily next to him, and Xavire remembered.

Doing his best not to disturb the other sleepers, Xavire crawled out from under the wagon, sheathed sword in one hand, and sat against a large, spoked wheel. Opening the coat of his uniform, he removed his glasses to wipe the lenses on his shirt, gazing out at the mess of indistinct blues. The rains had finally stopped. They'd left the ground wet, but not as sodden as he might have expected. The soil was thirsty. It had drunk deep. He stood up, stretching muscles that mourned the loss of his barracks bed, and replaced his glasses.

Thin mist lay over the Ardovikian Plains. It lounged on the gradual dips and swells of the land, obscuring a view that might otherwise have gone on forever. Rugged scrub vied with voluminous grass for every inch of ground, defied only by the occasional patch of moss-claimed rock. There were no trees, not even the thin, solitary figures of the ambush site. Xavire wondered if they had been saplings, the forest rebirthing itself beyond the gaze of Lord Darvled's Wall. He didn't know much about trees, having lived most of his life in the city, and wondered if they were a rarity on the Plains. A rolling sea of blue-green, cast in a muted light which danced on the dew; he thought this must be a landscape typical of Ardovikia.

Xavire let out a sigh as he fixed his sword to his belt, surprised to find himself contented. He'd never shared the wanderlust that drove Uslo and so many of his Claws, and could probably have managed another half a year at the wall without complaint, backwater or no. Before he left Valentica – before the incident – he had expected to live his whole life within its bounds. Indeed, he had welcomed it. The city was all the world he'd ever known or needed. Nevertheless, when he joined the Claws, Xavire soon discovered the ameliorating pleasures known only to the traveler. It went without saying that rough sleeping wasn't one of them. But the experience of waking like this, body sore, belly empty, looking upon a new land in new light, absorbing the total immediacy of it, before moving on in search of the next one, always the same but never alike – it was a worthy salve, if not quite a full recompense for his loss.

Certainly, it was good to be on the road again. Though as he turned to look down the line of covered wagons, he amended the thought. They weren't on a road anymore. They'd left it not long after sundown of the previous day, the same day they'd crossed the wall. The road which passed through the west gate went directly northeast, straight to Lord Darvled's armies and allies in central Ardovikia. The Claws, although going much the same way initially, naturally wanted to avoid running into any of the lord's forces. Their northerly dirt track had rapidly diminished, the undergrowth pressing from the sides and sprouting up its middle. At some points, it seemed to have disappeared completely, only to re-emerge after the caravan pushed through the invading grass, flattening it down and reconnecting the road for a time, until it finally vanished for good. From there it was hard going, their already-diminished speed dropping further as the front directed a path around rocky outcroppings and patches of boggy, waterlogged ground. Eventually the growing darkness and unrelenting downpour had compelled them to stop. Under the wagons and among the horses, the unlikely alliance of Claws and Plainsmen had huddled together, weathering the rain.

Many were still sleeping now, but Xavire saw that most were awake, assuming they'd slept at all. Those on their feet were engaged, it seemed, in one of two activities: taking the opportunity to get a first look through the contents of the captured wagons, or answering nature's call. Xavire knew which he favored for himself. His fingers fumbled with his belt buckle as he stepped away from the caravan.

"Xavire!" Uslo was calling him from the forward end of the column. "Good morning!"

"Morning, sir," he responded in a half-sigh, one hand raised in greeting.

"You've got to see this! In the first wagon! Come look!" Then Uslo ran back to the front, his youthful enthusiasm looking more than a little ridiculous on the tall Genezan.

"Yes, sir," he mumbled through a smile, shaking his head.

He began to make his way to the fore. More were waking up. They crawled groggily from under the wagons, no doubt disturbed by the sounds of those taking inventory above. While it was true that both Uslo and Xavire had been expecting more wagons to be crossing the wall with the supply train, the thirty they had captured were large and sturdy, each of them drawn by two horses and laden to the brim with everything a marching army could need. Not an army this size, it was true, but with care he felt sure they could make it last. In any case, once beyond Lord Darvled's sphere, they would be able to trade with whatever communities had emerged from the war. The orcs couldn't have destroyed them all.

Passing a group of Plainsmen, he saw Alea standing just inside one of the wagons, hunched over to keep her head from touching the canvas. She was directing the examination of numerous wide-based pots. Xavire called out a greeting, and she returned it. The ornate staff was still at her side.

"What have you found?" he asked.

"Olive oil," she called back.

"Preserves?"

"Some. Vegetables, mostly. The odd one contains fish. Most are just oil."

He nodded, but she'd already turned to talk with one of the elders. He continued on.

Two wagons down, another gathering was passing out some of the hardened bread Xavire had identified the day before. Several Claws were among them, and he was pleased to see members of the two groups talking to one another. As he passed closer, however, he overheard their mutual incomprehension, their voices edged with tension.

"They haven't gone bad, they're supposed to be like this!" Xavire caught Mattis's Lantorian accent among the hubbub. Searching him out, he recognized the Plainsman he was talking to as the one who'd been so protective of Cauhin on the wall. Solid and dark-haired, the Ardovikian seemed more interested in keeping Mattis and the other Claws away from the wagon than in conversing.

"What's going on, Mattis?"

Mattis looked round, his exasperation turning to relief.

"Sir! The Viks seem to think the bread is off! They're going through every crate and discarding perfectly good rations!"

Xavire craned to peer into the back of the wagon and saw he was right. The Plainsmen worked with hurried frustration, checking a loaf at a time and invariably judging each to be inadequate. In some cases, they were throwing bread aside. He heard a repetitive *thunk*, and spotted a young child hitting a loaf against the wheel of the wagon.

"Of all the damned... Alea!" Xavire cried.

At the sound of her name, the Ardovikians turned to look at him, their faces expressing an almost laughable innocence. Even the *thunks* stopped. He tried his luck.

"Everybody, stop! The bread is fine, it just needs softening with broth or oil! My men will make sure everyone gets their share!"

It was no good. Most had returned to what they were doing long before he'd finished talking. The *thunks* resumed.

"I've been trying to tell them that, sir, but–"

"Alea!" he interjected, turning to call back down the line. None of the Plainsmen looked round this time.

"Yes?"

Alea's head appeared over the Ardovikians, the red glass at the top of her staff seeming to hover close by.

"Could you please explain to them that–"

"Xavire?!" came a shout from the front. "What's taking so long? Come see!"

"Fill her in, Mattis," said Xavire, turning to set off again.

"Looks like there's no need, sir," said Mattis. The Ardovikians had once again stopped their foraging, this time listening with rapt attention as Alea's voice filled the air. Xavire saw comprehension dawn on several of their faces.

"Good," he said, speaking over his shoulder as he walked away. "Make sure it all gets packed up again!"

So much for taking care to make the supplies last, he thought. He would need to have a word with Alea later, to insist that the Claws be in charge of supplies. Otherwise, this was going to prove a very short expedition indeed.

Cauhin and his friend were standing at the front of the bread wagon, patting the horses' necks. As rough as Xavire's sleeping patch was last night, theirs looked to have been worse, with wet mud still visible on their rags. They watched Xavire silently as he passed. Seeing them there fanned his irritation. He stopped.

"Didn't feel like helping, eh?" he asked. "You must've been able to hear what was going on back there."

Cauhin stared at him impassively. The bruising from his head wound encroached on one side of his face, with the strip of material from Xavire's shirt having apparently been discarded. His friend, Fillam, avoided Xavire's eyes. "Sorry," he mumbled. Xavire waited, but Cauhin didn't react. If anything, his defiance seemed to grow harder.

"Fine." Xavire turned away, but not before adding in a flash of petty inspiration, "You've got mud on you."

"Thanks for saving us!" blurted Fillam. Xavire looked back, surprised. Cauhin was glaring at his friend, but now it looked like it was Fillam's turn to be defiant.

"Don't mention it."

"Xavire!"

"I'm coming, sir!" He saw Uslo a little way ahead, bouncing on the balls of his feet. Like the rest of them, the general bore the disheveled look of a disturbed night, his long hair tangled and his clothes wet. But as he caught up, Xavire saw that the fire in his eyes was burning as brightly as ever.

"Come on, you won't believe it!" The general was next to the caravan's front wagon, and Xavire now noticed that it was different to the rest. Its structure showed more steel reinforcement; the horses that drew it were larger, more stacked with muscle.

Xavire followed him around the back of the wagon. Uslo placed a hand on the canvas flap, grinning.

"Don't tell me to guess," warned Xavire.

"Wouldn't dream of it," said Uslo. He drew back the flap, releasing a charcoal smell.

Xavire's jaw dropped. "Is that…?"

"It is!"

The floor of the wagon was lined with straw. Along the sides and back were various boxes and barrels, some open-topped and filled with iron balls the size of fists. Various long-shafted tools lay among them, some with flat, circular ends, others sporting carefully trimmed sponges. And at the center of it all, its twin wheels painted red and its body black as a beetle's carapice, stood a prince of death.

"A cannon?!"

"Not just a cannon," said Uslo. He stepped into the wagon. "A howitzer!"

"Is it? How can you tell?" Xavire asked, following him in.

"See how it's fixed at an upward angle for longer range? The slight body makes it quicker to cool, too, meaning a higher rate of fire. Or so I'm told."

Xavire ran his hands along one of the red wheels, ludicrously large compared to the weapon itself. Its body was shorter than other cannons he'd seen, although judging from the size of its muzzle, not to mention the six or so iron cannonballs at his feet, it fired a respectable ten- to twelve-pound shot. Every inch of the weapon seemed to revel in lethal practicality, with the sole ornamentation found just above the vent hole, where the crest of the Lord Darvled shone resplendent on a small, brass plate. Xavire frowned.

"Howitzer... I thought these were Rhordian, designed by the halfmen of the League. But this looks to have been built in a Valentican foundry."

"Can you believe it, Xavire? A halfling-made weapon! The finest engineers west of Abercarr!"

"I admit, I'm struggling to," he confessed. It was quite a find, worth about as much as everything else the Claws owned put together. "Where did Darvled get the expertise to build it? And why only one in the train?"

It seemed Uslo wasn't in the mood for questions. Crouching down behind the weapon, the general sighed as he set his hands on the howitzer's body. "I've always wanted artillery..."

"It's a beauty," said Xavire, meaning it. "You've certainly made the find of the morning, safe to say."

The general grinned. "You know–"

A panicked yell reached them from far away. They froze, waiting. More yells confirmed the first, and Uslo stood up sharply.

"The rear of the train," said Xavire.

They leapt from the wagon, running back down the line as more shouts reached them, pierced by alarmed screams.

"What's going on?!" Xavire asked Mattis as they passed the bread wagon.

"No clue, sir!" he called, falling in behind them.

"Claws, up!" cried Uslo, drawing his sword and raising it high. "To me!"

Xavire kept his blade sheathed, gripping the handle in readiness as he hurtled along the column of wagons. The Claws around them responded quickly to their general's order. Others were already heading for the rear, their weapons bared.

The yells had stopped by the time they reached their source. Staggering to a halt, Xavire's bouncing vision detected no sign of a fight. Instead, a small group of Ardovikians stood away from the caravan, their faces pale and bodies primed to flee. They were staring at the second to last wagon.

"What happened?" asked Uslo. None of the two dozen Plainsmen seemed capable of answering. One woman came closest, however, holding up a shaking hand to point at the wagon, her words frightened and impenetrable. Xavire looked. Nothing about it seemed out of the ordinary. In contrast to the anxiety of the humans around them, its horses appeared calm.

"Whatever it is, sir, it doesn't look like an attack, at least," said Xavire through deep breaths. He glanced back. Over a hundred Claws stood around them, their crossbows loaded and their sword arms steady. More stood on the other side of the caravan, keeping their distance alongside an even greater gathering of Ardovikians.

"Yes," said Uslo, "but something has put the fear in them. Maybe Darvled's men were keeping something alive in there?"

Xavire shrugged. "War dogs?" But as soon as he'd said it, Xavire knew that was wrong. They would have heard barks long before now.

"Only one way to find out."

Xavire nodded, drawing his sword.

They approached slowly, Uslo and Xavire at the front. As they came within a dozen yards of the wagon, it moved. The Claws stopped dead, watching the some five-by-twelve-foot carriage wobble and bounce, the axles groaning in protest as something shifted its weight within. Something large.

"What in the Abyss was that?!" The voice had come from the other side of the wagon.

"Sir Guilliver?"

"Xavire?"

"Quiet!" hissed Uslo. They waited. The wagon didn't move.

"Now what, sir?" asked Xavire, a fraction above a whisper. He caught Uslo's eye, and the general looked at him seriously. Xavire saw the fire was still there, but it wasn't the childlike joy of the howitzer's discovery that burned. This was the other Uslo. The Silver Cat, claws out and back arching before a fight.

"Now we find out." Uslo turned to Mattis and the other Claws. "Wait here. Don't do anything unless I give the order." The Claws nodded, murmurs of 'Yes, General,' issuing from every mouth.

They stepped cautiously around toward the back of the wagon. Both Sir Guilliver and Sergeant Peris were approaching from the other side. Xavire waved them over before examining the back flap. As with all the wagons, the off-white canvas was bound tightly over arched iron. The flap had been untied, probably when the Plainsmen were taking a look inside.

Or, spoke an unwelcome thought, *when whatever is in there climbed aboard.*

"What do we think, sirs?" asked Peris, his crossbow set and loaded.

"We don't," said Uslo firmly. One hand pushed the unkempt length of his hair behind his ears. Forefinger and thumb then made a quick stroke along his mustache. His lips parted, and Xavire saw Uslo's teeth clenched in anticipation. "We don't think. We act." His eyes never left the wagon flap.

"On the count of–" began Xavire, but Uslo had already taken hold of the flap. The general flung it back, the material making a cracking sound as it whipped through the air. A second later, he had mounted the step and leapt into the wagon, sword outstretched. Cursing under his breath, Xavire followed.

Whatever they had expected, whatever horror they had feared or banality they might have hoped for, it wasn't this. First to greet them were the casks. Stacks of them, made from aged oak, each painted with the seals of southern vineyards. A number had already been tapped and sat dry on their sides. But it was what was lying beneath the emptied casks that caused their stomachs to tighten sharply, tucked into the narrow space between the untapped stacks.

An ogre.

Xavire glanced at Uslo. His grin had disappeared.

"What is it?" asked Sir Guilliver behind them. There wasn't enough room for more than two people to stand abreast on the wagons.

"It's–"

The ogre's head shot up. Recognition began to coalesce in Xavire's mind – but was quickly dashed by the sight of the blunderbuss's wide snout springing from beneath the empty casks, their sudden displacement emitting a drum roll of hollow clattering as they bounced aside. Xavire tried to yell a warning but managed no more than the first alarmed syllable before the air was knocked out of him. He fell from the wagon.

For a moment, Xavire was back in his nightmare, the mouth of the blunderbuss taking the form of a lidless void staring through him. Then Xavire hit something, and the fall slowed.

Sir Guilliver collapsed, grunting as he absorbed the impact. Xavire registered neither the knight beneath him nor the sprawled form of Uslo at his side. He seemed to have gone deaf, and though it was no longer visible, the gaping maw of the blackpowder weapon yawned before his mind's eye.

Why didn't it flare? he thought, dazed. His hand went to his chest, searching for blood. Instead, however, he found Uslo's arm wrapped around his torso. Pieces snapped into place. The general must have thrown them both from the wagon, whacking Xavire's ribs in the process.

Laughter – rich, delighted, far-from-sober – danced from within the carriage. They sat up. Uslo and Xavire stared at each other, their realization paired.

"Oh, no," came a voice, deeper than any man's, the words almost swallowed by mirth. "No, no, no. Mine bigger, see?" Peris had mounted the wagon after their fall, his crossbow held level. But now he lowered it, the other hand raised in resentful submission as he stepped back down to the plain.

The ogre slumped clumsily into view at the back of the wagon, crouched beneath the cover. Eyes of penetrating gray looked down at them, assessing the four men with open amusement. It was the female, the one they'd seen arguing with Warlord Rnmogyr when his tribe arrived at the wall. Her hair was loose, allowing a long, pitch-black mane to fall across the red-brown skin of her broad shoulders, confusing the patterns of pale tribal markings borne there. Carefree muscle lounged on each arm and strained beneath her fur-lined jerkin of studded leather. Xavire registered the almond shape of her eyes, the way her broad smile curved around wine-stained teeth the length of his fingers. But his attention was on her buckler-sized hands. Her hands, and her weapons. The left held the blunderbuss without threat, toying with the trigger as she rested the muzzle over her shoulder. The right, however, gripped one of the massive ogre crossbows, the shoulder rest pressed against her hip, the iron head of a ballista-sized bolt directed toward them.

"See? Bigger." The ogre laughed, attempting to throw back her head, only to have it bounce against the arched bow of the canvas cover. The iron creaked. Blinking in surprise, her mouth fell open as she contorted to examine the noisy metal. Something about it made her laugh again. Giggle, even. Then she let out a burp.

"She's drunk," said Sir Guilliver, pushing Xavire off his legs and getting to his feet.

"I believe you're right, sir," responded Peris with the barest edge of irritability, his crossbow still pointed to the ground.

"General?"

Xavire glanced to his right. The Claws' crossbowmen had their weapons trained on the wagon. They couldn't see what was happening and looked anxious for orders. He turned back to the ogre's crossbow, eyes following the bolt tip as it swayed back and forth across them. Chances were that any attempt to shoot her would see her skewer one of them, whether or not she was taken down in the process. Still, seeing the loaded weapon thrust in his face brought the command up into his throat. He clenched his teeth.

"Stand down!" Uslo was getting up, his sword left lying in the grass. "There's no need for any bloodshed!"

The Claws lowered their weapons, and in the next instant, the ogre stuck her head out to peer at them. Alarm spread across the faces of the Claws, and there was a *snap* as someone's finger slipped, the bolt lodging into soil at the skittish man's feet.

The ogre seemed not to notice. "You are not the same humans." Though slightly marred by the alcohol haze borne on her breath, her pronunciation was remarkably clear and confident, far more so than the Warlord Rnmogyr's had been.

"That's right," said Uslo, speaking slowly. "We captured the train yesterday."

"Stole?"

"...Yes."

Xavire stood up. Unlike the general, he kept his sword in hand. The ogre didn't seem to notice him at all. She was looking at Uslo, brow furrowed.

"...Don't remember."

"You didn't hear my men capture it?"

"No. I was sleeping."

"What?! You were sleeping?!" exclaimed Xavire. Her eyes turned to him, as did the massive crossbow. He tried to swallow, despite the dryness of his mouth, before continuing in a croaky voice. "We didn't exactly do it quietly!"

"I was sleeping. Ogres sleep deeply."

"Nothing could've slept through that!"

"They could when they've drunk a half-dozen casks of red, Almenara," murmured Sir Guilliver behind him, tone urging him to drop it. Shaking his head in petulant disbelief, Xavire dropped it.

"Why are you here?" asked Uslo. "Did Chantrille hire you?"

The question seemed to amuse her. "Chantrille hires no one. Urshal tribe works for Darvled."

"Of course," he conceded. "So, you work for Lord Darvled?"

She contemplated the general for a moment. Then her eyes drifted down, widening in apparent surprise at the crossbow she held pointed at them. The weapon lowered, and Xavire felt a measure of relief as his stomach unclenched.

"No," she said, quietly.

"No? Then you weren't supposed to be going north of the wall?"

She certainly wasn't supposed to be drinking that wine, thought Xavire, recalling the seals. Only the best for Lord Darvled's soldiers, it seemed.

"I have a purpose. I need to go north." She spoke seriously now, her humor forgotten.

"I see," said Uslo in an understanding tone. "But why hide on the supply train? Why not just climb over the wall? Surely that would be easy for your people, now that they guard it."

We should know, thought Xavire. He had sheathed his sword almost without thinking. Holding it seemed pointless.

"My father knew I wanted to leave. His warriors watched me. This was the only way."

Uslo nodded. "Warlord Rnmogyr is your father." It wasn't a question.

"Yes."

Xavire suppressed a curse. Of *course* she was the warlord's daughter. Who else but offspring could shout at Rnmogyr like that? Not that Xavire would've ever dared with either of his own parents. Not even in his dreams.

"Will your father come after you?"

The ogre shrugged. "Maybe." Her face suggested the question genuinely held no interest for her.

Abruptly, the ogre made to dismount from the wagon. They hurried to clear the way. The carriage groaned with her movement, and though the grassland muted the sound of her fur-lined boots hitting the ground, Xavire felt a single tremor dart up his legs. She looked around, both weapons now resting on her ample shoulders.

"You are not the same humans. You are going to join Darvled's army?"

"No," said Uslo, combining the word with an emphatic chop through the air.

"But you are going north?"

"That's right."

She nodded definitively. "Good. I will go with you."

Xavire caught Uslo's eye. He looked surprised. "Uh..."

"It would be an honor to have you travel alongside us, Warrior."

Alea had approached them from among the gathered spectators.

The ogre turned to face her, eyes flitting conspicuously to the ornate staff as she watched Alea give a slight bow of her head. After several seconds of consideration, the ogre returned the gesture. There was something oddly pleasing about seeing something taller than Alea, thought Xavire. Even if it was an ogre.

"I am Alea. This is Xavire, Sir Guilliver, Sergeant Peris, and General Dargent."

"Dargent," the ogre mumbled, glancing at the Genezan. "Sounds like 'Darvled'." A smile played on her lips.

"What may we call you?" finished Alea.

The ogre stretched her back, joints cracking audibly as she rolled her shoulders. "Nokragyrsh." The name sounded garbled, seeming to wallow too long in the ogre's throat.

"Pardon?" said Sir Guilliver.

"Nokragyrsh," she repeated. "It is difficult for humans. You can call me 'Nokrag'."

"Thank you, Nokrag," said Alea.

Nokrag nodded. "Now, I make water." And with that she strode off, moving behind the final wagon and out of sight.

"By the Abyss!" exclaimed Peris. They turned to look at him. The sergeant had climbed among the depleted wine casks and held one up to show them. "She drank *at least* half a dozen!"

"It was very good!" they heard Nokrag call. As if to emphasize her praise, the sound of a heavy stream began to emanate from behind the final wagon. "But we ogres like it stronger!"

"You don't say," said Xavire through an exasperated sigh.

"Well, that could've been worse," said Sir Guilliver, cheerily. Uslo was laughing behind one hand, thumb and forefinger smoothing his mustache.

Xavire jumped slightly as Alea touched his shoulder. He hadn't noticed her step toward him. "Is your forehead all right, Xavire?" she asked.

"What, this?" he answered, but her hand was there before his, and he flinched as pain leapt from her touch.

"Just a bruise," she murmured.

"Er..." Xavire didn't know what to say. Before he could think, however, Uslo interjected.

"It pains me to say it, Xavire," he began, wiping tears from his eyes, "but I think you were wrong after all."

Xavire raised an eyebrow. "Sir?"

"Howizter or no, *this* was the find of the morning!"

Behind the last wagon, the stream continued. Nokrag began to hum.

10

...However, while genuine, there is no evidence to suggest that such objects were unearthed at the same site – to the contrary, in fact...

Vespilo A., *On the Location and Identification of Primovantian Antiquity,* Appendix IX *'From the Gatekeepers'* - *The Mystery of Keatairn*

For three days and four nights, the horde surged across the human lands, leveling what little resistance braved its path. Far from diminishing Orod's forces, the triumphant orcs emerged from each battle with their numbers bolstered by yet more ax. Like birds flying south for winter or ghouls sensing fresh corpses, a bone-deep instinct drew the orcs for many miles around. Some came in groups of hundreds. Often they arrived alone, a constant stream of eager warriors. The Bloodtusk was forgotten, Orod's victory over him likewise. After so long a time of defeated vagrancy, all that mattered was this promise, this chance to once more inflict violence upon the civilized world.

Four days after sacking the fortress, the horde paused its onslaught, snatching rest from the small hours. While they slept, the Godspeaker Arlok searched. He'd snuck away from Orod with difficulty, the krudger rarely letting him out of sight. Arlok winced at the thought, a hand reaching under his cloak to cradle the latest bruise, this one spread across his left side. Orod's rage could be difficult to predict, but if he learned the Godspeaker was gone, if he had to send his greatax to find him, more pain would surely follow. Gritting his remaining teeth, he massaged the swollen flesh. He could take it.

Besides, the Godspeaker had other, more pressing concerns.

He looked out into the growing dark. Far from the orc camp, a figure was sitting atop an outcropping boulder. Like many others, the orc had arrived alone. Unlike the rest however, he had remained so, alternatively pacing and hopping around the camp perimeter, his rambling utterances lurching in volume between mutter and shout. The orcs of the horde ignored him for the most part. Occasionally they would watch him go by with cautious curiosity, other times they'd drive him off with the threat of a kicking. None of them could understand his cryptic declarations. But Arlok understood. It was fortunate that Orod hadn't learned of his presence – he might have understood, too.

Smoke began to drift around the boulder-perched orc, rising from a faint light before him. From between the Godspeaker's legs, Yip let out a crazed giggle. Arlok knew why. He could taste magic.

"Come," Arlok grunted. Using his staff to take the weight on his left side, Arlok began hobbling his way toward the fellow shaman. Yip skipped after, clapping his hands excitedly.

By the time Arlok reached him, the small fire was burning on its own. He stopped, examining the orc in its yellow light. His clothes differed greatly to Arlok's, consisting of a fine-spun tunic that had once been blue, now torn and caked in dirt, on top of which was bound a similarly soiled breastplate. In contrast to Arlok's bone headdress, the newcomer's head was bare, although he did have a number of bones threaded on rough string, hung loosely over the breastplate. All of it – clothes, armor, bones – was taken from humans. If there were any doubts on that front, the skull set into the head of the orc's staff was enough to silence them.

"Well-met," said Arlok.

The orc looked at him with distant eyes. Its staff lay across its legs, and a chewed thumb absently circled the eye socket of the human skull.

He's a Godspeaker alright, thought Arlok. He recognized the look on his face, the look of a mind whose tether on the world was tenuous. But there were always periods of lucidity, and that above all else he could not allow.

"Do you have a name?" he asked.

"…Name?" The newcomer's voice was dry, hoarse from the ceaseless and impenetrable proclamations. Arlok could smell his breath even through the smoke of the fire. It was rancid.

"Yes. A name. What do others call you?"

"Many things… many names… the last horde called me Shum."

Arlok grinned cruelly. 'Shum' was orcish for gore turds.

"Shum, eh? And whose horde was that? Which krudger?"

But Shum didn't appear to be listening. His far-off gaze had turned away from Arlok, settling on the camp beyond. Arlok glanced back. Only a few fires could now be seen among the horde, their flames low.

"They don't see you," said Shum.

Arlok looked round sharply.

"Who?"

"The horde. They don't see you."

"Isn't it always that way? They fear our connection to the gods. They don't want to see us. But Orod sees. Through me, he hears the gods." Arlok indulged a chuckle.

"Orod?"

"The krudger? Of the horde? The one you're staring at."

Shum said nothing. Even for a Godspeaker, Arlok realized, Shum was far-gone.

"Orod slew the Bloodtusk, broke the human fortress. And now..." Arlok was helpless not to grin again, "...now he brings destiny."

"Destiny... destiny of orcs..."

Arlok rolled his eyes, but before he could say anything, Shum began.

"The children of Garkan fall from his sight. The failure of the Grumtongue is the failure of all his wretched kind. Their defeat on the plains of men cannot be forgiven."

Arlok felt his heart stop. Shum's expression was still far-gone, but his words were certain, pouring forth in an unstoppable monotone. It was prophecy. *Real* prophecy.

"From beneath the rifted mountains, they will come. From vengeance, they are forged. They will bind their fallen brethren and bring an age of violence to this world. When all the land quakes to the hammer of the storm, lo, the Age of Orcs is come!"

Shum finished, head lolling, runtish jaw resting against his breastplate.

Arlok breathed out, his nerves alive. Then he laughed. "So that's what your 'gods' say, is it? Well, I think I captured the general idea of the thing, although I assume yours isn't talking about Krudger Orod."

Shum shook his head. "He goes to the night-teeth."

"...the what?"

"Darkness... bitin'... movin' with the mists..."

"Ah. You mean the shadow ones."

Shum looked up and appeared to consider this. "...They can't see you," he muttered, finally.

"Them too? Good. That's the idea, after all."

"Not them. Not the horde. The gods." Shum was looking at him again. "They can't see you."

At that moment, something entered the Godspeaker's eyes. Lucidity. He peered at Arlok, his expression becoming increasingly alarmed.

"How're you doing that?" he croaked. "How..."

There was a high-pitched giggle. Shum's jaw dropped open. It seemed he'd noticed Yip standing between Arlok's legs.

Sliding quickly from the boulder, Shum lifted his staff. One moment he was bringing it around, driving the human skull toward them, its sockets aglow with green light – the next he was swallowed by a brilliant inferno. Shum's scream lasted only a second before it was consumed, lost amid the roar of the flames. Arlok closed his eyes, savoring the heat. When next he opened them, the fires were gone.

An ash pile sat among smoldering grass. Arlok prodded it with the end of his staff. He was rewarded with a metallic thunk. Only a charred breastplate remained.

"That's how."

In the darkness of the eastern plains, Yip's giggling grew more deranged than ever.

11

...And that would be all there is to say about this mystery, were it not for your humble servant happening upon a potential solution in Drusus Messor's magisterial treatise Languages of the God War, *wherein he traced the emergence of the various dialects produced by the sundering events of that era...*

Vespilo A., *On the Location and Identification of Primovantian Antiquity,* Appendix IX *'From the Gatekeepers' - The Mystery of Keatairn*

They journeyed on without incident for two days. The rains had finally broken the unseasonable heat, and the train of wagons marched beneath a pleasingly temperate sky. Only the mists offered reason for complaint, never fully receding, their ebb and flow stalking across the land and leaving a damp quality in the air. In the caravan, a full inventory was taken of plentiful salted meats, matured cheeses, fruit preserves, oil, and bread – not to mention what remained of the wine, which was the finest to ever have passed Xavire's lips. A convoy for kings, as Sir Guilliver put it, and rightly so. Truly they could not have hoped for better.

Spirits were high. Already trust was beginning to sprout between the unlikely travel companions. Many of the Ardovikians were natural horse hands and were quickly tasked with a role in the animals' care. Alea, meanwhile, showed herself to be a master in the management of limited supplies, and she more than made up for the Claws' lack of a designated quartermaster. Nokrag was less impressed with Alea's regime. Seemingly oblivious to the cluster of curious Ardovikian children scurrying behind her, the ogress maintained a close eye on the wine wagon. Alea had recommended the southern vintages be placed under heavy guard, for peace of mind if nothing else.

The nights, however, were hard on Xavire. Each morning saw him awaken with a dulled mind and stiff muscles, his sleep disturbed by dreams he could not recall beyond mere residue of feeling, the sensation of being watched by unknown eyes. He could only conclude that crossing the wall and all attendant skulduggery to that effort had left its mark.

On the third day, the mist did not ebb. Like a veil over the land, it hung long and gray, swallowing all variance in its shadow. Low clouds stretched to every horizon, dispersing the light such that the sun could not be tracked. Trudging alongside the wagons, Xavire lost himself in the march, drifting in the fog of his sleep-deprived mind. It was with surprise therefore that he noted the dimming light when the order to halt finally came. The day was gone. It had seemed as though they'd just set off – it also felt like he'd been marching forever.

Xavire looked around, blinking at the surrounding grassland. Save for a narrow brook which cut across their path, the landscape was utterly indistinguishable to the one from which they had departed that morning.

"Fill up, lads! Let's get these horses watered!"

Sergeant Peris's call was repeated down the length of the convoy, breaking its formation. Xavire joined the unhurried flow of men and women bringing their flasks to the brook. His feet ached, the pain of each step registering acutely in his newly restored awareness.

Spotting Uslo and Alea at the brook's bank, Xavire adjusted his course to reach them. The general stood by his horse with his back to Xavire, fists on hips as he watched Volonto drink. Alea was talking to him quietly. She stopped when she noticed Xavire approach.

"Don't let me interrupt," he said.

Alea gave a slight shake of her head. "I was advising the general that we stop here for the night."

"We can manage a few more hours," Xavire replied. His feet throbbed in protest. "That said, it might be best to stop. This is the first water we've seen in days that wasn't stewing in a bog. Who knows when we'll next come across the like."

"There's that. And there's that." Alea tilted the head of her staff to the north, gesturing across the brook. Xavire looked.

"I don't see anything."

"The mists," she said simply.

"What about them…" he began, but he could see what about them. Around forty yards beyond the running waters, the misty veil became a fog curtain, heavy and indolent. The suddenness of the transition awoke something in Xavire. A disquiet. And a familiarity.

"We would be lost in there," she continued. "If we are not already."

"We are not," said Uslo flatly. He hadn't looked up once during the exchange.

"I'm glad. We are here for your sakes, after all. The Plainsmen have no need to make this rendezvous."

"Rendezvous?" Xavire's eyes snapped to Uslo. "What's she talking about, sir?"

"You mean you haven't told him, General?"

Uslo continued to look north as he answered, apparently ignoring Alea's remark. "We are to meet someone."

"Who?"

"Representatives."

"...Of?"

"Those who have purchased a stake in this venture."

Realization dawned. "The schedule for the supply train."

Uslo turned to meet his gaze, his otherwise neutral expression traced with defiance. "Information is never without price, Xavire."

"*Your* price, General," said Alea. "Yours and your Claws'. The Plainsmen have no part of it."

"On the contrary, my lady," Uslo replied. "They do, if they want us to come with them. Or perhaps you'd prefer they travel onward without our protection?"

Alea appeared impassive. "Perhaps that is the sort of man you are, General. Perhaps if I take the Plainsmen on without the Claws you will cut your losses and turn back. There are many who would." She stepped toward Volonto, placing her palm against the horse's flank and stroking it gently. "But I doubt it."

Uslo grunted. The fists fell away from his hips. "What say you, Xavire? Do we continue?"

Xavire glanced at Alea before answering. She was looking north into the fog. "I suggest we stop, sir. I assume these representatives can wait an extra day for us, at least. And..."

"...and?" Uslo prompted, after a second.

"And I don't think we should go into that fog." The feeling from his nightmare was back. Like he was being watched.

Uslo sighed. "All right. I suppose we'll have to wait for it to clear." He sat down on the bank, long legs stretched out before him.

Xavire crouched over the brook. He lowered his flask as best he could into the shallow waters, and the sound of spluttering *glugs* bounced atop the steady trickling of the stream.

"The scouting party will have hunkered down, I imagine," said Uslo. "With luck, we can regroup with them in the morning."

"You may not have to wait that long." Alea spoke quietly. She was still looking north. Xavire followed her gaze. Except for the wall of shiftless fog, he couldn't see anything. But he heard it. Volonto raised his head from the stream at the same moment, and Uslo sat up sharply.

"The scouts?" asked Xavire.

"Must be," said Uslo, getting back to his feet. He brushed off his breeches. "After all, who else could be out here?"

Neither answered. Together with the general and his steed, they stood in silence as the rhythmic patter of trotting horses drew closer. Shadows appeared in the fog wall, and then Sir Guilliver emerged, followed by six other horsemen. Xavire breathed out, feeling the muscles in his arm relax. He had been gripping his sword without realizing. Still, the tension didn't leave him entirely, Uslo's words seeming to echo inside his head.

Who else could be out here?

Weariness tightened its grip. Ignoring his throbbing feet, Xavire maintained the hold on his sword.

*****

The report from Sir Guilliver had changed things. Not for Alea and Xavire, who continued to advocate that the caravan should stop for the night. But it turned out the meeting site, the ruins of a town once called 'Cadalla,' was little over a mile away. Easily reachable before sundown. Uslo's delight was evident. He waited perhaps twenty minutes before ordering the march resumed.

The air felt heavy inside the fog, coating their lungs and confusing their eyes. Its smell made Xavire think of mildew, of its pale fur spreading through dead places. Much as he might try to think of something else, anything else, his mind was held in place by a gnawing unease. The sensation that his dreams were near.

Wiping a sleeve over the left lens of his glasses, Xavire glanced back down the line. He was at the front, walking alongside the howitzer-bearing wagon. Beyond the horses and fore wheels of the next wagon he could see nothing but swirling shades of gray. The deepest shadow he knew to be a cluster of Ardovikians staying close to the column. Where before the Plainsmen had been content to spread themselves wide, their movement parallel to the convoy, there was now simply no choice but to huddle together with the Claws, keeping a fixed eye on the wagon immediately in front of them. He faced forward. Uslo and the scouts were just visible up ahead, leading the way. Their walking motion was mildly disturbing; to Xavire's eyes, the fog confounded all distinction between mount and man.

Signs of Cadalla began to manifest around an hour later. At first, Xavire didn't notice the unnaturally-shaped rises in the grassland, their straight lines and crisp angles no more than ankle high. The occasional *click* of a wheel hitting exposed cobblestone also failed to register. Rather, it was the convoy's movement that finally stirred realization, the conspicuous twists and turns arousing his city-honed instincts. They were moving through streets. Increasingly narrow, increasingly winding, uphill streets. Even without the fog, he thought it would've been damn near impossible to tell by sight. Lord Darvled had not built his wall from quarried stone fashioned to purpose, but by appropriating whatever resources were in the vicinity. Villages, towns, cities; if they were in reach of the build site, then they were stripped bare, and not even gravestones escaped becoming masonry on the ramparts. Darvled had reduced Cadalla to its foundations, an imprint of its former self, with all sense of height and fullness left to mere inference. Less than a skeleton. A ghost. Xavire shivered. The Claws had probably walked its stones many times and never known it. And now, like the once plentiful roads of lower Ardovikia, it appeared that the city was deep in the process of being swallowed by the grasslands of the Plains. It wouldn't be long before no trace of it remained at all.

The narrowness of the pathway between one-time buildings reached its utmost and then suddenly disappeared, the road opening outward on either side as its gradual incline leveled out. Cobblestone *clicks* gave way to grassy *scrunch*. Even the air seemed clearer. Xavire thought it had to have been a plaza. It was very large. Perhaps it had even served as the central forum of the town. In any case, they had unquestionably arrived. He looked up, searching the obscured sky for any sign of the sun's position. Other than the markedly dimming light, there was none. But that was enough.

"Xavire."

Uslo turned Volonto out of the convoy's path, bringing the horse to a stop, and Xavire went to him.

"General?"

"This is the square where we're to meet the representatives. Or it could be, at any rate." Uslo glanced around. He was frowning in frustration. "Either we're in the wrong place, or they're late."

"We've reached the... we've reached the ruins at least," said Xavire. He had been about to say town, but that seemed almost disrespectful. Even 'ruins' gave too much presence. They had reached a ghost. "What do you want us to do, sir?"

"We will stop here. I have sent Sir Guilliver to set up a perimeter watch." Uslo dismounted smoothly. He stretched his joints, continuing to scan the surrounding gray. Behind them, the column of wagons and people shuffled past. "For all the good that will do."

"The scouts said Cadalla was empty before the fog rolled in. Chances are we won't get another good look until morning."

Uslo nodded. "True enough. All right, Xavire. Start coordinating the wagons."

It was a tight squeeze, but after a period of shouted instructions and careful maneuvering, they managed to pack the convoy into the plaza, the wagons arranged in a great circle around the masses. Crowds of the hungry and tired waited as food was divvied out. Welcome though a hot meal might have been, none had the patience for its preparation, and so hunks of oiled bread and hard cheese had to suffice. For his part, Xavire didn't much feel like eating. Sitting against the outward-facing wheel of a wagon, he chewed his share with slow deliberation. Anxiety fretted in his torso, clenching his stomach and prodding his guts. Occasionally he would glimpse movement in the fog, making him hold his breath; but it would just be one of Sir Guilliver's horsemen, quietly patrolling. Xavire didn't know what to make of his own unease. Part of him wanted to turn away and take refuge among comrades and Plainsmen. But every time he removed his gaze from the thick brume, a powerful instinct drew it back. It was as if only his eyes could ward off… what? He didn't know. Xavire sighed, adjusting his cap before letting his head fall back against the spokes.

"Xavire?"

Recognizing the voice, he croaked, "Over here!"

Alea stepped past the grazing horses of the adjacent wagon. Her hood was down, and her short cut of hair had frizzed in the damp air. Xavire greeted her, raising the hand containing the last of his oily bread in salute before popping the morsel in his mouth.

"Everything alright back there?" he asked through chewing.

"Yes. The fog has them a little unnerved, and there's not much room, but they are glad to be done for today."

Xavire nodded, his eyes having already returned to the gray cloud. He swallowed. "Good."

"And you? How are you feeling?"

"Fine," he lied, not looking up. His conscience insisted he add a truth. "I've not been sleeping well."

"That is not surprising."

Xavire met her gaze, raising an eyebrow.

"Most of the others are struggling," she explained. "For all they know, their pursuers are only one night's sleep behind."

He grunted acknowledgement and looked away again. "I guess I'm trying not to think about that."

Alea stepped toward him and crouched down, leaning on her staff. "Are you sure you're all right?"

Xavire smiled involuntarily. He was embarrassed by her concern. But when he glanced at her to repeat his lie, Xavire didn't see concern. Alea's mouth was drawn tight, and her eyes bore into him coolly, their hazel green barely showing in the low light. She was examining him as one might a cornered animal. Xavire blinked. For reasons he couldn't explain, he felt the urge to tell her about his unremembered dreams.

About the feeling.

Before the first word reached his lips, Alea turned her head away, frowning. He waited. She looked at him again.

"Do you hear that?"

Xavire listened. The tired murmur of the convoy, the chatter of many voices finding beds for the night. Beyond that, nothing. He opened his mouth to say so.

Then he heard it. Or rather, felt it. A buzzing in the soil. A distant rumbling. The light seemed to dip sharply, and the fog became a shade darker. Leering.

"Horses?" said Alea, standing up. She didn't see Xavire shake his head, didn't see his mouth work soundlessly as his body pressed back against the wagon wheel. It was something worse. It was…

But she was right. The sound had grown louder, and now there was no doubt. For the second time that day, it seemed Alea had detected the approach of mounted men. Only this time they were at a gallop. A charge.

Xavire hauled himself onto aching feet. "The rendezvous?" he suggested hopefully, voice still shaken from his moment of horror. Baying voices swooped in the air, yips and yowls.

"I think not."

"Attack!" Sir Guilliver's warning rang out across the plaza as his gray gelding burst from the eastern streets. "Claws up! To arms!"

Alea leapt to action, rushing back among the wagons. Xavire simply stood, staring out into the fog. He could see lights. Their sources were confused, forming a mass of diffused yellow that pulsed dimly in the gray swirl. There looked to be dozens of them, bouncing higher than any man. They were mesmerizing. And they were coming closer. Xavire's sword hung limply at his side.

"Xavire?! Move!"

He looked round blankly as Alea reappeared. She grabbed his arm and, with strength that didn't remotely surprise him, dragged him behind the wagon.

The horsemen appeared a second later, pouring into the square from every direction. Each held a burning torch. Some held two. A group of Ardovikians who had been wandering beyond the convoy screamed as they were ridden down. Unopposed, the horsemen began to set fire to the wagons.

"No!" shouted Xavire, adrenaline sharpening his mind and expelling the inertia from his limbs. He drew his sword. "Stop them! Don't let them burn the caravan!"

He moved to meet the attackers, heedless to whether his call was heard. There was no time for order, for formations or strategy. No time for nightmares. Ducking past panicking horses, he charged toward the first thing he saw.

The horseman appeared to be concentrating on his arson and didn't notice him until it was too late. Xavire swung horizontally, catching unarmored thigh and cutting deep. The vibration of steel on bone bounced up his arm. Blood gushed, its warm spray coating his face and glasses.

Xavire cursed. He must have hit an artery.

Backing away, Xavire was only distantly aware of his foe's pained scream as he made a desperate attempt to remove his glasses. They slipped in his fingers. He snatched instinctively, catching them before they were lost in the undergrowth.

The *clang* of colliding metal exploded above him. Sound retreated, leaving only a painful whine in his ears. Xavire looked up. Through the blur of his unaided eyes, he saw that the bleeding horseman had advanced toward him, and that his sword arm was recoiling as if from a deflected blow. Then Xavire was lurched sideways, a tall figure pushing past to engage the mounted man. He quickly wiped his glasses on his hip. He put them back on, and through the streaks of clotting red he saw Alea deliver an arcing sweep of her staff, knocking the attacker clean from his saddle. Without hesitation, she moved to the dismounted horseman and stepped down hard on his throat.

Heat washed over Xavire's face as the wagon's canvas ripped and roared. The material fell from its bows, rapidly igniting the contents beneath. Horses screamed. They began straining to bolt.

"Free the horses!" he shouted, rushing toward the animals. Either the order had already been given or others had the same idea, because a pair of Claws were already working to free the far horse. After a moment of fumbling at the clasp with blood-slicked fingers, Xavire made a quick hack with his blade, severing the leather binds. The horses sensed their freedom and ran, muscles quivering in fright.

"Duck!" cried one of the Claws, raising his crossbow.

Xavire ducked. The *thump* of a bolt impacting flesh seemed to reach him even before the *snap* that launched it. He looked around in time to see the would-be attacker topple, sword slipping from his hand. His left foot was stuck in the stirrup, and the horse dragged him face-down for several yards before it came loose.

The fighting was a mess. Fires raged in the outer wagons, their flames running amok through the dry carriage innards. The Claws had been taken completely by surprise but were somehow managing to muster resistance, Peris's crossbowmen picking off riders while swordsmen rushed belatedly to put themselves between torches and supplies. From what Xavire could see, their attackers were fewer in number than he had first believed, and they appeared reluctant to fight, by turns backing away and skirting any attempt to pin them down.

One of them was a short distance away, torch in hand and horse agitating beneath him. Raising his sword and gritting his teeth, Xavire charged. The rider's head turned to assess him. Xavire had time to make out a squashed nose set into a square face before his target heeled, taking himself far out of reach. Xavire stumbled to a halt, watching helplessly as the rider wound back his arm and hurled the torch into an already burning wagon.

"Fall back!" the square-faced rider called, casting a quick glance at Xavire as he prepared to ride into the fog. Smirking. "Fall b–!"

An enormous *clank* tore through the air, and in the next instant the man collapsed backward to the ground. The horse died instantly, a broad-headed bolt entering its rear end to burst from its lower neck, launching the animal's carcass from beneath its rider and crumpling it in a heap of meat.

Nokrag stepped out from between the wagons, her ogre crossbow held level. She had attached a wickedly serrated bayonet to the end, and her blunderbuss was slung over her back. Xavire gave her no more than a glance. As his mind made sense of the scene, he noticed something about the square-faced rider. Something incredible.

"Where are they?! Where?!"

Uslo was astride Volonto. The great palomino moved nimbly past the ogre warrior. Guiding the horse with his knees, the general brought him next to Xavire. His bastard sword was drawn, clasped in both hands.

"Xavire? What happened? Which way did they go?"

Xavire shook his head slowly. Disbelieving, he stepped around Volonto toward the prone and groaning man. He was wearing drab green. It was a uniform.

The uniform of Lord Darvled's forces.

*****

Xavire held his breath, smoke stinging his eyes as he and Uslo hauled the last crate from the smoldering wagon. They set it down clumsily. His muscles throbbed in pain. Gulping at ashen air, he lifted his glasses to blot tears against his arm. When he replaced them, a pair of black circles seemed to peer from his sleeve.

The salvaged items lay haphazardly in the center of the plaza, gathered at the feet of the Ardovikians. Many of the Plainsmen had helped, weathering the fires with impressive courage to recover or preserve as much as possible. The rest – hundreds of young children and elderly – could only watch, huddled among the hurriedly accumulated supplies. The mainstay of the Claws were beyond, readied in a perimeter in case their attackers should reappear. Those not on watch were helping Sir Guilliver and his riders get into their armor.

Looking out at the multitude of Ardovikian men and women, Xavire felt overwhelmed with the burden of their task. The Claws numbered little over two hundred soldiers, yet were charged with the defense of many times that. It wasn't simply the technical question that struck him. Rather, it was the sheer moral responsibility. He glanced over the supplies. By a minor miracle, both the howitzer wagon and the gunpowder it contained were untouched. The rolled-up company standard was safe, too – while not materially vital, its loss would have hurt morale among the Claws. Nineteen wagons in all had caught fire, with perhaps two thirds of their contents having gone with them. Not nearly enough remained for the journey ahead. Assuming they could even fight their way out of Cadalla.

Both Uslo and Xavire agreed – this wasn't over yet. It seemed highly unlikely that their attackers would launch such an attack without greater numbers in support. Otherwise, what would be the point? Although they were taken by surprise, the Claws had felled many and lost only those Plainsmen caught outside the perimeter. Then again, neither the Plainsmen nor the Claws themselves had been the targets, the wagons had. Had their attackers followed them here, or lain in wait? If the former, how had they overtaken them? If the latter, how had they known where they would be? And when? Even before the riddle of Lord Darvled's uniforms entered the fray, the questions were endless.

Xavire glanced at Uslo. The general met his eye. He looked calm, but Xavire knew that it was a show. That he was furious.

"I think it's time we have a talk with our guest," said Uslo.

The pair set off around the smoldering carriages, bare iron bows making them look like skeletons of their former selves. Those horses which the flames had forced them to set free were yet to reappear. If they ever would.

At the south side of the plaza, the square-faced rider sat propped against a stack of broken and moss-claimed masonry, chunks of stone no doubt deemed inadequate for Lord Darvled's Wall. He was the only one among his fallen comrades whose wounds hadn't proved fatal. His legs were bound together, his arms to his sides. A filthy rag

– gods knew where it had come from – was stuffed inside his mouth. Alea and Nokrag stood nearby, watching the prisoner in silence. Their presence made him appear very small. All three looked round at Uslo and Xavire's approach.

"I take it he has not said much." Uslo spoke with a matter-of-fact, not-quite pleasant tone.

Alea raised an eyebrow. "Nothing at all, in fact."

The square-faced man let out a burst of muffled expletives.

"Well, nothing except for that."

Uslo's smile didn't reach his eyes. Stepping away from Xavire, his hands moved to clasp behind his back, and his sheathed sword bounced against his hip. He walked past the prisoner slowly, looking out into the iron fog. By the time the fires had run their course, the sun had finally slipped away, leaving only a half-waxed moon to contend with the half-clouded sky. The prisoner followed Uslo with his glare, flattened nostrils stretched wide by defiant breaths. The general turned and stopped. For several seconds, Uslo contemplated him, the light casting a crescent ring of silver across the back of his head, framing a face of shadow. Then Uslo's hand flew out sharply. The square-faced man braced for the oncoming strike – but Uslo had already whipped the rag from his mouth. A flicker of surprise appeared in the prisoner's eyes. It was replaced by rage.

"My name is Uslo Dargent." Uslo paced back across to Xavire as he spoke, handing him the rag. "You are?"

"I'm the Grand Hegemon of sodding Basilea," the prisoner snarled, spittle launching from between his newly freed lips.

"So you are from Sathoi," said Uslo calmly. *That's right*, thought Xavire, impressed. It had been hard to tell through the snarls, but the accent was distinctive to the mountain city, not dissimilar to that of the Dragon's Teeth mercenaries they'd spent so much time with. "That will do."

The Sathoian's eyes narrowed. He said nothing.

"My man saw you attempting to give orders, Sathoian. Yet I see no indication of rank on your uniform." Uslo continued to pace slowly in front of him, not so much as sending a glance his way. "Your companions fought without discipline. Their horses were not bred for war. I assume you are all deserters."

"And what does that make you, *General*? Eh?"

Xavire resisted a smile. The Sathoian's riposte was revealing in ways he couldn't realize. For starters, it suggested that he knew who they were and where they had come from – but not that their contract had been nullified. He even knew Uslo's self-styled rank. Clearly the squashed-nosed Sathoian and his men hadn't come to Cadalla looking for just anyone.

"That assumption in hand," Uslo continued, choosing to ignore the slip, "I further assume that you place a healthy consideration on the preservation of your life."

The Sathoian laughed. It was an ugly sound. "Sure, use big words. Walk around in front of me until my neck gets sore. Get that ogre there to rough me up, if you like. I'm not going to talk."

Uslo stopped pacing. He turned again, looking down at the prisoner with wide eyes. "Well, of course not," he said, dangling what was to Xavire a rather obviously feigned admiration in his voice. He crouched down. "Look at you! You are strong. Tough. No one would doubt the blows you've weathered in your life."

Most of them aimed at the center of your face, thought Xavire.

"A man like you understands the value of pride. Pain is nothing to such men. Why, if I were to strike you now," he swung his fist out sharply, stopping a hair shy of contacting the prisoner's jaw. The Sathoian bared his teeth. Uslo grinned back at him. "I wager you'd spit the blood in my face."

Xavire saw Nokrag glance about, seemingly bored. Alea watched closely, however, her face set with determination. The Sathoian, meanwhile, appeared somewhat wrong-footed by Uslo's praise, perhaps taking it as genuine. He grunted, scowling.

"What do you want with me, then?"

"I want what you want. Life. Nothing waits for either of us on the other side. Nothing good, at any rate." He looked at the ground for several seconds, gently swaying on the balls of his feet. Then he looked up again. "Show us the way out of the ruins. Get us around the others who I'm sure are out there, and not only will I let you go, I'll give you a hefty compensation for your troubles. You won't even have to say a word."

The Sathoian scoffed. "What kind of moron are you? There's no way out! You're gods-damn surrounded!"

Uslo tilted his head as if to consider this. Then his face lit up, and he snapped his fingers. "You can talk us past them! I cannot believe they hold you in anything but the highest regard–"

"What?! Are you mad?! Even if I were stupid enough to try such a thing, they are loyal men! *I* am a loyal man! We fight for the Butcher of Eprye!" He yelled, eyes popping in deranged fury.

Uslo nodded slowly. The Sathoian glared at him, breathing heavily through his mouth. Uslo stood up, turning to the group.

"Anyone heard of this 'Butcher of Eprye'?" he asked. Xavire shook his head.

"I have," said Alea. Uslo looked at her.

"A general?"

"A bandit. A murderer."

"He won't intend to let us go?"

"She. Her name's Jathina Maem. And no."

Uslo nodded. "So we fight our way out."

"Wait! You can't!" The Sathoian looked panicked. "Y–You'll all be killed!"

"And what difference would that make?" asked Uslo coolly. The interested act was gone. Now, there was only contempt.

"They want someone alive," said Alea. She looked at them each in turn, continuing to put the pieces together. "That explains why the attack was so small, and why it was directed at the supplies. They're trying to make us desperate. To make us give up whoever it is in exchange for our lives."

"You– no–!" There was an audible *click* as the prisoner brought his teeth together. He finally realized he had said too much.

"Who could they want?" asked Xavire. Uslo shook his head.

"I too am curious... but even if we could know, it's irrelevant. Whoever it is, they can't have them."

"But they don't know that," said Nokrag. "They don't know what we know."

Uslo grinned up at the ogre. This time it did reach his eyes. "Exactly. They'll have to present their demands. And that's when we make our move."

"She'll kill all of them! The children, too! But if you just give her what she wants, I swear–"

"Xavire." Uslo jerked a thumb at the prisoner. Xavire nodded. He drew his dagger.

"No!" In the wake of his repeated slips, the Sathoian had lost all trace of his rage-induced composure. Only fear remained. "Wait!"

Xavire stepped toward him.

"Stop! She'll let you go if you give her what she wants!"

"Who?" said Xavire, crouching down. The Sathoian hesitated. Sighing, Xavire raised the blade to his throat. "Who does she want?"

"Alright! Alright." Xavire lowered his dagger, and the Sathoian took a deep breath.

"You're right. She won't let you go. Even if you hand them over, she'll want to kill all of you anyway. But if you play this right, if you give her–"

"Who?!" Xavire shouted, pressing the tip of the dagger into the prisoner's throat until it drew blood. "Who does she want?!"

"The guide, of course! The damned guide!"

Xavire blinked. He looked over his shoulder at the others. Though their faces were hidden in moonshadow, he sensed their incomprehension. He turned back.

"Guide?"

"To the treasure! The guide who's leading you to the treasure!"

Several seconds of silence followed. It was broken by a groan from Alea.

"That's enough, Xavire," said Uslo quietly.

The Sathoian's eyes went wide as the dagger came up–

"No! Hold on–!"

–and Xavire shot his other hand forward, pushing the rag back into his mouth. He stood up.

"This changes nothing," said Uslo. "We knew she wanted someone alive, and we knew she was planning to kill the rest of us in any case. You don't get the name 'Butcher' for less."

"It does, however, suggest our contacts for the supply train schedule sold us out. Sir." added Xavire.

Uslo sighed. "Sold us out or were themselves betrayed. We have no time for that puzzle."

"Puzzle?" said Alea. "It seems clear to me. You told others of our plan, and whether by lapse or design, these criminals have likewise been informed." Anger simmered beneath her words.

"I believe we can agree that deciding what we do next is more important than recriminations over what has already passed."

"You're going to find treasure?" asked Nokrag. "How much? What's my share?"

Muffled laughter filled the air. They glanced at the Sathoian. Tears glinted mutely on his cheeks. He appeared to have come quite unhinged.

"Xavire," said Uslo. Xavire turned to him. "Did the pikes survive the flames?"

"Yes, sir." The tight-bound bundles were too lengthy for the wagons and so had been carried separately by the men.

Uslo nodded. "Go give the order to don shields and arms. Then get back here quickly. Bring Sir Guilliver and Peris." He looked at them all, meeting their gaze one by one. Xavire saw a momentary strand of moonlight penetrate the clouds to shine silver on his skin.

"I have a plan."

*****

"*Uslo Dargent!*"

The booming voice was dampened slightly by the misty air, yet the words were carried with enough force to reach them clearly.

"*By crossing the great wall… you and your men have violated the law of Lord Darvled…*"

"It's coming from the north," said Xavire.

"Then that's where we attack." Uslo was helping fix the last of Volonto's barding in place. Black scorch marks marred the bronze plate in swollen blotches. Recovering them from their burning wagon had been a close thing. Uslo pulled the strap tight. "Help me up."

"*…and are declared to have trespassed against him…*"

There was something odd about how the voice kept pausing, reflected Xavire as he pushed Uslo into his saddle. That, and it didn't sound like the speaker had any understanding of the meaning of the words he was bellowing.

Volonto grunted with impatience as Uslo settled in. Xavire handed up the general's helmet, de-plumed by the flames. "Be careful. We have no idea how many of them are out there."

"Indeed, we do not," said Uslo as he fixed it in place. "But with luck, we'll be striking directly at their leadership."

"*…By the lord's authority… you are hereby compelled to relinquish your guide to the Ardovikian Plains…*"

"Do you ever worry that lady luck might be trying to cut us off?" asked Xavire. He lifted the black-leather scabbard containing Uslo's bastard sword. Grasping the handle, Uslo turned to look at him.

"Never. That hag owes us a lifetime's worth." Even with his face in shadow, Xavire knew he winked.

Though Xavire's amusement was genuine, his laugh sounded grim in his ears. "And since when did that matter?"

"It will tonight." Uslo spurred Volonto, and the warhorse set off, causing the bastard sword to be dragged from its scabbard. Swinging it deftly upright, Uslo steered his way around the horde of gathered Ardovikians toward Sir Guilliver and the adventurers.

"*…Should you comply with this order… his lordship gives his guarantee that…*"

Slinging the empty scabbard over his back, Xavire turned and stepped smartly toward the Claws. The Sergeants Peris and Eumenes watched him approach. Behind them, one-hundred-and-forty men stood to attention in the dark, pikes up, round shields offering the faintest glimmer of bronze.

"Everyone ready?"

"Aye, sir."

"Good. Eumenes, you take the west pikes, I'll take the east. We'll have to spread thin, encourage them away from the flanks and into the center. That's where your crossbowmen will cut them down, Peris. Remind the men that we're acting as a rearguard. When we turn back the enemy's assault, I don't want anyone chasing off after them. We hold."

"*...you will be permitted safe passage south... however...*"

"It's going to be difficult to tell who's who in the dark," said Peris.

"If they're coming from the south, kill them. Simple as that."

They nodded.

"Let's go."

Xavire and Eumenes parted in opposite directions. His orders passed discreetly along the ranks as he moved, and he made a quick glance at the mass of Plainsmen to their north. Alea had faced a challenge in convincing the elders of this plan, but the younger tribesmen and women had embraced it with fierce conviction. Maem's raiders had killed thirty-two of their number. Four elders were among them and, more painfully still, one young child. Xavire saw the dull glint of looted iron in several hands, recovered from the murderous dead. Although the plan wasn't for the Ardovikians to fight, it was nevertheless reassuring to see they would if it came to that. The Plainsmen wanted revenge.

"*...as such, you and your abettors will face summary judgment...*"

From beyond the Plainsmen, the vague and fog-shrouded forms of the adventurers started to ride out north. Xavire thought he saw the top of Alea's staff raised high at the front of the horde, a short distance from the enormous silhouette of Nokrag. The staff swept down silently. The Ardovikians set off after the horsemen, slowly at first, building speed. Lifting his arm, Xavire held it upright for several seconds, watching as the ripple of movement finally reached the last of the tribesmen. He made a long chopping motion, and immediately began a quick walk after them. The Claws followed.

*****

Cauhin gripped his improvised club, recovered from among the remains of a burned-out wagon. Movement slowed as the sound of combat washed over the Plainsmen. He was toward the back. Despite his protests, Riuen and the other adults had forbidden him from the front where the chances of fighting were highest. Not even Alea stood up for him, and Cauhin had nursed frustration as he and his people followed the Claws' horsemen along a wide, ruined street into the mists. Now, listening to the battle and held fast by a tight-packed throng, frustration was forgotten. He only wished that he could see what was happening.

A horn sounded to the north, cutting across the clashes of steel.

"Keep moving!" Alea's cry was hurriedly repeated down the broad column. Similar shouts rose up from behind, the Claws' leadership issuing a command to the soldiers to spread out as they advanced. Unthinking, Cauhin strained to turn and look.

"What are you doing?!" Fillam was right behind him. His sister Rheyall, seven years younger than them both, was clinging to his back. Their mother and father were at the front. "You're going to trip me!"

"I was just–" Cauhin stopped to listen as another blaring note from the warhorn whipped through the air. It sounded taut, as if the blower's lungs were on fire.

"Stop!"

The column stopped. Cauhin turned around, squeezing past Fillam and craning his neck to look over the others. Behind them, the Claws were continuing to march in the dark. Cauhin glimpsed the tips of their towering spears as they fanned out, twinkling in the dim light like metallic insects.

"What's happening, Fillam?" asked Rheyall. She sounded scared. "Why did we stop?"

"They're getting ready to fight..." mumbled Cauhin, listening intently as the Claws directed themselves over and around the low-lying ruins. The night air continued to be filled by the uproar of clashing horsemen at the front, but Cauhin thought he could sense something building beyond the pikemen. Something that was coming this way. The Claws stopped moving. An order was barked and the steel spearheads disappeared with a final rippling flicker as they lowered into a phalanx.

"It's alright, Rhey-rhey," said Fillam softly. "The warriors will protect us."

"Yes..." said Cauhin. There was shuffling along the outer sides of the column, those Ardovikians who were able to fight forming a circle around the rest. "Yes, we will."

Cauhin began pushing through the throng, heading straight for the Claws.

"Cauhin, wait! Don't..." Fillam's words were swallowed as Cauhin slipped past the huddle of children and elders, improvised club held flat against his leg. He didn't belong with them. He should be with the fighters. Fillam had to stay with his sister, Cauhin understood that. But regardless of what their elders said, both lads were old enough to defend their people. To be warriors.

Getting through was difficult. Most of the Ardovikians were going the other way, trying to pull back from the Claws' formation. He took deep breaths, holding them as he wedged his way shoulder-first. The Plainsmen pressed into him from his right, pinning Cauhin against the others and halting his progress. With breathless cursing, he twisted his neck in an attempt to see the cause. Nokrag stepped into view, moving quickly along the column. Alea followed. The crowd had parted to let them pass. Cauhin heaved against the crush, provoking complaints; he ignored them, levering his body through at just the right moment to stumble into the space behind Alea.

When he straightened up, he saw she was looking at him. He met her gaze with defiance, hoping she couldn't see the heat in his cheeks. After the briefest moment, she gave a nod.

"Come on."

The three of them reached the column's end. The Claws were arranged only a few steps away with their backs to the Ardovikians, three ranks of them spread wide and straight. Those armed with the strange, horizontal bows were in the center. Nokrag and Alea stepped forward to join the back rank, and the Claws shuffled to make room. Spearmen stood to either side of the bowmen, still as stone, their shields up and long staves pointing out. Looking down the line, Cauhin spotted Xavire pacing behind the left flank, his head turned toward his men. Seeing the bearded Southerner stirred a familiar and incomprehensible feeling.

Xavire is going to save you again, came the thought in his head. Cauhin's brow furrowed.

No, he answered it firmly. *I'm going to save myself.*

Hands flexing on his club, Cauhin steadied his feet. He glanced around at the other tribesmen and women. Not one of their grim faces turned to look at him. Their attention was directed south. Cauhin followed their collective gaze. Behind him, the clamor of battle at the north end continued to fill the night air, but Cauhin once more thought he could sense something up ahead. A gathering in the dark.

It seemed he wasn't the only one.

"Ready, Sergeant!"

Xavire's call was at once detached and unassailable, assured of control without any trace of dominance. It didn't sound anything like what Cauhin imagined of warriors before a battle. Yet it was bracing, somehow.

"Yes, sir! Crossbows, ready! First rank, aim!"

Cauhin saw movement as the men responded, leveling their weapons at the darkness.

"Loose on your order, Sergeant!"

"Sir!"

For what felt like an age, all was still. Cauhin squinted, peering between the Claws and into the tenebrous mists beyond. Nothing. Not even the whisper of movement. His eyes drifted to Alea. She held her staff in both hands and had it planted upright in front of her. Her face was down, forehead pressed against the metallic blue pole. Although he couldn't see her lips, Cauhin felt a sudden and irrepressible certainty that she was silently talking. He saw her head lift sharply, looking out into the dark.

Cauhin gasped. In one moment the darkness held sway, and in the next, what little light there was grew bold, leaping playfully to their eyes. What it revealed sent a jolt throughout Cauhin's body. Framed by the extreme radiance, a veritable wall of horsemen spanned the ruined street and fanned out on either side beyond. They had been stalking toward them under cover of misty darkness, and now they bustled with confusion, the stunned riders pulling back on the reins.

"Sergeant!" shouted Alea. To his credit, the sergeant's reaction was instant.

"Loose!"

There was a concerted *crack* of discharging cords. Cauhin caught a flash of iron in the air, exaggerated by the mysterious light, and then yelps of pain and anger went up from the horsemen.

"Second rank, aim!"

The front rank of archers went down on one knee as the second tracked their weapons on the enemy. In the distance, Cauhin heard a whiny voice screeching the order to charge.

"Loose!"

Another volley flung forth. Riders fell from tumbling mounts, the bodies tripping up several of those behind. Horses on either side of the roadway struggled to build speed across the hazardous ruins hidden in the shadowy undergrowth. They began to converge back toward the open span of the central street.

"Third rank, aim!"

The horsemen charged down the road. Like a flooded river fed from all sides, they surged toward the line of archers. Cauhin's body began to shake. The momentum was too great. They would crash over the Claws and run straight into the Ardovikians. Straight into him. But the Claws showed no sign of concern that he could see. The second rank had crouched down with the first and were fixing some sort of metal object to their weapons. They began using them to draw back the string, the near-synchronized motion producing a succession of rapid clicks.

"Loose!"

More projectiles flew, disappearing into the tightly packed mass. It seemed to Cauhin that they couldn't possibly miss, and yet the charge didn't falter, unhurt riders quickly guiding their mounts past those that fell. They had crossed more than half the distance.

"First and second, aim!"

The second rank, still fixing their small arrows into place, stepped forward hurriedly into the spaces between the men of the first, cutting off Cauhin's view. This would be the last volley, he realized with quiet panic. He barely registered Xavire's voice ordering the spears to advance, nor its immediate echo on the opposite flank. A steady drumming began to beat.

"Loose!"

The roll of *cracks* was twice as loud as before. The two ranks crouched, and Cauhin saw that their volley had struck hard, stalling the charge behind a slew of plunging horses. On either side, Cauhin finally noticed the advancing spearmen, their formation halfway turned toward the road. His heart cheered – but now the horsemen were resuming the push for their line.

Too many, he thought. *There're just too many. And they're too fast.*

"Third rank, aim!"

There isn't time! thought Cauhin desperately. He held the club out in front of him, less like a weapon and more like some form of talisman as he willed the riders to slow. *They're going to hit us. There isn't–*

"Get down, humans! Cover your ears!"

Nokrag's voice boomed in his head. Cauhin looked up at her, stupefied, as she stepped into the center of the road behind the Claws' formation. The oversized version of the horizontal bow was slung over her back, and in her hands was the strange contraption whose function he didn't understand, a wide-mouthed tube of metal bound to a length of wood. He watched with oddly detached interest as the Claws' archers pinned their palms against their ears, huddling low to the ground. Beyond them, the horsemen were perhaps only forty feet away. Thirty. Twenty.

Nokrag raised the contraption, and a burst of flame erupted from its end. The light seared Cauhin's eyes. Silence smothered him.

Blinking hard and lowering a hand that had risen late, Cauhin tried to see past the bright marks on his vision. Nokrag's weapon had sent the horsemen into chaos, many of their mounts rearing and bucking in an attempt to flee, leaving those behind with no time to avoid crashing into them. A rider slipped past the turmoil only to take an arrow to the face. The Claws stood up and were now firing independently. With the road choked, riders began steering their charge outward – straight into the advancing spearmen.

Pain started to build in Cauhin's ears, sound returning in a high whine that pierced his temples. Though it seemed far away, he could already make out the roar of triumph from the Ardovikians around him as they watched the pincer movement of spear formations press in on the funneled enemy. Long staves assailed the horsemen, precision thrusts impaling riders and denying them any chance of counter attack. Stumbling backward, the enemy began to flee.

Cauhin felt an ache of protest in his throat. He realized he was shouting, club raised above his head and tears in his eyes. Why were the enemy running? He wanted them to come back. He wanted to fight them. It looked to him as if the enemy still numbered in the hundreds, and that, despite the Claws' efforts, there couldn't be much more than two dozen of them in the dirt. Why were they running?

Riding hard, the horsemen disappeared into darkness as the mysterious light effect faded to normality. On the road, the two groups of spearmen met and merged, adjusting the line until it had smoothly curved into a long, outward facing semi-circle. The drum beat stopped, and the spears were raised to stand vertically.

Cauhin saw Xavire trudging back toward the archers. Both Alea and the stern-faced sergeant moved to join him. He could see Xavire's bearded face. Cauhin grimaced. Before he knew it, he was striding toward them, stepping past the oblivious archers.

"...safe bet they won't try that a second time," Xavire was saying. "I'm guessing they'll want to surround us once more, use their numbers to overwhelm us. Unless we can get moving soon, we won't be able to stop–"

"Why are you letting them run?"

Xavire turned his face toward him, eyes hidden behind his glasses. He said nothing.

"Why don't we go get them now? They're fleeing! We can kill them!"

"Cauhin." Alea's voice was firm.

"What?!" he said, rounding on her. "I heard what he was saying! Those men killed my people, and he wants *us* to flee!"

"Go back and stay with the young ones."

Cauhin recoiled. Her words had hit him like a slap in the face. Mouth wide, he stared at her for several seconds. She looked away, and his jaw clenched.

"This is because of you!" he seethed through grinding teeth. "We'd never have come to this place," then shouting, "you don't care about us at all!"

Without waiting to observe the impact, Cauhin stormed back toward his people. He was shaking. Where the final part of his accusation had come from, Cauhin didn't know. Did he believe that? Perhaps the burden of keeping Alea's lies had become too great. One lie for the Claws, another for the Plainsmen. His lies as much as hers. Justified, necessary; it didn't matter. He no longer wanted anything to do with it.

The Claws stared at him with amused puzzlement as he passed back between them. Cauhin kept his head down, face hot with mingled anger and shame. He heard the three behind him resume their discussion. Two short horn blasts sounded to the north.

Suddenly, a hand was in his path. A large hand.

"Do you wish my advice?"

The ogre's voice seemed to resonate throughout Cauhin's body, voiding his mind. Still staring at the huge palm, he found himself nodding assent.

Nokrag placed a giant finger under his chin, drawing his face all the way up to look at her. "Head up. Always. You said your words. Don't regret. *Learn.*" She withdrew her hand, watching for his response. Cauhin stood speechless, fascinated by her almond-shaped eyes, their piercing gray visible even in the darkness. He was distantly aware that her face should be terrifying, the sharp fangs barely held within a broad maw. But for some inexplicable reason, it filled him with calm. Pushing his shoulders back, he gave another nod. She returned it.

All was quiet. Even the battle to the north seemed to be over. Passing back through the column of Plainsmen – now contracted into a circular mass – it wasn't long until he rejoined Fillam and Rheyall. Fillam clapped him hard on the shoulder.

"Idiot," his friend said, visibly relieved. Cauhin shrugged, forcing a smile.

"Yup."

"Is it over, Cauhin?" Rheyall held her brother's hand, having dismounted his back. After a quick glance at Fillam, Cauhin shook his head.

"Not yet." Movement caught his eye to the north. The indistinct outlines of the Claws' horsemen emerged into view, returning from their fight. *Soon*, he thought, gripping his club.

But not yet.

*****

Sir Guilliver's sword arm burned, deflecting yet another blow coming from his left. The blades locked together, steel and iron screaming as they pressed into each other's hilt. Twisting in his saddle, he swung his free arm up, smashing his gauntlet into unarmored wrist. His adversary gave a yelp and let go of his sword, the weapon slipping into the shadows as it fell between their parallel mounts. In haste, Sir Guilliver made an unrefined hack. The sword's tip hit his foe's shoulder at an angle, bouncing along bone and sending waves of fire up Sir Guilliver's forearm. He grimaced and tried to ready a second strike. His arm resisted. It seemed to weigh of stone. By the time he managed to raise it, his enemy had produced a long, curved dagger. It sprang up like the head of a viper, catching Sir Guilliver's downward slash and sweeping it aside.

Drawing back, the hedge knight gulped hungrily at the cool air. It stank of exertion. He cast an eye over his opponent. The low light didn't permit much save the glint of small eyes, the snarl of errant teeth. Like the others, the man wore Darvled's uniform without armor and controlled his horse with the awkward competence of the self-taught. A brace of blades was bound tight across his torso. His left arm, drenched in blood from Sir Guilliver's misaligned hack, was somehow keeping its hold on the reins. The man yanked them hard, urging his mount to close the distance.

They're relentless. Sir Guilliver's thought was subsumed in weariness. The Claws' cavalry had as good as won the engagement; any could see their enemy was outmatched. Yet the bandits would not give up. All around him, the so-called Butcher's horsemen continued to fight in a series of static brawls. Momentum was dead on both sides – there was only the grind.

Sir Guilliver pulled his speckled gray around, readying his sword for a final blow. The two horses' heads came together, and Sir Guilliver's steed lashed out, teeth snapping from beneath its barding. Gelding had done little to curb the animal's ferocious streak. Defying its rider, the other horse strained to pull away. Sir Guilliver heeled. His warhorse leapt forward, bringing him side-on to his struggling foe. He saw the man's small eyes widen in surprise as he chopped cleanly from the left. The eyes disappeared, carried to the ground with the tumbling head.

From the south came a *bang*. Blackpowder.

Alarm reared in his chest. Turning away from the decollated body, Sir Guilliver sought out Uslo among the melee. The general was ten feet away and caught between two attackers, not so much keeping them at bay as pursuing them on both sides with soaring sweeps of his bastard sword. Moving to assist, Sir Guilliver reached them as one caught Uslo's counter-swing beneath the head of her handaxe. With a cry of vindication, the other readied a strike on the general's unprotected side – both cry and strike were cut short as Sir Guilliver pushed his sword through the would-be attacker's lungs.

By the time he'd freed his weapon, the enemy were finally falling back. Uslo's other attacker was among them, her axe either lost or abandoned. Several of the adventurers were urging their mounts into pursuit. Snatching up the horn which hung across his chest, Sir Guilliver gave two quick blasts – break off. There was little chance the Claws' armored mounts would catch their lighter foes. Drawing up next to him, Uslo removed his helm.

"General, it sounded like–"

"It must've been the ogre," Uslo gasped. He was drenched in sweat. "They've come under attack." He turned his horse, head moving quickly as he scanned the dark field. He pushed back his hair. "How many did we lose?"

Sir Guilliver looked over the regrouping adventurers, running a hand across his hair in mirror of the general, despite the fact that it was tied back. They seemed to have come through well. "Hard to say. Certainly no more than ten."

"All right. Let's go back and assess the situation."

"What about the enemy's supplies? We might not get another chance to capture them."

"We cannot be sure they are out there, and we cannot risk looking. Those bandits held us here for too long." Uslo took a deep breath through his nose, expelling it through pursed lips as he continued to examine the men. Then he nodded. "It isn't over yet, lads! The night is young!"

To the cavalry's relief, they soon saw that Xavire and the infantry had repelled the attack. The column of Ardovikians was now a circle, the obscured faces of its outer defenders granting only the barest acknowledgement of the returning men. On the far side, the Claws infantry faced into the fog-ridden night, themselves almost entirely swallowed by its gloom. Sir Guilliver looked up at the sky. Not a single star pierced the heavy cloud. The moon was gone.

"Where's Lady Alea?" asked Uslo, addressing the nearest of the Plainsmen. No answer came. "Never mind," he sighed. Then he raised his voice. "Everyone! The way is clear, but it will not stay so for long! We go!"

Movement began to spread throughout the convoy as people gathered up what little they had in preparation for the march. Sir Guilliver set the adventurers into their forward formation, ready to vanguard out once more. Uslo was looking out over the convoy, and he moved to join him.

"It seems likely they'll try to attack again," said Sir Guilliver.

"Likely? I would say inevitable," corrected the general. "We have used our one surprise. Now, we must use haste." Uslo turned his mount away from the Ardovikians and toward the cavalry. "Worry not, my dear Sir Guilliver. If these bandits are half as disorganized as they seem, then I doubt..."

"...Yes, General?"

Uslo said nothing. He was looking out into the darkness. Sir Guilliver couldn't see his face.

"...Uslo?"

"We're too late."

"What?" Tension snaked through aching muscle as Sir Guilliver spun his head, searching for any sign. "Where? I don't–"

"General Dargent!"

All turned toward the voice. From the black mists to their west, a lone rider approached, torso rolling atop the steady walk of a tall horse.

"General Uslo Dargent! I've come to talk!" It was a woman's voice, drawling and authoritative.

"Over here, Jathina Maem!" Uslo called. She turned toward him and stopped. There was a moment's pause.

"General!" she answered, finally. "I'm glad you know who I am. Saves us some time. If it's all the same to you, I'll have you come to me. Wouldn't want your men getting any ideas, eh?"

Uslo met Sir Guilliver's gaze from across the darkness. Sir Guilliver shrugged. It seemed they had no choice. Handing his bastard sword to one of the adventurers, the general nudged Volonto to motion and set off toward Maem. Sir Guilliver began to follow, but Uslo held up a hand, signaling he wait.

"Bring him along, General, if he makes you feel safe!" Maem barked a laugh.

That's some eyesight, thought Sir Guilliver. Beneath the disaffected tone of her words, he sensed she was furious.

"A generous offer. I think I will." The general sent a nod over his shoulder. Sliding his hastily cleaned sword into its sheath, Sir Guilliver urged his gelding to catch up.

"I'll hang back and keep an eye out for trouble," he said quietly. Uslo didn't respond. He seemed to be looking past Maem, scanning the obscured horizon.

"That's... some armor, General," said Maem as the pair drew up, Sir Guilliver stopping ten feet short of them. "Shame we're in darkness. I imagine it looked more impressive in the firelight."

Uslo was continuing to turn to and fro in his saddle, peering into the night. He settled back. "I take it you'd have me believe we are surrounded again?"

"Right in one." Then Maem sighed. "I wish I could show you, but believe me when I say they're close. Much closer than last time. If you try to run again, your men won't get twenty paces before being crushed from all sides."

At this distance, Sir Guilliver couldn't make out much of her aspect apart from a round face and thick, shoulder length hair. Her right hand was doing something strange, swaying back and forth at her side. Twirling something.

"Tell them to come forward," said Uslo. "Let me see them."

"In time."

Now it was Uslo's turn to sigh. "Disappointing. I hoped the 'Butcher of Eprye' would know the value of a show of force."

"You hoped I would give you a look at my force, more like. Just what were you thinking, General? Did you really believe you could fight your way out?"

Uslo shrugged, running a finger and thumb along his mustache before he answered. "It wouldn't be the first time I've done it, and I see no evidence to say I can't do it again. Now, if it is all the same to *you*, I'll be leaving."

"Don't be a fool," she hissed, the disaffection rupturing. "I'm not fu– ah, well would you look at that!"

As Maem spoke, the clouds parted, revealing a well of sky with the bright, crescent moon at its center. Cool light bathed the ruined town in its glow, banishing darkness from the mists. Shouts went up from the convoy, the voices torn between alarm and despair. Stomach clenching, Sir Guilliver put a hand to his sword.

"There you are," Maem gloated. She could be seen clearly now; the sneer on her lips, the long dagger twirling between her fingers. "Silver light for the Silver Cat! And they say the gods have no sense of humor. Satisfied, General?"

Uslo turned slowly, face impassive, his sweat-soaked skin shining with moonlight. Sir Guilliver followed his gaze. He needn't have bothered. It only confirmed the obvious. The moment the light had fallen upon Cadalla he had seen the long line of horsemen behind Maem, stretching beyond the limit of his peripherals. Hundreds of them, covering every approach, every ruined road, street and alley. They were trapped.

"All right," said Uslo, turning back to Maem. "Let's talk."

*****

As a cascade of moonlight touched upon the ruins of Cadalla, so too did Xavire fall. It seemed the world had given a lurch, shirking his purchase. Everything spun.

"Xavire!"

Alea's voice seemed to come from far away. He dimly recalled that she had been by his side a moment ago, that they'd been walking quickly. Why, he couldn't remember. His cheek was flat against the dirt, his glasses dislodged from his nose. But he could see. Gods, he could see. A halting breath escaped his lips. A silent scream.

The images vanished as hands grasped his shoulders and rolled him onto his back. Alea was leaning over him, her face a blur.

"Xavire! What's wrong?!"

"It's here!" he gasped. "It sees us!"

"What are you saying? What sees us?"

"Nuh- nuh-," he swallowed.

"...what?"

Xavire pushed himself up, resetting his glasses to see her face. "This will sound insane..."

"Speak."

He nodded. "Something's coming. We– we have to get everyone ready, we have to warn Uslo–"

"Uslo already knows, Xavire. He is talking to Maem now."

"Not the bandits! The..."

Xavire baulked at what he was about to say. It was as if his consciousness were sliced in two, with one half submerged in sleep and the other painfully awake, each raging against the other in denial of what both knew to be true. Worse, the certainty was dangerously close to slipping away. He felt sick.

"...nightmares!" The word emerged as little more than a whisper.

Alea's eyes widened. She quickly glanced up at the sky. Xavire looked. The gap in the clouds was shrinking rapidly. The light would soon be gone.

"Get up," she said firmly. "Move!"

Hooking her arm under his, Alea hauled Xavire to his feet and began to drag him into the anxious throng of Ardovikians.

My cap, he thought, putting a hand to his head. Too late. It must have come off when he fell. Ahead of him, Alea was saying something over and over, likely telling the Plainsmen to move aside.

"Wait!" said Xavire, though his body offered no resistance. "We have to warn–!"

"No time! Move it, Xavire!"

She was right. Back on his feet, Xavire could see the light fading, could sense the malevolent hunger of the coalescing darkness. Something was moving to surround them all, Maem's men included. He saw shapeless forms contorting in the fog as they circled the circle. Terror gripped his throat. What would he and Alea do to stop them? What *could* they do?

"Come on, Xavire!"

His legs had weakened again, and Alea turned, bringing her face down to his.

"Don't look at them! Just keep your head down!"

Hope swelled in his chest. "You can see them too?"

"No! No one else can see them yet!" Then she began to pull him again, one arm keeping her staff pinned upright against her shoulder. He followed her advice, leaving her to guide him through the crowd, his eyes taking shelter in the shadows at their feet. Alea was speaking, but it no longer sounded like telling people to make way. Her voice was low and monotonous. Xavire thought she was praying.

The light went out. Darkness was total. For several seconds, Xavire heard nothing except the motion of his breath and the shuffle of his and Alea's short steps. Even her murmuring had stopped.

Then came the scream.

Bodies shunted into Xavire, compelled by blind panic to flee the source of the sound. But its source was everywhere, emanating from all sides in a singular wail. It wasn't despairing. It was hateful. Almost immediately, the scream's unwavering drone was joined by the sound of a battle taking place beyond the Ardovikian throng, confused yelling mingled with the tortuous cries of man and horse. This time there were no clashes of iron and steel, no commanders directing the fight. In their place was something else. A chorus of roaring, torn from inhuman throats.

Jostling around Xavire and Alea intensified. The Ardovikians began to cry out, calling the names of kin into the dark. In a way, the all-encompassing blare of their terrified voices was a relief – it drowned out the slaughter beyond.

A cluster of Plainsmen collapsed onto them. Xavire spat a curse, managing to avoid falling as they passed. He and Alea had been pushed apart. He tried to call to her, but his voice was lost in the storm. Then someone grabbed hold of a patch of uniform at his shoulder. Grasping the arm in turn, he fought his way toward her.

"We cannot go any farther!" said Alea once he reached her. "We have to do it now!" She was shouting into his face.

"Yes!" responded Xavire, having not the faintest idea what she meant. They were pressed together. She felt like iron.

"Turn around!"

Xavire turned until his back was to her. Her free hand gripped his shoulder. Over the surrounding din he thought he could hear snatches of Uslo's voice, exhorting the Claws to form a defensive circle.

"You need to lift me! Get ready!"

She began to push him down before he could respond. Crouching low in the pitch black, it occurred to Xavire that if another cluster were to run into them now, he would be knocked flat and crushed. But none did. Alea straddled his shoulders. He hooked his arms around her legs to hold her steady, and the world went mercifully mute as her thighs clasped over his ears. Taking a deep breath, Xavire began lifting her up.

Alea was heavier than he expected, even considering her height. But her balance was even, and Xavire was soon standing straight, his legs braced beneath them.

What now? he thought. Plainsmen continued to elbow past, ignorant of their precarious effort. Worryingly, a new sound was emerging, unhampered by the muffling of Alea's legs. It was a sort of buzzing, an uneven hiss that brushed needles along Xavire's spine. As if someone were whispering it directly into his ears. He gritted his teeth. What exactly was Alea doing?

Then he saw it. White light, dim and delicate, was falling around him, around only him, extending no more than a couple of feet in every direction. The hissing stopped. Movement petered out, and in the narrow trench afforded by bunched-up robes, Xavire witnessed the faces of the Ardovikians turn to gaze up in wonder, their mouths agape. The light was coming from Alea. And it was getting stronger. Straining his head back what little he could, Xavire looked.

Alea held her staff high in both hands, pointing its head to the black clouds above. It was glowing from top to bottom, every inch giving off a radiance of rapidly building intensity. Within seconds, the staff itself was gone, all distinction between its gold and silver workings lost behind the sheer luminescence. It stung his eyes, and when he looked away, Xavire saw the staff's light reflected against the clouds.

An unseen force impacted them. It seemed to have been borne on a screeching shout which even Xavire could hear. Plainsmen crashed into one another, in some cases being lifted off their feet. With intermingled surprise and despair, Xavire realized he was going to topple. He managed to take two quick steps back, his torso laboring to keep Alea steady. The light dipped sharply as she removed a hand from the staff to grab a fistful of his hair. He registered the pain only distantly. They were going down.

Fortifying arms – he couldn't tell how many – appeared at his back. His fall slowed to a stop. In front of him, a young woman reached out to take hold of his coat. Together with those behind, they heaved him upright, continuing to hold him and Alea straight. More screeches buffeted the Plainsmen, driving into them, causing Alea's robes to whip back and forth. Xavire stood strong, shored up by the dozens of Ardovikians, their footing growing firmer as more joined the huddle. Keeping ahold of his head, Alea raised the staff once more, the light roaring back to life. Her thumb pressed hard against Xavire's forehead.

A feeling of calm detachment fell over him. Like a dream.

Xavire closed his eyes and felt Alea give a shout, felt the force of it run through her body. The light flared beyond his eyelids. It was suddenly as though his entire being were made up of a thousandfold tiny rivers, all of them aflame. Then a deep and bone-rattling *boom* exploded above, leaping through the earth and generating a mighty blast of wind. The bracing hands fell away as their owners were thrown to the ground. The light was gone.

He couldn't keep standing. Lowering himself in a shuddering jerk, Xavire set Alea on her feet, from which she immediately fell to her hands and knees. He could hear her breathing in great gasps over the moans and groans of the Plainsmen – other than that, it was quiet.

"Are you alright?" he asked, pushing his glasses up from the tip of his nose.

Alea made a quick wave over her shoulder. After a couple of deep breaths, she turned to look at him. "Fine," she said flatly. Her olive skin glistened with sweat. Xavire blinked. The pitch darkness was gone. He could see her.

Head turned up, Xavire slowly got to his feet. The air was clear. The clouds had been banished in every direction, thrown outward to reveal the night sky. Stars gleamed in the infinite depths, their shine outdone only by the sundered brilliance of the half moon.

With dreamlike detachment, Xavire turned his eyes to Cadalla. Nothing. No mists. No… things. Not even Maem's horsemen. Just the bewildered looking adventurers – most of whom were still on their horses, a few unsaddled by Alea's blast – and the prone Plainsmen, who were gradually standing up. Actually, he thought as he peered out at the ruins, maybe Maem's horsemen weren't gone. It looked as though…

"They're dead," said Alea. She stood up. "The Butcher thought she had us closed in, but in the end, her forces were surrounded too. Lucky for us – if her bandits hadn't been there to slow them down, we'd all be dead."

"And what exactly *did* they slow down?" asked Xavire. His stomach churned, and he had to fight down a retch. He wasn't sure he wanted to hear the answer.

Alea fixed her eyes on his. It was the same look she had given him before, in that moment before Maem's horsemen burned the wagons. The look that seemed to invade.

Uslo's voice cut across the night air, the general giving orders to get the train moving. Xavire raised a hand in acknowledgement before turning back to Alea.

But she was gone.

12

...Messor noted a curious and short-lived tendency among the people of the Lantor region, then called Lantis, to apply elven suffixes to the roots of their own distinct Primovantian dialect...

Vespilo A., *On the Location and Identification of Primovantian Antiquity,* Appendix IX *'From the Gatekeepers' - The Mystery of Keatairn*

The curved spearhead flashed toward him, snagging Orod's shoulder. Pain flared. With a snarl, the krudger brought his axes down in a wide arc, severing his attacker's arms at the elbow. The soldier staggered back, wailing over his stumps. He buried his weapon in the weeping man's skull.

He was becoming annoyed. The fight still offered its immediate pleasures. Its satiating carnage. But from the back of his mind, an irritant had steadily grown, extending its barbed tendrils across all else.

The humans weren't breaking.

Another one charged forward, the skillful weaves of his sword setting Orod on the defensive. Catching the blade in the butt of one axe, the krudger hooked it with the other before wrenching both aside. The sword snapped. In a single hack, he split the human from shoulder to hip.

They were scared, of course. He could see it. Could smell it. And with good reason. They had no hope of victory, now. All that remained for them was a brutal death at the hands of his ax. Yet despite this, the human army continued to hold its ground. It was enough to make his orc blood boil.

From his enemy's backfield, one of the human horns gave its thin cry – more joined it a second later. Curious, Orod turned to face the source of the sound. A group of mounted men bore toward him, visible over the heads of his orcs. The sight of them rebirthed the krudger's grin. Most were on horseback, their long spears leveled toward his hastily bracing greatax. They were joined by several of the strange, monstrous dogs whose riders could apparently do little more than hang on as they bounded across the field. But it was the figure at their head that so enthused the krudger, the one whose presence sent anticipation to the far corners of his being. Sitting tall atop a muscular horse, the man's chest was bound in bright plate, his shoulders draped in furs, his arms bare and strong. In his hands he brandished an impressive battleaxe, and his face was as long-bearded as the hated dwarf masters. Orod licked his lips. In just one look, he knew with bone-deep certainty that this was the humans' leader, called, according to Arlok, a 'lord' – more, he knew that this man thought himself a warrior. Orod would enjoy correcting him.

The charge barreled its way through the greatax, crushing the first ranks beneath hoof and paw. Those beyond struggled to get out of the humans' path, panic making them easy marks for the riders' spears, while the giant dogs pounced wildly from orc to orc, catching heads in their jaws before breaking their necks with a sharp shake. Adjusting his grip on the axes up to their shoulders, Orod strode toward the lord. He saw him split the head of an orc with the battleaxe, watched as he prised the weapon free. Then his eyes turned to Orod. Recognition flared.

He knows what I am, thought the krudger. *He knows, and he fears.*

Except, much to Orod's fury, there was no fear in the man's gaze. Only a righteous hate.

The human pointed his battleaxe at Orod in the clear expression of a challenge. Stride unbroken, the krudger raised one of his own in response. Then he bared his bloodstained teeth and rushed.

Alarm flashed across the lord's face. Too late, he tried to wheel his horse toward the oncoming orc, spurring hard for a charge. Winding his arm, Orod slid his grip along the haft until he held his axe above the pommel, aiming to bury it in the horse's skull. Unleashing a triumphal roar, he–

The world spun. Plunged into wet earth, Orod rolled twice before coming to a stop. Pain hummed in his side. Something had bowled him over. Something big.

He lurched upright. A ring of fangs leapt out from amidst the blur. The krudger dove sideways just in time and heard the *snap* of a massive maw closing mere inches from his head. Twisting around, Orod staggered back several steps before planting his boots in the mud. One of the axes had fallen from his grasp, but he didn't dare look for it. His eyes were set on his assailant.

The giant hound stared back at him. It had placed itself between Orod and the lord, front legs crouched to pounce, its hackles high and its teeth bared. Lumps of black clot clung to niveous muzzle, and in its ice-blue eyes Orod sensed a profound intelligence. Glancing up at its rider, the krudger recognized an elder warrior, gray-haired and with a fresh score across his face. The veteran was effortless atop his mount, the movements of both man and animal perfectly harmonized. His sword arm was steady.

Another Bloodtusk, thought Orod. *Another old beast for me to put down.*

The enormous dog-mount growled. Orod growled. Then it lunged for him, cocking its head as its jaw was flung wide. Orod leapt into the attack, swinging his remaining weapon from the shoulder. Its edge met the top row of teeth, shattering them as it drove into the gums. The hound gave an agonized wail, its long incisors snagging Orod's leg as it pulled away.

The pain of his parted flesh reached the krudger as if from across a great distance. He leered at the dog and its rider, relishing the hesitation that had entered each of their gazes.

Spotting the duel, the orcs around him began to chant, the rhythmic bark quickly joined by wardrums as it spread throughout the horde.

"*DOOM! DOOM! DOOM! DOOM!*"

This would not be like the Bloodtusk. Orod would not evade, he would not give ground. Back then, in that fight, he had been named 'doomed one' – now he was the doom.

"*DOOM! DOOM! DOOM! DOOM!*"

With eyes on the hesitating rider, the krudger stepped out of his boots. Cool wetness pooled between his toes. He took hold of the rupture in his leggings and pulled. The material resisted, its thick lace stretching at the seams. From atop the gargling hound, an expression of bewilderment came over the veteran's face. Orod laughed. With a final jerk, he tore the hide garment away.

Orod closed his eyes and breathed deep. His naked skin pulsed beneath the cling of red blood, the combined voices of his orcs swelling around him.

"*DOOM! DOOM! DOOM! DOOM!*"

Dog and rider let out a battle cry. Orod felt warm spray from the beast's maw. Then, in a lightning motion, the krudger wound back his axe and hurled it, opening his eyes only at the last possible instant. The weapon went up past the gnashing snout of the hound, completing a single rotation as it sailed toward the rider. Orod didn't watch. Immediately and with a full-throated roar, he lunged forward, dropping low and using his arms to propel him across the sludge. The beast raised a long-clawed paw to swipe at him – there was a sickening *thunk*. Above them, the veteran's battle cry had cut dead.

There was no more than a split-second pause in the hound's attack – it was all Orod needed. Leaping from all fours, the krudger sank his teeth into the animal's neck. Its mournful wail gave way to snarls as it struggled to free itself, its claws raking across his flanks.

Orod hung on, wrapping his arms around its muzzle, pushing forward with his legs. He closed his throat as an arterial flood rushed from the wound, spraying outward around the corners of his mouth. Releasing his jaw, he spat quickly before biting again, chewing his way frantically into the enormous gorge. The hound's struggling weakened. Finally, it collapsed into the mud.

Orod stood, savoring the taste of blood. Every part of his body seemed awash in pain. But he would not rest. The battle wasn't over. He still had the humans' lord to deal with.

Spotting the corpse of the veteran, sprawled in the muck with the Tragarian axe in his face, Orod began toward it. Before taking so much as two steps, however, he stopped. From amid the swirl of ongoing combats that surrounded him, two figures had caught the krudger's eye.

Lashka and the lord were fighting. She was wielding the krudger's axe, the one he'd dropped when tackled by the hound. The lord's horse was behind them, slumped awkwardly, Lashka's glaive driven deep into its breast. As Orod watched, his mate unleashed a flurry of strikes, each more furious than the last. The man blocked them all, but only just, twisting the great head of his battleaxe back and forth. His face was drenched in sweat.

For a moment, the krudger was held by indecision. Part of him seethed at the thought of anyone else claiming such a kill; but another relished the sight of Lashka in action, hungered to see her culminate.

Before he could make up his mind, Lashka discharged an arcing blow powerful enough to fell a gore – and committed a fatal mistake.

"NO!"

It was too late. Helpless, Orod watched as the lord stepped back from the mistimed swing before burying his battleaxe in her chest.

A haze descended over Orod's mind as he charged. Hearing the orc's roar, the lord tried desperately to pry his weapon from Lashka's ribcage. The battleaxe came free a split-second before Orod crashed into him, impact launching it from the lord's grasp. They fell heavily. Orod felt his foe begin to grasp at his throat, followed quickly by a firm and frantic thumb against his windpipe. He ignored it. Teeth bared, the krudger pushed himself up to straddle the lord's chest. Then he laid into him, raining blows onto the bearded face with the base of his fists. For a second, the grip tightened on Orod's throat, and then it released, the lord's hands moving to shield his exposed head. Orod carried on regardless, hammering until he felt the crack of bone.

Beneath shattered hands, the lord gave a muffled moan. Slowly, Orod drew the useless appendages aside, revealing a broad and battered face. The lord's nose was broken, the pink skin rapidly turning purple all around it. The gold circlet on his head was bent. Orod leaned over, and stared deep into the man's mud-brown eyes.

He could see fear. He could see it, and he felt nothing.

Silent as the dead, Orod sat back, clasped his fists together above his head, and brought them down.

*****

Another battle was over. With the death of their lord and his retinue of riders, the humans had finally fled. Or rather, they had tried to. None escaped the gore riders' pursuit.

Standing alone among the carrion, Orod absently caressed the head of his axe, long-since recovered from the dead dog rider. He could hear his remaining orcs ransacking the human camp in the distance. Wind enveloped him, and his wounds ached warmly against its touch.

All around, a sea of birds kept a wary distance from the naked orc, bickering loudly as they decided which patch of dead flesh to pick at next. More circled overhead. Watching them ride the eddies, Orod felt a strange certainty that he had seen some of them before, that they had followed his horde from the east. His mind retraced the journey from here to the river, from the river to the Steppe, to the Howling Peaks and all the way back into the flooded lands of Tragar. To the revolt, to the slave pits. To darkness.

He looked down.

Lashka's body lay at his bare feet, a yawning rent in her chest. The rage he'd felt at witnessing her death had been unlike anything he'd ever experienced. But his fury was sated. Now, he felt nothing. A vague regret, perhaps.

Orod turned his gaze to his axe, still grasped in Lashka's hand.

She was... strong, he thought.

He leant over to take it. Her hand was cold. Stiff. He pried it free.

Not strong enough.

Orod turned away. It would be the last time he thought of Lashka.

His weapons returned to him, the krudger paused as he passed the body of the human lord. Though splattered with muck and blood, there was no denying that it was a fine pelt around his shoulders. With care, Orod took the great length of fur and bound it around his waist. He hung the twin axes at his hips.

Bolirm and Arlok watched him from what had been the human backfield. Each maintained a wary distance from the other as they waited for the krudger.

"Goblins're gone," said Bolirm as Orod moved into earshot. "Ran off durin' the battle."

Orod slowed, tilting his head as he considered this. He found the news neither surprised nor angered him. He shrugged.

"They'll get what's coming to them. In time." He stopped, meeting Bolirm's gaze. "What about you? Goin' to leave, too?"

Alarm gripped the orc's features. "What? I..." Then his eyes narrowed. "...No."

Orod nodded indifferently, already turning to the Godspeaker. "Well?"

"Your victory is total, krudger. It was faith that drove your orcs to fight like troll bruisers."

"And hunger," grunted the krudger. "I pushed them hard, and they fought hard. How many do I have left?"

"Less than we'd hoped, I'm afraid. Little over a thousand ax." Arlok sighed. "The cost was high."

"It was necessary. Only the strongest can be part of my destiny."

Orod strode between them toward the plundered human camp.

"These thousand are the strongest. They proved that today. With this victory, there're no other armies to stand in my way, nothing between here and the power that awaits me. Already I've surpassed the so-called great invasion, and once I cross the rest of the human lands, I'll have done what no other krudger could. I'll gather the mightiest of hordes, one so large that each orc here will be krusher to ten-thousand others. They will come to me."

Orod stopped. The rows of tents stretched out before him, most hanging frayed on their supports. His orcs moved among them, relishing the wanton destruction. Bonfires were beginning to burn hungrily in spite of the morning's rain. He reflected that orcs were good at fire. They shared its purpose.

Orod lifted his gaze, ignoring the walled town in the distance to scan the western horizon.

"There'll be no walls that can stop me, no cage to hold us. The world'll suffer an Age of Orcs. And then it will end."

13

...By way of example, he showed how the words 'vivelirn' (librarian) and 'sparirn' (warrior) would be formed from 'vivel' (book) or 'spar' (sword), and the elven 'irn' (keeper of)...

Vespilo A., *On the Location and Identification of Primovantian Antiquity,* Appendix IX *'From the Gatekeepers' - The Mystery of Keatairn*

The wind was high on the Ardovikian coast. It blew from the west across waters known to the southerners as the Straits of Von Terel, and to Cauhin's people as the Bitter Sea. It battered waves against the rock-strewn beaches, the rhythm of their breaks like a tireless chant. It filled the wind-thrown air with salt and sea-rot, once a strange smell, now familiar. A quarter mile from the shore, Cauhin shivered. It was cold.

The caravan left the ruins of Cadalla almost two weeks ago to the day. After hastily recovering all they could from the bandits' supplies and their own, they had forged northwest to the coastline. From there, they followed its northeasterly contour, diverted only by the occasional patches of mist spied at distance across the flat plain. A consensus had emerged among the Plainsmen, built by whispers: it was restless spirits who had attacked that night, ghosts of the dead city revenging themselves upon an intrusion of the living. The explanation was satisfying in several ways, the most important being that it put the horror far behind them, which in turn removed the need to discuss the matter further. Even so, none wished to brave another fog any time soon.

Shivering again, Cauhin pulled his cloak tight as he looked out at the gray-blue mass which stretched across the entire west. His first sight of the sea was ten days ago, and it had left him vaguely disappointed. Nothing about it appealed to him, nothing drew him forward. Even so, that day he'd walked down to the beach with the other initiates of his kin – who were old as well as young – watching the bitter-cold waves reach toward them, icy fingertips submerging feet to drag feebly at ankles. Without saying a word, Fillam had plunged his head in to drink. Then he'd leapt up in panic, eyes wide with innocent hurt as he spewed. No one had told them differently, but it didn't surprise Cauhin to learn the water was undrinkable. *Otherwise,* he thought, *all of life would come to its shore*. It seemed to Cauhin that the sea wanted no such thing.

Turning away, Cauhin stepped closer to Nokrag, putting her large form between himself and the wind. The ogress glanced around in acknowledgement of his presence, then turned her gaze north again. Cauhin looked.

It was the first settlement they had come upon in five days. It was small, and it was poor. Clinging to the banks of a long and wide estuary, the village consisted of around a dozen conical constructions made from thick, grass-wound thatch. Only their top halves were visible, protruding above an irregular driftwood palisade that divided them from the open plains, extending a short way into the water on either side. Cauhin guessed the bases of the huts were broad, housing many. Or perhaps not; patches of unworked farmland surrounded the settlement, and there were no fishing crafts in the estuary. Cauhin doubted the village could feed a lot of mouths. If that was right, he wondered what they could offer in trade.

"They say they don't have anything," said Nokrag as if in answer to his thoughts.

Cauhin gawked up at her. "You can hear them from here?"

A large finger dug in her ear and flicked away what it had found. "I can hear enough."

Somewhere between twenty to thirty yards away, Alea, Elder Nyrona, Uslo, and Xavire talked with four members of the small community. Two of them were warriors armed with bone-tipped spears, probably tusks, while the other two appeared to be authority figures of some sort. They were younger than Cauhin would have expected. Perhaps their own elders didn't want to come out.

"Maybe the next village will be bigger," speculated Cauhin. Uslo was talking, his hands extended in gentle gesticulations. The leaders shook their heads.

"There is no next one," said Nokrag. "They say theirs is the last settlement on the coast before the hills, and that nothing lives in them but goblins."

Cauhin said nothing. It was bad news. Supplies were running low. The attack on the wagons had destroyed much, and everything they'd recovered from the bandits' carts was unfit for long journeys: soft bread that too soon succumbed to weevils and mold, fruits which spoiled within the week, meats which were insufficiently salted, and so on. They had eaten what they could, while they could, and thereafter portions had been drastically cut. There was no time for hunting – not that it had stopped a number of Plainsmen from breaking off to try their luck at catching rabbit, or even spear fishing along the coast, to limited success. Underfed and overexerted, the caravan had wended its way listlessly from one coastal settlement to the next, trading their empty carts and some of the animals for what little the villages could spare. Mainly fish, it turned out. Hungry though he might be, Cauhin was sick of fish.

"What is it about human tribes and walls?" asked Nokrag.

"What do you mean?"

Nokrag glanced at Cauhin. "Look at them, cowering in there." She pointed past the group of eight to the settlement's semi-circular palisade. Gaps in the driftwood were spread along its length, and several dozen faces peered out at them, hands pressed against foreheads to shield their eyes from the sunlight.

"Their wall offers them no protection. Anyone could go around and enter from the water – or even easier, they could hack their way through." She looked at him seriously. "I ask you help me understand."

Cauhin smiled. Nokrag always spoke to him as an equal, when in truth, her intelligence surpassed that of anyone he'd known, except maybe Alea's. Throughout their many conversations, the ogre's grasp of Plainsmen's dialect had progressed from none to competence in a staggeringly short amount of time. Never again would Cauhin credit those stories which depicted her race as slow of mind.

"I don't know what to say… anyway, it isn't just humans that use walls. The dwarfs are famous for them. And I think there's even an elven city called 'Walldeep.'"

"You speak truth. But what about that one there?"

He shrugged. "It makes them feel safer, I guess? If they had the materials, I'm sure they'd build it better. Like Darvled's Wall."

Nokrag tilted her head, appearing to contemplate this. As was often the case when he looked at her, Cauhin's eyes were drawn to the tribal markings on her right shoulder, glimpses of interconnecting spirals beneath wind-blown hair.

"It is not only this wall, then," she said finally. "It is all walls. I do not understand them. They are fixed, yet they can be crested. They may be strong, yet they can always be broken. That is a thing we are often hired to accomplish. Your human tribes build walls, and then others pay us to break them in siege."

"*My* tribes don't build them."

"But they hid behind one."

Cauhin felt his smile falter. Her tone had changed almost imperceptibly, and something about it disturbed him in a way he couldn't name.

"We had no choice," he said flatly.

Nokrag grunted. "We ogres do not use walls. When enemies come to our lands, we face them as warriors. We do not hide like you humans. We do not cower like those over there."

Cauhin's chest went tight, and when he spoke, it was with indignation. "What do you expect? That they tear it down? Face us with bone spears? The plain was flooded with orcs, it was hide or die! And now the land is devastated–"

"You speak to me of floods and devastation?!" growled Nokrag. "Me, an ogre? If it had been a flood of orcs on the ogre lands, we would have killed them all or died trying, just as my kin killed them on these plains of yours! And 'devastated'? We have walked many days now, and I am yet to see anything remotely like the damage dealt by the melted sea to my home. *That* was devastation! This!" She cast her great arms about her. "This land is untouched! It is fierce! But most of all, it is unworthy of cowards and their walls!"

Without another look at him, Nokrag stalked away. Cauhin watched her go, torn between shock at the uncharacteristic outburst and hurt at what she had said. He wiped his eyes against his cloak, teeth gritted. He should have said something else. Something… stronger.

Turning to go and join Fillam among the wagons, Cauhin took one last glance at the group of eight. A small jolt of surprise leapt in his chest. Alea was looking at him, her face impassive. He hadn't approached her since that night in the ruined city, nor she him. They held each other's gaze for several seconds. Rumor among the Plainsmen said Alea herself had offered the prevailing explanation for what occurred in Cadalla, and that was reason enough for Cauhin to doubt. He wanted to talk to her about it directly, to demand to know if she was lying to his people once more. But he was afraid. Not of her answer, but of his motivations, of the longing to be in her confidence. To go back to how things were before.

You could apologize, he thought to himself. He missed her. More than he could admit to himself, he missed her.

Cauhin closed his eyes. No chance. An apology would be a lie, and Cauhin was done lying.

His eyes opened. Alea was no longer looking at him. He walked away.

*****

Two days later, as dawn light began to stir in the east, Xavire moved among the sleeping caravan. Bodies clustered together for warmth beneath the starry sky, and he stepped around them quietly, making his way to the front of the train. In the distance, small campfires warmed the sentries, occasionally revealing the shape of a sleeping or grazing horse, unhitched from its cargo. The wind had relaxed that night, granting a brief reprieve from its seaweed smell. In its place, the travelers were treated to the faint odor produced by the newly-acquired periwinkles. After careful insistence, it had turned out the small settlement could trade after all, though only at an extortionate rate. Uslo had grumbled, but they agreed it was better than nothing.

Xavire reached the front wagon. Uslo would be asleep inside, bundled next to his bombard. Members of the Claws were underneath, their shields resting upright on all sides in an effort to see off the winds, now unnecessary. Stepping around it, he peered into the morning gloom.

More nightmares. Since Cadalla they were always the same, dreams laden with the same stalked feeling as before, now filled with the glimpsed shapes in mist. For the others in the caravan, the horrors of that night dimmed with each mile – for Xavire, it seemed they followed his every step.

"Xavire?"

Xavire jumped at the whisper, though he quickly recognized it.

"Over here, Alea."

She stepped around the wagon. It appeared she was long up, that she had perhaps not slept at all.

"Good morning." Slivers of starlight gleamed on her staff, but her face was shadow.

"Good morning," he answered quietly. It seemed she was aware that it had happened again. He turned his gaze north.

The Ballamor Hills, as the villagers had called them, began less than a day's journey ahead. Mounds of black against a deep blue sky, the hills would fail to impress in any other part of Upper Mantica; in fact, thought Xavire, they would barely be worth naming at all. After weeks of travel over featureless flatland, however, the Ballamor range seemed to rise above the Plains with all the grandeur of the Tarkis Mountains.

He turned his attention back to Alea. "Can we walk?"

She nodded. They set off slowly, walking in silence for about a minute, heading out from the caravan toward the coast. Xavire didn't want them to be overheard.

"The same?" asked Alea.

Xavire nodded. "The same." He sighed. "Eight days since the last time. I'd started to hope it was finally done with me. Whatever *it* is." He felt tired. Even in his own ears there was a numb quality to his voice, as if his words came from far away.

"Still only in sleep? You haven't had any more… intuitions while awake?"

That brought him back a little. "Intuitions?" he scoffed, glancing round. "Does jumping at shadows count as intuition?"

"Xavire."

He sighed again. "No. Nothing. Not like that night."

Now it was Alea's turn to sigh. He suspected it was relief. Somehow, Xavire had been able to sense their attackers in Cadalla minutes before they arrived. 'Nightmares,' he'd called them. It had taken a little coaxing, but on that very next morning, she convinced him to tell her what little he remembered about his dreams. About the feeling.

"And you still cannot recall anything of the dreams themselves?" she said.

"Nothing new." But he began anyway. "Something chases me. I can't see it when I look back, but it's there, just out of sight. I keep running… I hear it calling, demanding to know…"

"What?" In each instance of the dream, Xavire's pursuer seemed to want something, though he could never remember it. "What does it want?"

"… I don't know."

"Think, Xavire. It could be important."

He said nothing for almost a minute. Alea waited.

"It's looking for something, something specific. But… it doesn't seem to know what it is."

"It doesn't know what it's looking for?"

"Sort of. It knows the thing it wants, but not how to describe it. It's like… like an instinct."

Alea nodded. "Good. Keep going."

"That's it. There's nothing else."

They'd reached the dunes overlooking the beach. Gentle waves reflected the early dawn light, their low crests glimmering as they caressed the shore.

"What were they?" asked Xavire. "That night in Cadalla?"

"Things that live between. Lost souls and tenuous beings. Sometimes we sense them, usually as children. Most of us will go through our lives never knowing of their existence. But they're there, just out of sight. Much as they want to enter our world, they can't stay for long, often only for a few seconds. Maybe minutes. When the conditions are right, however…"

"So, what? It was our bad luck to be there when the conditions were right?"

"Most would call it good luck – they took care of Maem's bandits."

"That's one way to put it..."

"They were strong that night, it's true, but we were lucky. Somehow, those mists held a door open for them – they weren't strong enough to remain without them."

"But one night they could be?"

Alea nodded.

Xavire looked out over the sea. The wind was picking up, and he drew the red hemming of his overcoat tight across his chest. "Will they come again?"

"I don't know."

"What do we do?"

"The only thing we can: avoid the mists and continue to examine your dreams."

"For intuitions."

"Yes."

Xavire let out a long sigh. He glanced at her, unable to hide a forlorn expression. "Forgive the self pity, Alea. But I just... I just can't stop thinking why. Why *me*? You're sure that nobody else is having similar dreams?"

"We've been over this, Xavire. I suspect at least half the convoy are still having nightmares about the things in Cadalla, but I haven't heard of anyone else sensing the attack when it came, as you did."

"Right. I remember."

"It could be that others are out there and are keeping it to themselves." Something about the way Alea said it suggested she thought it unlikely.

"Yes, fine," muttered Xavire. "And if I *am* the only one?"

Alea took a moment to consider. It was a question he had asked before, one she could not answer. Or perhaps would not.

"I have had one thought. It is possible that you possess... a sensitivity."

"For?"

"Sorcery."

Xavire looked round, expression caught halfway between appalled and horrified.

Alea laughed. "I only said it is possible."

"Even so, I'm sorry I asked." He managed a laugh. Although her suggestion that he possessed a link to the arcane was unwelcome, it nevertheless made him feel a little better. Sometimes even the worst answer really was better than none. "But wouldn't that mean you should be having the nightmares, too?"

It was the first time Xavire had made any reference to what Alea had done in the battle at Cadalla, and he was glad to see her smile in response. "There are many kinds of magic, Xavire. *If* I'm right about you, then yours would be an uncommon sort. In the extreme."

Xavire smiled wryly at her. "Any chance I'll accidentally turn someone into a newt?"

Alea laughed. "Again, *if* I'm correct, then chances are you would never have known. Such sensitivities are normally discovered in early training, and I cannot imagine any practitioner would wish to take on an apprentice of your years."

"So... no newts?"

"No newts. Only the greatest wizards can learn without training, and I fear your greatness is wanting, Xavire."

"Thank the gods for that."

Xavire clapped his hands together, rubbing them for warmth. He turned his back to the sea. "Come on. Let's start to rouse them. I need some broth in me, although I've never eaten boiled snails before. You?"

"I have," she said. They began to walk back to the caravan.

"I admit, I'm a little bit repulsed by the thought. What are they like?"

"They are... distinctive."

"Oh, don't!"

*****

Deep into the second day of travel through the Ballamor Hills, they came to a road. As the man who found it explained to Sir Guilliver, it was discovered by chance. The man, one of the adventurers, had dismounted to relieve himself. With modesty rarely seen among soldiers, the brimming fellow wandered away from the group toward what appeared to be a deep, dense thicket of spruce and blackthorn. Beyond spiny branches, he glimpsed the mottled gray of flagstone. The scouts cut through and, to their astonishment, discovered one of the finest roadways they'd ever seen – certainly finer than anything they'd expected to come across outwith the Successor Kingdoms, or Rhordia to their east. Broad and level, the road seemed to belong to another world, its smooth stones unclaimed by the surrounding wilds, its path untroubled by the hills.

Leaving the other scouts behind to await the caravan, Sir Guilliver explored the southward stretch, finding it shortly ended in a small harbor, its stone jetties flung out over a cove inlet. There were no crafts of any kind. It was abandoned. With nought else to do but ponder this mystery, he returned north, finding the caravan had not long caught up to the scouts.

"The people in that village didn't say anything about... well, any of this!" exclaimed Xavire, his arms spread wide. "What do you think it means, General?"

"You took the words right out of my mouth, Xavire," said Uslo. "Perhaps you can give us an answer, Lady Alea? What does this road mean?"

"It means, good sirs, that we are going the right way."

Sir Guilliver felt his eyebrows climb. Alea's expression was bright, her voice cheerful. From the moment the ex-knight learned that she hailed from the Brotherhood, was a lady of their esteemed Devoted no less, he had never doubted this expedition; now, for reasons he couldn't account, he felt a vague suspicion.

"Excellent!" Uslo clapped his hands and gripped them together emphatically.

"I beg the lady's pardon, but if this road takes us to our destination, why didn't you tell us about it?" asked Sir Guilliver. "What if my scouts had missed it?"

Alea turned to him. "I was confident you and your and riders would happen upon it, Sir Guilliver – if they had not, then of course I would have told you all before long." Her voice had remained pleasant, but Sir Guilliver thought he caught a hint of irritation flicker across her face. Unease growing, he smiled.

"Of course. Forgive me."

Reaction to the road varied among the other travelers. For the Claws, the toil of clearing the caravan's route along overgrown valleys had seemed unending; the relief they felt at the road's discovery more than made up for the mystery of its being there. For the Ardovikians, however, there was no such consolation. It seemed to Sir Guillliver that the road disturbed them greatly, with most choosing to forge a route alongside rather than tread its stones. Uslo, for his part, was delighted. Leading the men in a rendition of *My Heart Dwells upon Swell of Ocean Fair* – one of several sea shanties he had obliged them to learn in the original Genezan dialect – the incongruous lyrics bore a wistful melody up from the caravan and over the hills.

Heels to the road, the convoy made rapid progress, cutting through the range like an elven galley through high waves. By evening, they'd covered the same distance as the previous two days combined. Sir Guilliver suggested they ease the pace; people were tired, primarily as a result of hard rationing. Uslo would not be deterred.

"We're close," said Uslo, perched high in his saddle atop Volonto. "I can feel it."

"Close to where? The valley from the Plainsmen's story? How do you know?"

"Patience, my friend," said Uslo, running thumb and forefinger across his mustache and casting a wink at him. "Patience."

It rained softly throughout the next day, drops so thin as to be almost imperceptible but for the cold dampness they left in clothes and hair. Despite the added discomfort, the caravan's good progress continued. Even a downed beech tree provided only a slight hindrance, its gnarled upper branches found stretching across the road, its roots unearthed by a great shift in the hillside soil some months past. The Claws chopped it back and collected the firewood.

Two hours later, around mid afternoon, Sir Guilliver saw it. Fear, the same fear that lingered in the minds of everyone since that night in Cadalla, seized his chest. Leaving his scouts on watch, he rode back and reported a cloud of fog on the northern horizon, its dense form hanging heavy across the road. Sir Guilliver could see the shadow fall over Uslo's mood as he told him. With no way to circumvent the mists, the general called a halt. Camp was readied, a tract of fern flattened and bonfires set to dry the travelers. All agreed it was best that as few learn about the fog as possible. With that in mind, Uslo ordered a cup of wine be given to every man and woman at sundown, 'to warm their spirits.' The officers had gone with the story that they'd stopped the caravan early for an overdue reprieve, and as far as Uslo was concerned, that meant drinking. If the acting quartermaster had any objections, she gave them no voice, not even when one cup inevitably turned to several.

Despite there being no cause for festivities – the opposite, in fact – and in spite of his long-standing estrangement from alcohol, Sir Guilliver realized he was having fun. He spent most of the evening sitting with Xavire and other Claws, half-listening to a drunken Nokrag regale the Claws with the grand feats of her clan. The ogre's character was almost unrecognizable once drink passed her lips, her serious measure swept aside by a boisterous brag, one whose loudness was matched only by her wit. It was all so absurd. Supplies were lower than ever. They had no idea how much longer remained until they reached their destination, nor what exactly they'd find there. And yet, for all that, there was an air of celebration in the camp. Perhaps the discovery of the road cheered people more than Sir Guilliver had realized, or perhaps the wine was just that good. Perhaps the explanation was simpler still: they were celebrating because they needed to.

Sometime past midnight, Sir Guilliver's curiosity won out. Filling a cup, he went to find the Lady Alea. The easterner was sitting alone on the other side of the road, warming her hands by a small fire, her staff resting against her shoulder. She looked up at his approach, doubtless warned by the soft grumble of horses as he slipped past the wagons.

"Good evening, my Lady!"

"And to you, Sir Guilliver." Her hood was back, and in the flickering light of the fire, he saw an eyebrow rise. "If it pleases you to simply call me 'Alea.' I no longer have titles."

"Then I would ask you call me 'Guilliver,' for these days I am likewise innominate."

She nodded.

"I asked that Plains lad where I could find you," he continued. "He thought you might be here."

"Fillam?"

"No, the other one."

Alea nodded again, her face remaining impassive. "Is there something I can help you with, Guilliver?"

Sir Guilliver blinked. He had a purpose, of course, but he hadn't intended on coming right out with it. Staring at her for several seconds, he tried to recall the pretext to his plan. Then he remembered the wine cup in his hand.

"I brought this for you." He held it out.

A smile formed on Alea's lips. Only her lips. "Thank you." She took the proffered cup and waited as Sir Guilliver sat himself across the fire.

"It's the last of the wine, I'll have you know."

"Glad to hear it. Not partaking, yourself?"

He shook his head. "Not for many years."

She nodded. Though he had no qualms about explaining his relationship to alcohol, he was all the same grateful for her not asking. Enjoyment of the taste was certainly not the issue, and his mouth watered slightly as he watched her take a sip. Alea's eyes widened as the wine hit her tongue. She gave a soft hum in her throat.

"Good?"

"Yes," she said. She sipped again and sighed. "Very good."

Over on the road, one of the horses was nickering. They looked over. A pair of Ardovikian women moved from wagon to wagon, checking the reins and straps, putting handfuls of straw in the animals' nose bags. Save for scraps, they no longer had anything better to give them, and they couldn't afford to risk setting them loose among the hills at night. But the horses seemed grateful, chomping happily while their bonds were adjusted as needed.

Alea said a greeting. The women murmured quietly back and moved on.

"How can I help you, Guilliver?" she asked, no longer meeting his eye. She was, he realized, as suspicious of him as he of her. Of what he was about to say next.

"I would like to ask you something and – forgive me, Alea – I would like you to be honest."

"If your question is about the road, I already gave an answer, and it was an honest one, whether you liked it or not."

"Fine. I accept that answer as honest. But don't pretend you've been completely straight with us on every question. I'm not saying you've lied – and I'm not saying for certain that you haven't, either."

Alea's eyes flicked to him briefly, her nostrils flared in anger.

Shouldn't have said that last bit, thought Sir Guilliver.

"All I meant is I suspect there are gaps in your answers. Intentional gaps." Sir Guilliver thought perhaps her lips tightened – otherwise, her expression was impassive once more.

"I know that you won't tell us where our reward is, or even really *what* it is, beyond the tenuous suggestions of some Ardovikian legend."

Alea's eyebrows rose slightly.

"Yes, Uslo told us the story back in Darvled's Town. The one about the hunter chasing a ghost or some such. He believes it describes a Primovantian trove, undisturbed artifacts from before Ardovikia was flooded by Winter's ice. Having heard the story, I can't see why he would think that at all – the tale was vague at best. Yet he is convinced."

Sir Guilliver leaned forward. He waited for her to meet his eye before speaking again.

"Did you know that's what he thinks?"

"Yes."

Sir Guilliver nodded. "Is that because you told him so?"

"No."

Although this surprised him, he believed her. "And what exactly *did* you tell him?"

"I informed Dargent that the Plainsmen could lead the Claws to the valley in the story of Eranie the huntress. Once there, he could explore the underground caves and take whatever he found for his own. Whether or not he will find relics from Primovantor, I do not know, but it is plausible."

"All in exchange for us getting the Plainsmen across the Wall."

Alea said nothing. She continued to look into the fire.

"Uslo is very... content, right now. All except for the mist up ahead, I mean." Sir Guilliver paused long enough to shake the unwelcome thought from his mind. "And it's not just that we've entered the hills, where he no doubt thinks we'll come across the valley with the underground caves described in the legend. It was the road that most uplifted his spirit."

"I would have thought everyone pleased to be on level roadway," she answered.

"Not like Uslo."

Alea shook her head. "I cannot speak to that, nor to the origin of his convictions. I can say, however, that it has seemed to me that the general felt this tale was in some way corroborated, or that it corroborated something else. Perhaps you should ask him."

"Perhaps I will." Sir Guilliver leaned forward. "Because wherever we're going to, it isn't the valley from the Ardovikian legend."

She looked up at him sharply. "What?"

"Alea... the Ardovikians didn't lead us along the coast, you did. It was obvious that most of them had never stood on a beach in their lives. Nor did they lead us to these hills. I saw the confusion as we approached them, I saw you convincing the reluctant elders. And the road – well, the road was the clearest sign of all. They were alarmed by it. Not a one among them welcomed it, never mind *expected* it."

Alea made no move as he spoke, gave not the slightest reaction. All the same, in that moment Sir Guilliver knew he was right.

"The Plainsmen don't know this area, and they don't know where we're going. The same cannot be said for you, Alea."

"What do you expect me to say?"

Sir Guilliver shrugged and scratched his chin. "Not sure I expect anything, really. Maybe you'll deny it, or maybe you'll come clean. Don't worry, though. I know I asked you for honesty, but it doesn't matter either way." He stood up slowly, legs protesting from a day in the saddle, and looked at her. "You are a good person, Alea. Xavire told me you were a Devoted of the Brotherhood? Their honor is without peer, as is their duty toward the *good* of this world. Whatever you did, whatever lies you've told or truths you've bent, you did it to help some of the most unfortunate souls this side of Tragar. What's more, you did it without hope of any reward that I can make out. You've used us in the process, of course, but there's not much to be done about that now."

Alea's eyes were wide in surprise. "Sir Guilliver, I–"

"For now I'll trust that you're leading us to somewhere close by which fulfills your deal with Uslo, even if it's not quite the place you claimed it would be. But know this. If you aren't – if your plan is to string us along, far beyond these hills – then the moment the Mammoth Steppe is in sight, I will make certain that we part company. You'll no longer have the Claws at your disposal."

"I see..." Alea looked down for a moment. Then she stood up slowly and met his gaze. "Thank you."

Sir Guilliver smiled and gave a dismissive wave of his hand. "Ah, come now. I was a knight once. I have a soft spot for noble causes, and they rarely come without an ignoble clause or two to muddy the water."

"Even so, I thank you."

"You're welcome." Sir Guilliver looked at her. She was smiling. With a self-consciousness he'd thought relegated to his youth, he bowed lightly.

"I will leave you. Sleep well, Alea."

"And you, Guilliver."

This time, the smile reached her eyes.

Walking back through the still reveling Claws, Sir Guilliver gave himself a quick shake. It was time to rejoin his scouts. As he made for his horse, he saw that the rest of the Claws had begun to flag, Nokrag having called it a night and stoppered what seemed to be a bottomless source of entertaining tales. The bonds among his fellow mercenaries felt strong, reaffirmed in the way only merriment can provide. However, as he rode out into the northern gloom, something nagged at him. Some flaw in the picture. It wasn't until he looked on the fearful mists again that he realized what it was.

The Ardovikians hadn't joined in. They hadn't drunk the wine.

*****

When consciousness returned, Xavire was aware of two things. The first was that he was dreaming; the second, that someone was shaking him. Peris's voice reached him.

"Xavire. Wake up. The general is asking for you... We have a problem."

Tension snaked along resting limbs. *The mist*, he thought. *That must be it. We're back in the mist*. For once, his dream had been a pleasant one – perhaps a little too pleasant. Alea's face dissolved before his mind's eye. Fishing out his glasses, Xavire sat up as sharply as his body would allow. He looked around, rapid blinks fighting back sleep. Blue-gray lay across the campsite, confirming his fears – but no, it was only the dim light of dawn. There was no fog, and not even the incessant drizzle of rain remained from the day before. The air was clear.

"What problem..." he managed, one hand at his temple. His head thudded dully with the threat of a hangover. When would he learn not to drink wine on an empty stomach?

"It's the Plainsmen," said Peris. Xavire turned to look at the sergeant, who was still squatting next to him.

"What about them?"

"They've been stealing," Peris said quietly.

"...Come again?" said Xavire, matching his volume.

"They've taken horses. Supplies, too."

Xavire twisted around, looking along the line of stationary wagons. Around half were missing their animals, and the cargoes of several open-topped carts were notably depleted. He was stunned.

Alea, he thought. *Did she do this?* He stood up carelessly. Peris rose with him, holding an arm to brace his ascent. His stern grip made it seem more like criticism than assistance – Xavire wouldn't have expected it to be otherwise.

"Did anyone see them do it? Where did they go?"

"Nowhere, yet."

Xavire looked at him questioningly. Without a word, Peris guided him in a turn until he was facing south. The Ardovikians – all three thousand of them, it seemed – were gathered in a mass beyond the last wagon. Three dozen horses were among them, improvised saddles in the various stages of being fixed across the animals' backs. They appeared to have been built from the cannibalized collars, reins, and girths of the now horseless wagons, and were loaded with supplies. The Plainsmen stood ready to leave, seemingly indifferent to any attention from the waking Claws. But they weren't gone yet. They were waiting.

"They did it in the night. The sentries saw them, but assumed they were just getting on with their duties. Only when they saw those harnesses being put on did one of them get suspicious enough to wake me."

"Does the general know?"

"Look there," answered Peris. He pointed to a huddle near the Ardovikians. Xavire saw Uslo among them, engaged in intense discussion with Alea and a number of elders. "I went to him first. He told me not to wake anyone but you. Doesn't want whatever this is to get out of hand." Peris let go of Xavire's arm. "Although it's a bit late for that."

"What do you mean?"

"Everyone's waking up."

He was right. Across the tract of ground, packed together around the smoking ash beds of the bonfires, the men of the Claws were groggily getting to their feet. Already Xavire could see the confusion on their faces, some looking over at the emaciated wagon train, others at the gathered Plainsmen. Those still sleeping were being shunted awake by comrades, and a babble of voices began to build, pregnant with anger.

"Damn it," muttered Xavire. "Gods damn it all." He looked to Peris. "Alright. Find Sergeant Eumenes. Keep the men in order. Any that step out of line will be flogged. I'll swing the leather myself."

"Aye!" snapped Peris. There had never been a flogging in the Claws – withholding wages typically proved sufficient, both as punishment and disincentive – but Peris was ex-Valentican military. Old guard. Walking quickly to join Uslo, Xavire wasn't sure which disturbed him more – the prospect of holding the whip, or the eager approval in Peris's voice.

As he approached the last wagon, Xavire spotted Nokrag through a tear in the canvas. She was sitting inside. Her blunderbuss lay disassembled in her lap where she delicately wiped a strip of cloth across its parts. She looked round as he passed, asking in her familiar rumble, "Still going north?"

"That's the plan," responded Xavire, slowing. "You?"

"Yes." She spat into the cloth and resumed wiping, throwing a nod toward the ongoing dialogue between Uslo and the elders. "What is being said makes no sense."

"Is that right..." At this distance, the speakers' voices were deeply muddled in the general hum of the Plainsmen.

"Yes." Nokrag looked back at her work.

When he reached them, Alea was deep in discussion with a stern and brittle-looking elder – Xavire recognised him as Ottrid. Xavire directed himself to Uslo, stepping close and speaking as quietly as the hum permitted.

"You called for me, sir. What's going on?"

"I don't know. I can't get a clear answer."

"It looks like they want to leave?"

"It certainly does." The general sighed. He looked tired. Overnight, the shadow of stubble across his neck and jaw had crossed the fine line into becoming a beard, revealing patches of gray hair in the morning light. "I assumed this meant we'd as good as arrived, and that the Plainsmen believed their end of the bargain fulfilled. Were that the case, perhaps I could've forgiven all the supplies they've taken. But Alea says it's not. That's just about all she's said..." he grumbled.

Xavire's jaw clenched. He glanced at Alea. Watching her talk, listening to her characteristically calm tone, one might be forgiven for thinking that she was simply engaged in clearing up a minor disagreement. But the strain of breath behind the words betrayed her urgency. Elder Ottrid, for his part, looked back at her with frigid antipathy, unmoved by her appeal. All at once, Xavire realized how simple it should have been to understand the Plainsmen's speech, requiring perhaps no more than a handful of evenings spent in conversation with them for his ear to make the adjustment. But none of the Claws – not even Uslo – had made the effort.

"Lady Alea," began Xavire, "perhaps–"

She held up a hand to silence him, her talk continuing without interruption.

"Believe me, Xavire, I've tried," said Uslo. "She won't– hey, you there! Young lad!"

Uslo practically leapt away from Xavire. When he returned a moment later, his arm was around Cauhin, having managed to pull the youth from among the Ardovikian crowd with good-natured insistence. "Cauhin, son of Hunlo! How wonderful to see you!" Despite the bonhomie in the general's voice, Cauhin's face was pale, his wide eyes lacking their usual defiance and darting between Xavire and Uslo. He looked sick. "It has been too long since we last talked, my friend. But it will have to wait – now I need you to tell me what is happening, yes? Go on."

"I c-c-can't..."

"Can't hear? Come, let's take a step closer. There, that's better. But– what's wrong?"

Cauhin was shaking his head, and Xavire realized he knew. Whatever was happening, Cauhin must know all about it. After all, when Alea first approached Uslo with the proposition back at Darvled's Town, Cauhin had been there too. At the same moment of realization, Xavire recalled Cauhin's outburst during the fighting in Cadalla. Though the words were lost, he remembered the anger, most of which had been directed at Alea.

"General... Uslo–"

"Hold on, Xavire. Listen, Cauhin, just ask something for me, yes? Ask the elders if we are nearing our reward. Ask them."

Alea and Elder Ottrid had stopped talking. Both were looking at Uslo and Cauhin.

"I can't..." repeated Cauhin.

"Why not?"

"Leave the boy be, Dargent," said Alea, the words clipped to command. Uslo's brow furrowed. He let him go, and Cauhin stepped away, head down.

"Enough," said Uslo quietly. "I've been patient. My men have been patient. But no more. Someone is going to tell me what's happening."

"Really, General, how dramatic," said Alea with genuine exasperation. "There's nothing to be concerned about. If you'll allow the elders and I to finish discussing–"

"Why have they taken horses? Why do they presume to strip the wagons for parts and help themselves to our supplies? Someone better give me an answer right now!"

"Listen. I understand how it looks–"

"Do you?"

"–but I assure you," continued Alea, almost in a shout, "I am taking care of–"

"I will tell." The deep voice cut across Alea's words with finality. They turned to its source. Nokrag approached at a stride, crossbow and blunderbuss slung over her back. "This deceit bores me."

"Deceit?" repeated Uslo, confused. "What is it that you know, Warrior of Urshal?"

"Only what I overheard." Nokrag's gaze was fixed unwaveringly on Alea, her lips a hair shy of snarling. Stepping aside to accommodate the ogre, Xavire glanced back at Alea, her stance unwavering beneath Nokrag's towering glare. Even so, Xavire sensed her resignation.

"The tribe of the Plains no longer wish to follow the road. They say they are leaving these hills and will travel east into the heart of the land. The witch was trying to convince them to continue with us. She said the Plains are not safe. That is the truth – any other is deceit."

Silence followed as Uslo and Xavire processed this. Alea stared up at Nokrag, unmoving save for an eyebrow raised at her description. The elders looked on with visible lack of understanding.

We've been played. Through the suddenness of the realization, through its betrayal, Xavire found he wasn't surprised. Nothing had been as it seemed, and on some level, he'd known it all along.

"So..." said Uslo, stretching the vowel. "So. They want to go inland. Is that because the treasure is that way?"

"I did not hear mention of treasure," said Nokrag.

Uslo waved an impatient hand. "Fine. Not treasure. Our reward. The valley of legend, beneath which lay marvels. Did they mention anything like that?"

"No."

"General," said Alea finally. "It's time I explain something."

"One moment, if you please."

Too late for that now, thought Xavire.

"Nokrag, would you ask the elders if we're going the right way to the valley, the one from the legend of… what was it now… Eranie? Tell them it's the one with the underground caves."

But there was no need for Nokrag to ask. The elders had already reacted with confusion to hearing Uslo mention the name of the huntress and, despite the odd manner of their speech, Xavire had to assume some among them understood more than they let on. Their mouths dropped open, their eyes went wide. Ottrid spoke, and through the thick accent, his meaning stood clear.

"The story of Eranie is for children! It has no place! Why you would ask such a thing?!"

Stunned, Uslo turned to Alea. "How can they not know anything about their end of the bargain?"

"They do not have an end. I do."

Before Uslo could respond, Ottrid gave an accusatory and vindicated shout. The once cold dislike on his face now burned with revelation, and he gave it voice in the Plains dialect, gnarled finger pointing at Alea. Whispers snaked through the Ardovikians.

When the elder finished his rant, Nokrag explained, "They appear to have known that the witch made a bargain to buy their freedom, but not its form."

"Call me 'witch' again, ogre."

Nokrag shrugged but said nothing.

Uslo didn't appear to be listening. He was looking off into space, a closed fist against his mouth. He lowered it with a dismissive gesture. "You told me the Ardovikians knew of treasures on the Plains, that they would lead us to them. You were lying?"

"Yes. I alone."

Xavire glanced back at the Claws. The men held their weapons in hand but stayed back, watching the discussion at distance. Xavire gave silent thanks they were too far away to overhear.

"In that case, where have you been leading us?"

"To your reward."

"I… I don't…" Uslo sighed. "Are you saying that *you* know of the valley? The one the Plainsmen now say isn't real?"

"I believe that I do."

Swinging his gaze back to Alea, Xavire barely caught his voice from breaking in surprise. "What? First you admit to lying, now you say it was true?" Alea's eyes met his, her expression revealing nothing.

"Why should we believe you?"

"You believed when you thought the Plainsmen knew the way. Why not believe me now?"

"They... but, their stories..." said Uslo.

"Exactly. You're a believer in stories, Uslo Dargent. I don't mean to call you naive – not at all. I doubt the sons of Geneza can be lured by any old fable. But you believe in the power of legends, in their wisdom. I knew it before I met you, from the way Cauhin described you to me."

Uslo glanced at Cauhin. He didn't meet the general's eye. Patches of red bloomed on his otherwise blanched cheeks.

"I thought – I hoped – that you would believe the Plainsmen an honest people. And you would be right to do so. But the Plainsmen don't know of any treasure, General. Not the sort that would interest you. I allowed you to think otherwise, yes, but I never planned to cheat you. Because I *do* know a place, a location so alike the one described by Eranie's legend, that it might just be it after all. Before I heard her story, I knew it by a different name – *Keatairn*."

Astonishment lay open on Uslo's face. "What did you say?" he breathed.

Alea smiled. "So you have heard of it as well. I'm guessing your contacts were the ones who made the connection?" She stepped toward the general, lowering her voice. "If we follow this road, I believe you will find what so many have sought on the Plains for hundreds of years! Lost since the days of Primovantor!"

"And if we don't?" said Uslo.

"Then I'll remain in your debt. Until you deem it paid."

At that moment, as if conjured by her pact, three horsemen rounded a bend in the northern road, visible over the heads of the Claws. Sir Guilliver was at the fore, pushing his gelding to a fierce gallop, the clacks of iron shoes against flagstone building like oncoming hail. The men standing on the road quickly stepped off to make way.

Reaching the convoy, the riders drew to a halt. Neither the depleted wagons nor the gathered Ardovikians seemed to attract their notice, standing in their stirrups as they scanned the faces of the Claws. Sir Guilliver spotted Peris.

"Where's the general?!" he shouted.

"Over here!" yelled Uslo, stepping toward him.

The gray gelding began to move again even as Sir Guilliver's head snapped round. For a fleeting moment, Xavire misread the wild look on the Imlarian's face for alarm – were they under attack? But as Sir Guilliver cantered over to meet the general, he realized that it was something else entirely – elation.

"A settlement, sir!" blurted Sir Guilliver, horse dancing beneath him. "There's a settlement up ahead, the likes of which you won't believe!"

"Up ahead? Did you ride out further?" asked Uslo.

"Not at all! The fog had cleared by early morn–"

Xavire winced at the mention of fog, but he seemed to be the only one.

"–and when the light came over the hills…" Sir Guilliver made an expansive motion with his arms. "There it was! We mounted up and returned here immediately!"

Uslo looked up at the still-agitating knight, visibly stunned by this latest in a morning of revelations.

"It appears we are much closer to our goal than even I knew," said Alea, moving toward them. Xavire watched her as she passed, noting the relief in her smile. Though he would never dare call her a witch as such, she nevertheless seemed blessed with a magician's timing.

Uslo turned to her. "Is it?"

Alea nodded. "It must be. We're almost there."

"Almost there?!" cried Sir Guilliver. He laughed heartily. "I do beg your pardon, Alea, but we're practically on top of it!"

*****

Not thirty minutes later, Xavire finally laid eyes on their goal. It was a difficult sight to accept. The settlement seemed to share little with its surroundings except for the road, which drove straight for it like a loyal hound to its master. Embedded in the mouth of a shallow trough valley, a striking scene of symmetrical lines and architectural dominance bristled between the flanking ridges, whose sheer elevations were themselves so alike as to suggest them a product of human meddling. A stone wall, squat and sturdy, traversed the valley floor, neatly extending to the twin slopes on either side; beyond, the town stood tall, many of its buildings at least a story higher than the wall which guarded them. Xavire recalled his surprise at first seeing the road, the feeling that it didn't belong. That was nothing compared to this.

The town's gate was open, its portcullis up and doors wide. Though their approach would have been obvious to any observer, no movement could be seen along the battlements, much less in the yawning gateway. Uslo and Sir Guilliver took the cavalry ahead. Marching at the fore of the convoy, Xavire watched as the horsemen approached at a canter, finally stopping around a hundred yards short of the walls. He listened as Uslo called out in various tongues. The general even tried the simple Ardovikian greeting they had all come to learn. No response was heard.

Xavire turned to look down the depleted trail of wagons. Their column had gradually lost form as the men spread outward to get a clear view of the settlement, and neither Peris nor Eumenes were making any effort to get them back in formation, a leniency Xavire saw no reason to overturn. Beyond and obscured from his sight, the Ardovikians followed at a distance. Though Xavire could only guess as to what had changed their minds, he imagined it was the possibility of seeing the place of their legend which had ultimately swayed them. Amidst the ambiguous soup of feelings he now held for the Plainsmen, he found he was glad; for the sake of Alea, if nothing else. Turning back to the north, he watched as Uslo led his adventurers through the open gateway.

The crash of falling water grew steadily brighter, and it took until they had almost reached the square gatehouse for Xavire to discern its source. Low on the east side of the town's wall, a river gushed through a wide arch and immediately vanished, dropping into a trench not quite obscured by long grass, from which it appeared to snake its way southeast between the hills. The outlet disappeared from sight as Xavire passed the oak doors of the humble gateway, and then he stepped into the settlement. Humble became grand, a plaza some fifty yards deep and twenty across lined by the same unbroken surface of keen flagstone which had brought them here. The road resumed at the far side, rounding an eastward bend out of sight.

"What in the…!"

Xavire turned to the speaker and saw his own astonishment mirrored in Peris's face.

"Is it just me," said the sergeant, "or does it look like…" he couldn't seem to finish.

"The Ven," confirmed Xavire. "It's the spit of it!"

Valentica's Venerable Quarter, or 'the Ven' to locals, was host to among the oldest structures in the city, most dating from the latter days of the Primovantian Republic. Columns of smooth, white marble lined its buildings on the street side, black veins twisting an inscrutable journey from base to peak. Balconies ran along their top, their iron railings delicately coiled into floral shapes, and were shaded by flat roofs. Inside, their structures would center around an open courtyard with nothing but sheets of fine linen hanging in the doorways. It was an ill-fitting style even for Valentica, originating further south where presumably weather was fair all year round. This far north, however, set against a thin blue sky and with cold wind flowing freely through their form, the buildings seemed absurd.

Stunned, the two Valenticans stepped out of the convoy's path, eyes never leaving the uncanny structures that surrounded the town's entrance. They weren't the only ones taken aback by their sight, and a hum of awed voices rose from the Claws as more crossed the threshold. Approaching the nearest column, Peris removed a leather glove to place his palm against the marble.

"How?" said Peris, voice cracking. The sergeant wet his lips. "I thought everything on the Plains was destroyed by Winter and her glaciers. How did these survive?"

"Almost everything," said Xavire absently. "The cities in Rhordia came through..." He recalled what Alea had said to Uslo, a word the general appeared to recognize – Keatairn. Was that the name of this place? He would have to ask Uslo about it.

"We should keep moving," said Xavire. Behind them, the convoy was continuing to file down the boulevard.

"Hold on." Peris stepped between the columns and pulled one of the large double doors. It opened shrilly. He put his head inside. Xavire waited, eyebrow raised in question as the sergeant rejoined the convoy a minute later.

"Didn't look like it was looted," said Peris. "Just... empty. They must've abandoned it in a hurry. And they didn't have time to take everything with them, or else were so rich that the silverware wasn't worth taking."

"Who knows what else they left behind..." said Xavire, excitement sparking in his chest. They shared a look. Behind the sergeant's martial cool, Xavire saw that Peris felt it too.

As they left the plaza and followed the easterly turn of the street, the ground beneath them began a gradual downward incline. There were no longer columns on the buildings to either side, but the Primovantian theme remained prominent, with outer walls coated in the same weather-dulled stucco and balconies hemmed by coiled iron. The buildings were shorter than those in the plaza, few more than two stories high. Oak doors and thick shutters kept the north winds out, and when he looked up past the balconies, Xavire saw the overhang of slate on pitched roofs.

The road leveled out as Xavire and Peris reached Keatairn's river. Up ahead, the caravan had turned north along the adjacent street, drawn toward the tall spires of what looked to be a temple at the settlement's far side.

Xavire glanced over the river. It was held within a levee and ran a rigid line across the town, its breadth never varying along the entire stretch as it traipsed silently toward the railed drain in the town's south wall. The crashing sound of its plunge into the free wilds, heard so clearly when they had approached the town, was here muted by the thick stonework. Stepping away from the procession, Xavire clambered up onto the levee's knee-high wall. He looked upriver, and along the quarter-mile length, Xavire saw two wood-and-rope bridges projecting from the embankments. A third rope bridge hung broken on either side, its lines dragging in the current. The bricks along the inside of the levee were water-worn far above the surface level, and on the river's far side, one of the older looking structures was slightly tilted.

"Any sign of the general?" asked Peris.

"None. Wait..." Several mounted figures had appeared at the street's end where it turned west toward the temple spires. "I see him. They're signaling us to keep coming." Xavire hopped down from the levee wall. "We best get to the front."

Uslo and the trio of adventurers waited unmoving in their saddles throughout the time it took Xavire and Peris to reach them.

"What do you make of it, Xavire?" asked Uslo, his expression unreadable. Hands on hips, Xavire glanced back as he considered his answer. At the river's south end, beyond the much-reduced trail of carts and wagons, he saw the first of the Plainsmen continuing to follow. There was an evident divide between the wary elders and the more inquisitive youngsters, with the former clustered in the middle of the road as far from the buildings as possible, while the latter dashed from doorway to doorway, peering through any that opened or else pressing their faces against windows. Watching the emerging Plainsmen, it dimly occurred to Xavire that Nokrag, normally so conspicuous, was nowhere to be seen.

"It's incredible, sir," he said finally. "I'm at a loss. The hills hide the town from sight on all but the south side, I'd guess, but even then I don't understand how a settlement of this sort could exist unknown to the world."

"Not to all the world, Xavire."

"Evidently, sir." He thought of Alea. Did Xavire ever have questions for her, too. "I'd appreciate being brought up to speed on this 'Keatairn' business."

"In a moment." Uslo rubbed the back of his neck, brow furrowed in concentration. "And what of the people?"

"Seems they left in a hurry. Sometime during the orc invasion, I'd wager. Perhaps the orc hordes passed by close enough for the citizens to decide to abandon their town rather than risk being surrounded. Haven't seen any evidence of looting though. Orcs mustn't have found this place after all." He looked at Uslo. "Anyway, shouldn't I be asking you? You seemed to know what you were expecting to find. Was this it?"

Uslo glanced across the river, running his gaze along the waterfront. "Yes." He paused a moment, then reached into his saddleback to produce a hard-faced tome, its leather binding stained deep blue. Opening it to a marked page at the very back, he handed it to Xavire wordlessly.

Xavire glanced at the faded title – *On the Location and Identification of Primovantian Antiquity*, by Amulius Vespilo – and then began to read. The passage was short, an appendix covering little more than a page. Xavire finished. He read it again. Then he looked up, meeting Uslo's gaze as he handed back the tome.

"This says there's no such place," said Xavire flatly.

"It does."

"It says it's just some language... thing."

Uslo nodded.

"But you never believed that," added Xavire.

"I believed we would find a hidden settlement that was the source of many Primovantian antiquities sold throughout Pannithor, and that it would also be the site of the Ardovikian legend of Eranie and the ghost. I believed each story would explain the other, you see?" Uslo shook his head, eyes flicking apologetically to Xavire before returning across the river. "Madness, even for me. I knew only an incredible place would prove a match for such an incredible idea. And this really is... incredible."

Xavire didn't know what to say. Were it any other circumstance, any other place... dismayed wouldn't begin to cover it. But Uslo was right. This place was incredible.

There was a sound of shifting leather and boots on stone as Uslo dismounted. "Sergeant Peris, have the wagons stop here alongside the river. Then split the men into groups of ten or so. I want the whole town searched before nightfall. Start here and work your way south."

"Understood, sir," answered the sergeant. "Anything in particular we should be looking for?"

"Whatever's of interest. Foodstuffs. Wine. Gold." Uslo flashed a comradely smile, and then his expression was impassive once more. "People, too, although I doubt there's much chance of that. Make sure you check the cellars, Sergeant. Xavire, come with me. Let's see what you think of this."

They set off, Uslo leading Volonto by the reins as Xavire followed them around the river's sharp westerly bend. River and street merged after only a short distance, the waterway disappearing from sight beneath an arch to run under the uphill street.

"The people here dammed it for irrigation not far past their north wall," said Uslo. "Looks like the valley was good farmland before..." he glanced back, and Xavire raised a questioning eyebrow. "Well, you'll see."

They rounded a bend, coming up onto the flagstone of yet another broad plaza, and it was there Xavire finally beheld Keatairn's temple. Erected at the top of a nine-stepped platform, its facade of bleached stone stretched across the entire west side of the square. In its center, a ten-foot wide portal of stained glass depicted the six most revered Shining Ones: Fulgria of the White Fire; Domivar the Unyielding; Kyron of the Hunt; Fotia the Twin-Soul; Eoswain the Comet; and, above them all, Mescator, Father to Domivar and God of Justice. The remaining minor deities were shown separately, on two smaller portals below and to either side. The steeple tower, visible the moment the Claws first saw the town and throughout their journey along its riverfront, was set above the temple's northwest corner, rising to around one hundred and eighty feet high from base to spire. Above the temple's central body, a dome of weathered bronze caught the late-morning sun in its cool verdigris. Though not as grand as even the smaller cathedrals of Valentica, the temple was in every respect a remarkable structure. Had he not already come to expect as much from Keatairn, Xavire felt certain the mere sight of intricate iron embossment on the large double doors would have floored him.

"Impressive, no?" said Uslo.

Xavire had scarcely begun to respond when something caught his eye. He blinked.

"Do you see that, sir? In the door there, sticking out of it?" Without waiting for Uslo's answer, Xavire strode across the plaza and climbed the temple steps. The object, embedded right-of-center in the left door, refused to make any more sense the closer he got – only when he was standing directly before the temple threshold did its protrusion become clear.

It was an axe. Not a wood chopper's tool – a battleaxe. The head was broad, choked with rust. It was mounted on a bone handle, perhaps the femur from a young horse or cow.

Or from a man.

Mouth suddenly dry, Xavire ignored the protest issuing from his empty stomach and grasped the handle. He pulled. The handle shifted slightly at its joint to the axehead, but the weapon itself remained buried in the temple door. Whoever – whatever – had put it there was strong.

Xavire let go and turned to face Uslo, who had approached the foot of the temple steps. There was no confusion on Uslo's face, no surprise at seeing the axe.

"This is... but..." tried Xavire, to no avail.

Uslo nodded. "Seems you were right about why the people left. But there's plenty mystery yet." The general pointed to the street leaving the plaza's north end. Xavire descended the steps to get a better look.

At the end of a short avenue, the open gates of a wooden palisade marked the upper limit between town and valley farmlands. Except 'open' wasn't the right word – the gates had been torn apart, their timber splayed on the cobblestone like the fingers of a broken hand. And not just the gates, Xavire realized – on either side of the avenue, buildings stood in silent distress, their doors and windows smashed, their innards pulled out, much of them carried by rainfall into the gutters. But by far most concerning to Xavire, as he made his way mindlessly across the plaza, was the blood. Its shadow was splattered high on the stucco walls. He came closer and saw its stain on filthy garments that had gathered in the gutter. The blood was more than dark.

It was black.

*****

The adventurers returned not long after. They had followed the trails of blood and destruction that wound, seemingly at random, out from the broken gate, down alleys, and across the ground floor of homes, none reaching further than a third of the way into the settlement. What looked to have begun as looting had become a battle of sorts, and a baffling one at that. The men came across weapons, shields, even the occasional helm or strip of mangled armor. And, of course, blood. Lots of blood. Less on the open streets where exposure saw it thinned, but wherever the fighting had moved inside, the floorboards or throw rugs were thick with months-old coagulation. Its color was the black of orc and goblin races. But strangest of all were the bodies – there were none. No limbs, no bones. Not even a tooth, as Sir Guilliver put it. Of anything pointing to the involvement of men, not a trace was found.

The Claws' horsemen regathered in the temple square as Sir Guilliver gave his report. The general listened without interrupting, then, as soon as Sir Guilliver was done, he instructed that the adventurers take the wagon horses and their own mounts past the northern palisade to forage and rest. Those men not attending to the animals began to clear the debris from around the gateway and were mid-way through this task when the Plainsmen arrived.

Instinctively, Xavire looked for Alea's tall, robed form among the first Plainsmen to appear, and failing that, for the blue-and-gold shine of her staff. But he spied neither.

"Where's Alea?" he asked the nearest elder. The old woman ignored Xavire, side-stepping his approach and following her kin north toward the broken gateway. Xavire hadn't considered how the Ardovikians might react to the blood on the buildings leading up to the northern palisade – after what they'd pulled in the night, he wasn't sure he cared – but he certainly would not have expected them to be calmed by the sight. Yet it seemed they were exactly that, their whispers rising to chatter as they pointed to the dull stipples. Some even let out derisive laughs. Xavire couldn't begin to guess why.

"Has anyone seen the Lady Alea?" he tried again. No one looked his way.

"General!" It was Sir Guilliver's voice coming from beyond the palisade. Uslo was inside the temple, and unlikely to have heard the call. After a moment's hesitation, Xavire decided to check it out for himself.

"One moment, sir knight!" Slipping through the oblivious crowd of Ardovikians, Xavire stepped around the few remaining strips of debris from the broken gates and across the threshold. He cast his eyes over the new horizon. Unlike the sheer cliffs to either side of the town itself, the two-mile stretch of valley to Keatairn's north was nestled between gradual slopes, lush with the sporadic gold and green of abandoned fields and vacant pastures. He heard the gentle spill of water to the east and spotted some two-dozen yards away the broad dam Uslo had mentioned, the irrigated river disappearing beneath the earth on its journey toward the still stricter confines of the town's waterway. A wide dirt road followed the river upstream to the fields, and the Claws' horses padded about the bank, chargers and polers alike enjoying the freedom of an undisturbed forage. All the same, the adventurers kept close by, their eyes on the surrounding hills. The riddle of the blood had set the horsemen on edge. Xavire understood – discovering an orc axe in the temple door had been far from pleasant – but was ultimately unconcerned. Whatever occurred here looked to be almost a year in the past. The likelihood of death-by-orc was, it seemed to him, no greater now than before.

"What is it, Sir Guilliver?"

The Imlarian was crossing the dirt road to meet him. "Look there, Xavire." Without breaking stride, Sir Guilliver turned and pointed north. A large shape was coming down the road, rapidly closing on a half-mile's distance.

"Nokrag?" asked Xavire.

Sir Guilliver nodded and stepped up beside him. "She ran past us when we were first coming through the town. Said something about a scent. The general wanted to know when she returned."

Xavire mumbled his acknowledgement. The ogre was running at a leisurely pace, long legs propelling her almost as fast as a galloping horse. Much as he tried to resist, he couldn't help imagining an army of her kind charging toward him. It was the sort of thought that caused things to loosen. "Alright," he said finally. "I'll go get him."

*****

Inside Keatairn's temple to the Shining Ones, light from lancet windows flickered with dust before illuminating long pews, their bare wood darkened and worn. The empty rows faced toward an altar draped in gold-fringed teal, perched atop a raised circle of marble some two-foot thick and ten wide, set into the recess of an apse in the far wall. Leaving the door ajar behind him, Xavire's gaze was drawn up to the apse's semi-dome, where a grand fresco told the familiar tale of the birth of Pannithor and the arrival of the ancient Celestians, the images flowing out onto the ceiling and culminating in the shattered Fenulian Mirror directly overhead. Few would dispute that Keatairn's temple was as impressive inside as it was out – or at least would have been, in its day. Alcoves along the four walls were bare of whatever relics their plinths once held, and save for its unswept cover, the altar was bare. Since it didn't appear that the orcs had got in – not enough wanton destruction – Xavire thought it safe to assume the locals had taken their religious objects with them. Apart from the entrance, the only other door was set into the northwest corner, where it presumably led up to the belltower.

"Yes, Xavire?"

Uslo was standing before the altar, hands clasped behind his back as he looked over to Xavire. He wasn't alone.

"Sir Guilliver sends word, sir. Nokrag is coming back." Xavire's eyes stayed on Alea, and hers on his.

"Ah, good. I am eager to know what had her so animated. Let us go."

"If you do not mind, General," said Alea, "I'd have a word with Xavire."

"Suit yourselves," said Uslo, already setting off. He gave Xavire an affectionate clap on the shoulder as he passed, then shut the door behind him.

Xavire turned to look up at the portal windows above the door. The inverse image of the Shining Ones gazed past him, tinted frames morphing the clear sky beyond into a profusion of color. "The Plainsmen still plan on leaving today, I take it?"

"Yes." Alea's voice was buoyed with resonance from the temple's acoustics. "I tried to persuade the elders that they should stay here a few nights at least, but they're eager to depart the hills."

"You'll go with them."

"Where else would I go?"

Xavire turned, meeting her gaze across the nave.

"I don't know. To find another cause?"

"I'm not yet finished with this one."

"No, I suppose not." Xavire pictured the trail of Ardovikians marching out onto the Plain. For some reason, the young Cauhin's face stood out most of all. "It'll be a long journey before they're safe. If they ever can be."

She said nothing, continuing to meet his gaze. He held it for a moment, then looked away, setting off around the temple walls.

"Do you think their story about that huntress is true? Do you think this is the place?"

"Stories rarely bother themselves with truth. And for the ones that do, it often doesn't turn out to be the truth we think it ought."

Xavire laughed. Its sound bounced merrily along the temple ceiling. He grinned over at Alea and saw she was smiling.

"What sort of an answer is that?"

She shrugged. "This is Keatairn, of that I'm certain. The people here sold countless Primovantian relics across Pannithor, and I think it's a safe bet they built their town atop ruins from that age. Perhaps the Plainsmen came across the town's ancestors long ago, after which this strange place found its way into one of their stories?"

Still smiling, Xavire sighed. "I thought you might say that. Doesn't answer everything, though."

"Nothing ever can."

Xavire gave a hum of acknowledgment. He reached the front of the nave and shifted his sword along his belt to sit on a pew, looking up again at the overhead tableau. It was a long time since he had been in a place of worship. Long enough that he'd forgotten how it used to make him feel. Peaceful, and small.

"General Dargent is satisfied, at any rate," said Alea, still standing atop the marble platform. "He holds our bargain fulfilled."

"Of course he does," said Xavire seriously, meeting her eye. "Uslo's not the sort of man to take prisoners out of spite. Or hold grudges. It's the last thing he'd do."

"You have great respect for him," she observed.

"I do. We all do, in the Claws. Plenty don't understand it. Including you. Don't deny it – you probably think he's a fool. But Uslo Dargent is a great man." Xavire looked up at one of the lancet windows, folding his legs and resting an arm on the back of the pew. "Even if there aren't any underground chambers full of 'marvels' like the story said – gods know, I still have my doubts – we'll carry on. We won't give up on him."

Out of the corner of his eye, Xavire saw Alea move to slowly sit next to him, felt the bench shift with her weight. "Why not?" she asked.

Xavire turned and looked into her oval face, her tanned skin dry from days of travel, her short hair windswept and greasy, her hazel eyes as fierce and exhilarating as the day they met. All at once, he was painfully aware of the space between them, the pounding in his chest. "Because Uslo would never give up on us," he answered.

Alea smiled sadly. "That's not much."

"It's everything." He could taste her breath.

Xavire stood up more sharply than he'd intended. "In any case, I'll be sorry to see you go," he said with a glance toward the temple doors. "Would be a shame to face those… 'things' again without you there to… well, you know."

"Oh, I wouldn't worry about that," she said, standing slowly and brushing a hand over the back of her robes. "I don't believe the mists will let them through again for a long time."

"That's not what you said before."

Alea shrugged. "Call it a feeling. The nightmares should stop, too – most likely for the rest of your life. But if they do come back, best take it as a sign."

"To do what?"

"To get far away from wherever it is you find yourself." Alea placed a hand on his arm and squeezed. Then she began to make her way toward the temple doors. After a moment, Xavire followed.

*****

Nokrag found evidence of the orcs all throughout the northern valley. First, it seemed the greenskins had attacked, destroying farmhouses and burning fields; then they had fled, their arms and armor scattered among the wild-growing crop much as they were in Keatairn's alleys; as in the town, there were no bodies. Such information was of secondary concern, if indeed it provoked any concern at all. A little while earlier, Sergeant Eumenes had offered tersely that the fight occurred between the orcs themselves, after which the victors simply ate the vanquished. Given the well-known orcish tendency to eat their foes, Xavire thought it plausible. Regardless, it seemed certain both that the orcs had run into a bad time, and that they weren't here now – that was enough.

Of greater interest was Nokrag's discovery of a pastoral trail at the valley's end, by which they could leave the Ballamor Hills and get back onto the open plain within the day. Not to the Claws, of course, who had come as far north as they ever intended, but to the Plainsmen, who immediately prepared for their departure. Whether or not this was the valley of Eranie and the ghost didn't matter; there was no appetite among the clans to stay a minute longer than necessary in this mysterious and deserted town.

Alea, Nokrag, Uslo, and Xavire had gathered outside the northern palisade to watch as the procession of Plainsmen set off in good spirits past the broken gates and out into the valley. To watch, and to say farewell.

"You are sure you won't stay with us a while, at least?" said Uslo to Nokrag, having failed to formally recruit the ogress into the Claws. "If we find our bounty here, you've more than earned a handsome share."

"I will say again that it is tempting, General Dargent. But no. My purpose is in the north. I will go with the Ardovikians."

"In that case, it has been an honor, Warrior of Urshal. I hope our paths cross again – though never our swords." Uslo bowed low. Nokrag waited, exchanged a nod with both the general and Xavire, and joined the Ardovikians.

Uslo turned to face Alea. They looked at each other in silence for several moments. The general opened his mouth to say something, appeared to think better of it, and bowed again.

"May the Ones light your path," he said as he straightened up.

Alea nodded. "And yours, General."

Uslo left, heading back through the gateway into Keatairn.

"Well," said Xavire awkwardly. He took a breath, and sighed. Then he let out a laugh. "I'm not sure what's left to say."

Alea smiled. "Then say nothing." She raised her hand to his cheek. "You're a good man, Xavire. Too good to be a sellsword. The wound in your heart blinds you, but I hope one day you see it."

Xavire was stunned. *I never told her about my past*, he thought desperately. *She can't know.*

Reaching behind his head, Alea pulled him forward and placed a firm kiss on his forehead.

"And you need a new hat," she added, tussling his hair and flashing a playful grin. It dawned on Xavire that he'd never wondered about Alea's age, having simply accepted the seniority suggested by her gravitas; yet he now felt an inexplicable certainty that she was no older than he.

Before Xavire could think what to say, Alea had stepped away, pulling up her cowl and plunging into the stream of Plainsmen. She was too tall to disappear completely, and the red globe at the top of her staff bobbed alongside her hooded head, shimmering as it caught the sun.

Xavire shook his head and sighed. As he turned to go, he spotted Cauhin's tangle of red hair at the edge of the procession. He called to the lad, who stopped, looking over at him with wide eyes.

"Fair journey! Stay safe out there!"

The young Plainsman frowned. "…Thanks," he said flatly. Then he set off, his pace quickened.

Xavire watched him go. Then he shrugged.

His stomach growled as he headed back into Keatairn. No more work today. Time he got something to eat. Perhaps, if he felt so inclined, he might even get a little sleep.

*****

The pastoral trail only went so far into the hills, weaving between sheltered meadows grown fat with herbage. One was covered with apple trees, their fruit small and bitter. It wasn't long before the Plainsmen had no choice but to leave the meandering path and attempt to find a way past the steep scree dividing them from open plain. They no longer had wagons or carts to worry about, but the horses posed a problem. Some suggested that the animals be left behind and their cargo divided among the Plainsmen. In the end however, Nokrag was able to find a suitable, if narrow, route, and the procession of three thousand continued with horses in tow.

Cauhin walked slowly, Fillam matching his pace. The pair stopped often during the course of the some four hour trek, by turns sitting on outcropping rocks or foraging wild berries as their kin trudged past, until eventually they fell in with the rear of the column, where Riuen conscripted them into helping guide the pack animals. So it was that the two youths were the last of the Ardovikians to reach the final crest of the final hill, last to see what came next. They stopped to take a breath, wiping berry-stained fingers on their tunics as they looked out across the Shadow Lands.

The dead rest poorly in the Shadow Lands. That was the sum of his mother's response when a younger Cauhin asked her about the expanse of country in Ardovikia's northwest. The soil disturbs them. Adults would often tell children that if they didn't sleep still, if they tossed and turned and woke their parents, the Shadow Lands would prepare a bed for them. Fighting his instinct to fidget beneath the family's bear pelt, the young Cauhin would conjure visions of a land untouched by sunlight, where spindly trees would creak and groan in the wind, and where the ground would open beneath his feet to pull him into endless, sleepless black.

But the Shadow Lands looked nothing like his childhood conjurings. Rather, the landscape spread before them was simply the Plains he'd always known, with boundless open grassland, unbroken save for the patches of shrub clustering behind dips and rolls in the earth, their roots submerged in bog. From the base of the hill, the caravan of Plainsmen stretched out northward, fleet of foot once more atop the familiar ground and eager to put the hills in their wake. Casting his gaze across the green horizon, Cauhin recalled the ambivalence he had felt weeks ago upon first seeing the sea. Now he understood why. The Ardovikian Plains were his sea, he needed no other. Uslo Dargent could keep his floating city.

Nokrag was sitting among the grass a short distance from the column, apparently waiting for the Plainsmen to emerge over the crest. Cauhin waved, signaling that they were the last. She raised a hand in response and stood up. There had been no further mention of their argument outside the fishing village. Cauhin breathed deep, the familiar sedgy scent of the open plain filling him with confidence. He planned to talk to her later and finally ask her to teach him. Teach him to be a warrior. To fight. He had made his decision long ago. At the inevitable parting of ways, Cauhin wanted Nokrag to take him with her.

"Ouch!"

Fillam had clapped him on the arm, and Cauhin grinned, raising his fists as he turned to get revenge. But although Fillam's arms were up, they were grasping rather than punching. Cauhin caught hold of them by the wrists. His friend's face had gone starkly white, his mouth flapping wordlessly. Cauhin felt a surge of apprehension.

"What..."

He saw it. Far on the southeast horizon, a dark shape crept across the Plain, rippling forward like tiny hairs on the back of a black caterpillar. Neither he nor Fillam had seen anything like it. But both knew. They knew as if their ancestors were there to whisper it in their ears.

Fillam's voice returned. "I'll go get Lady Alea!" he cried, and he bolted down the hill, giving wide berth to the horses still making their descent. Cauhin, wondering why he hadn't spotted the shape sooner, stared after him dumbly. He saw the Plainsmen call out as Fillam dashed by, heard his friend shout the one word they feared above all others.

"Orcs! ORCS!"

The Ardovikians stopped dead. Families grabbed hold of one another. The few weapons in their possession were drawn. But though they cast about in all directions, none save those on the hillside could see the horde.

Cauhin's eyes returned to the distant shape. Orcs. The things that destroyed his tribe. That murdered his parents. With hands balled tight at his sides, Cauhin lost track of how long he stood there. He didn't notice the caravan begin to move again, quicker than before. He didn't notice Riuen coming back up the slope to get him.

The Plainsman placed a hand on his shoulder. "Let's go, lad. No need to worry. The greenskins are heading toward the hills. Long as we keep on, they won't even know we were here."

"The hills..." mumbled Cauhin. He looked up into Riuen's stony features, rigid frame around kind eyes.

"Cauhin!" It was Fillam. His friend ran breathlessly back up the slope. Cauhin spotted Nokrag beyond him, her hand raised against the sun as she contemplated the distant horde.

"I'm fine!" Cauhin called, finally coaxing some movement from his legs. He set off toward Fillam. "It's alright, I'm coming!"

But Fillam kept running up the hill, shaking his head. "...can't... nowhere..." he gasped.

"Woah there, Fillam!" said Riuen, "No need to–"

"She's gone!" Fillam cried, stopping to hunch over his knees, sweat dripping from his brow. "No one's seen... must've..." he fought for air, "...must've fallen behind!"

"Who?" asked Riuen.

"Lady Alea!"

Cauhin was already remounting the hill, dashing up to the crest and looking out beyond. All was still, gray scree and thicket. There was nobody. He glanced back and shook his head. Fillam's face showed dismay, and even stony-faced Riuen appeared troubled.

She must've gone back, he thought. Cauhin scanned the southwest hills, willing his eyes to find Keatairn, but from here, the town lay hidden in its valley. Alea wouldn't be lost, wouldn't be anywhere she didn't choose. She must have a purpose. Did that mean she already knew about the orcs? Cauhin couldn't see how – the horde had only just come into view. She couldn't have gone back to warn them. Which meant that…

"The orcs will kill them," said Cauhin, the words seeming to spill over his bottom lip in a low monotone.

"The southern men are strong fighters, lad, you can't know that they–"

"There're too many! They'll all be killed!"

Without so much as a backward glance, Cauhin set off into the hills at a run. He heard Riuen shouting after him, but his words were overwhelmed by the pounding of blood in Cauhin's ears. Ignoring the gradual and winding trail they'd used to guide the horses, he bounded down sheer drops, knees braced as he rode the shifting earth.

I have to get back! I have to warn–!

Suddenly, Cauhin's legs were knocked out from under him. Flung backward, he collapsed onto something. Something bony. It grabbed hold of him.

"You… can't…" Fillam wheezed into his ear. It briefly occurred to Cauhin that, having taken the brunt of his fall, Fillam must have been in a lot of pain. The thought was quickly lost in anger.

"GET OFF!" he yelled, prying Fillam's hands from around his torso. He could hear the dull thumps of footsteps rapidly approaching and hauled himself to his feet. Looking back up the slope, he saw Riuen bearing toward him. More worrying still, Nokrag was right behind. Her long and sure strides would see her outstrip a fleeing mountain goat, never mind a youth from the plain.

"You can't!" repeated Fillam, gripping Cauhin's rags by the fistful. "It's too far–"

"Someone has to warn them!" shouted Cauhin, all too aware of the unbridled panic in his voice. It was too late. He could never outrun Nokrag.

Seeing that Cauhin had stopped, his pursuers slowed their descent. He waited for them to reach him and then spoke quickly.

"I'll keep trying! You'll have to tie me up!"

"Why, Cauhin?! You don't know you can save them!" Fillam was still sitting, still holding on tightly to Cauhin's clothes.

"They'll die! Lady Alea will die! Don't you care?!" he spat, the words slick with a venom he instantly regretted.

Fillam's face went from stung to furious in an instant. "Of course I care!" he yelled, attempting to get to his feet. His legs betrayed him, causing him to let go of Cauhin and slide haltingly back onto his rear end. Cauhin felt his anger vanish. He tried to pull him up, but Fillam batted his arms aside. "Just because I don't charge off to get myself killed, doesn't mean I don't care!"

"Fillam..."

"Enough." Nokrag leaned between them. She pulled Fillam to his feet. "*I* will warn the Claws." She spoke with finality, no doubt thinking that the end of the matter.

"I'm still going." Cauhin met Nokrag's gray eyes with as much determination as he could muster.

"Don't be a fool, lad," said Riuen. "Nokrag says she'll take care of it."

"Like I said. You'll have to tie me up."

Riuen stared at him for several seconds. His eyes narrowed. "If that's how it is..." He stepped toward him. Cauhin braced, knowing he wouldn't be strong enough to break free when the Riuen got hold of him, but ready to try regardless.

"Stop."

Riuen stopped. All eyes turned to Nokrag. The ogress was still looking at Cauhin, an enormous thumb pressed against her chin as she considered.

"You are sure about this, Cauhin? Orcs will soon be spread throughout these hills. Could be we will die."

Cauhin shook his head. "Doesn't matter. I have to go. Don't ask why, because I won't answer. If anyone understands that, Nokrag, it's you."

The ogre nodded. "This is so. All right. You may come."

"But that's madness!" exclaimed Riuen, his once gravelly voice almost a screech. "He's only a lad!"

"I was told the people of your tribe are full-grown with thirteen winters." said Nokrag.

"Well, yes, but–"

"Then Cauhin has made his choice."

A heady mix of pride and excitement tumbled in Cauhin's chest. It was dashed when Fillam spoke.

"I'm coming."

"No," said Cauhin.

"I'm thirteen, too! If you can–"

"You have a family, Fillam! You can't leave them! Would you leave Rheyall without even saying goodbye?!"

Fillam opened his mouth, and Cauhin knew what he was going to say. Fillam was going to tell him that they were brothers, that he was his family, too, and Cauhin couldn't bear to hear it, not because it would change things, but because it wouldn't.

Perhaps something in his face conveyed Cauhin's plea, or perhaps Fillam sensed his answer. He said nothing.

"Cauhin's right," said Riuen. "You need to go on with the others, Fillam. Tell the elders where we've gone." Cauhin began to object but had barely uttered a sound when Riuen growled, "Don't you *dare* tell me what I can and can't do, lad! Think you're a man now, eh? Well, any man tells me what to do gets put on the ground. I'm coming with you."

"We have wasted enough time. Keep up, both of you." Nokrag set off down the slope. Riuen placed a hand on Fillam's shoulder and nodded grimly to Cauhin. He followed.

"Ouch!"

Fillam had thumped his arm. Cauhin made to tag him back, but in a flash, his target leapt forward to embrace him, almost knocking them both off their feet.

"Don't die."

"I won't," said Cauhin, hugging him back.

They parted. "And find Lady Alea." Without looking back, Fillam turned and ran back up the hill.

Lady Alea…

Jaw clenched tight and fighting tears, Cauhin watched until Fillam had disappeared over the crest. Only as he turned to follow Nokrag and Riuen did his vision finally begin to swim. He barely noticed. His mind's eye was elsewhere, subsumed by monsters – orcs pouring through Keatairn, devouring everyone in their path. The face of one victim stood out above all others, and it wasn't Lady Alea. It was a man, bearded, spectacled, amber-eyed; Xavire.

The man who had saved his life.

*****

"…and so then Lord Talgia turns to the young knight – did I mention his name? 'Jerrome' I think it was – he turns to him, and he says–"

"It's you to call, Sir Guilliver."

"…It is? Oh, yes. Escalate, I suppose."

There were groans around the table as the Imlarian dropped three silvers on the pile. Sir Guilliver, in his first time ever playing Sparthan Spearwall, had yet to lose a round. Worst of all, as far as

Xavire was concerned, was that despite their repeated explanations, he clearly had no idea how to play. Xavire watched as Sir Guilliver toyed with his coin, willing a trace of intent to reveal itself. The horseman set the pile down with a bright *clink*, eyes merry as he looked about the table.

"Now, where was I..."

Sighing, Xavire matched the bet. His cards were far from inspiring – hunter and a blade, both blue – but Sir Guilliver's luck had to break some time. Sergeant Peris, having lost most of his coin in the previous round, disengaged, as did Eumenes. Uslo hung on in there, however, allowing the third card to be flipped on the Spear.

"...but of course, there wasn't a unicorn in sight, never mind a pink one, and– what's the card?"

"Dictator," said Xavire.

Sir Guilliver let out a triumphant laugh. His hand went belatedly to his mouth, and he feigned a cough. "Oh, really? Well, I guess I'll escalate again..."

"Oh, the Abyss with this!" said Xavire, throwing his cards in as he stood up from the table. He grabbed his empty flagon. "Anyone want another?"

None did, and Xavire set off toward the cellar, moving sideways to slip past the one-hundred or so Claws currently reveling in the makeshift parlor. Though the building in Keatairn's west side didn't look like any tavern he'd ever seen, the discovery of twenty-two barrels in its cellar was enough to seal its fate. Scouring the nearby streets, the Claws had packed as many tables and chairs as they could find into the ground floor, and when that was full, they expanded the operation to the empty structures on either side. Fires were lit in hearths, stews were boiled up, flagons were filled, and the men settled in for an unforeseen second night of drinking.

He began to descend the cellar steps, but someone was coming up the other way. He moved back to let him pass. The man's eyes were fixed on the dubious stack of cups and flagons he had piled in his arms, each filled to the brim.

"Need a hand there, Higgins?"

"Not to worry, sir," Higgins responded without so much as a glance his way. "We're onto the fourth barrel. Looks to be all cider, sir."

"Gods, I hope not," mumbled Xavire, taking a moment to reassess if he truly wanted another drink. Nothing gave him a worse hangover than cider.

"Beverage, coming through! Move yourselves!" The throng parted, then swallowed the laden man.

"Watch out, chaps!" laughed a voice. "His arms are full, but Higgins's got a mean kick!"

"Too bleedin' right!"

More laughter. Xavire grinned. One more drink.

Dunking his flagon into the open barrel, Xavire looked around the low-ceilinged cellar, dimly illuminated from the top of the stairs. It was one of only six they'd found in Keatairn. In a town likely prone to flooding, Xavire thought it made sense that there were so few. Of course, that also made the prospect of finding underground caverns filled with treasure seem even less likely. Before the revelries commenced, the Claws had spent close to four hours exploring every nook and cranny of the settlement, and so far the most wondrous thing they'd found was here in this cellar.

Xavire placed his loaded flagon down with care and set about fixing the lid back on the barrel. It wasn't all bad news. The mysteriously absent people of Keatairn had left behind enough mundane items of quality – fabrics and garments, tools and cutleries – that the Claws could recoup their loss. And though Uslo was reluctant to part with it, if they found a buyer for the howitzer, they'd be in a better spot still. Obviously the Claws wouldn't be able to return south for a while. But they could cart their scavengings to the east, go somewhere like Rhordia or Letharac, and after that, find some work guarding merchant trains. Xavire thought a week of fishing and hunting ought to restore their supplies for the road. And in that time, they could continue to look for anything that might yet be hiding in Keatairn. Any secrets. As Uslo said to him, a place like this was bound to harbor a few. The general hadn't given up yet, and that was enough for Xavire.

Weaving his way back to the game, Xavire was halfway across the parlor when he heard a roar of triumph go up from the table. He arrived to find a delighted Uslo leaning across to collect his coin. Eumenes had stood up, red-faced, and was unleashing a string of Sparthan at Sir Guilliver, who for his part wore an expression of poorly-feigned innocence.

"What did I miss?"

"He was dissembling!" laughed Uslo. "He has been playing us the whole time!"

Xavire's mouth fell open. He looked at Sir Guilliver's cards. "Tower and a blade… you had nothing!"

"A mistake, I assure you," hummed the ex-knight, visibly struggling to hold back a grin. "I just can't seem to remember all the rules–"

"Liar!" barked Eumenes. The Sparthan strode off, muttering darkly.

"I think there was something about the privy mixed in there," said Uslo. "Poor chap. Beaten at his people's game. But he is on to you, Sir Guilliver! You have played before! Confess!"

"Not at all! But I am a quick study!" Sir Guilliver sighed. "How did you know I was dissembling, Uslo? I had the others fooled."

Uslo grinned and ran his thumb and forefinger along his mustache. "You should know by now, it takes more than innocent eyes and a flapping mouth to fool me."

"Tell that to the eastern woman, sir," grunted Peris. Xavire looked round at him in surprise, but behind his clipped goatee, the sergeant was smiling. Uslo laughed.

"Now, now, Peris. It's only the first day. Let's see what we turn up, eh? Keatairn may yet reward us for our troubles."

"And you think we'll find it underground, sir?"

"I do. Just like in all the best stories." The general had collected in the cards and began dealing the next round. "After all, where else were they going to put it?"

While Uslo was speaking, Xavire had noticed a figure pushing his way to their table with urgency. The light revealed Mattis's face as he reached them.

"Apologies for interrupting, sirs."

"Not at all, Mattis!" said Uslo, patting him on the arm. "Would you like to play? Pull up a chair!"

Mattis began to decline, but Peris spoke before he did. "He's still on duty, sir. Have something to report, Mattis?"

"Yes, sirs, Sergeant. We've spotted something coming down the north valley. It was… fast. I think it's the ogre."

"Nokrag?"

"I believe so, sir. It – she – was still some way distant when I left, but given the size, and the speed…"

Uslo met Xavire's eye.

"Do you think something could have happened to the Plainsmen?" asked Xavire.

"It's not impossible," said Uslo slowly. "Those villagers did tell us there were goblins in the hills. We did not see any signs of them, but…."

None spoke. Around them, the mix of laughter and drunken boasts from the Claws seemed to grow slightly more raucous. Or perhaps Xavire was simply more aware of it. Still meeting Uslo's gaze, he pushed his drink away. The general nodded.

"Sergeant Peris," began Uslo, his chair legs scraping as he stood up sharply, "close up the cellar. They've had enough for one evening. Organize lodgings before it's dark. Sir Guilliver, see how many of your adventurers are sober enough to ride and bring them to the temple square. Xavire, let's go."

Uslo, Xavire, and Mattis walked quickly, using the temple spire as a guide through the still-unfamiliar streets. The air was cool outside the hearth-warmed and stuffy parlor, and light from the evening sun cast the smattering of unburdened clouds in shades of yellow and violet. Reaching the northern plaza, they continued on past the gates of the broken palisade to join the gathered sentries, and they looked out into the valley.

"It's her," said Uslo. "No need to ready your weapons." There were murmurs of agreement from the sentries as they returned bolts to quivers. Nokrag was running even harder than when Xavire last saw her approach and had already crossed more than half the distance from the valley's end. There was something about her shape that didn't make sense. Xavire squinted.

Is she carrying something? he wondered.

She was. But they wouldn't see what until she reached them minutes later, sweat bright across her brow. Taking deep breaths through large nostrils, Nokrag squatted down to let two figures dismount from her back.

"They did not keep up," she grumbled.

Xavire recognized one to be a hard-faced Plainsman whose name he'd never learned, and the other… he blinked in surprise.

"Cauhin?" said Uslo, stepping out to meet them.

"General Dargent!" responded the youth, rushing forward. "Is Lady Alea here?"

"Alea…" Uslo glanced back at Xavire, his eyebrows high. "Didn't she leave with you?"

"We thought so, but–"

"She did," said Xavire firmly. "I saw her."

Cauhin shook his head. "We couldn't find her. She must have come back!"

"Mattis?" said Uslo. "Could she have slipped by you?"

"I don't… I mean, of course it's possible, sir."

Possible is right, thought Xavire. The memory of Alea's face rose in his mind, amused dimples shadowed by saffron lamplight.

"Curious… well, I'm sure she'll turn up, so no need to worry yourself, young-"

"The witch is irrelevant," said Nokrag. "We did not come for her."

Uslo turned to her. He clasped his hands behind his back. "Speak, Warrior of Urshal."

*****

Things moved quickly after that. From what Nokrag had described, Uslo predicted the orcs would soon enter the Ballamor Hills south of Keatairn, the thousand-strong horde pressing over and around the arduous slopes. The result was that the flagstone road south, which had so smoothly delivered them to the settlement, and which was their only means of leading the wagons out of the hills, was likely a deathtrap. There was only one option: leave the train behind, priceless howitzer included and follow the Ardovikians north. Those Claws who were still sober were put to work emptying the wagons of whatever could be carried, while the rest were sent to dunk their heads in waters drawn from the river. In less than thirty minutes, the temple plaza was abuzz with activity as the company prepared to leave.

Watching from the top of the temple steps, Xavire felt a curious sense of connection with the people who had lived here before. They, too, must have experienced a feeling like this, he thought. This impotent anger. This loss. They didn't just leave behind their homes. They left their futures, their plans and hopes. All to an unseen enemy, as alien and uncompromising as a storm. Or a flood. It was, he supposed, the story of Ardovikia. And now they too were caught up in it, stripped not only of their wagons, but of their dreams, pecuniary though they were.

They were almost ready to move. Turning away from the square, Xavire stepped inside the temple. Though there were still hours to go before day's end, already the dip in light had put much of the interior in shadow. Xavire squinted across the nave. He knew Uslo was here, could hear his muttering amplified by the building's acoustics.

"General?"

The muttering grew louder, and he caught a snippet.

"...doesn't make sense..."

Xavire sighed through his nose. Uslo's response to Nokrag's warning had been immediate, unemotional, and perfectly pragmatic. There wasn't time for anything else. Once the cogs in the machine of their departure were set moving, however, the general had withdrawn to the temple, with instructions not to fetch him until the last moment. Xavire understood. After all they had done, all they had risked, they were to be hounded from their prize by an army of orcs.

Orcs! Hadn't the war routed them? And why here, of all places? Why now?

None of it made sense. In the end, all that could be said was that Lady Fortune had dealt them her cruelest hand yet.

"Uslo? It's time to go."

"Hold on, Xavire!"

The words were followed by the screech of stone being dragged on stone, and Xavire spotted the general emerging from one of the alcoves on the south wall. There was a deep *snap* as Uslo set the empty stone plinth down.

"What are you doing?!"

"Never mind that," Uslo gasped. "Open the doors wide, then help me carry this to the light! Quickly, Xavire!"

Uncomprehending, Xavire pulled back the double doors and ran over. Together they hauled the plinth into the center of the nave. Xavire now saw that six others were already there, set amongst the pews.

"Here, put it down."

"Why did you–"

"Look!" Uslo crouched down and blew dust off the top of the plinth before wiping with his sleeve for good measure. "Do you see it?"

Xavire did see it. A shape, delicately carved into the stone surface.

"Is that... High Primovantian?"

"It's high script, but not a word – gibberish! Either one syllable or a meaningless pair. There's a different one on each. I noticed that even though there are ten alcoves, there are only six plinths. There was no symmetry to their placement, no order that I could discern. So I looked closer and found these!" He ran his finger along the carving.

"Alright. Are they something to do with the six Shining Ones on the portal?"

Uslo shook his head. "I assumed that too, at first, given the portal. But no. If you read them phonetically in the order of their original placement, it spelled out a *sentence*, Xavire." He rattled off a string of High Primovantian, complete with declamatory baritone. "It means *Keepers of the Gate*! Do you see, Xavire! Old Vespilo was right!"

"Vespilo? You mean the scholar?"

But Uslo dashed off, practically leaping over pews to re-examine the other plinths.

"Yes. This one here... and this goes there..." He clapped his hands and let out a laugh. "That's got to be it!"

"Got to be what?" Xavire glanced back at the open doors. They shouldn't be wasting time. "Uslo–"

"The key! There's a gate in here, Xavire! If I'm right, then we'll have proven this is where Eranie hunted the ghost!" Uslo turned on the spot, running his gaze along the temple walls. "Ten alcoves, six plinths..."

"Uslo!"

"What's going on?" Sir Guilliver was standing in the doorway. "We're ready to go out here, sirs."

"The general, he's..." Xavire had no idea what to say.

"Come in, sir knight. No, wait! Fetch half-a-dozen men. Xavire, help me with this one."

Xavire shot a shrug at Sir Guilliver, then moved to assist. The sooner they tested whatever this was, the sooner they could get moving. *When it doesn't work*, he thought, *and if Uslo still won't come, then I'll drag him out of here by that Abyss-damned mustache....*

They set the plinth in the alcove to the right of the apse, pushing its base into a neat-fitting recess.

"Good. On to the next one!"

"What are you making them say?" asked Xavire.

"I'll tell you when it works," said Uslo with a wink.

Sir Guilliver led several men into the temple, Mattis among them.

Uslo moved to stand by the remaining plinths. "All right, men! Pair up and listen closely. The order needs to be just so."

Under the general's direction, they began shifting the plinths. Uslo seemed to think that a word could be formed from an uninterrupted sequence of plinths, while an empty alcove denoted the space between them. And then, what? A gate would open? It seemed a ridiculous fancy, especially with orcs only hours away. But each time Xavire heard the *snap* of stone into a recess, his excitement grew. What if Uslo was right? What if they'd found it after all?

"Hold on that last one, Xavire!" Xavire and Sir Guilliver stopped and set the final plinth down in front of its alcove. Lifting his glasses, he used his sleeve to collect the sweat from his eyebrows. When he replaced them, he saw Uslo was lifting the altar off the marble platform in the temple's apse.

"Something tells me this will be in the way," he explained. "All right. Place it!"

On the count of three, Xavire and Sir Guilliver hefted the stone. The sound of it slipping into place echoed lightly throughout the temple interior. Xavire held his breath and listened. Turning slowly, as if any sudden move might spoil it, he gazed first at the marble platform, then up at the overhead fresco.

Nothing.

"What are we expecting?" whispered Sir Guilliver.

Xavire sighed. "It doesn't matter," he said, louder than he needed to. Uslo was staring at the marble platform, arms across his chest and chin down in contemplation. "General. We have to go."

"One moment!" Uslo hissed. He put his face in hands, spoke into his palms. "Lantor… Vespilo said the name *Keatairn* came from a dialect in Lantor…" Uslo looked round, eyes wide. "Mattis?"

"Here, sir."

"You're from Lantor. What's the most obscure word for 'hunter' in your dialect? Quick, man."

"Well… that would probably be *persegit*, sir."

"I see… so if we assume… what's the word for 'path'? *Camhi*?"

"It's a bit old-fashioned sounding, sir, but yes."

"In that case, we need to swap that one, and that–"

"General!" Xavire pleaded. "Sir, we don't have time for this!"

"Last card, Xavire!" Uslo grinned at him. "If we don't flip a Royal Drakon, I'll disengage quietly!"

"Oh, I'll make it loud," muttered Xavire as he and Sir Guilliver pulled the plinth back out. This time they had to take it to the opposite end of the temple. Xavire saw that a number of Claws had gathered at the open doors, their mass slowly spilling across the threshold as more clustered in to take a look. He cursed through gritted teeth, feeling his hand begin to slip. They reached the alcove, and in a now well-practiced movement, set it in place. Mattis and his companion set theirs not three seconds after.

In that instant, Xavire knew Uslo had been right.

It began with a single, barely perceptible sound, a mechanical *click* beneath their feet. The temple floor began to vibrate. Pews buzzed against the flagstone, rattling like bones, and then the grinding started; a crunching, jarring peal of deafening proportions. Throughout the temple, hands rushed to cover ears. The marble platform was moving. Drawn by an inconceivable force, it slid back into the apse wall.

It was opening.

Entranced and with palms still pressed to his ears, Xavire crossed the nave, watching the circular platform as it disappeared inch by weighty inch. It stopped as he reached Uslo's side, a deep *boom* emanating from below. Xavire lowered his hands.

The passageway was ten-foot wide and lined with broad steps, the stones sagging in the middle from decades of use. Though its darkness was total, there could be no doubt that the passage ran deep. They could smell it.

"Uslo... Sir..."

"Yes, Xavire?"

He met the general's eye. "What did you write with the plinths?"

Uslo grinned. "I wrote 'Path of the Huntress'."

The murmur of many voices alerted Xavire to the rest of the Claws. They had begun to gather behind them, peering into the passage, news of it quickly spreading back through the men. From the sounds reverberating inside the temple, it seemed damn-near every soldier in the Claws was within its walls. He could even see Nokrag's unmistakable form standing in the entranceway.

"The cave from Eranie's legend," said Xavire weakly. "Sir, you found it."

"No, Xavire," said Uslo, grabbing hold of his shoulders. "*We* found it! We found our treasure!"

Uslo's words were like a spell. Xavire felt its power reach into him, delivering a cocktail of clarity and lust that sent a shiver down his spine.

Our treasure...

The words echoed among the Claws, igniting elation and greed.

"Our treasure!" repeated Uslo, facing the men. "It is here! What say you, my Claws? Will you take it? Will you fight for it?!"

"Fight! Fight! Fight! Fight!" The chant roared up from the men, seeming to buffet against the fresco ceiling which returned it in a choral frenzy. "FIGHT! FIGHT! FIGHT! FIGHT! YEEEEAAA–"

Their chorus broke into a cheer, and a sea of swords and daggers were thrust into the air. Uslo grinned at Xavire, and he grinned back. They would not run. They would not flee before the orcs. Dargent's Claws would dig in.

They would fight.

14

...In a flash of inspiration, your humble servant recalled the middle-Ice-Era term for a portcullis – 'geata'. Assuming a minor degradation of the word and appending the 'irn' suffix, one arrives at a tantalizing possibility – 'Keatairn' is not a place, but rather a person, a 'gatekeeper' to be precise, itself a word often used to describe the criminally corrupt...

Vespilo A., *On the Location and Identification of Primovantian Antiquity,* Appendix IX *'From the Gatekeepers'* - *The Mystery of Keatairn*

The sun was low by the time Orod first saw the hills through his waking eyes. From the flatland of the plains they rose, steep and steadfast, ranging the entire horizon from north to south. Like a wall around the world. Like a cage. He pushed on, and as his horde reached the nearest of the scree-strewn slopes, the departing light cast the western sky in a blaze of orange. The hills were burning, just as they had in his dreams.

They left the carts behind. Even the war drums were soon abandoned. The hills gave no passage willingly, and the horde had to fight for every step, by turns hacking through dense and thorny thickets or braving the treacherous slopes. Twice they were stopped as the ground moved beneath them, rockslides dragging scores of orcs and gores into hidden ravines. While there were no clouds to blunt the full moon, it was little compensation for the lack of daylight. Many wondered aloud if they shouldn't wait for morning. But their krudger would not stop. Here was a power to break the world. It seemed to infuse the air around him, calling him forward, binding his every thought. He was close.

Deep in the heart of night, slick with sweat and muscles flaring with the effort, Orod crested a final, perennial-choked ridge – and he saw it. The settlement cowered behind stonework, infesting the maw of a sheer-sided valley. A road ran up to it from the south, while a trickling river seemed to weep through a grate in the wall, its shallow waters winding southeast down the web of ravines. There were no lights in the windows of the buildings, no torches along the ramparts. It was silent.

The krudger grinned. He had found it. The final cage. His orcs would consume, burn, raze this place to the earth. They would dig through the bones of civilization to find what it had imprisoned beneath, and he, Orodrazk, would unleash its power. This was where the Age of

Orcs would begin.

But first his horde would have to reach it, and crossing the river proved more difficult than expected. The soil of its sharp embankments was wet and loose. It seemed the waters were running shallower than usual. Orod was first to cross, and as his column of orcs navigated the ridge and trudged over the silted trench, he stood alone on the stone road, gazing hungrily at the settlement. Its gates were open. Obsession corralled the krudger's thoughts, and yet, from within its enclosure, he began to wonder.

Labored breathing revealed the Godspeaker's approach.

"Can you feel it, Godspeaker?" said Orod without turning. "The power?"

"I can, Krudger Orod." Arlok's voice seemed to slither through the dark.

"Describe it."

"…What?"

"The power. Describe it to me."

It was a moment before Arlok spoke. "It will… unleash a wildfire. Mighty warriors will gather from across the world, enough to tear down the noble peoples. But surely you know this as well as I, Krudger. The gods themselves have shown you the way."

Orod laughed. "That's true. Although the answer makes another question." He turned, and in the moonlight saw Arlok flinch.

"What question?"

Orod smiled. He set his hand on one of the axes at his hips, tracing the nail of a finger along its edge. "Since I'm guided by the gods, and since the power is now mine, why do I still need you?"

Trembling, the Godspeaker held his gaze for several seconds, the rattles of his bone headdress tickling the night air. Then he averted his eyes, hunching low over his staff. "I am yours, Doom of the World. I submit to serving as you see fit."

Orod tilted his head, weighing the display. Before he'd made up his mind however, he found his eyes drawn down to two waist-high orbs. The goblin Yip was at Arlok's side, stretching tall, its wide grin alive with lunar glow. It was gazing somewhere above Orod's shoulder. He turned to follow it and saw a great hill rising before him, taller than the rest. A trail of narrow and uneven stone steps wound its way up the nearest face.

Something about the hill gave him pause. Something to do with the way its trail cringed next to the road, the apparent aimlessness of its path. It seemed… false. As if it wanted nothing more than to be overlooked. Orod moved toward it, the Godspeaker forgotten.

Dismounting the flagstone road, he set his bare foot on the first–

Orod froze. Then he stepped back sharply, spinning to face the settlement. He could hear something, the acute snaps of metal on stone, hundreds together, rapidly building in both speed and intensity. He saw movement in the gateway.

"Humans!" he roared, drawing one of his axes. "They're attacking! Get ready!"

The horsemen let out their battle cry. Spilling through the gateway like a raging torrent, the near four-dozen riders fanned out to a v-formation, never slowing as they made for the orcs. Fewer than two hundred ax had crossed the river. None were ready. The cavalry crashed into them, swords glinting in the moonlight, momentum driving their steel to hack cleanly through flesh and hide.

"Fight! Kill them, you worms!" cried Orod, rushing toward the fray. The charged orcs scattered. Those still on the hillside began to spill down its ridge, piling into their kin as they struggled to escape the river trench. The humans never stopped moving, sweeping along the bank, felling any ax who made it out. Orod was near twenty yards distant when one of the riders gave a blast of a horn, and the horsemen pulled away as one, flowing together smoothly as they made for the gateway.

Orod dragged himself to a halt, calling, "Gores! Get after them! Don't let them get behind their wall!"

Quickly mounting their swine, the gore riders rushed down the slope, trampling orcs as they burst over the riverbank. By the time they were across, their enemy had reached the gatehouse, and the mass of black-haired boars grunted and screeched, surging after them.

Orod barked a triumphant laugh. The humans were too slow. They wouldn't be able to close the gate behind them in time.

The horsemen passed through, the timber doors of the inner gates began to swing closed. They failed. The first of the gore riders slammed into the half-shut doors, flinging them wide. Some three-hundred orcish cavalry piled around the narrow gateway, crushing together as they tried to force their way through. Crude a method as it was, it was working, the throng of the gores rapidly shrinking, draining through the open gates.

In the riverbank, stable routes were found in the silt. The trickle of ax became a stream. "Come on, get out!" called Orod, grabbing one orc by the arm and hauling her out of the trench. "Get through that gate!" The mingled ax and greatax began to steadily amass before the settlement. Moving to join them, Orod looked up and down the battlements along the length of the wall, scanning for any signs of their foe. Nothing. Over the eager shouts of his horde, he could hear fighting inside the settlement, the clash of weapons, the pained squeals of orcs and gores.

The last gore rider pushed through the gateway. Ax began to follow. Suddenly, a screech of scraping metal cut across the clamor, followed immediately by the clanking roll of a chain mechanism. With ponderous and implacable certainty, twin portcullises slammed down at each end of the gateway, crushing orcs beneath their iron spikes, trapping another twenty or so between them.

"Get it open!" called Orod, shoving his way forward. Orcs inside and out grabbed hold of the heavy wood frame, straining to raise it. It didn't budge, appearing to be locked in place.

"Don't lift, break it!"

The orcs began to chop at the barrier, their swings impeded by the growing crush as the rest of the horde continued to join them. Pushing past the surrounding ax, Orod brought his weapon down in a heedless hack. Despite the full-bodied *thunk* it produced, the krudger cursed. The wood was strong. Beyond the gateway, the sounds of fighting raged on, the orcs' roars awash with fury – they sounded impotent.

"Move! Out of my way!" The krudger pulled back from the gateway, looking along the unmanned walls. It would take too long to cut through, and longer still to assemble the gear for his orcs to climb over. He needed another way.

"Godspeaker! Where are you?! Move it, you runts! ARLOK!"

Arlok bowed low as the krudger emerged from the horde. He had barely moved since the attack began. He was shaking.

"I want that gate open!"

"Please, Krudger Orod, I'm not sure I have the strength… the journey has been hard… why not order the orcs to build– urk!"

Orod grabbed him by the throat. "Orcs don't build, Godspeaker," he growled, anger simmering in his voice. "Or did you forget? We destroy. Now break open that gate before I break your skull!"

Arlok nodded. Orod released him. Raising his staff, Arlok pointed it toward the gateway. "Your ax are too close–" he wheezed.

"NOW!"

The Godspeaker closed his eyes, and the Abyssal skull atop his staff began to emit a red glow. Orod turned. All sounds of battle had stopped. There was only the dull *thuds* of axes on timber, the restless shuffling of the waiting horde. Then all at once, the night was rent by light as the portcullis burst to flame, spitting from the gateway in a furious *whoomp*. Orcs inside and out screamed as the fire consumed them. The surrounding ax strained to pull back from its scorching heat.

Orod ran. The wood of the portcullises banged and popped, clattering to the flagstone as their frames crumpled. Burnt flesh sweetened the air. Quick as it had come, the blaze wasted away, stripped of arcane propellant. By the time Orod pushed past his orcs, the flames were gone. Their afterimage flickered against the darkness, against the smoke that swirled like fog in the stone passageway, obscuring whatever lay beyond. It was silent. Axes clasped in each hand, Orod turned to face the horde. He raised them over his head and roared.

Baying for blood, the orcs charged into the settlement.

*****

Bolirm rested a hand on his coiled slave-hook at his belt, running the cord between his fingers. Standing atop the ridge where Orod first laid eyes on the settlement, he and the other ex-slaves watched as the horde crammed through the still-smoking gateway. His skulks had been acting as rearguard during the long march from the battle in the east and had finally crested the rise just in time to witness the Godspeaker's magic. Bolirm squatted down, eyes narrowing as he peered over the wall at the moonlit buildings beyond.

He was surprised to see a settlement out here. There had been plenty in the lands surrounding the last battlefield, towns ripe with plunder and lacking any defense, now that the humans' armies were crushed. They could've spent many moons ransacking the region, hunting all who tried to evade the orcs' hunger. But the krudger had marched them west and brought only what they'd pillaged from the human camp – plenty enough to keep them fed, of course. But not to sate them. Flush lands had given way to barren, to a rough and featureless expanse not much different to the Steppe. Occasionally they'd spotted some vestige of civilized races, perhaps a strip of roadway and a rotting line of fence, or the skeletal remains of ravaged hovels, always overgrown. They had even passed a crumbling tower, its stonework blackened by flame. The sight of it had stirred something in his gut, an irresistible, blood-borne intuition. For all the emptiness around the tower, its damage was surely no more than a year old. It was like a marker, filling his mind with its psychic scent. Other orcs had been there.

Bolirm had wanted to get away. To leave the horde. Being rearguard meant the opportunity was there, and it seemed a safe bet Orod would care about as much as he had when the goblins split off. But still he sensed the other ex-slaves would not follow him. For whatever reason, they remained loyal to the krudger. Now, however, as they watched silently from the hilltop, Bolirm thought he could finally detect a fissure forming.

"A trap..." said one. There were murmurs of agreement from the others. Bolirm said nothing. All could see the scores of dead orcs along the riverbank. He waited.

"Humans knew we was comin'," said another. "They was ready."

"Orod's gone in. He gotta have a plan..."

Silence. Bolirm stood up slowly. He rolled his shoulders, producing a run of clicks in the joints. Their eyes were on him. He could feel them.

Turning his gaze from the settlement, he pointed to the cliffs that overlooked it from the east. The valley hills seemed to provide a natural barricade, and few of its slopes appeared trickier than those directly to either side of the town. It would be arduous, doubly so in the dark. But they'd dealt with worse.

"We're goin' to climb that," said Bolirm, loud and firm despite the smog-scarring of his voice. "We'll get around the humans. Hit them from behind."

Muscles braced in his arms, ready to round on any who voiced dissent. He turned to look. Across the narrow hilltop, close to one hundred and sixty orcs looked back, their faces impassive. The brands on their jaws shone pale in the moonlight. None spoke. Then the smog-scarred orc gave a nod. One by one, they began to move down the ridge, circling toward the ravine that separated them from the cliff face.

The time was coming. They were almost his. Bolirm restrained his smirk as he joined the procession.

*****

The krudger didn't take a breath as he passed through the gateway, the call to charge unceasing in his throat. His blood was up, its hateful fire consuming him. The humans were trying to stop him. They wanted to lock his destiny away, to return him to his chains. *He would kill them*. Dark shapes loomed in the smoke, orc and lumber charred beyond distinction. He leapt over. The stone was hot beneath his bare feet.

The first orcs burst from the smoldering passageway. Moonlight stung their eyes, their feet coming upon unexpected ground, strange obstacles in their path. But there was no slowing down, the push of the horde at their backs was relentless. They were spilling into a broad space, flanked by long and open buildings. Drawing on air rank with the stink of gore, Orod's gaze snapped to a group of figures at the far side. There weren't many, six or so, watching the orcs from horseback. All at once the scene between orc and man rushed into focus. Carnage stretched out before them, the flagstone obscured beneath hundreds of bodies. No gore riders had survived.

"Humans!" roared Orod, advancing over the corpses, axehead leveled at the horsemen. The krudger's fury was redoubled, his vision reduced to a tunnel through green haze. "GET THEM!"

The ax charged. Their cries bounded against the buildings, echoing back in atrocious cacophony. Rushing ahead, Orod's muscles began to burn. He was practically wading through meat, skirting the tremendous forms of the dead and dying gores, trampling their fallen riders. Along the far side, the humans sat stock-still, their horses fretting before the oncoming tide. Only when the horde was halfway across did they turn, spurring their mounts down a wide street before quickly splitting off into two alleys.

"That way!" he yelled, the words vanishing quickly into the roar of the horde. They had seen them run. Vaulting the last of the carcasses, the orcs pounded after the humans.

In that moment, the krudger could think of nothing save the taste of red blood, the prospect of his fangs sinking into pink flesh. In the minutes to come, however, he would recall a troubling fact – of the mass of bodies beyond the gateway, none had been men.

*****

Rows of slate shimmered in the moonlight, an archipelago of yellow and green lichen spread far across their tiled sea. Working his way along the slanted surface, Sergeant Peris crouched low, one hand on the roof's ridge, the other gripping his crossbow. His quiver hung light against his hip. Almost half its bolts had already been spent.

The men ahead slowed as they reached the improvised walkway, a pair of narrow boards fixed together and set over a back street.

"Keep moving!" he hissed. Peris could hear the first of the orcs beneath them, crashing down the alleys in pursuit of Sir Guilliver. As his men moved carefully across the breach, the sergeant scanned the surrounding rooftops. Clusters of Claws, four including Peris's, stalked along the contours, following the path of the horde below. Those across the street to the east traversed their own gap, and through it the sergeant caught a glint of steel in the night. Weapons upright, the pikemen were quick-marching away from the square and down to the river and its rope bridges, their route isolated from the orcs.

A trumpet sounded in defiance of the horde's ferment. Sir Guilliver was leading them on. Somehow, despite the alarming manner in which the orcs had broken through the gateway, it was all working.

Peris's silver goatee twisted around a scowl. How typical of their luck that the orcs would have magic. And when the eastern woman had just left them, no less. There was nothing to be done about it. As always, they would just have to place their faith in the general and hope his plan would see them through. It was a familiar feeling in the life of a Claw.

The man ahead stepped onto the walkway, crossing over the back street in a pair of nimble strides. With resentful awareness of his years, Peris followed slowly, eyes level. Between their barked warcries, he could hear the orcs' grunts of exertion below, the clatter of their armor. They stank like old meat.

He reached the far side and hid the pleasant swell of relief behind a curled lip. They had mounted a long length of adjoined buildings. It would be a while before he'd have to do that again.

"Quickly! Over there!"

The Claws scrambled over to the west side and spread out. Small stacks of shingles, torn from the roof less than an hour before, were set at regular intervals. The men began to dislodge more. Peris looked to the building opposite and waited as the group there took up position.

"Steady..." He drew a breath, lifting his free arm overhead. Just as the order reached his throat, a yelp burst from the man to his left. The tile he was trying to free had suddenly come loose, and the man was toppling toward the edge. Cursing through his teeth, Peris lunged, grabbing an outstretched hand as the man's boot stepped back into night air. Legs braced on the exposed battens, the sergeant watched as the extricated slate slid over the side and out of sight. They heard it crash below.

"NOW!" he yelled.

Slate in hand, the Claws looked over the edge and began hurling them into the throng of orcs. With a groan of strain, Peris pulled the man back.

"Thank you, Sarge!" he gasped.

"Watch your footing, Higgins, for gods' sakes!"

"Yes, Sarge!"

Pained cries mingled with furious howls in the street below. Peris looked down. The sharp-edged shingles were more viciously effective than even he could've supposed, slicing through flesh or bursting heavily against helms. They couldn't miss, so tightly packed were the orcs in the enclosed street. He saw many greenskins trying to slow, craning their necks toward the source of the attack. But the horde pushed on, trampling any who wavered in its path.

Gods, he thought, *there are so many.*

Peering up the street, the sergeant could see the shingles raining down along its length. The third group were now in place at the far end, while the fourth had just about reached their spot beyond its bend, overlooking the route through which the orcs would continue to be funneled. Adjusting his crossbow to hang across his back, Peris picked up a tile from the nearest stack.

"Look sharp, Higgins! It's time to earn your pay!"

*****

The night was cold. Arms tight across his chest, Cauhin blew out a deep breath and watched as the plume passed through the belfry's lancet aperture into silver light, dispersing in the southeasterly breeze. The temple below was marginally warmer, the southerners having lighted the sconce-borne torches along its walls. But he didn't want to go down. In there, he would have nothing to do but wait for the battle's conclusion. He would lie on one of the pews, fully aware of the yawning tunnel beneath the apse, while Eranie's tale would circle his mind. He would see nothing. Here, however, atop the bell tower, he could damn-near see it all.

The southerner's horn sounded again, closer this time. Beyond, the din of the oncoming horde continued to grow in intensity, suffusing the settlement in its savagery. The Claws' archers were arranged along the edge of a distant run of rooftops, flinging indistinct objects at the street below. Although he couldn't see the orcs, Cauhin imagined them as a raging river, one that crashed against its banks, scarring the land as it surged toward its goal.

Riuen let out a gravelly sigh. Cauhin glanced round. The Plainsman was leaning against the wall. In his hands was a hideous battleaxe he had pried from the temple door, its handle fashioned from a single bone, its head rusted. Without meeting Cauhin's eye, he lifted the weapon in one hand until it was over his head, then tapped it against the bell. The dome of verdigris brass barely moved, emitting a slight and ugly chime.

"We should go."

Cauhin frowned. "Go where?"

"Away. As far as we can."

Cauhin thought for a moment. His muscles – not only in his legs, but everywhere – still ached. "You said we shouldn't leave in the dark," he said finally.

Riuen grunted a laugh. "And would you've come if I said otherwise?"

"But you didn't."

"Well, I was wrong."

Cauhin turned back to the aperture, leaning forward to rest his elbows on its cold stone. Below, in the temple square, the southern horsemen were arranged in neat rows. The horses' breaths were heavy, continual blossoms of white vapor forming between the ranks. He had watched them arrive only minutes before, trotting three-abreast from a street on the town's west side, General Dargent leading them back from their foray beyond the south wall.

Cauhin heard Riuen step across the belfry, felt him brush past to join him. There was a moment of quiet as they looked out, listening to the pitiless roars.

"I never expected to hear that sound again," said Riuen, his voice about as soft as a slow-turning grindstone.

Cauhin said nothing. He didn't know what he'd expected. About the orcs, about finding Alea. About any of it. So much had happened in the last day alone. It was too much, too many things to fit into such a small amount of time.

His gaze drifted from the temple square down the street on its eastern side, toward the wide stone bridge that spanned the river's north end. Three figures stood along it, their profiles distinct even at a distance. Nokrag and Xavire stood at the bridge's center, each with one foot on the low parapet. Dargent had not long joined them and had remained astride his warhorse. Between all three was a curious contraption, an iron tube set between a pair of large, spoked wheels. Cauhin had seen it only once before, yesterday, when the southerners were taking the wagons across a tricky ditch in the hills. They had moved it separately, and he remembered thinking that it looked something like the wide-mouthed weapon Nokrag had used at Cadalla. The one that spat thunder.

"You believe you owe something, is that it?" Riuen had followed his gaze.

"Don't we?"

"Not we. You. And you don't."

"I..." Cauhin didn't know what to say. Riuen was right. If he should feel anything, it should be that he had done his bit, fulfilled his debts to all concerned. He had come to warn them, had tried to find

Alea. No one could reasonably ask for more.

But... he hadn't really come for that, had he? Nokrag could have delivered the warning alone. He and Riuen had just slowed her down. No. There was something more he needed to do. Something he couldn't have put into words if he'd tried. It was like a word on the tip of his tongue. Only not a word. A feeling.

Cauhin's eyes were fixed on Xavire, now bent over and fiddling with the wheeled-weapon.

There was something more.

Suddenly, there was a sharp build-up of hooves on stone, and six more horsemen galloped into the square below, arriving along various streets and alleys. The one at their head he recognized as Sir Guilliver, the metal horn still clutched in one hand. While the rest fell in with their fellows in the square, the blond-maned knight carried on in the direction of the north gate, dropping his horn to cast a wide wave at the general before he disappeared from sight.

"They've finished luring the orcs," observed Cauhin.

Riuen grunted. "It'll be over soon. One way or another."

The orcs sounded closer than ever. The rooftop Claws were moving again, following the horde's flow as it rounded to the east. Cauhin wished he could see what was going to happen next, but save for the north bridge, buildings blocked the entire riverway from view. If all went well, he wouldn't get a chance to lay eyes on a live orc. The dead ones would have to do.

More sound reached him from directly below, not the chaotic clatter of horses, but the regimented clicking of boots. Cauhin peered down and saw yet more Claws filing into the square, thirty or so of the long-spear infantry. They moved smartly, weapons upright, the spearheads dulled to moonlight by a layer of blood.

Everything was in place. Drawing his ragged furs against the deepening chill, Cauhin watched.

*****

Blood sprayed across Orod's face. He slowed, momentarily blinded in one eye. A slab of shale had split the skull of the orc to his left, pitching its lifeless body beneath the rushing horde.

Something was wrong. Throughout his pursuit of the horsemen, an irresistible rage had clouded the krudger's mind, steeped it in the image of the humans charging from the gateway, of his gore riders dead. But as he quickly wiped the blinded socket against his upper arm, its frenzied fog thinned, and thoughts previously denied now raced across it. The horsemen, having fled down seemingly random and disparate routes, had reunited along this twisting road before vanishing around the last bend. There was nowhere for them to have gone – nowhere for anyone to go, in fact, save the empty street and its easterly curve. Objects cluttered the many diverging forks and alleys, crates and other constructs stacked high across their entranceway. Surging after the sound of horn blasts, the horde followed the open path that lay before them, utterly heedless of those closed to it. The overhanging roofs on either side drowned them in shadow. It was as if they were in a tunnel. Orod looked up, and all at once felt a profound recognition, one rooted in the earliest memories of his existence.

The orcs weren't chasing. They were being herded.

"Stop! Stop running, you shum-brained runts!"

The orcs in earshot tried to halt, but they were few amid the furore and quickly found themselves pressed on, the krudger included.

"I told you to stop!" he roared, emphasizing the command by slamming the pommel of his axe into the nearest maw. It was no use. They were submerged in their fury, continuing to stream past unabated. Another slab crashed over the shoulder guard of a nearby greatax, bursting in a shower of needle-sharp shards. It was Tragar all over again. He had come so far, had crossed the face of the world, only to be held by yet another web of obsidian black. Craning his neck, he looked at the humans above, their silhouettes appearing and disappearing along the narrow sliver of starlit sky. Only he didn't see men. He saw the dwarf masters, their broad and spiteful faces, their eyes red with Abyssal fire.

Orodren'val... doomed one...

"No!" he cried, axe raised in defiance. "I am 'The Doom!'"

"DOOM! DOOM! DOOM! DOOM!"

Roaring his name and gripping his axes at their shoulders, Orod rejoined the rush of chanting orcs. He had broken his chains before – he would not be caged again. As the krudger pushed his way toward the fore, the rage reclaimed him in its fog.

Rounding the lane's end, the orcs emerged into open night. As they spilled onto a wide and empty street, the horde found itself faced with a stone-banked river that cut across its path. Men were arrayed on the far side. They were standing some twenty feet from the waterway, thirty or so spanning the front rank, the full number hidden beyond. Circular shields were raised against the orcs, and moonlight played along their connected wall of brass and steel.

Orod's lips curled back, teeth bared in a snarl. Then he filled his lungs.

"Kill them!"

Bloodlust swelled in the orcs' cries. With no crossing in sight, they leapt over the stone levee, surging down the trench of sloped masonry into ankle-high waters before charging up the opposite side. The waterway was deep, its walls slick. As Orod stepped over the levee to follow, he heard the humans strike up a drum.

"Get up there! Now, scum!" Landing in the churn, the krudger pushed the orc ahead of him with his forearm. More continued to crash into the trench around him, filling it rapidly. An instinctual cohesion took hold as the ax below supported those in front, pressing them up the embankment. In seconds, the first two dozen reached the edge. The orc ahead clambered over, and Orod hooked the heel of his weapon onto the side, heaving himself up.

The humans gave a collective shout. Suddenly, no more than five feet from the river's edge, a swarm of spearheads leapt up from the flagstone. The humans shouted again as they thrust forward, the long spears impaling the orc vanguard and driving them back over the edge. Orod twisted sharply, letting the punctured warrior fall past him before leaping up onto the levee. Another shout – spearheads pounced toward him. The krudger let out a furious bark, swinging the cheek of his axe to bat them aside. An opening appeared between the staves, but as he made to charge through, he saw yet more steel leveled. There were layers of them. For each rank he passed, more spearheads would riddle his path. The humans were out of his reach.

During his split second of realization, the humans let out another of the concerted shouts. Roaring frustration, Orod defended, sweeping his weapons in desperate arcs as the spearheads thrust out. One spear glanced off the head of an axe, the deflected point nevertheless scraping across his exposed side. The pain was hot. Still swinging, Orod stepped back onto the river's levee. With a final warding hack, he turned to the teeming trench.

"Move! Get out my way!"

Despite being crammed into the depleted river, the orcs had sense enough to scramble out of the krudger's path as he jumped back down. Fewer now were joining them from the other side, the sight of the over-full trench causing them to finally resist the push of the horde behind them.

"Spread out!" called Orod, shoving orcs on either side. It didn't matter how long their spears were, the humans couldn't defend themselves from all sides. "Get around them! Crush them!"

The orcs began to spread along the trench, traipsing through the mud basin. The human drum continued to beat, not a deep pound like the war drums but a sharp, irritating *snap*. Grinding his teeth, Orod looked up at the stream of orcs coming in over the side.

"You lot, too! Why aren't you spreading up there?! Go along the road!"

"Can't do it, Krudger," responded one, standing on the embankment. "They've blocked–!" The orc's jaw fell loose, his eyes glazed. He toppled, skidding down the side before ending face down at Orod's feet. The white fletching of a bolt projected from the back of his skull.

Humans – the ones that had followed the horde from the rooftops – were gathered atop the riverside buildings. They were armed with crossbows and were launching projectiles into the green mass below.

The krudger felt his anger seethe. The humans were so few! How *dare* they challenge him!

"Go up again!" he called, dismissing the crossbows as he turned to join the flow of orcs moving north along the river trench. Those furthest ahead had to have gone beyond the spear formation by now. "Attack!"

The orcs scaled the incline, many using the downward spikes on their shields to drag themselves over. Orod heard the humans let out a shout in perfect unison as the orcs were cut down.

"Keep going! Bury them in green!" He needed to see what was happening. Pushing through the spill of ax, Orod climbed the west embankment and looked out. The roadway was indeed blocked, at least three rows of beastless carts and wagons packed tight to obstruct the orcs on either side of where they had emerged. Looking across the river, Orod saw that the human spears were expanding their formation, reducing their ranks as more stepped forward to fill the gaps. So far they were managing to keep pace with the orcs. But they couldn't do it forever, and every rank they moved to the front thinned the bristling of their spears. Orod grinned, his anger sweetened by impending triumph. The defenders numbered a little over a hundred at most. His horde was too big to be stopped by them for long.

A bolt whistled past his ear as he turned to his ax. "Faster, my ax! Into the river! We bring the humans their doom!"

"DOOM! DOOM! DOOM! DOOM!"

Already the last of his orcs were arriving, ignoring the gauntlet of crossbows as they charged the trench and leapt into the buoyed deluge of their kin. Six hundred orcs surged outward, north and south, faster than the humans could expand their line. Soon, scores of his warriors were mounting the far embankment across a vast front. Pressure built on the spears, and the krudger saw his foes begin to pull back, restoring the ranks as they formed a semi-circular defense, their drum increasing the pace of its *snaps*. Soon they would be fighting on all fronts.

It was time to break them. Hefting his axes, Orod prepared to charge back across the bare stones of the riverway.

"Now, my ax! Charge–!"

Orod's ears stung as a roaring explosion burst from the north, echoing sharply off the town's masonry. He had already stepped over the trench edge, and as he skidded haltingly to stop in its depths, the krudger looked. At the north end, just shy of what looked to be a wooden palisade set along the settlement's upper bound, he saw a stone arch bridge. A plume of gray smoke hung above it.

Blackpowder.

Drum and warcries were cut dead. As booming echoes faded into the valley, the krudger heard a rushing sound. It was coming from above. Before he so much as rolled his eyes up in their sockets, there came a *bang* of iron colliding mightily with stone. Orod cast about for any sign of the cannon's wrath. Despite the deafening impact, it seemed the shot had fallen some way from the horde.

There was a burst of deafening *cracks*. It seemed at once to sound from somewhere further down the trench and from beneath their feet, and for as much as four seconds, heavy tremors raged along the masonry; they stopped as quickly as they'd come.

In the stunned silence, the krudger looked south. His orcs choked the dry river as far as he could see. They looked back at him, twisted and toothy maws hanging open. The same question hung across their faces, hovered in the dim glints of their eyes.

What the shum was that?!

*****

Xavire uncovered his ears. His legs were locked upright, feet straining inside his boots as if to grip the bridge's stonework.

"It missed."

Uslo was behind him, resplendent in his plate, mounted atop Volonto. Incredulous, Xavire turned, air slipping from his lungs in a prolonged hiss. Through the gap in the red-bronze helm, he saw that the general's expression was as flat as his tone, save perhaps for a slight tightening of his lower lip.

"If I might beg your indulgence, sir," Xavire began, the words cracking. His throat felt dry. He swallowed quickly and tasted rather than smelled the howitzer's sulfur. "I think that a lesser concern, particularly when compared to, oh, I don't know, *the floor shaking*!"

"It was not like any earthquake I have known," said Nokrag. Her brow was drawn in deep, the rest of her features obscured in shadow as she contemplated the masonry beneath them. "It cannot be an accident that it happened after we fired."

"I'm only saying it's a pity. They're bunched up so nicely, after all."

Xavire turned back to face the horde. The greenskins who had left the trench were still engaged with Eumenes's pikes, the sergeant's drills showing as the men steadily withdrew their formation from the waterway. Those orcs still inside it seemed momentarily frozen in confusion, although that wouldn't last.

"Sir Guilliver will've heard it firing, General. I think we can at least be sure of that."

Uslo gave a mighty sigh. He ran thumb and forefinger across his mustache. "You are correct, of course, Xavire." Volonto's shoes clacked on the flagstone as the general turned him about. Then he let out a laugh. "And one cannot have it all!"

Xavire opened his mouth to give a gentle retort, but Nokrag cut him off.

"We must leave now."

Rid of their confusion, the greenskins' warcries filled the night once more. Those closest to the bridge now appeared to be charging toward it, and over the orcs' heads, Xavire saw a particularly fearsome specimen pointing his weapon at them, yelling in deep and hammering tones. He guessed it to be the warlord.

Uslo heeled Volonto toward the temple square. Lifting the howitzer's trail in both arms, Xavire prepared to wheel it off the bridge. Suddenly, one of Nokrag's giant hands snapped around it.

"I take, you go! Run!"

There was no questioning the command in her voice. Holding his sheathed blade against his hip, Xavire ran. He heard the squeak of the howitzer's wheels as Nokrag came behind him.

From somewhere beyond Keatairn's northern palisade, a flash bloomed, and the blast to end all blasts rang out in the valley.

*****

It was him. The humans' leader. Their 'lord.' Orod knew it with the same certainty as before, when he saw the bearded one charging onto the battlefield back east. And just like before, he was going to kill him.

"There!" he yelled, aiming his axe at the trio of figures atop the bridge. The lord was on horseback, clad in plate armor that tinged its moonlit shine with an orange hue. "Forget the spears! Get *them!*"

The orcs roared approval, surging along the trench once more. Almost immediately, the lord rode away, leaving the others to trail after him. One looked too big, like an ogre. They wouldn't escape; Orod saw his orcs had passed beyond the barricading carts on the street, and began urging them to get back over the–

Tension leapt through every part of the krudger's being. An explosion had ripped across the night, far louder than any artillery. He'd heard such blasts before, when the dwarf masters opened new mines. Not a discharge – a demolition.

The orcs' loping strides slowed. Then they stopped. In the explosion's wake was another sound, this one unlike any Orod had known. It was a... rushing. A roaring, but not one made by throat and maw. And it was growing.

In the moment the rushing reached its apex, the woodwall burst apart. For a moment, it looked to the krudger as if moonlight itself had torn past its lumber, crashing down the trench before spilling over and around the stone bridge, sprays of silver crowning every step. Then the darkness of its underbody loomed in his mind – he realized what it was.

Confusion struck the orcs. They broke in near every direction, cohesion lost beneath the surge of panic. They collided, they tripped, they brawled, they bit. Orod didn't waste time with orders – he began to hack his way through, the Tragarian axes felling any in his path as he fought to escape the water's onslaught. But there was no escape. It was spilling down the streets to either side, its waves crashing over the levee to roll high across the flagstone. As Orod hooked the heel of his axe to haul himself out, the river swallowed him.

Cold held the krudger, flooding across his flesh and deep into his lungs. In its darkness, he felt himself being carried far, felt the impact of other bodies below and above him. Twice his journey was interrupted as he became caught in an unseen crush, each lasting a handful of seconds before he was snatched up and trawled onward again. Orod fought, kicked, struggled. In the flood's embrace he held on to his axes, gripping them to the end. They were part of him. Amid the smothering cold, the memory of his master's dying face burned bright in his mind's eye, weapons the dwarf had worn with pride now buried in his chest, grasped evermore by Orod's hands.

As the final dark began to take him, the krudger's onward motion made an abrupt shift. He was falling.

*****

Awed, his road-stubbled jaw hanging open, Sir Guilliver beheld the aftermath. He had been gripped from the moment the river tumbled free, stock-still on his gray gelding. His paralysis endured long past the time it took for the waters to break the town's palisade and return to their rightful thoroughfare, denied to them hours before by the sealing of the dam. It had been a rather panicked affair in all, what with the hedge knight hastily igniting Nokrag's carefully laid fuse before riding to a safe distance, only to wonder if he'd messed the whole thing up as the seconds trickled by. Just as he'd begun to seriously consider returning to the dam, the blackpowder barrels unleashed their might.

The barrage of tidal crashes were abated. Sir Guilliver's open mouth finally shifted, resolving into a broad grin. He could hear voices. The Claws were cheering.

"Yah!"

The gelding leapt to motion, galloping down the farmland paths toward the settlement. Ankle-deep water lounged on the road outside the gateway and was cast high behind him as he passed. He followed the broad street, and when he arrived in the temple square, it was to the sight of horses rearing and swords being brandished in celebration, the sound of staves clattering on shields as the men roared hurrahs.

"Victory, my Claws!" Uslo's cry rode the cheers like a galleon on high seas. Sir Guilliver drew up among the mercenaries and saw that the general was returning from the direction of the waterway, bastard sword aloft as Volonto pranced beneath him. "The river has shown her wrath, and it is to our favor!"

The cheering redoubled. Grin spread from ear to still-ringing ear, Sir Guilliver reached out to clap the nearest horseman on the back. His heart felt like it would burst with pride. Though all in the Claws had risen to this moment, none had been as magnificent as his adventurers. Their charge and baiting retreat at the south gateway was to his mind the stuff of legend. Through the ranks he spotted Nokrag's unmistakable bulk, the howitzer deposited next to her. She had a large hand on Xavire's shoulder.

"But we're not done yet, lads! Form up! It's time to assist the good sergeants and dispose of any greenskins who yet–"

A pained cry cut across Uslo's words. The cheering faltered and, as the cry morphed into a scream, stopped dead. It was Xavire. His eyes were wide behind his glasses, their whites stark even under Nokrag's shadow. The ogress was hunched over him, Xavire's torso clasped between her broad palms.

"Hey!" shouted Sir Guilliver, heeling his mount toward the pair. "Unhand–!" But Nokrag was lowering him slowly down to the flagstone. She must have caught him as he fell. Dismounting, Sir Guilliver ran to their side and reached them just as the general drew up.

"Xavire!"

Xavire stopped his cry and pulled in a shuddering breath. Kneeling beside him, Sir Guilliver lifted his head, locking their eyes.

"What's wrong?!"

"C-c-c–"

"He could not breathe," said Nokrag.

"–come!" Xavire spluttered. "They've come back!"

"What's that?"

Nokrag stepped back as Uslo joined them. He leant over the prostrate officer.

"What's he saying?"

Xavire's eyes snapped to Uslo. His mouth began to work, opening and closing soundlessly.

"He must've taken a blow to the head, or else come down with something fierce," said Sir Guilliver. "I recommend we move him inside the–"

"Talk to me, Mister Almenara! That's an order! ...Xavire?"

Xavire swallowed, and a measure of the panic left his face, his eyelids finally re-emerging to blink. In a hoarse voice, he let out a single word. A terrible word.

"Fog..."

Xavire's head sank to the floor, the moon reflecting briefly in his glasses. His eyes rolled back. He'd passed out.

Sir Guilliver looked up, trying to catch the general's eye. But Uslo was facing away. His gaze tracked past the temple and over the surrounding buildings. Following its course, Sir Guilliver saw there was indeed a thin mist forming along the western cliffs.

Uslo stood up.

"Bring him inside the temple."

Sir Guilliver moved back as three men came forward. After counting down, they lifted the limp Xavire in a smooth motion and carried him toward the temple steps.

"Sir Guilliver, I want you to lead the cavalry into the valley."

"But surely you can't think–! It's only a touch of mist!"

"Take them to open ground. Try and protect the cart horses, if you can, but don't get trapped out there. If they come for you, keep moving."

"If *what* come? You mean those–! General, how could he even *know*?"

"It is too fast," said Nokrag, looking east. "It does not move right."

Sir Guilliver looked. More mists were forming to the east, seeming to seep from the rock face itself, merging together into thick and silver fog. Glancing back, he saw the same thing happening to the west. To either side, the fog fell quickly, building speed as it rolled down the slopes. Like waves.

The general called the pikes to formation as Sir Guilliver vaulted into his saddle.

A scream. It came from across the river, clear-pitched and hateful, a sound that caused his back teeth to grind. Sir Guilliver had heard such a sound before.

Xavire was right. Gods, *he was right*.

"Ready, adventurers! Into the valley! General?"

Uslo approached, handing him Volonto's reins. Sir Guilliver took them.

"Aren't you coming, sir?"

The general shook his head. "The infantry can't get out in time. I won't leave them."

The thirty-odd pikemen had arranged themselves in a circular phalanx, shields locked and spears out. The mists were now tumbling over the nearby buildings. High above, Sir Guilliver realized that clouds were beginning to blot out the moonlight, and under their gathering darkness, he saw the shadows writhe within the fog.

"Go, Imlarian!" With open palm to one and flat of sword the other, Uslo gave a sonorous *whack* on the horses' rumps. The animals grunted displeasure as they sped off, shoes clattering along the flagstone.

"To me!" called the knight. He looked back just before the adventurers fell in behind him. The general was stepping through a gap in the pikes' formation.

"Sir Guilliver!" shouted one of the horsemen. Sir Guilliver swung his gaze forward. Ahead of the palisade's gateway, a waft of mist was stretching across the street, billowing out from a narrow side alley. He fought down the urge to pull his reins. There was something inside.

"Don't stop!" he cried, dropping the gelding's reins to draw his blade. "We press on to the valley!"

Lights swirled in the deepening fog, sickly and blue. They moved in pairs. Like eyes. Just as he braced to pass through, something leapt out at him. Sir Guilliver barked a horrified warcry, sweeping out with his sword. Only after the blade had rent the unnatural flesh could his mind begin to lend the creature form. Cloaked in a rippling darkness, the thing's skin was red as an angry newborn, and it had arms and legs like a man, each ending in a brace of dagger-long claws. Its maw hung at least a foot wide, a veritable forest of teeth surrounding a swollen tongue. It had no eyes. Not on its head. Instead, dozens of the paired lights peered out from inside its cloak, each set upon a mournful and pleading face, held within eddies of endless black.

Pained, the creature let out a piercing hiss. Sir Guilliver passed through the fog. As he crossed beneath the gateway, he released Volonto. The charger continued to gallop north across the puddle-strewn road, and Sir Guilliver slowed, drawing his gelding off the track. His body was shaking, wracked by a previously untapped font of primal fear. Adventurers streamed past. He looked back. He could hear more of the hissing, spluttered and gargled across numerous swollen tongues. There was a rash of yells from the men who'd yet to come through. A horse screamed.

One of the horsemen burst from the fog and under the gateway, barely staying upright in the saddle. A creature was hanging on to him, its clawed hands slashing at the back of his cuirass, those on its feet buried in the horse's flesh. With a yell, Sir Guilliver spurred to meet them, bringing his sword down in a tall arc. The creature fell away, split from eyeless head to shrouded nave.

The adventurers ahead were stopping. They gathered atop the incline that ran alongside the sundered dam.

"Onward!" shouted Sir Guilliver, spurring the gelding to pace. "Keep going, damn it!"

The horsemen began to move again. "What about the others, sir?" one called. Most of the adventurers had made it out. But not all.

Sir Guilliver glanced back. The gateway was gone, swallowed in a fog that was continuing to swell, pushing up the valley behind them. The paired lights hovered at the frontier, eyeless faces and long-clawed hands reaching beyond as they pursued the riders. He shook his head.

"We can't do anything for them!" The words stung in his ears, all the more painful for their truth.

They were on their own.

15

...It can therefore be proposed that the expression 'from Keatairn' has a forgotten and euphemistic origin, expressing the idea that an object comes, quite simply, 'from those with access to it,' at one time signifying that it was acquired by iniquitous means, and now perhaps that the provenience is simply unknown...

Vespilo A., *On the Location and Identification of Primovantian Antiquity,* Appendix IX *'From the Gatekeepers' - The Mystery of Keatairn*

Some time before, when the mists had yet to flow down across Keatairn, when the river Keata was still held behind its dam and when the howitzer had only just seen itself hastily wheeled out onto the stone bridge, Arlok climbed. The wizened figure, his breathing haggard and his joints protesting, followed the old steps, the winding trail that gradually worked its way up the base of the tallest hill in the range, ending not far short of its broad and doming peak. Only as the last of Orod's six-hundred or so ax warriors piled through the charred gateway of the south wall did he reach the final step, whereupon he paused, leaning heavily on his staff.

He was exhausted. Drained, in so many ways. The physical toll was bad enough, and were there eyes for him to fool, he'd have no need to feign its wear. But it was the mental strain that punished him now. Even Yip, whose mind was normally wracked with lunatic energy, looked near empty, hauling his perpetually-hunched body up the last of the steps behind him, eyes drooped and glassy. They had come so far, had spent so much. But it would all be worth it. Arlok gazed up ahead at the twisted mouth of a cave, set into a wall of sheer slope.

He was close.

Drawing determined breaths through his nose, the Godspeaker shuffled toward the cave. He peered into its gloom, headdress rattling softly as he leaned across the portal. Then he placed his staff upright against the threshold and went inside. The narrow cavern drifted left for several yards, ending in a sharp right turn. Arlok looked around it. Blocked. Sealed by a cave-in.

Not ideal, he thought, returning cautiously along the jagged stone. *But little more than an inconvenience*. He had plans for just such an obstacle.

The proximity of Arlok's prize restored a measure of his vigor. Slowing only to cast a contemptuous glance at the Abyssal skull atop his staff – now surplus to its limited requirement – he stepped outside and moved to the center of a patch of flat ground, the precipice of which overlooked the settlement and the valley beyond. Arlok stopped. There were no sounds along the hillside, no insect chirps, no nocturnal calls. Nothing to challenge the battle below. He lifted an arm, and long, gnarled fingers probed the front of his headdress, locating the smooth oval of obsidian gemstone that hung against his forehead. It hummed beneath his fingertips. In a swift motion, he pulled it free and dropped it at his feet. The dull *thump* of impact in the grass was too weighty for an object of its size.

Yip watched the Godspeaker closely as he backed away from the stone, a sliver of anticipation quivering along the goblin's lips, the barest hint of a whine in his throat. Arlok met his gaze, and Yip froze.

"It is time." Arlok's words were neither orcish nor of the Tragar dwarfs. They were smoother in sonancy, crueler in tenor. It was a tongue from another plane. "Bring them forth."

Yip's features became glut with delight. The runtish creature leapt forward, skipping toward the dropped stone. Arms and face raised to the night sky, he released a squeal of unbridled and joyous mania. Deep within the obsidian, a red light began to glow. The gemstone jittered in the grass, bouncing with sparks of heat that singed the turf around it. Slowly, it began to ascend, glowing brighter and brighter as it climbed. Yip was changing, too. Dancing around the ovoid, light flared from blazing cracks along his form, a web of fire that hissed and spat. Tall horns sprouted from his brow, ridged like an ibex. His green skin morphed to a devilish red. His nose shrank.

Six-feet from the ground, the obsidian gemstone burst. There was a *whoomp* of displaced air that left an uneven ring of flame expanding in its place. The temperature rose sharply. Arlok felt its pleasing warmth against his skin, felt it caress the depths of his lungs. It smelled of brimstone. He closed his eyes to savor it. To relish it. When he opened them a second later, it was to see reality undone.

Hovering over scorched soil, the portal continued to burn along its frayed edges, encompassing a space some eight-feet high and five wide. It was shaped less like a door than a gash, an agonizing tear in the fabric of the world. Steam issued in great gouts from beyond, near obscuring an island of bare and blackened rock surrounded by broiling waters. He could hear them bubbling, could glimpse the great plumes of sulphuric vapor issuing from a place deep below the surface. A place far deeper than mortals could ever know.

"Well?" he called after several moments, straining to elevate his voice over the waters' ebullience. "What's taking so long?"

From somewhere outside the fiery outline of the portal, two steam-blurred figures moved into view. Tall as men, their bodies were lithe, their graceful movements honed to ensnare the eye. They passed through one after another, traversing a distance of nearly four-hundred leagues across the face of Pannithor in a single stride.

The emerged figures stood side-by-side before the threshold, the first with hand on hip, the second holding the chain leash of a three-headed mastiff. Physically, there was little to differentiate the sororal succubi Zenarei and Zexori. Both had long hair, blacker than the night, penetrated at crown by a pair of smooth horns. Their faces were tight-angled and stern, full lips wrapped around sultry smiles. Their eyes were sulfurous, flashing bright amongst skin of rousing red. Garb was a different matter. Zexori's radical contours were entirely held within shapely-cut robes of midnight blue, while Zenarei was barely garbed at all, wearing what could only be described as ornately-armored undergarments and tall, gloss-leather boots. The sisters' arrow-headed tails swayed behind them.

"It's cold," said Zenarei, pouting.

"It'll be a lot colder once that closes. Do you have it?"

"We have it," purred Zexori. Her pet, a hellhound, pointed its three snouts in the direction of Keatairn. One of the heads growled.

Arlok sighed in relief. The plan could continue. "Then hurry up and bring it through! The portal won't last long!"

Zenarei stuck out her forked tongue as they stepped aside. Turning to the portal, she placed two long-nailed fingers at the corners of her mouth and whistled. Immediately, more figures appeared from outwith the portal's bounds, and soon a procession of lower Abyssals were moving through.

Arlok's lip curled in disgust. Stooped and shuffling, the lower ones had always been a wretched sight. The flooding of their home in the First Circle seemed to have drastically worsened matters. Red skin hung pale and gaunt across their bones. The fixed grins on their devilish skulls, brimming as ever with uneven teeth, now resembled the grimaces of tortured men. Most walked on bare, three-toed feet; some ambled awkwardly on goat legs. Shards of naked bone projected through flesh at their shoulders, while for a few, the ossein spikes even jutted out along their spines. All wore a mishmash of whatever armor and weaponry they could scavenge – a battered chest plate here, a rusted shield and scimitar there. Clots of black ichor glistened on their blades and seeped from cuts in their exposed skin. At least the lower Abyssals' compulsion for violence hadn't been dampened by the waters, Arlok reflected.

Around a dozen came through in all. The last four carried between them a length of heavy chain and were using it to draw something behind them. Seeing the shackling irons provoked a flash of concern in Arlok, quickly igniting anger – but it was doused just as quickly when the one they bound emerged. It seemed the manacles were mere precaution rather than necessity.

As the enchained being was guided away, a great shadow moved to fill the portal. Ducking to pass its ram horns, the creature's cumbrous steps shook the hillside soil. The demon, a moloch of the Sixth Circle, towered over the others, glaring at them each in turn. Though it shared the fundamental aspect of its Abyssal kin – crimson skin, devil's face and horns, eyes that radiated with the life-sustaining heat of their infernal home – the moloch was tall as an ogre and still more bulked. Naked save for a mail loincloth, its front clasp was fashioned from the skull of a rival, and a razor-pronged trident was grasped in its massive fists.

"I see you've continued to deepen your talent for taming pets, Zexori."

The moloch's lips curled back, revealing the full extent of its tusks. It snarled.

"Careful, now," chided Zexori, placing her free hand on the moloch's elbow. "His name is Gig'Thanas, and he is not my pet." Her fingers began to walk along the beast's skin. "He's my… *companion*."

As soon as she spoke, the burning edges of the portal flew inward, producing a brief sound of sucking air before vanishing entirely. The heat lingered for several seconds, then dispersed.

"Brr! You weren't wrong!" said Zenarei, a shiver seeming to run from shoulder to bare shoulder.

"I see Yipposhix'Zal is looking… well, he's looking as ever," said Zexori. The warlock had rolled onto his back near the cave mouth, a gurgling giggle issuing from deep in his throat. Zexori's gaze turned to Arlok. Her eyes narrowed. "Why are you still in that form?"

Catching Yip's mad eye, Arlok nodded. Yip made a quick gesture. Unlike the warlock's transformation, there was no light, no burning glow within a morphed being. Rather, it was as if a veil of shadow-borne illusion fell away. Where before there was a horn-adorned headdress, there were only tall and curving horns; where there was a tattered brown cloak, there was a cape of exquisite black satin, held between spiked shoulder guards; where there was only ragged loincloth, there was a gilded mail cuirass and enormous, black iron greaves; and, at the center of it all, where once there stood a hunched and withered orc, there now stood straight the unyielding form of Kolra the Tormentor,

Demon Champion of the Fifth Circle.

Kolra looked across the gathered. The lower Abyssals fell to their knees, avoiding his eye. Gig'Thanas and the sisters, in contrast, seemed unimpressed. Feeling the curious pull of her pet on its leash, Zexori turned to look out at the settlement. The sounds of fighting continued to reach them. A smile unfurled across the succubus's black lips.

"A battle?" she purred.

"There were men here when the horde arrived." Kolra's voice was deep and resonant. Only its slithering quality remained. "The orcs are doing what they do best."

Zenarei laughed. It was a sound at once cruel and enticing. "I must say, my Lord Kolra, that was some feat! Directing the orcs all the way here, massacring all those men in their path! The Circles are positively burning with rumor about it and little else. Tell me, how *did* you convince the greenskins to do it?"

Kolra smiled. "You know I'd love nothing more than to tell you, my dear, but a soon-to-be god must have his secrets."

"Aww," she pouted, fingering the coiled whips at her belt. "Such a tease."

He chortled softly. "Let's just say I selected a particularly impressive specimen, and that I gave him..." Kolra paused, running a firm hand along his restored jawline. He could still feel the echoes from Orod's strikes. Resisting the urge to kill the orc had been the hardest part. It felt good to be himself again. "...a dream. The rest played itself out from there. More or less."

"Incredible. Such ambition! Lord Anag'rha'su was beside himself, you cannot imagine."

Oh, I think I can, thought Kolra, a vision of the archfiend's furious face appearing before his mind's eye.

"Quite so," agreed Zexori, glancing back. "Stealing the World Render's most powerful portalstone *and* his favorite warlock?" She gestured toward Yip, who was currently running his hands over his horns, a dreamy quality to his grin. "Do not misunderstand, we're delighted it went so well, but when we heard he sent Zunun'Nuuth the Hunter after you both..."

"And yet you were waiting in the First Circle when I called."

Zexori's smile was tight. "Well, for a plan *this* ambitious, even a slim chance was enough. And then there were the rumors of the horde, of course."

"Of course. But I'm glad you understand the stakes, and that your... *faith*," Kolra couldn't help but sneer as he spoke the word, "held true. When we are finished here, Anag'rha'su can rage all he wants – we three shall reign over him in the Wicked Ones' favor!"

Zexori nodded absently. She began to examine her nails. "What, er, what did happen with Zunun'Nuuth, my lord?" The moloch Gig'Thanas stomped across to the cave as she spoke, crouching to look inside.

"He caught up to me soon after I left, if that's what you're asking."

"And?"

Gig'Thanas moved on, disinterested. Kolra nodded to the abandoned staff.

"He's there."

Zexori stared at the skull for a moment. Then she let out an angry hiss, looking away. Zenarei laughed.

"Pay her no mind, my lord. She'd long desired to put the Hunter on her torture table."

"Speaking of which," said Kolra as he turned to give due attention to the chain-bound being. He stepped toward it. "Is it…?"

Zenarei took the chain from the still-kneeling Abyssals and gave it a quick tug. "It is."

Kolra's grin was broad. Pathetic as the bound one looked, this was not the fundamental wretchedness of the lower Abyssals, but rather that of a great and powerful being brought low. Broken. Appearing like a tall and muscular man, with a plainly even face and small horns on its bald head, one might first mistake it for a demon of Kolra's own sort. But an ethereal quality instantly dispelled such comparisons from the mind, as if the being were only partly present in this world – true enough of all Abyssal denizens, but still more so of this one. Tiny flames flickered along its fingers and feet, the former bound by chains against its chest, the latter simply bound. It hovered several inches from the ground. The grass below withered in the heat.

"You think we showed faith by waiting for you on the surface," said Zenarei. She placed her palm at the center of Kolra's bare chest. "What word but devotion could describe those who snare an efreet of the Fourth Circle?" Pushing the nail of her index until it drew black blood, Zenarei slowly dragged it down toward his nave. Leaning close, she whispered, "What word but worship for those who find a way to break one's will?"

"I shan't pry as to your secrets, my dear," whispered Kolra, reaching out to touch the efreet. It flinched away. Kolra felt his joy swell. "But know that you and your sister's reward shall be without measure."

Zenarei tittered hungrily in his ear. She held up the efreet's chains. Kolra took them.

"I assume that these…?"

"Just a reminder. It could melt through them in an instant. But it won't. Its spirit is gone."

"I see that." Kolra pulled gently on the chains as he moved toward the cave mouth. The efreet followed, unresisting. "No doubt it longs for a different release? Something more permanent?"

The efreet met his eye. Kolra thought he could see a glimmer of attention rise up through its despair.

"Yes," said Kolra, forcing a sympathetic smile. "Come. Here lies the path to sweet oblivion." He placed a hand on the demon's head, lowering it under the cave's threshold. Then he and the others stood back. Well back.

"Unleash your fire, efreet. Open the way for us and you will find what you seek." Kolra glanced at Gig'Thanas, currently staring south into the hills. "Oh, and make it wide," he added.

The efreet turned to face into the cave. For a moment, it simply hovered there, the minute flames on its feet and hands casting a flickering orange along the jagged walls. Then all at once there was a roar of ignition as its entire form flared with white light. Heat washed over the onlookers, and Kolra turned his face away. He felt the chains fall slack. Peering through narrowed eyes, he saw the rock around the cave rapidly turning red. Molten droplets began to fall, soon converging into rivulets. In less than a minute, a stream of lava was snaking its way from the cave mouth, the cavern walls widening as the runoff seeped away. With gradual inevitability, the efreet began floating further into the hillside.

Zenarei sighed, crouching to warm herself by the molten glow. "Nothing to do now but wait, I suppose."

She was right. Although, they would not have to wait long, thanks to the efreet's power, its life-ending flame. A good thing, too. Without shedding mortal blood, whether in battle or through ritual sacrifice at a scale beyond their current means, no Abyssal could maintain its presence this far from the Circles for long; with the portalstone spent, there was nothing else to sustain them. Watching the efreet work, Kolra found to his surprise that he was somewhat shaken by the sight of it. Such incredible strength.

It will be as nothing next to my own, once this is over, he thought, stoking anticipation. *My name shall be among gods!*

From the settlement below, a boom of detonated blackpowder rang out across the valley. None of the demons acknowledged it, nor the odd rumbling that followed the shot's impact. Only Zexori was still watching the battle. A second explosion was heard shortly after, this one far larger.

"They've destroyed the town's dam," said Zexori. Then, a little later, "It seems your orcs are losing."

Kolra sighed. Prying his eyes from the cave – the glow of its rock had dulled around the broadened mouth as the efreet's light moved ever deeper – he stepped across the lava to join her.

"You need not concern yourself, my dear Zexori. Victory or loss – it makes no odds." He paused, watching with mildest interest as the freed river crashed over the greenskins. It seemed that Orod truly had expended his usefulness. "Their purpose now was to provide distraction, for which men will serve just as well."

"Distraction?"

"Yes, from the– ah, look there."

Kolra pointed to the slopes rising over the west of the town. Runnels of unnatural mist were already beginning to appear, the crude intelligence of the shadow ones inescapably drawn to the scent of mortal suffering.

Zexori's eyes widened as she beheld the gathering fog. Her lips settled into a smirk, doubtless savoring the prospect of what awaited the men below.

Stepping away, Kolra came to stand in the hardening cave mouth, a basalt heat caressing him from below. Whoever those men down there were, they'd find their victory short-lived.

Orod is not the only one who's doomed, he thought. Delighting at his joke, the demon laughed.

*****

Nokrag drew back the flintlock on her blunderbuss. Around the temple, fog gushed from side streets and swept across the river to the east. Eerie lights swirled within, projecting silhouettes of incomprehensible limbs and maws. The last of the Claws' horsemen left the temple square – and they appeared.

Lights flew toward the Claws. There were cries from the struck men. Nokrag saw one fall.

"Shields!"

Dargent's call was answered instantly, the semi-circular ranks of Claws ducking behind their round shields. And not a moment too soon. The creatures that emerged – spectral and hollow, their malformed bodies glowing with ethereal tendrils, their eyeless faces dominated by broad, jeering grins – hurled their arms forward again, launching a barrage of compact and luminous mist. The missiles made no sound as they impacted, instead bursting silently apart to scatter across the mercenaries, provoking more yells of pain.

One of the baffling projectiles went high, sailing over the heads of the Claws to where Nokrag was standing on the temple steps. She lurched sideways. It glanced across her greaves, and she drew a sharp breath through her teeth. Despite the thick leather, the mist seemed to leech painfully into her leg. Its burn was ice-cold.

"Hold, lads! Steady! Drag the wounded back!"

Another mist volley fell against the Claws. Above them, the clouds had closed over the night sky. The glowing specters and their luminous missiles were the only sources of light. And they were advancing.

"On my order, pull back to the temple! Eyes front and mind those steps!"

Looking south, Nokrag saw five or so of the specters moving to get around the Claws' formation. They were clustered closely together. Mistake. Bracing the blunderbuss on her hip, Nokrag unloaded at the flanking group. Blackpowder smoke stung the air as the shot cut through them. The specters flew apart. Or they seemed to – a second later, four of the five reappeared, their ethereal forms swirling back together.

"Ready! Back!"

The pikemen responded with a collective shout as they stepped back, the rear rank mounting the temple steps.

"Again!"

Nokrag stepped up under the temple's doorway. She could hear the horsemen under attack north of the square. From the building clatter of horse shoes, more than a few were turning back. Letting the blunderbuss hang at her side, she swung the crossbow from her back and in the same moment retrieved the lever from her belt. As she finished winding the cord to its latch, the pikes took another step. The outer men were now up against the open double doors on either side of the doorway, a couple breaking off to bear a wounded comrade inside.

"Front rank, hold here! The rest get inside–!"

The general's command was cut short by a horse's scream.

Here they are, thought Nokrag. She set a bolt in the crossbow's groove. Though the mist was everywhere now, it was thinner, the thick gushes having spread to fill every nook and cranny of the town. The lights shifted constantly between pale greens and blues, occasionally dipping to sickly violet. Against the swirl of colors, the shapes of a dozen horsemen burst into the square, crashing inadvertently through the advancing specters. Evidently not all the Claws' riders had escaped in time, and those who failed were falling back toward the temple. They were pursued by what looked to be phantasmic shadows, flying after them at head height, slashing at them with clawed and spindly arms. Two of the phantoms caught hold of a rider on either side. The man's terrified screams were quickly lost as they dragged him into darkness.

"Belay that! Expand the front! FORWARD!"

The combined bark of the pikemen rebounded sharply across the stonework. In seconds, their tight-packed ranks were unmade, the formation shifting with mechanical precision to swell the semi-circular front outward. Nokrag set her crossbow stock to shoulder, tracking one of the flitting phantoms. Even when the creature paused, she couldn't bring herself to loose. It felt as though her mind was out of step – or rather, that the phantom resisted purchase. With mingled distress and frustration chafing, she removed the bolt and strode down the steps.

Up ahead, Dargent was calling to the horsemen, ordering them to get behind the pikes. Wheeling their animals in a panic, the riders spilled haphazardly toward the temple, making desperate sword strikes at their pursuers. A storm of spectral missiles cut across them. Nokrag saw one of the horses take a succession of silent bursts. The animal collapsed lifelessly to the flagstone, seemingly dead before impact. Phantoms fell upon its flung rider.

"Open the line! Let them through!"

A corridor opened among the leveled pikes. The horseman – five remained in their saddles – raced for it. Planting herself at the center of the Claws, Nokrag fixed the long, serrated bayonet to her crossbow. She braced. The luminous projectiles continued to pelt the pikemen's shields around her. Another rider fell, his steed split along its flank by phantom barbs. The horsemen passed through.

A chorus of pained hissing filled the air as the phantoms met the Claws' pikes. Dargent's men quickly closed the line behind their comrades. Several phantoms made it through, and as the horsemen swerved out of her way, Nokrag launched forward, cleaving her bayonet across night-cloaked forms. The pair before her let out shrill rasps, their lank bodies dissolving, their cloaks dissipating into the darkness. Before they were even half-gone, another pushed through them, its claws aimed at Nokrag's eyes. Flinching aside, she felt the freezing talon rake along her cheek. A missile streaked past. By its light, she saw the phantom's face hovering less than a foot from her own. The sight of it seized her in ice, and she watched in helpless alarm as it drove its teeth into her shoulder. Her paralysis lasted only a second, needles of hot pain pushing through her fear. Reaching up, she wrapped a hand around its torso and *squeezed*, the pain increasing in her shoulder as the phantom struggled. Nokrag felt the *pop* of bones in her fist – it went limp. The body faded to nothing before she could wrest it free.

The Claws pulled back again, a cloud of phantoms held off by their pikes. Nokrag saw the general drawing his bastard sword free from one that'd slipped through. He met her eye.

"Get ready to close the doors!" he called.

Nokrag nodded. Shifting her crossbow to her back, she bounded up the temple steps to unhook the first of the double doors from the outer wall. The surviving horsemen had ridden in ahead of her and were dismounting in the nave.

"You!" she boomed, moving to the other door. "Be ready to close these behind your tribe!" Torchlight inside the temple revealed the fear in the horsemen's faces, but they nodded, plate armor clanking as they rushed to the threshold.

Behind her, the men in the square unleashed their collective shouts to a rapid rhythm. With the second door freed, Nokrag turned to see them packed against the steps once more, the thrusts of their pikes growing ever more wild as the incomprehensible mass of specters and phantoms built against them. Dargent's head was craned, his torso twisting to see the doorway.

"Now, Dargent!"

"You heard the ogre, lads! On my order, back rank moves inside! NOW!"

Lifting the long staves, the men peeled off, quickly mounting the steps before turning to lower their weapons again as they backed under the threshold.

"Ready! NOW!"

The maneuver repeated. A phantom slipped past the thinned pikes – Dargent put his sword through it.

"Front ranks, withdraw together! NOW!"

The last of the Claws began backing up the steps, pikes still held level. Sensing weakness, the phantoms surged.

"Drop pikes!" yelled Dargent. "Doors!"

With a final thrust, the pikemen let go of their staves. The doors swung in. Nokrag reached out to drag some of the men back as she pulled the heavy door around, immediately feeling the roll of impacts on the other side. Even with four of them on the other door, the men were slower, and a phantom pushed through, its dagger-claws quickly finding the nearest man's throat. The gurgling mercenary staggered back. Before his attacker could invade further, Nokrag grabbed the handle and yanked it closed, severing the phantom at the torso. Its cold flesh fell across her arm before vanishing. An iron ring in each hand, she held the doors shut.

"Get the bolts!" called Dargent, quickly pushing forward to do it himself. There were only two between the doors themselves, with two more sliding down into the flagstone. Nokrag let go, and they stepped back. The doors rattled violently. Dust trickled from their hinges. After grabbing the rings again, she quickly let go to instead press her palms against the doors, bracing her legs.

"They're pushing," she observed. "Means we can block it."

"We'll use the pews."

Nokrag looked at Dargent blankly, but he was already moving toward the timber constructs – pews, she supposed – that were arranged along the temple's interior.

"You two, move the wounded up the back. Everyone else, stack these at the doorway! Hop to it!"

Nokrag drew back, helping to slide the first pew into place. It quickly became the foundational piece below a bulging mound, the old wood groaning with every addition. Over the next two minutes, the mercenaries dragged the long constructs across the stone floor, handing them off to another group to place them on the amassing pile. By the end, only the ogre had the strength to heave them atop it. With the sweat thick on her ample brow, she set the last one down, the impact producing a sound like a gunshot. Its echo trilled briefly through the temple acoustics, soon swallowed by the ceaseless thumping of bodies on the doors.

She turned to look at the Claws. They were spread across the now clear space, shields held slack, the roughly half who still had their pikes leaning heavily upon them. The four riderless horses – one permanently so, the throat-slashed man having perished sometime in the last minute – quivered in a far corner. Despite the bangs and scratches from outside, Nokrag could hear the shudders in the mercenaries' cider-tinged breaths, many being pulled through rattling teeth. One strode away to vomit into an empty alcove. She knew how they felt, even if her ogre pride wouldn't permit her to show fear before the humans.

"That should hold them, wouldn't you say?" Dargent was shaking too, forcing deep breaths through his nose. His helmet was off, and hairs along his mustache stood rigid at odd angles. "There's a lot of them, but they didn't seem all that strong."

"I believe so. We must look for other–"

"Help!"

The shout, heavy with accent, came from the passage in the temple's northwest corner. In its mouth were steep wooden rungs, twisting up into darkness, ultimately leading to the tower, she presumed.

All at once, Nokrag remembered Cauhin.

It seemed Dargent had the same thought. "Someone get up there!" he called. But Nokrag was already rushing over, Claws practically having to dive out of her path. The Plainsman's plea repeated as she reached the arch. She ducked under, twisting to look up. Through the darkness, she discerned a pair of figures descending the spiral stairway. One was moving wrong, or rather wasn't moving much at all. She put her boot on the third step and immediately heard it emit a sharp *creak*. Even if she had been able to fit, there was no way she would get up there.

"What happened?" she called, employing the Plainsmen's dialect. The figures paused for the briefest moment before redoubling the descent.

"I don't know!" came Riuen's rough-throated response. "We saw the Southerners celebrating and were about to come down. That's when the lad, he... he..."

"What's he saying?" said Dargent behind her. His sword was sheathed, and he was holding a burning torch. Nokrag stepped aside for its light as Riuen's legs came round the final bend, Cauhin's hanging limply at his side.

"It's as though he's asleep – only I can't wake him!"

"Like your man, General," she explained, reaching in to help bear the man pup down. "It appears Cauhin cannot waken." Taking him carefully from Riuen, she saw Cauhin's eyes shifting rapidly behind slack lids.

Dargent nodded, his expression equal parts calculating and concerned. "When did this happen?"

Seeing the Plainsman's confusion, Nokrag added "Did he fall when the mists began to appear?"

"I think so, yes."

She nodded, looking to Dargent. "Same as your man, it seems."

"I see..."

She carried Cauhin over toward the open apse, beside which lay Xavire. It seemed one of the Claws had folded their coat under his head. As Nokrag set the youth down next to him, Dargent removed his own overcoat to do the same, fully revealing his red-bronze cuirass beneath. Once in place, he put a hand on Cauhin's chest. Nokrag saw Riuen stiffen, but the Plainsman said nothing.

"Heart's beating fast." Handing his torch to a nearby mercenary, he reached over to Xavire's neck. "And so's his. They're both breathing cleanly." Dargent moved his hands to their brows. "No fever. Chilled, if anything, but whatever this is, they don't seem to be in any immediate peril." As he spoke, the general removed Xavire's glasses, folding them with care before slipping them into the unconscious man's pouch.

Dargent stood up and looked toward the obstructed doors. "Other than the peril we share with them, that is." He was silent for several seconds. Nokrag watched patiently as Dargent removed a glove, using the freed thumb and forefinger to flatten down his mustache, all while his eyes never once left the stacked pews. He appeared to give himself a shake.

"Claws! Stand ready around the entrance! Pikes to the front!"

There was a smattering of movement as the Claws arranged themselves.

"Hold on there, Bedric. Leg all right?"

"The pain's dulled, sir, though I can't move it none. Those... things hits me right in the thigh – hurt like nothin' I felt before, sir, but I can't see a wound or nothin'."

The general set a hand on the hobbling mercenary's shoulder. "Alright. Hand off your pike and sit down." Dargent nodded to another laying nearby, a cap placed across his face. The man's hair was pure white.

"Is that Venjen?"

"Yes, sir. Dead. Took one to the face."

Dargent nodded soberly, patting the man's shoulder again. Then he walked back across the temple, moving to where the surviving horsemen sat with their fallen comrade.

"My condolences, friends. Issum was a good man..."

Nokrag stopped listening. She crouched over Cauhin, massaging the patch of numb skin on her upper leg as she watched his eyes flit back and forth. "Did you close the way behind you?" she asked Riuen.

"What?"

"The tower. Did you shut it?"

"...I don't remember."

Nokrag sucked on her teeth, thinking. The phantoms could fly, but they didn't seem very smart. They hadn't flown over the pike formation, and by the ongoing hammering on the doors, they weren't seeking other ways in. But even so...

She stood up. "Check."

After a quick glance at Cauhin, Riuen rushed up the spiral stairway. Nokrag strode over to Dargent.

"But most made it out with Sir Guilliver?"

"It's hard to say how many, sir, although certainly a good number–"

"How did you open that?" Nokrag interjected, gesturing to the descending passageway at the far end of the temple.

"I beg pardon– oh, yes. It's the plinths, you see?" The general swept his finger along the alcoves in the inner walls. "They are marked with symbols which needed arranging to form a phrase, and only the exact right one would do. Forgive me, Warrior Nokrag, I'm not sure now is the time–"

"Can it be opened from the other side?"

Dargent blinked. "Possibly… I did see some sort of mechanism a little way down."

"And are there other ways inside this building?" asked Nokrag.

"I believe not."

Nokrag nodded. "You must close that hole. Might be they try to come through there. Them, or something else."

A sharp *crack* bounced through the temple air above them. It was quickly followed by a roll of tinkling *crashes* on the pile of pews. Spinning toward the entrance, Nokrag's gaze was drawn up to the portal window above. Ghostly lights shone dully beyond the colored glass and, through the face of a depicted god, a long-clawed hand grasped toward them. It seemed the phantoms had decided to seek other ways in after all.

"I *was* inclined to agree with you, Warrior Nokrag, but on second thought…"

More glass fell from the portal. Below, through the mass of stacked wood, something slammed against the temple doors. Something big.

Nokrag drew her crossbow from her back. "We go underground."

"Everyone, fall back to the passage!" ordered Dargent, his martial timber rebounding throughout the temple. "Get the wounded down first! You lot, lead the horses! Go!"

Four phantoms tried to push through the portal at once, their furiously hissing faces directed as much at each other as at the men. Nokrag set a bolt in the groove and raised the crossbow high, ignoring the Claws as they ran around her. Even with such an easy target, the same feeling of mental misalignment began to take hold. She waited. Something hit the doors again, louder than before. Seconds passed. She heard Riuen insist he carry Cauhin, heard the general convincing the Plainsman to go into the passage with the others. *Slam.* Several of the pews were shunted from the pile, clattering noisily onto the flagstone.

"Now, Warrior!" the general called, his voice sounding some distance within the passage. "I have to close it!"

One of the phantoms pushed through. Nokrag squeezed.

The bolt tore through the phantom's eyeless face, casting a splatter of viscous blue gore onto its fellows behind it.

Nokrag didn't wait to see what happened next. She ran back toward the passageway, arms levering the crossbow's cord in the process. The Claws had taken their torches, and the only light in the temple flickered up from the passage depths. She had hardly reached its top step when the doors gave an almighty *bang* behind her, exploding in a bloom of shattered woodwork. Wind struck her back with such force that she almost toppled, forcing her to lunge over a half-dozen of the narrow steps. It pushed past her and down, knocking the mercenaries into one another. Their torches went out. Turning into the gale, Nokrag looked out over the top of the steps and beheld what had come.

In the absence of torchlight, the temple was illuminated by a bilious blend of purples and greens, revealing a trio of black-robed horsemen standing just inside the threshold. Their mounts were large. Very large. And, she realized with no small horror, they weren't standing at all. They were hovering, six legs each and not a single one touching the floor. They were *burning.* Unnatural flames licked across their pallid flesh, glowed within beak-like maws. The riders held long, double-handed scythes, and their cowled heads turned back and forth, scanning the interior. It was altogether a sight so terrible that Nokrag felt her muscles sag in despair. Wind assailed her face. It smelled of flame-scorched bone.

"The mechanism won't close!" Dargent's words gave valiant struggle against the wind. "Lock shields! Prepare to defend yourselves!"

As one, the riders spun their heads to Nokrag. They spurred hard. Rearing, their beasts unleashed earsplitting screams.

Instinct roused her. Raising her crossbow – she couldn't remember setting the bolt – Nokrag aimed for the central rider. The jarred feeling surged with a vengeance – in the same instant, an idea. Her gaze shifted to the left row of alcoves. Without further thought, she loosed her crossbow. There was a piercing *clap* as the steel bolt hit stone. The plinth rocked back once, rolled along the alcove wall, and fell out onto the flagstone.

The moment the plinth's weight shifted, the temple was filled with a cacophonous grind of hidden mechanisms. The passage began to close. Not fast enough. The three riders were charging, swooping across the space toward her. Nokrag staggered back, quickly slipping on the overly narrow steps to fall forward. Pain exploded in her ribs. As she shimmied down backward, she heard the whine of a blade cut through the air. Nokrag looked up to see one of the riders leaning into the passage, arms outstretched, the end of its scythe embedded in the stone where her head had been a split-second before. Dislodging its blade, it guided its infernal mount in further before raising to strike again. Eyes locked on the instrument of her death, the daughter of the Urshal snarled.

"Get back, soulless devil!"

A single pike thrust forward, plunging into the rider's chest. It wailed, throwing back its head in agony. The cowl fell back, revealing a skinless skull. The pike withdrew, and the rider tried to ready its retaliation. But there was no longer room – the heavy platform was pressing in. As it closed over, the last thing Nokrag saw were the three mounts peering through the gap, snapping their beaky maws in frustration, the ill light in their throats winking. There was a grinding *thud*. All was dark.

Nokrag began to rise to her feet, instead turning to sit awkwardly as the burgeoning welts made themselves known.

"I owe you my life, General Dargent," she wheezed into the darkness.

"Undoubtedly," came Dargent's similarly breathless response. "That said, your warning about the orcs saved all our lives, and if you just did what I think you did, then..." He took a deep breath. "Then I believe it is I who is quite hopelessly in *your* debt, Warrior Nokrag."

She gave a short laugh. "Might be I saved us. Or trapped us."

Light, yellow and glorious, flared to life as one of the men reignited their torch. Soon all ten or so were crackling again.

"There must be another way out," said Dargent quietly, although she thought his tone wasn't exactly assured. He glanced along the nearby passage wall where a rusted lever projected acutely from the stone. "Or maybe that only works to open it from this side?"

A shriek of otherworldly frustration reached them from above.

"We can test it later," added Dargent quickly.

"Agreed."

"What now, sir?" asked one of the Claws, proffering Dargent a torch. The general took it in exchange for the pike.

"We won't stay here. This place isn't defensible. From either direction." He looked down the broad tunnel. Nokrag followed his gaze. Even to her ogre eyes, the steps continued to descend beyond sight. Dargent nodded, seemingly to himself. "Nothing else for it. We'll go down. Find somewhere to hold out until morning. Keep the pikes at the rear as we go, wounded and horses in the middle, the rest with me at the head. The Warrior Nokrag may march as she chooses."

"I go at the front."

"Then let's be off."

As she walked cautiously between the Claws, Nokrag set the crossbow on her back and began reloading her blunderbuss. She had to hunch forward; even then, the smooth stone of the passage ceiling was close enough for her hair to drag along it.

"Who knows," said Dargent as they reached the front of the column, a whisper of anticipation lurking in his voice. "Maybe we'll spy some of the treasure down here."

Nokrag raised an eyebrow, giving genuine consideration to the thought. The tiny balls of iron shot chimed dully as she poured them down the blunderbuss's barrel.

"Alright, Claws, we'll have to take it slow for the horses' sake until we get off these steps. Ready?"

The men affirmed.

"Onward."

"If we do find treasure," said Nokrag some minutes later, her eyes down as she traversed the human-spaced steps, "I'm taking first claim for my share."

"And a handsome share it shall be. Tell me, Warrior, will that perchance prove sufficient to address my debt?"

"No. But the debt will no longer be hopeless."

*****

It was behind him. The boy ran as fast as he could down the corridors of his home, bouncing off wood-panel walls as he rounded its corners.

"WHERE?! WHO?!"

Its voice wasn't the rasped gargle of before, but a united chorus, a meeting of endless voids. A nothing that pulls. He heard its scuttling movements, so close the sound seemed to scratch the back of his neck. But he didn't stop, didn't look back once. The house continued forever, twisting in on itself in senseless loops. He didn't know how long he'd been running. It felt like forever.

"Too close!" Desperation entered its many voices, pervading the highest whine to the lowest wail. "Another huntress has come! Must stop it! Mustn't be shut out again!" It seemed to be speaking to itself.

"WHO IS IT?!" they screeched.

The boy skidded to a halt. Ahead at the corridor's end was a familiar sight, a street cat known simply as 'the huntress'. She was sitting with her back to him, light shifting inexplicably around her. The stripes on her tabby coat danced under saffron illumination, swirled in shadows. The tip of her wiry tail was stiff with tension.

"TELL US! GIVE US THE HUNTRESS! OR WE WILL TAKE HIM, TOO!"

The light around the cat flared blindingly, forcing the boy to squint. It relented as quickly as it came, and when he opened his eyes, it was to find himself standing outside, in the alley behind the house, baking under the hot noon sun. Broken and discarded crates littered the alley entrance – a cat lay dead in their shadow. Not a tabby. Not the huntress.

A silver cat.

Recognition – unknown as it was profound – roared within. "No!" cried the boy. "You can't!"

The void laughed. For the first time, the voices almost sounded relaxed.

"Can't? CAN'T?!" It laughed harder.

All at once, the strangest of feelings overcame him. It was as if one eye continued to see the alley, while the other... something else. Something dark. But there were lights in the dark. If he could just focus, if he could block out the sun...

The boy put his hands over his eyes and saw that he was standing on a broad, descending stairway, its steps sunken in the middle from centuries of use. It was dark, but there were lights coming down the passageway toward him. Torches, carried by a troop of fighting men. Xavire immediately recognized the two figures at their fore – the larger could only be Nokrag, while the man at her side was...

"General!" Xavire ran up toward them, taking the steps three at a time. It felt effortless. "General Dargent!"

Uslo gave no response. He held the torch ahead of him, its light catching against his cuirass, shimmering on the central working of a rampant battle cat. It cast a play of shadows across the pale canvass of his face.

"It's me, sir! It's Xavire!"

There was no reaction. Xavire stopped. The general should've been able to see him by now, never mind hear his call. Something was off. Xavire could hear his own voice, same as ever, but it seemed otherwise disconnected from the world around him.

"Uslo?"

It was the echoes. Or rather, the lack of them. The tunnel's space was replete with the reverberations of boots and horseshoes. But his words produced nothing. Uslo had almost reached him, and as Xavire stepped aside, he saw the general's deep brown eyes scanning the darkness ahead. They passed straight through him. Xavire wasn't here. Not really.

"*Can't?*"

Xavire froze. The voices, at once as insubstantial as a thought and as real as a whisper behind his ears, sent sickening realization down his spine. Turning his head slowly, he peered into the darkness below.

It was there. He could see its eyeless face, its torn grin. The void had set its gaze on Uslo.

The general staggered, dropping the torch. It clattered on the stone steps, bouncing end-over-end three times before rolling swiftly on. For a split-second, Xavire saw the sheen of its light against aberrant flesh. Then it vanished.

Nokrag prevented Uslo from falling. Most of his arm was in her fist. "What's wrong?" she rumbled.

"I… I'm not sure…" Without the torchlight, Uslo's face was lost in shadow.

"General?" said one of the Claws. The column had stopped. Uslo straightened up and waved a hand over his shoulder.

"I'm all right. Not sure what happened there, but I'm all right."

Nokrag let go. Giving himself a shake, Uslo pointed down to the distant torchlight before turning to the men.

"Looks as though the stairs relent up ahead. With luck, we can stop for–"

Vertigo snared the boy as he felt himself fall. He threw out his hands from his face – and lurched to a stop. The glass of the window alcove was ice-cold against his palms. Thick fog hovered beyond, seemed to press on it.

"We can hurt more than him," hissed the voices. The fog contorted rapidly, spinning in a whirl of steely grays. Its center opened. He saw men with crossbows in a dark room, the doors and windows stacked with assorted furniture. The eye of the fog winked, and there was another, larger group of soldiers, these ones holding long spears and shields. They were standing in a tight circle with their backs to one another, staring out into night-soaked mist. Many dead lay about them, men and monsters both.

Tears streamed down the boy's cheeks. "I don't know what you want!" he cried.

His perch fell away beneath him. He landed hard on wooden floor.

"YOU KNOW!" they screamed.

The boy looked up. The huntress sat at the corridor's end, her tail stiff, her back to him.

"WHO?! TELL US OR ELSE THESE ONES DIE!"

He opened his mouth uselessly, unable even to repeat his protest.

The huntress stood up. Slowly, she turned to meet his gaze. Eyes, sharp and fierce, inspected him from within her oval face.

And he knew.

The dual sight swept over him. He tried to fight it, he knew he mustn't let–

Xavire blinked. He was standing in a narrow tunnel. There were no steps, no torches in either direction. The darkness was almost total. Almost, but for a dim red glow coming from inside an adjacent passage. Over seconds, the light grew steadily stronger, and before long the source emerged. It was an orb, set atop a silver-blue staff. The figure that held it was tall, dressed in thick robes, a cowl drawn up over her head. Sweat glistened on sun-kissed skin and, as she turned to look along the tunnel, he saw her hazel eyes pass through his own. Xavire's heart leapt.

The world blurred, twisting around–

There was a bright snap *and the* rip *of fabric as the chair gave way. He collapsed, sprawling on the common room rug, one leg sticking through the broken slip seat.*

"YES! THERE!" Its voices burst all around him. The boy – who now knew that he was something else, too, even if he couldn't remember what – covered his ears, eyes squeezing tight. But he could still hear them all, their shrill words booming inside his head.

"HOW DID IT HIDE FROM US?!" Panic swept across its tones, obliterating the moment of jubilation. "TOO CLOSE! MUSTN'T LET IT SHUT! MUStn't be trapped… not again…" The voices diminished rapidly, racing away toward distant perception. Mercifully, they slipped into silence. But he could still feel them.

After a time, the boy sat up, blinking around the empty room. He uncovered his ears, freed his leg from the chair. He stood.

Guilt wracked him, shaking him to his core. Guilt, and relief. The relief was the worst. Somehow, he had committed a great betrayal. Though it hovered just outside his grasp, he was sure of it. The certainty sickened him.

"Xavire?"

With a jolt, he spun to the doorway. An older lad, red-haired and spry, was standing in the corridor, a look of surprise on his freckled face. His surprise couldn't come close to that of the boy. Everything about the arrival was at odds with their surroundings – the dirt on his face and arms, the mishmash of distressed pelts and rags, the wild and bitter smell cutting across the familiar background of lemon-scrubbed hardwood. Yet there was something familiar, too. The stranger's sharp brow furrowed as he considered the boy.

"I don't owe you anything."

"What?" said the boy, startled at the depth of his own voice. "Hey, how'd you know my name's–"

"I said I don't owe you anything! If you're here for that, you can forget it! I don't care if you saved me, I won't betray her!" His top lip, shaded by thin hair, was curled in anger.

"You're Cauhin," said the boy. The recollection brought calm, negating the impact of Cauhin's strange outburst. "What're you doing in my house?"

Instantly, Cauhin's expression became puzzled. "Your house*? This is the Refuge." He turned away to gaze along the corridor wall. "I thought I was the only one here, 'cept for Derraz. He was chasing me. Said he was looking for… hold on, that can't be right." Cauhin turned back to the common room, peering at the boy through narrowed eyes. "You killed him at the pits, the day we…"*

"Something chased you, too?" The boy felt this was important. He held his breath.

Cauhin nodded slowly. "He was looking for her."

"Who?"

"Alea."

Her name seemed to shunt something aside. In an instant, the boy's childhood home vanished.

Cauhin and Xavire stared at each other fixedly, as if they each feared the slightest move might cause the world around them to change again. Then their eyes flicked aside. Slowly, they turned to look.

"Xavire? Are you seeing…?"

"Yes."

Claws surrounded them. Most were facing away, loosely arranged in the middle of a broad chamber, those without torches clasping pommels as they considered the dark passages set into the surrounding walls. In the center of their circle, mere feet from Cauhin and Xavire, several men were standing around four horses. Xavire noted the plate armor of Sir Guilliver's adventurers among them. A couple of others were crouching nearby over prone figures.

"…too narrow if we run into a fight. Golloch's bollocks, should we need to come back, turning the horses would be next to impossible."

Hearing Uslo's voice, Xavire stepped around the men until he came into view. The general was directing torchlight into one of the passages as he conversed with a hunched Nokrag.

"Then we continue down," she said, nodding toward a wider tunnel, appearing to be a continuation of the descending steps that had brought them into the chamber. "Although with these passages behind us, we can not be as sure that something does not follow."

"Indeed."

"They can't see us, can they?" observed Cauhin, moving to his side.

"No. I believe not." His memory was strangely fuzzy, but something about the disconnection, about the way it felt, was nevertheless familiar. "They can't see us, can't hear–"

"Riuen!"

Cauhin rushed over to the crouching Plainsman, reaching out. However, just as he was about to grab Riuen's shoulder, the youth recoiled. The little color possessed by his Ardovikian complexion vanished.

"What is it?!"

Cauhin pointed, jaw flapping. Xavire leaned over and saw a pair of prone bodies, carefully laid out on the floor.

"It's…! They're…!"

"Us," finished Xavire flatly. The sight of himself was met with a plunging feeling in his stomach, quickly followed by cold and total numbness. He was shocked, certainly – but unlike Cauhin, he was not surprised.

One of the Claws was pacing. He passed through them. They felt nothing. Cauhin and Xavire stepped back.

"Do you think we're dead?" asked Cauhin, his voice dropping to barely above a whisper.

Xavire shook his head. "No. I could see them – us – breathing. It looks more as though we're asleep."

"So, what, then? This is a dream? I've never dreamed anything like this before. It feels too…"

Cauhin met Xavire's gaze. *Real*, thought Xavire. *It feels too real. But it didn't always.*

"Do you remember anything before now? I *think* I was somewhere else, but I just can't seem to–"

"The Refuge," said Cauhin, suddenly. "I was there, being chased by Derraz. Except…" His eyes widened. "Except it wasn't really Derraz. It was hiding in him, but when I saw its face there was–"

"Nothing."

Cauhin swallowed. He nodded.

"Yes..." said Xavire. "Yes, I can remember something similar. *That* was the dream. This is more like something in-between."

"And we're here together? You're not my dream?"

"As much as you're mine, I'd wager."

Cauhin tilted his head to consider this. Then, without a word, he moved over to Riuen, stepped carefully around the now sitting Claws and Plainsman, before reaching toward his own prone body.

"Ouch!"

He jumped back, his legs passing through Riuen. The sight of it made Xavire's head swim.

"Are you alright?"

"It burned me!" Cauhin massaged his fingers. "But it was cold! Coldest thing I ever felt!"

That thing, the empty voice, is keeping us out, thought Xavire. More memories came back to him. The dreams had returned. What was it Alea had said? Something about getting as far from wherever he found himself as possible. *Too late for that, now,* he thought.

Xavire froze.

Alea.

"It was looking for Alea!"

Cauhin's brow furrowed momentarily. Then he gasped.

"That's right! It wanted her! Only… it didn't know it wanted *her*. But I knew, I knew that somehow I could show her to it, and that I had to keep…" Cauhin trailed off, apparently spotting the look of horror that had claimed Xavire's face. "You showed her to it, didn't you?"

"I think… I think I…" Xavire could see her in his mind, peering around the passage bend, lit by the sparse illumination of her staff. Guilt consumed him. "I did."

Cauhin didn't seem to be listening. He was looking up, scanning the bare rock of the chamber ceiling. From across what felt like a great distance, Uslo gave the order to march. Riuen draped Cauhin's listless form over his back, Xavire was carried between two men. The Claws began to move.

"We're under the town, aren't we? These must be the caves in Eranie's story."

"Why does that matter? Didn't you hear me?! That… thing is going to find Alea!"

"That 'thing' is a monster."

"The ghost from the legend?"

Cauhin nodded.

Xavire attempted to grasp this. He failed.

"So?!"

"So, it was afraid of Alea! Don't you remember?! She must've come here to kill it!"

Torchlight was fading fast, borne into the descending passage by the Claws.

"It called her a huntress," said Xavire quietly. "It was afraid something would be shut, that it would be trapped again..."

"We have to help her."

Xavire stared into his face, little more than a dimly outlined silhouette. Yet, somehow, he could see him perfectly. Cauhin's expression was determination itself.

"How?"

"I don't know, but... but I can *feel* it down here! Can't you?"

Xavire could. It was a slim thing, a bare tingle at the furthest reach of perception. But the moment he noticed it, he knew what it was. There was nothing else it *could* be.

"I can. I think..." he raised his arm, pointing to one of the narrow passages. "I think we go that way..."

"Right! Come on!" Cauhin dashed toward the passage.

"Hold on! How will we–!"

"We have to hurry! It might've already got to her!"

Cursing under his breath, Xavire ran after him. As he crossed the corridor's threshold, his shoulder collided painfully against its uneven frame. Distant, but it was pain all right. It seemed that even in their disembodied state, they couldn't pass through everything. Amidst all that was happening, this was as solidly familiar a fact as Xavire could hope for. He'd have gone so far as to call it a relief.

*****

Orod drifted between darkness and oblivion. Weight pressed him. He tasted blood. With mind blank, he attempted to draw breath – pain thrust him to consciousness. It came from everywhere, every nerve in his body seeming to cry out in furious protest. Gritting his teeth, he forced air into his lungs. The smell was old. Damp and lithic. Familiar.

His pain seemed to produce a ringing inside his skull, and he became aware that one side of his head was pressed against cold rock. Forcing back a groan, he lifted it slightly. There were sounds. Loud ones. They blended in echoes, an effect compounded by his internal ring; but as the noise washed over him, Orod gradually managed to separate its sources: metallic clashes, the grunts and thumps of fighting, a hissing rush and the bursts of falling water. Beneath it all, moans of dying orcs.

Something was on top of him, holding him chest-down to the rock. A corpse. Orod tried to dislodge it, pushing off with his forearms. The effort yielded little, and so he reached forward, feeling past the fire in his nerves for inconsistencies in the ground's surface. The grooves were shallow. He pressed the tips of his fingers hard and dragged himself forward. A cold spray began to fall across his back as the limp body rolled from on top of him. Slowly, haltingly, Orod got to his feet.

One eye was blood-clogged. Orod cleared it clumsily. He could feel his heart thudding across the swollen half of his face. Each breath brought dagger-like pain to his side, no doubt from a broken rib. The spear wound continued to seep beneath it. Pressing his fist against the flow, the orc peered through intermittent vision. A scattering of figures dotted the darkness ahead. Two of them seemed to be circling each other, their breaths heavy and menacing. One of the pair let out a bark, launching itself forward. The metallic clashes resumed, answered by cavernous echoes.

Orod looked up. Far above, almost directly overhead, was a hole. Water poured steadily over its jagged edge, its streams surrounded by mist. The clouded night sky could be glimpsed beyond, barest source for the vanishingly spare illumination below. But it was enough. Orod had been born in the darkness of underground places.

Underground…

Memory returned. The human lord had unleashed the river. He had baited Orod, had trapped him. His orcs had been swept away, dragged until… He recalled the cannon, the way the ground shook after it had fired. Its shot must have torn open the cavern ceiling, with the quaking that followed produced by the massive crumbling of rock. And now he was here.

Orod's rage began to burn, fueled as much by the pain as by humiliation. He reached for his axes but found they weren't hanging at his sides. Alarmed, he looked at his hands. He had held to them as the river carried him along its trench. They were gone, dropped as he fell. Knowing it was in vain, he turned to search the site of his landing and saw what remained of his horde.

Beneath the cascading mist, the pile of bodies rose precipitously against the edge of a sheer drop. It couldn't contain even half the orcs that must have fallen through. Most were dead, but a few twitched uselessly, their pitiful moans seemingly without end. Orod watched as several corpses tumbled limply off the cliff, falling into an impenetrable black.

From behind him came the *crunch* of blunt iron driving through bone, followed by the feeble *thump* of collapsing flesh.

"Any of you other runts want to have a go?" The orc's voice brimmed with contempt. There was no response. "Thought not. That means *I'm* the krudger, now. Got it?"

"No."

"What's that? Who're you?"

Orod turned and looked upon his challenger. It was one of the greatax. While it appeared the orc had lost the double-handed weapon typically wielded by that elite rank, as well as his helmet, he was nevertheless an imposing brute, being tall and bulked, clad in a solid mix of iron plate and leathers. Orod met the dull sheen of the challenger's eyes.

"I am the krudger," said Orod flatly.

There was a pause. Then the challenger's lips drew back.

"Orod?" He laughed. "Garkhan's spit, you *are* a tough lump of shum. Though... not lookin' so tough now." The orc raised his weapon, a battered handaxe, and pointed it to the dead behind Orod.

"Look what your 'destiny' came to, eh?"

Orod said nothing, his gaze unflinching. The challenger lowered his axe.

"Always knew there was somethin' off about you. Never should've trusted a slave, made me sick just–"

Orod lunged.

Too late, the challenger brought his axe up in a panicked strike. Pain lanced up Orod's arm as he caught the blunt edge in his hand, and they crashed bodily, sending them to the ground. There were sharp *clangs* as the armored orc's pauldrons hit the ground in near perfect unison. Grabbing his opponent's head in his hands, Orod slammed it back. The impact of skull on scabrous rock produced a *crack*. The greatax howled. Orod took a moment to straddle his foe and then slammed the head again, and again, and *again*.

The howling stopped.

Orod stood up. The thrill of combat sweetened his pain, sent vitality to every corner of his being. He filled his lungs, welcoming the stab in his side, and let loose. Long after he'd stopped, the cavern rang out with his roar.

The krudger ran his gaze across the onlookers. There were more than he'd first thought. Perhaps as many as twenty orcs watched him warily from amidst the disused scaffolds and mine carts. He stared them down in turn, securing his domination. Then he leant over the dead greatax and began to strip its iron plate. Orod hadn't only lost his axes in the flood, but his pelt as well. Everything he had taken from the world, gone. He'd had enough of skins and hide. It was time to return to what he knew best. In the shadows, nothing but iron would touch him.

Greaves, breastplate, pauldrons, bracers – with the pieces bound tight against his flesh, Orod stepped toward the waiting orcs.

If they hadn't held on to their own, all of them had at least managed to scavenge some weapon or another. It would have to do. His fury couldn't wait.

The orcs fell in behind him as Orod walked toward the nearest passage, an arched tunnel set into the rock face. Broken rail track ran straight into its total dark. As he reached its threshold, Orod spotted a length of chain coiled on the floor. He gathered it. The metal was thick with rust, nicking his hands.

With intimate familiarity, the krudger fixed the chain across his chest, wrapped it around his upper arms, bundled its ends around his fists.

"What do we do now, Krudger Orod?"

Facing into the tunnel's darkness, Orod grinned.

"Now, we hunt."

*****

As he dashed along the winding stone passages, there were several thoughts Xavire attempted to avoid. The first was how he seemed able to see Cauhin in perfect clarity, while all else – the tunnel walls, the floor, the odd boulder for him to stub his foot on – was cloaked in the fathomless dark of the underground. At one point he had tried to remove his glasses, only to discover that, for the first time since adolescence, he wasn't wearing any.

The second unwelcome thought was how easily they were finding their way. Despite the frequency of forks and junctures – sensed but unseen – not once did either of them show a moment's hesitation before selecting their path. On an unspeakable level, Xavire felt as though he had run these passages many times before. It was another idea he did not wish to explore.

Finally, inevitably, there was the monster. The empty voice. He could feel it moving ahead of them, a buzzing void, inescapable, yet impossible to grasp. Xavire wondered if it could feel them, too, if the sensation that allowed them to follow in turn revealed the followers themselves. More so than the others by far, this thought proved hopelessly unavoidable.

Through the tunnels behind him, Xavire heard the last vestiges of a distant echo. He shivered. It sounded like a roar.

"Ouch!"

Xavire stopped. Cauhin was standing up, rubbing his shoulder. It seemed in his haste, he'd overshot a bend, colliding with the rough-hewn stone of the passageway. It wasn't the first time.

"Careful, there. You're going too fast, don't want to–"

"I'm fine."

"Of course." Xavire believed it. Such pain faded quickly for them. Like echoes. "All the same, maybe we should slow down."

"*It* isn't slowing."

He's right, thought Xavire, reluctantly turning his attention to the monster. Its buzzing had grown more agitated. It was getting close.

Light washed over them. Xavire blinked rapidly, hands shielding his eyes as they adjusted.

"Wha–?" His mouth fell open. Cauhin held aloft a burning torch, its flames tall and seasoned. The Ardovikian's face was bright with pleasant surprise.

"Where did... *How*–?"

"Haven't you ever had a dream where you realized it? Where you knew?"

"But... but we're *not* dreaming!" *Aren't we?* he thought.

Cauhin shrugged. "I know, but I wanted to see where I was going and I thought of this, and here it is, just like in dreams! You try."

Speechless, Xavire held out his hand. When was the last time he'd realized he was dreaming? He couldn't say. Certainly a long time ago. Strange as this experience was, it wasn't like any dream he'd had before. Nevertheless, he half closed his hand, imagined it held a stave, the end bound in twisted–

"Ah!"

The warmth of flame swept across his face. Xavire let go. The torch vanished before it hit the floor.

"I think we'll just use yours."

He looked around at Cauhin, but the youth was staring into the passage ahead. Toward the monster. Xavire immediately knew why.

It had stopped.

"Come on!" urged Cauhin.

They ran down the passage. With the light's aid, there were no more obstacles to hinder them or turns they couldn't judge, and they raced along increasingly even corridors, making straight for the monster. Its buzzing swelled with every step and soon seemed to shake them somewhere behind their eyes.

Just as the buzzing surged to an impossible peak, a pained cry reached them from up ahead. They stopped, staring at each other. Cauhin's torch was gone.

There was no doubt.

"Alea!" yelled Xavire.

They rounded the bend and saw her.

A pentagonal intersection of passageways lay before them. Alea was on hands and knees. Her staff appeared to have rolled beyond her grasp, and in place of its red glow, a violet light pulsed against the surrounding rock, igniting dendritic veins along the ceiling surface with sickening magenta brilliance. The monster loomed over her, shimmering in Xavire's perception, dozens of spindly appendages connecting unreasonably to the bottom of an emaciated torso, tight with perse flesh. Its eyeless face looked down at Alea, and its torn mouth frothed with the hunger of the void.

Fear, more profound than Xavire had ever known, enveloped him.

"Oh, gods!" Cauhin's voice pitched and trembled. The sight seemed to strip him of his defiance. "Oh, gods, what do we *do*?!"

Xavire drew his sword. It hadn't been there before he reached for it.

"Unhand her, fiend!" Xavire cried, his voice barely holding together.

The monster gave no reaction to Xavire's injunction, and still none as he charged down the passage toward it. Bringing his blade high, Xavire piled momentum behind a heavy overarm hack. The steel sang as it sailed for its mark. It hit the monster – and vanished.

Xavire had just enough time to look despairingly at his empty hand before one of the monster's many limbs swept out dismissively, catching him square in the chest. The pain was cold and immediate, an explosion that so drowned his awareness, Xavire failed to notice himself being thrown back down the passage to land in a crumpled heap against the far turn.

He resurfaced to the sound of his own wails. Through blurred eyes, he saw Cauhin's terror-struck face leaning over him. Xavire clamped his teeth shut.

"Help me up," he wheezed.

With Cauhin pulling his arm, Xavire managed to work his way up the wall behind him, until finally he was more or less able to stand. The pain was fading, but only in the most tortured increments. He felt drained. All at once, Xavire was acutely aware of how far he was from his own body.

In the intersection, Alea's arms were shaking. One collapsed. She rolled onto her side.

"We can't help her," said Cauhin. Tears were streaming down his cheeks. "Can't we help her?"

Xavire tried to speak. No words came. He wanted to look away, but his eyes were locked on Alea. She had stopped crying out.

We'll be next, he thought. Selfish though he knew it to be, at that moment he welcomed such an outcome. Anything to rid him of the guilt.

"Sorry, lad," Xavire croaked finally. "Some monsters can't be slain. Not by us."

He closed his eyes, overcome by the need to see something else, *anything* else. When Xavier opened them again, it was to see a thoughtful Cauhin looking at him.

"Not us..." Cauhin's brow drew in. He straightened up, pushed his shoulders back. "In the legend, it was scared. It was afraid she would kill it!"

"Who?"

"Eranie!" Defiance returned, Cauhin faced the monster. He lifted his left arm toward it, hand closing on air.

"We need a weapon it fears!"

And then Cauhin held a bow unlike any Xavire had ever seen. It was tall, almost as tall as the youth himself, made from dark wood that curved elegantly above and below the grip. Thick spines abounded its length, each the length of his thumb, their needle-fine points directed outward from the archer. For all its apparent symmetry, there was something about the design that defied artifice. It seemed almost organic. As if it had grown.

Cauhin raised his right hand. Instantly, a green-headed arrow appeared, nocked tight against the bowstring. With a sweep of his arm, he drew and loosed. The arrow soared in a perfect arc before burying itself in the monster's chest.

Screams pierced their ears like knives. It recoiled, clawed hands pulling at the arrow, its manifold legs working furiously as it scuttled away into one of the passages. The cries quickly diminished, and in their place, Xavire heard Alea draw a deep and shuddering breath.

Xavire stared at the young Plainsman in awe. "By the gods, lad, you did it!"

Cauhin was already running down the corridor as he spoke.

"Hurry!" he called.

Steeling his still-shaky legs, Xavire went after him. Alea had recovered her staff, and Xavire reached her as she used it to push herself to her feet.

"Alea? Can you hear me?" He tried to touch her arm and quickly withdrew when his hand vanished into the robes. It was the same as with the others. He looked round for Cauhin and saw him standing by the monster's passage, a freshly conjured arrow leveled at its depths.

"It's going to keep coming!"

"How did you hurt it?" asked Xavire.

"This is the Thorn-bow! It's what the hunter Eranie used to chase it down here!"

"*The* Thorn-bow? From your legend?"

"How I imagined it, anyway." Cauhin glanced back at him. "Hurry and make another! I don't think I can hold it off alone!"

Xavire stared at the bow. His mind clamored with what felt like a thousand questions, each more unanswerable than the last. Weakly, his chest still aching from where the monster struck, he raised his arm in imitation of Cauhin.

For the slimmest instant, a Thorn-bow flickered into his grasp. It vanished decisively.

"C'mon, Xavire!"

Xavire could sense the monster in the dark. Cauhin was right – it was coming back.

"Don't fear it! Whatever you do, don't–!"

"Oh, sod this!"

Xavire adjusted the position of his hands, squeezing his eyes shut. He felt a weight appear in his arms.

"What's *that*?!"

Xavire opened his eyes. In spite of everything, he grinned.

"I never was one for traditional bows!" he said, setting the stock against his shoulder. The crossbow was made from the same mysterious material as Cauhin's bow, its limbs bristling with the same thorn phalanx. The string was set, a green-headed bolt in the groove.

Cauhin's laugh had an edge of madness. Xavire knew how he felt.

Violet light bloomed in the passage depths. The monster appeared around a bend, hurtling toward them.

"Steady!" called Xavire, but already the monster was unleashing a frustrated shriek. It retreated.

"Aha! That's it! Run away, beast!" Xavire wanted to be sick.

"Xavire, look!"

Xavire followed Cauhin's glance in time to see Alea leaving through another passage.

"Follow her!" said Xavire, dashing toward the passage. "We might be hurting it, but she's the one it wants!"

"Right! We have to keep it away!"

Alea strode purposefully through the underground, slowing only to run her fingers over the passage walls by each juncture. Her way was lit once more by the staff's red glow.

"That... thing," said Xavire, his eyes on the bend behind them. It seeped violet light. "What do your people call it?"

"*Mulach-oid.*"

Xavire looked back at Alea. She was moving quickly. Even as a… whatever they were, following with their backs to her was difficult.

"What's that word mean? Ghost?"

"I think 'nightmare' is closest in your tongue."

Xavire nodded. It seemed appropriate.

"But that isn't exactly it."

"No?"

Cauhin shook his head, a smile faltering on his lips. It ended up more like a grimace.

"It means 'the dream that hunts.'"

*****

Nokrag's people were well accustomed to cold. In the ogre lands, chill winds arrived with scant variance from across the northern glaciers, bracing and fresh. Not like here. Underground, the air's bite seemed to sap, and every step brought the mercenaries further into its numbing stagnance. She let out a great breath and observed the eruption of torch-lit vapor. It streamed around her face to fly back up the tunnel behind her, as if making a desperate bid for the surface.

A short time after passing the nexus of diverging passageways, Nokrag spotted lights ahead. They were faint, barest glimmers of sepia-stained luminance appearing at irregular intervals along the tunnel walls. As the distance shrank, she identified them as a series of lamps, unusual in design, although she would admit to hardly being an expert. So bare was their glow that, when finally Dargent and his men could discern the bulbous frames, the light of the torches rendered them inert by comparison.

The ones at the bottom were brighter. As the troop debarked the protracted stairway, the cavern ceiling rose dramatically, vanishing into darkness. Relieved murmurs escaped from the men. They were glad to be back on level ground. Those with pikes could finally carry their weapons vertically after the awkward space of the tunnel. Even Nokrag let out a sigh, stretching her neck and shoulders as she looked around. They had emerged on a broad platform whose limits on one side were marked by the ascending buttress of bare rock, and on the other by around a dozen of the curious lamps, each standing waist-high – an ogre waist, that is – atop metal rods. Their light was sufficient to reveal the ground about them and no more. Or rather, they revealed where the ground ended; an inconsistent cliff made its abrupt appearance less than a pace beyond the line of lamps.

"Get the wounded on horseback," said Dargent. The animals were perhaps the most relieved to leave the tunnel's steps – the need to painstakingly guide them down had slowed progress to a crawl. But now they could show their worth, and the mercenaries helped their comrades up, the one with the bad leg settling into the saddle, Xavire simply lain across another. Riuen shook his head firmly, hunched under Cauhin's limp weight, the orc axe still clasped in one hand.

"Suit yourself, my good man. Warrior Nokrag, if it pleases you." The general gestured for her to follow. They walked toward the line of lamps, moving along the bare rock face from which the tunnel sprang. Nokrag looked up. The rock rose steeply, dissolving into obscurity.

"Can you see a ceiling to this place?" asked Dargent. Though he spoke quietly, his words were nevertheless trailed by a hum of acoustic resonance.

"No."

"I see. But there's no question we're still underground."

They shared an awed silence. Ogres possessed an altogether different sense of physical scale, as far removed from that of men as the concept of time was to elves. Here, however, the enormity of the space overcame all such difference.

"And what about there?" They reached the lamps, beyond which the ground dropped away sharply. Nokrag leaned forward, scanning the ocean of black. Dargent held his torch over the edge.

"I can see the other side. It is not far. But down there," she looked back, meeting his gaze. "Nothing."

The general kicked a pebble off the cliff. They listened. Nokrag heard a dim *snap* of impact. Only the echoes made it back to Dargent.

"Deep, then."

"Very," she confirmed.

Dargent nodded as he set off along the lamps, tracing the cliff's edge. He paused once, looking as though he wanted to touch one, only to think better of it.

"It appears as though our journey continues straight along the cliff," said Dargent finally. "No narrower than the passage down, by the looks of it, although these lamps don't continue beyond here. We take it two-abreast, hugging the cave wall. And slow."

Side-by-side, Nokrag and Dargent were closer to four-abreast, but still they led the way, following a sharp southward curve around the yawing gorge. Contrary to the general's assessment, Nokrag soon saw that there were more lights ahead. A lot more. It wasn't long before the men could see them, too. After unknown minutes of cautious progress, the shape of what lay ahead gradually became clearer.

"It is a settlement."

"Indeed? An old mine of some sort, would you say?"

"I do not know such places. I can not say."

The cliff's path opened out onto a wide plateau, lamps spread across its surface. Most were broken or spent, and the glowing few showed little. Only by the men's torches could Nokrag identify the box-like shapes as carts, some still heavy with dark ore, as well as the strange criss-crosses of wood and iron upon which they were set. Scaffolds in various states of decay had been set into the cliff to work their way down its face, while at several points the carts' tracks swooped over the edge at steep gradients, continuing to descend out of sight.

"As I thought," said Dargent, his eyes alive with curious delight. "A mine. Looks like it was a massive operation in its day, which was antediluvian, certainly – perhaps even pre-God War! There's no way the people of a town such as Keatairn could've worked something on this scale. Only Ancient Primovantor can account for it."

"Or dwarfs," offered Nokrag.

"Much the same, Warrior! Legend has it that in the Time of Light, the noble peoples lived harmoniously. Men, dwarfs, elves, all working together in peace. Now that I think about it, I'm not sure if your people are mentioned in Man's histories of the period... a gross oversight, if so."

The general paced along the nearest track as he spoke, inspecting it eagerly. After a while, he stopped. Torchlight cast flickering shadows across a thoughtful expression. He passed thumb and forefinger across his mustache.

"None of these appear to lead back the way we came... whoever built all this must have had another method for bringing ore to the surface. I bet if we follow any tracks going up, we'll find–"

"We are still to reach the settlement."

"...Forgive me, Warrior, I don't follow. Is this not what you meant?"

"No."

Dargent cast about. "Then where–?"

"You will see. It is... big." She grinned down at him, and after a moment, he returned it. If there was anywhere they'd find treasure, it was there. Anticipation welled in her, mounds of glittering things conjured in her mind.

They continued on. The road – for there was indeed a road of sorts, its contours guiding them out and around the mining site – had changed almost imperceptibly, the more-or-less even surface giving way to a grit-strewn upward incline. The darkness ahead of them seemed to wobble, as if the troop were peering through murky waters. Only Nokrag could discern the looming dimensions of what awaited them. She said nothing, however, waiting for the men to confirm it for themselves. Light from the general's torch reached the first structure. Several of the mercenaries gasped.

A lancet archway some three-stories high spanned the road with flawless symmetry, its pale stone reflecting the light in a shower of igneous sparkles. And it wasn't alone – more arches ranged out to either side, each connected to the next, identical dips and crests curving inward to form a circular facade as they melted into the dark. But it was those above that seemed to rob the men's breath; between every arch pair, a third sprouted above, joining the others to either side, those in turn supporting another, on and on until their pointed outlines disappeared into the cavern ceiling, which was here low enough for Nokrag to glimpse the tips of its many stalactites.

The air around them hummed with expectation, no less from Nokrag herself. Only Riuen appeared reluctant before the arches, the Plainsman's gaze fixed on the floor before him. Without a word, Dargent led the way into the city.

Nokrag had visited but a handful of large human settlements in her time. It was, however, enough for her to decide that most converged around the same ugliness, a seemingly compulsive destruction of open space as more and more inhabitants squeezed all manner of their lives together. But she recognized the differences, too, the various styling of east and west, of cold and temperate climes. This one looked like Keatairn. From the height and form of its precise structures, through the airy layout of broad doorways surrounded by columns, terraces, and lancet windows, the architecture of the city below held striking resemblance to that on the surface. There were differences, of course, and not minor ones. Unlike the valley-squatting Keatairn, the underground city was arranged around an enormous column of natural rock, which Nokrag could dimly make out over the tops of nearby buildings, and which itself appeared to be pocked with various towers and structures. Where Keatairn's aspect lay incongruous to the surrounding landscape, even to an ogre's eyes it had to be said that everything here seemed to more or less accord. But there was another difference, one so arresting it all but banished the others from Nokrag's attention. It drew a hiss of disgust through her lips.

The city was a ruin. Hardly surprising, with all Nokrag had seen. Rather, it was the *manner* of ruin that so bled her of hope. For all the damage wrought by time, at least tenfold could only be attributed to pillage. The columns were bare and ragged, whatever ornamental stone that once decorated them having been stripped away. Those doors not removed hung broken in their portals, and piles of broken tools and masonry were carelessly scattered across a ground which, Nokrag now realized, must once have been paved with flagstone.

If the rest of the troop's hope wasn't immediately dashed by the edifices that greeted them, they were certainly tarnished. Stepping away, Dargent approached the nearest structure. Crude holes appeared regularly along the face of its stonework, doubtless opened with pickaxes. The general placed a hand inside one.

"They took the iron clamps..."

He entered the building.

The mercenaries talked in hushed tones as they waited. Wanting to block out their words, Nokrag moved to sit on a cylindrical stone at the road's juncture. She guessed it had once borne one of the likenesses that smaller races were so fond of. Perhaps it had even been made from precious metal.

It is a big settlement, she thought. *There might yet be treasures unclaimed.*

Nokrag continued to nurse such notions until Dargent re-emerged. The general approached his men. She listened.

"...stripped clean. A thorough job, too. It's likely the people up in Keatairn have been at it for generations. But this is a big place, there's no reason to think they got it all–"

Nokrag stood up sharply. She could hear something other than the general's attempt to bolster his men's motivation. It was moving in the cavern beyond the arches, stalking across the underground, casting barest echoes through its wallowing dark. Many things.

And they were coming their way.

*****

Slag proceeded down the hillside steps, innumerable seams of fiery brilliance revealing the furore within. Although searingly hot, its surface had nevertheless hardened to a degree such that Abyssals could walk upon it. The devils savored what they could of its fire on their cloven feet, and of the scalding air that flowed in distorted waves from ever deeper inside the cave. They waited.

Finally, the heat of the cavern air dwindled. The *cracks* of melting stone died out.

Kolra the Tormentor stepped up to the cave mouth. It was wider now, and taller, a consistent corridor that curved toward the hill's heart, smooth save for a scattering of nascent stalactites. Head held high, he led them into the short passage. The Abyssals rounded its sole bend and saw what remained of the efreet.

In many ways, the creature was near unrecognizable, its once muscular body having shriveled, its glowing red flesh now charred to piteous black. The last six yards or so of its work, melting through the blockage set by the cave's protectors, appeared to have proven the most arduous, and it had collapsed against the cave wall, utterly spent. The rock around it continued to glow, the odd molten rivulet dribbling slowly toward the floor.

However, it was what lay beyond which drew Kolra's eye. Violet light, sickly and bruised, swam with liquescent burden around the efreet's crumpled silhouette. The sight of its source filled the demon champion with hunger. Grinning from ear to devilish ear, he strode past the dead or dying efreet – he cared not which – and into the domed chamber.

"Is that...?" breathed Zenarei at his ear, her hands closing around his upper arm.

"Yes."

The Abyssals spread themselves along the curving chamber wall, heads turned inward, their rapturous stares rising up the length of the central object. Even the perpetually scowling Gig'Thanas, more disgruntled than ever at having had to crawl behind the others, beheld it with something akin to awe. The gate had a slender frame of smooth, dark stone, the tip of its lancet arch thrusting to a point just shy of the ceiling. At almost twenty-feet high and six across at its base, it dominated the chamber. And it was open. Liquid light fell in a silent cascade, an amaranthine torrent that cast its violet illumination across the demonic spectators.

Kolra sighed. He had it. At last, he *had it*.

"My, my," said Zexori, stepping forward. "The material, it's..."

"Pure, stabilized portalstone," finished Kolra. "No need for ritual here, for sacrifice and invocation. This gate goes all the way back to the so-called 'Time of Light,' vanishingly scarce in its day and without doubt the last remaining of its kind. Built with the knowledge of the Celestians themselves, perhaps even by their hand, and certainly for their purposes. Stop!"

Zexori had continued to approach the gateway, and she stopped, looking back with bare impatience.

"Do not go near it. We cannot risk alerting the shadow ones to our presence." Kolra nodded toward a robed corpse not far ahead of the succubus. What remained of the man's flesh had a desiccated look. His hands were pressed over his eyes.

"I see. As you wish." Zexori drew back and tugged the chain of her hellhound. The beast's heads were attempting to sniff at the corpse.

The demons around Kolra shifted uncomfortably. Much as it grated him to admit, he understood how they felt. At first, the gateway had done nothing but captivate. But other senses were quickly beginning to make their challenge. Mauve mist obscured the floor in its immediate proximity, one of many possible sources for the nauseatingly saccharine scent, the rest being the invasion of alien flora that brimmed from cracks in the stone, glowing fungi, flowers that seemed to grow inside-out. Even for a denizen of the Abyss, whose home in the Circles violated the reality of the mortal plane, something in the chamber's space felt... warped. As though he'd lost his balance. Kolra blinked hard, trying to clear the swimming quality from his vision, and realized that it wasn't a product of his vision at all.

Forcing his thoughts to order, Kolra brought his gaze back across the chamber, locating the only other object of interest. He circled toward it, giving the gateway a wide berth.

"You're sure you can direct it?" asked Zenarei as she followed.

Kolra laughed. "Oh, I intend to do more than that, my dear. Far more."

She let go of his arm. "What do you mean?"

This time, the demon champion gave no answer, leaving her as he continued toward his goal. *She can work it out for herself*, he thought.

It was a pillar. Tall as he was, every inch of the dull black stone was covered in runes save for its perfectly flat top. Kolra began to circle it, examining the surface under the gate's light. A pair of spent lamps rested together at its side – he shoved them away with his foot.

"Aha," he growled, pleased. Four of the runes glowed with blue light. Kolra saw Zenarei approaching, watching him closely.

"I must sever the corruption tethering it while the shadow ones are distracted. It shouldn't take long. Whatever fool used this hadn't the slightest idea what he was doing," he explained, his words rich in condescending delight. "It's not even fully open – ajar, you might say!" He laughed.

"My Lord, what you said before... Can it be... Do you mean to..."

Kolra looked round. Zenarei's expression was controlled, but the drained color gave her away. Kolra smiled wickedly.

"Now you see. A more ambitious plan than even you could imagine, eh, Zenarei? Just think of it! Far from Kolosu and their Basilean pawns! Even the Green Lady will be powerless, her forest surrounded by our fire!"

Kolra turned back to the pillar, continuing to search as he spoke.

"I will not simply direct the gateway to the Abyss. Rather, I will bind it to the Seventh Circle! It will tear open a new Abyss, right here, on the Ardovikian Plains!"

"The Seventh?! Impossible! Every attempt to reach it has failed! Rivers of blood spilled in vain, every spell nullified, every portal–"

"Ah, but those were *our* portals, *our* spells. This, Zenarei, this is *Celestian* magic! Beings mightier even than our Wicked masters, and certainly stronger than the accursed Domivar and his prison! None have attempted to use *their* power, because none ever found anything more than a broken vestige of it! But I–" He looked at the succubus. Her eyes were wide, her body shaking at the magnitude of the idea. "I shall be the first *and* last!"

Zenarei smiled. "You shall be a god," she sighed, "second only to the Wicked Ones themselves!"

Kolra placed a hand on her face. Slowly, he increased his grip until he held her skull tight.

"And you, cruelest Zenarei, shall be my queen."

Her mouth opened, inviting. Kolra leaned forward.

The demon froze. He'd detected something out the corner of his eye. A figure, warped by undulating vision. Slowly, Kolra lifted his head to look.

At the top step of a broad, spiraling stairway that emerged up into the floor along the nearby chamber wall was a man. Tall and hooded, he wore thick robes, well-worn from the road. In one hand was a silver staff, its head adorned by an orb of red glass.

In distant awareness, Kolra noticed Zenarei frowning at him. He released her.

"I hope I'm not disturbing your moment."

The sound of the voice was met with a burst of hissing from the Abyssals. They quickly began to work their way around either side of the gateway. Kolra stared through narrowed eyes, uncomprehending.

Not a man. A woman.

"Who're you?!" exclaimed Zenarei. She eyed the staff warily. "Witch!"

"Don't call me that."

The Abyssals had crossed the chamber, and Zenarei stepped back to join their semi-circle around Kolra and the arrival, unhooking her whips.

"Yipposhix'Zal!" barked Kolra. The warlock stepped forward, meeting the champion's gaze with mad eyes. Kolra pointed.

"Burn her!"

With evident and baleful glee, the warlock lifted his arms, leveling every one of his long digits at the woman. There was a sudden roar as fire arced through the air, engulfing her in its inferno. Warmth prickled across Kolra's face as he looked on, his grin wide – it vanished not a moment after the fire.

"No! It cannot be!"

Pure light, faint but unwavering, surrounded the woman. It seemed to radiate out from the silver of her staff, its red orb offering only the slightest glow. Her hood and robes were gone, burned to ash by the flames, and their absence revealed an armor set of such resplendence it stung the demons' eyes to behold. Gold bands trimmed each of its master-wrought plates, the steel somehow resisting the corrupt light of the gateway. Her tunic was white, her cloak celestial blue. Kolra looked at her oval face, met her fierce eyes. And he understood.

"You shall not have the portal, demon!" In a swift motion, the sisterhood warrior swung the head of her staff against the floor. The orb shattered with a *bang*. When she raised it again, it was with a long koliskos spearhead in its place. "In the name of the Grand Hegemony, I stand against you!"

"Curse you and your Shining masters!" barked Kolra. His hand dove for his saber. "*Get that Basilean whore!*"

The minions moved in. Several of the lower Abyssals charged ahead, weapons raised and screeching fury. The Basilean dispatched the first three with a great sweep of her spear, deflecting the blow of a fourth with enough force to send the rusty blade from its grasp, before making a quick stab between the ribs of a fifth. Carrying the momentum through, she spun to launch a back kick at the face of the disarmed demon – the crack of its neck breaking reverberated between the chamber walls.

All five of their bodies hit the floor together. The Abyssals paused.

"Who's next?" she taunted.

The demons looked to Kolra. Before he could select a volunteer, white light flashed blindingly from the Basilean's spear.

One hand over his eyes, Kolra staggered back toward the pillar, his saber making warding sweeps.

"Stop her! She must not be allowed to interfere!"

He heard Zenarei's whips cracking in the air, felt Gig'Thanas's strides pulse through the stone floor. There were cries of pain from the lower Abyssals; the hellhound's heads were barking furiously.

Kolra opened his eyes, blinking away the last of the glare. Save for the moans of dying lower demons, the sounds had stopped. The Basilean had fought her way toward the portal arch only to become completely surrounded. Her face was bleeding on one side from what looked to be a lash wound. Gig'Thanas loomed over her, the koliskos spear pointed at his mountainous and freshly-perforated flesh. Zexori was clutching an arm. One of the hound's heads was dead.

"What are you waiting for?!" yelled Kolra. "Kill her!"

Gig'Thanas nodded. He stepped forward, trident raised.

Suddenly, childish laughter echoed throughout the chamber. The moloch stopped, its small eyes rolling back and forth. Kolra cast about with it, momentarily dumbfounded. It seemed to be coming from everywhere. Another voice joined in, its mirth layered in perfect synchrony. A woman's, its sound at once melodious and malevolent, rich and hollow.

Realization dawned even as Kolra looked toward the gateway. The mist at its base was thickening, spreading out across the entire chamber, while behind the cascading light, a shadow had begun to form…

The Basilean barked a laugh. "How unfortunate!" she called over the echoing voices. Her tone mocked. "Looks as though our moment's to be disturbed after all!"

A third voice, deep and ancient, joined the laughter – and the shadow ones appeared.

*****

Xavire's hands were shaking. Standing on the top step of the long, spiral stairway, he tried in vain to keep his crossbow steady, trained at the bend below. Vertigo hit him in waves as the very air seemed to heave around him, threatening to pitch his exhausted mind into darkness. Just out of sight, the monster fretted and seethed, its light impossible to distinguish from the violet radiance filling the domed chamber. But he could feel it. It was preparing to pounce.

"Alea was lying to us! Did you see her?! She lied to all of us!"

"Gods damn it, lad, focus!"

"But– but who *is* she?!" Cauhin's knuckles were pearl-white on the Thorn-bow. "She was speaking to… to *them*!"

Xavire clenched his teeth, overwhelmed by the sense he was going to be sick, if such were even possible in his current state. Despite the urgency of the monster before them, despite its buzzing behind their sockets, his eyes strained to look across the chamber. It took near everything he had left just to hold them on the stairway.

Abyssals! Here! Devils from childhood tales, who mothers warned would snatch naughty children away! Alea taunting them, emerging from infernal fire, clad in–

Xavire glanced again, the barest flit of his gaze. She was fighting them, a lone warrior against more than a dozen fiends, cloak soaring, armor shining pure as she cleaved through crimson flesh. There was no mistaking the gold inlays of wings and stars upon her plate, nor the distinctive blade of the koliskos spear. Alea – if that was her name – was not of the Brotherhood at all. She was Basilean.

Suddenly, the sound of fighting stopped. Xavire risked another glance.

Abyssals surrounded Alea on every side, their grotesque forms swaying with the portal's light. Her stance was defiant, the spear held firm. Her torso pumped breath to a steadfast rhythm.

Xavire cursed as he looked back to the stairway.

"What's happening?!" Anguish bled Cauhin's voice thin.

"Just don't look!"

"She can't fight them all! She'll die–"

"*Don't look, Cauhin!*"

With a bark, the demon leader gave the order to kill her.

Just then, a burst of laughter shot across the chamber. Xavire swung his head to and fro, jaw hanging in dismay. It sounded like a child. The unseeable source was bouncing between the walls, at one point seeming to fly straight between them. A second laugh began to whir after it, rhythm matched to the first, a mellifluous cackling–

"Xavire!"

Xavire snapped his gaze back down the steps. The monster was coming, its countless legs splayed across the passage as it hurtled toward them. Cauhin loosed. The monster lurched its torso aside and the arrow cut through spindle limbs, provoking a wail – but did not slow it. After a moment of horrified inertia, Xavire tracked his aim to its empty face. He squeezed.

Too late.

The monster flung out an arm and knocked the weapon from his grasp, crossbow and half-launched bolt vanishing instantly. It barreled into them. Freezing agony flooded Xavire once more as the impact sent him flying. He rolled twice before striking the dome wall.

Curled into a ball, Xavire groaned. A wearied dark encroached upon his vision, fought to claim his exhausted mind – his pain anchored him, allowed him to mount a last gasp of resistance. He forced his blurred gaze across the chamber. Things were pouring from the portal, large and small, throwing themselves at the red shapes of the Abyssals. A cacophony of unnatural roars blared against the stonework, shot through with the clash of weapons. Xavire blinked hard, and the scene flew into focus.

Shambling, half-naked creatures, their slender forms seeming to mock those of men, were everywhere assailing the demonic minions, locking the Abyssal sabers with all manner of sickles and scythes. Among them strode a three-armed brute the size of Nokrag, its skin a fathomless and glistening black, its eyeless face dominated by a drooling maw. In one of its arms – Xavire quickly realized they were in fact bundles of tightly wound tentacles – it hefted an enormous butcher's knife, bloody from splitting a lower demon. The enormous moloch let out a roar before slamming into it, and the chamber shook with the weight of their struggle.

"Where's Alea?!" called Cauhin, barely audible. The youth had pushed himself to his knees, one arm clasped across his chest. It seemed he'd somehow held on to the Thorn-bow. "I can't see her! Xavire?!"

Xavire couldn't either. Something else had just come through the portal. Something big. His mind balked before the cephalopodic monstrosity. It was floating upright, tendril limbs hanging several feet above the floor, its lower body ringed with mouths. The rest of it seemed to be made from countless layers of folded muscle, across which arced flashes of putrid luminescence. The muscles were pulsing. Two of its mouths slid apart from one another, and a single, serpentine eye blinked open in the space between. As one, the mouths let out a screech.

"There!" cried Cauhin the moment the screeches let up, pointing. Xavire looked and caught the sweep of a koliskos spear, blood trailing as it sundered the remaining heads of the Abyssal hound. Its succubus owner screamed furious vengeance. Producing a curved blade from her robes, she launched herself at Alea, who had no choice but to try to fend off the hail of strikes. Flares of light, each joined by a dizzying *bang*, were now rebounding across the chamber, diffusing an ozone stench – the screeching squid was firing lightning from its eye. Gouts of hellflame soon followed as the Abyssal warlock commenced a sorcerous duel.

The buzzing behind Xavire's eyes gave a warning throb. The monster. It was excited. Lifting his gaze, Xavire saw it perched in the slim space between the top of the portal arch and the domed ceiling. Looking straight at Alea.

Xavire tried to push himself up and immediately collapsed. He felt so empty – which, he supposed, he was.

Where Xavire failed, Cauhin succeeded. The young Plainsman lurched to his feet, a conjured arrow set to the Thorn-bow.

"Up there, Cauhin!"

"I see it!"

Alea pushed her attacker back into a cluster of the scythe-wielding thralls – the monster dove. Cauhin's arrow struck before it was even halfway down, sinking deep into its flank and pinning it to the wall.

Unheard to any others, the monster's agonized cry drowned their ears. It wrenched itself free and scuttled around the chamber dome, seemingly torn between the two threats of Cauhin and Alea. Though Cauhin's legs were shaking, he was managing to keep his aim steady. As the monster dashed back and forth along the wall, Xavire noticed a trail seeping out after it, an inky black substance that hung in the air. It was bleeding.

"That hurt it, lad! You really hurt it!" Disbelief wrestled against the triumph of his words.

"Just remember it's scared!" called Cauhin. "Don't think about anything else! *It's scared*!"

A flicker of pure silver drew Xavire's eye. The demon leader had easily dispatched the thralls attacking him and was reaching toward the strange, rune-covered pillar – Alea charged at him. Her spear leapt for the demon's outstretched arm, who withdrew it at the last moment. They began to fight.

Scared or not, the monster made up its mind. With an almighty cry of frustration, it surged for Cauhin. The youth drew to ear, tracking the creature along the chamber wall. Just as he was about to loose, a stray blast of lighting exploded in the air above, bathing them in light – the arrow flew wide.

The Thorn-bow vanished as Cauhin staggered back, throwing up his arms.

"Ahhh–!"

Xavire had no memory of when he'd stood up, nor when the cold pain had left him. He thought only of the monster, the being that had stalked him for months, the primal fear that crawled across his nights. It was so close, a bare second from snaring Cauhin in its mortal embrace.

And it's scared.

No sooner had the crossbow reappeared in Xavire's grasp than the string gave a *snap* of release, shunting its bolt straight into the monster's featureless face. Ink blood erupted from the wound in great plumes, stifling gargled wails. Within moments, it flooded the space around them. Xavire was blind.

"C-C-Cauhin!" coughed Xavire. Smokey blackness assailed him, rife with the scent of mold, the taste of ash. "Cauhin!"

"I'm alright!" Cauhin's voice trembled. But then he laughed. "It's running away! You got it!"

It was true. Xavire could feel the monster growing ever more distant as it fled back down the stairway into the depths of the underground. Relief enveloped him. He'd dealt it a grave wound – it wouldn't be back.

The cloud dispersed. Xavire ran to help Cauhin up.

"Look!"

He turned in time to witness the moloch pull its trident from the body of its butcher foe; an instant later, the screeching squid wracked the giant with lightning, an arcing bolt that caused its eyes to burst from its head; the screeches shot up in pitch as fire consumed the squid's form, flames propelled by the cackling warlock. All the while, Alea and the demon champion continued to trade blows in a furious clash of saber and stave. The champion was a formidable figure, seven-feet of satin-caped brawn, regally crowned with twisting horns. His blade was a blur, leaping skilfully between feints and unrelenting strikes, defying mortal endurance. Alea was equally impressive, the graceful sweeps of her spear backed by unwavering grit. Neither gave ground, and neither won it.

"Do you think she can kill it?" asked Cauhin. Xavire barely heard him – the portal held his attention, pulled it into the unending downpour of light. Something else was coming through, revealed by a rapidly growing shadow. It had the outline of a human woman, sharp shoulders and narrow waist, a slender gown apparently draped across its frame. The shadow raised its arm – a clawed hand emerged, scrawny and perse.

It seemed the demon champion noticed it, too. Making a broad sidestep, he shifted the fight until Alea's back was to the portal before launching a renewed barrage of blows. Xavire realized with horrified certainty that the demon was trying to hold her attention – Alea wouldn't see it.

Dismay surging over him once more, Xavire watched as the rest of the shadow came through. Floating just over the flagstone, the creature was no woman and wore no gown. It was blank flesh, as featureless as the empty-voiced monster, its body formed in replica of a feminine silhouette. It cast its eyeless gaze across the chamber until it came upon Alea and the champion. Slowly, the creature began gliding toward them, claws outstretched.

Alea let out a triumphant bark – she had managed to slash her spear across the champion's chest. But her victory was a ruse, felt Xavire. The demon was feigning weakness. A distraction.

The creature sped up, closing to strike. Suddenly, its head sprung open, cleaving a jaggedly horizontal line from top of crown to bosom.

Inside were teeth.

Useless though it was, Xavire cried out.

"ALEA! BEHIND YOU!"

*****

The city hummed with the layered *claps* of quick-marching soldiers and horses, not to mention Nokrag's own thudding strides. Without pause, she led the Claws down whichever street took them further into the settlement and away from whatever followed. She could still hear it. It sounded like a swarm, masses of bodies slithering across the settlement's ruin. Like snakes. Nokrag hated snakes.

Up ahead, the great column loomed ever larger over the underground edifices, the ground's incline gradually rising as the troop drew closer. Nokrag had described the column to Dargent when they set off, since it seemed not one of the men was able to distinguish the enormous rock formation from the cavern's dark. She'd told him it was their best chance for finding another route to the surface, and that they ought to head directly for it. He'd agreed. Which was as well – if he hadn't, she would have gone anyway. Alone. Nokrag hadn't crossed the humans' wall only to die fighting in this darkness. Not without prospect of reward, at any rate.

Prospect, it seemed, was slim.

While the matter of their unseen pursuers was chief among the ogre's thoughts, the question of treasure lurked close behind, eying up the surrounding streets. What she saw stoked a bitter disappointment. Even the men, blind as they were, their breathing heavy as they strove to keep up, couldn't have failed to notice the same as she. The inner city was as ravaged as its outskirts. The walls were stripped of ornament, the roadways torn up. A thorough job, to use the general's description. Not all the damage was man-made; some buildings seemed to have fallen foul of time long before any plundering occurred. Their collapsed masonry spilled over the streets, forcing the mercenaries to seek alternative routes. She guessed the plunderers had not been so deterred, something suggested by the rickety constructs that clung tenuously to many of the ruined facades, repurposed from the mines to give access to the isolated upper floors, or else walkways across the debris. Nokrag had tested a ladder at the base of one – it shattered beneath her boot like boiled bones. Even if she were to have abandoned the men and their horses, the walkways were useless to her.

Forced to circumvent yet another toppled building, Nokrag was about to direct them up a narrower side street when the general called a halt. She looked back to see him steer his horse out from the column. Dargent had mounted up behind the unconscious Xavire, one arm holding the limp man upright in the saddle, the other the reins.

"Why?" she asked, packing the lone syllable with irritation. She wanted to get out of here.

"I beg but one moment, Warrior."

Dargent dropped the reins to take a torch from one of his men. Then he heeled, cantering all the way to where the debris blocked their path, to a slanted scaffold wedged against the ruined building. The horse slowed, allowing the general to carefully place the torch among the dry scaffold's bindings before riding quickly back. Flames were spreading along the timber by the time he rejoined the troop.

"What can I say? I thought the place could use a little light! And something to distract our stalkers, with any luck." He adjusted his grip on Xavire, who had begun to lean precariously.

"It will not distract for long," said Nokrag. She looked over the mercenaries' heads, listening. "*If* it does."

"Perhaps not, but no harm in the attempt. This side street looks like it bears us away some – maybe those... maybe they won't know which way to follow."

"They know." Nokrag set off again.

Woodsmoke followed them up increasingly convoluted routes, with more paths blocked by torn masonry than not. For a while, its scent was the only reminder of the fire's existence, as light from the incipient flames failed to impact the dark, until suddenly it tipped into a tall blaze, projecting an orange glow over the tops of the buildings. Though faint, it proved enough to reveal the column to the mercenaries and many of its details to Nokrag. The shapes she'd guessed to be structures were mere remnants, open wounds clinging to the rock face. Some must have been bridges in their day, huge stone walkways that led out over the settlement. All were broken, most abruptly shorn a little way from the column. Their collapse was likely responsible for much of the damage below. But of greatest interest to Nokrag were the tunnels. They were everywhere – some large, like those leading out to the bridges, many small, visible among the interior remains of buildings once set into the column's lower half.

It would be a long climb, but it was bound to lead to the surface.

"We're close," observed Dargent. Xavire bounced slackly before him in time to the horse's steps. The general jerked a thumb behind them. "What about our friends?"

"Closer," grunted Nokrag.

"Do you think we can make it?"

Nokrag said nothing. She didn't know.

Staring straight ahead, the general expelled a deep breath through his nose. "We can't let them catch us on the move. We'll have to choose somewhere to mount our defense."

"They are too many."

"Even so." He stopped. The Claws stopped with him.

Nokrag looked back at the troop. They were watching her.

A surge of mingled fury and frustration washed over the ogre. What was she doing here? Why did she come back to Keatairn? To save the humans? To fight orcs? Either was perfectly honorable, as far as her people were concerned – so long as she came away with something shiny for it. Preferably a pile of somethings. Had she really thought there would be treasure?

The sound of massed pursuit was clearer than ever. It no longer made her think of slithering bodies. They were scuttling.

Even the humans must hear it now, thought Nokrag. She scanned their faces. Human faces were easy to read. Nervous. And steady. They were an all right sort, really. For men. She had enjoyed their wine, and the company that went with it, particularly Cauhin. Nokrag sought him out, quickly spotting the limp red-head slung over the back of the other Plainsman, Riuen, who was somehow bearing the lad's weight and keeping hold of an orc battleaxe. Cauhin's headstrong nature, his leaps between wild temper and reflection, reminded the ogre of her younger self. She wished him no ill. But her purpose in the north was bigger than the humans, bigger than herself. She could think of no reason why she shouldn't leave them and go on ahead.

Except…

Except the things following them – stalking, as Dargent said – alarmed her. Nokrag feared them, and her fear hid behind anger, masked itself with excuses. No ogre of Urshal tribe ran for fear's sake, no less the daughter of Warlord Rnmogyr. She refused to let fear choose.

What I wouldn't give for a swallow of Steppe Root, she thought.

"We can seek a place to resist," said Nokrag finally, looking back toward the column, "but we go to the rock column. Might be we reach its passages. Come! Quickly, humans!"

The men didn't argue. Together they ran up and out the slender alley, the ground leveling off as they emerged on a broader avenue. One way led back toward the scuttling, the other toward a single arch of broken bridge, standing tall over the far end. The buildings on either side were long crushed beneath the collapsed sections, producing mounds of rubble, but there was space enough between to pass under the arch, putting them within spitting distance of their goal.

Nursing a triumphal growl in her throat, Nokrag quickly reached the destroyed bridge and strode under its arch. The column was there, a straight shot beyond the tunnel. She sped up, pounding along the grit floor. They would reach it after all. No buildings stood between them, no rubble. No… anything.

Nokrag's heart thumped with realization. She skidded to a halt, the grit rasping under heavy boots.

A drop. Its edge cut diagonally across their path, the nearest point some two-dozen yards from the bridge section, with the column perhaps three times as far away. She could see devastated architecture far below – it seemed some sort of subterranean shift had caused an area of the city to slump. The tall opening of a passage taunted her from across the gap, set into the column's enormous face.

"Stop!" she called. The Claws were filing through the arch and around the debris, Dargent at their head. He drew hard on the reins.

"Dead end?"

"Dead drop."

"Right." The general stretched upright in the saddle, craning his neck as he peered into the dark. "But that there looks promising, no?"

Nokrag followed his gaze. Several dim lights hovered in the darkness, running the length of an intact walkway between city and column. More bulbous lamps, the first they'd seen since coming down here.

"It does," said Nokrag, bitterly. They had come so close.

"Excellent. About face, lads! Back—!"

"No."

Dargent's questioning look lasted a second. He understood.

"How long?"

"Now." Nokrag emphasized the word by fixing the serrated bayonet to her blunderbuss, producing a *click* as it locked in place. Like the slithering before, the scuttling had stopped. It had been replaced with a predator's silence.

Dargent dismounted, heaving the unconscious Xavire down and laying him next to the debris.

"Wounded, here! Keep the horses over there! FORM UP!"

His martial shouts slapped off the cold stone, activating the Claws. The limping man led the horses back, while the rest began to fan across the space of the arch, those with pikes dropping their large shields so as to field their weapons two-handed from the back rank. Nokrag saw the Plainsman Riuen move hesitantly through the commotion, not showing the slightest intention to set Cauhin down.

"What's happening?"

"They have found us," she answered.

"And we can't run?"

"There is nowhere to run to."

If it were possible, the man's stony face became harder. He lowered Cauhin next to Xavire before hefting the orc axe to his shoulder.

"Then we fight."

Nokrag nodded. They stepped forward together.

The torches were wedged upright into the surrounding rubble. Dargent had put on his helm. In the distance, the general's fire appeared to have spread, its flames throwing a stream of embers up into the underground air, casting a faint and hellish glow across the city. By its light, Nokrag could clearly see their enemy appearing at the far end of the ruined street. Tension raced along muscle, blood pounded in her ears. They were different to the things above. They were horrifying.

She wasn't the only one who saw. The mercenaries' breaths quickened. Several groaned. There was a light rattle of steel as one of the dismounted horsemen began to shake in his armor. In the distance, the ruined city began to sound with unearthly voices, the screams and bellows of hungry maws.

Dargent drew his sword slowly, stretching out the bright *scrape* of metal. He then picked up one of the pikemen's shields, tested its weight, and moved to join the front rank.

"Claws! As men of war, you have fought for fortune, you have fought for glory! You have fought for me! To a man, you have done me honor! But this will not be an honorable fight! I can offer no fortune, no glory in this darkness!"

Over the heads of thirty men and beyond the arch, Nokrag watched the swarm come closer, moving in unhurried strides, long claws caressing the space before them. They were like the phantoms without cloaks, eyeless and wide-mouthed, their flesh angry and tight. Their bodies were more sinew than spindle, however, and they walked on long, inverse-jointed legs. An extra pair of limbs projected out from their backs and over their shoulders, each ending in a single, black spike. Nokrag drew back her flintlock.

"But those are the concerns of men! In this fight you are beasts, cornered and furious! A single battle cat will fight like ten when so pressed, and now so must you!"

"Your general speaks well, men of Claw-tribe!" boomed Nokrag. "This enemy hunts with fear! Do not let them! Take their weapon and feed it to rage!"

"Roar, my Claws!" cried Dargent. "Show them the cornered beast!"

The Claws roared. Nokrag and Riuen roared.

The enemy roared as it charged under the archway.

*****

Alea's arms rang with pain, steadily amassing under the weight of each deflected blow. The Abyssal champion was by far the most fearsome adversary she'd ever faced – and this from a list which included more molochs than were currently present. Crushingly strong, the champion moved with a speed belied by his size, his curved saber as likely to sweep neatly around her stave as to strike it with bone-jarring force. It took everything she had just to hold her own, every iota of focus, every ounce of will. But she held it. By the grace of the Shining Ones, she held it. What was more, the demon had begun to tire. How could he not, so far from the Abyss? If Alea could only persevere, if she could endure just a little longer, she would find her opening and smite him like so many devil-kin before.

The champion deployed a downward hack; Alea dodged, launching a lightning riposte of her spear; the attack was parried, the saber turning in a bid to bite her face; she lifted her stave sharply, knocking the blade high. The forceful rebuke seemed to take the champion by surprise, and he was slow to bring his weapon down. Twisting the spearhead up, she aimed to split her foe along the abdomen. The champion stepped back just in time to avoid evisceration, though not far enough to prevent a deep slash along pectoral muscle.

"Aha!"

Blood gushed between the demon's fingers, a red so dark it bordered on black. His saber hovered before him even as indecision claimed his features. This was it. Her opening. Now she would–

Alea! Behind you!

Every nerve plunged into ice. Ducking low, Alea spun, simultaneously sliding her grip toward the head of her weapon. The creature grasped for her, claws raking the space occupied a split-second before by her head – she drove her spear through it.

The creature screamed. Sound retreated from the chamber, swept under a storm of piercing tones that sent needle-sharp pain into her skull. Alea gritted her teeth, concentrating. The stave of her spear pulsed with white light, the blessed weapon abhorring the corrupt flesh that enveloped it. All at once, a flare of righteous brilliance burst from within the abomination, banishing it utterly.

Without so much as a breath, Alea reeled around and up, straining to catch a saber strike. Its metallic *clang* whined in her ears; the sound cut short as the champion punched her square in the face.

Iron flooded her tongue, tears her sight. Staggering back, her legs betrayed her, and Alea fell to one knee. She pressed the shoe of her spear against the stone floor, let it hold her as she hastily cleared her eyes. After a handful of helpless, heart-pounding seconds, she looked up in time to see the Abyssal champion press the final rune on the pillar.

"No!"

The demon threw her a satisfied smirk. He reached his free hand up to the pillar's flat top and pushed.

In the space of an instant, the chamber roared to life, its walls rippling and turning, the ground shaking violently. Alea pushed herself to her feet, held by a surge of panic as she attempted to ride the motion. Vision bouncing, she looked toward the portal. Its torrent of light twisted inside the lancet arch, contorting, seeming to resist.

What remained of the shadow creatures let out final, futile cries. The portal's light ceased its flow, and then they were gone.

*****

"Not them! Not the night-teeth!" The orc's eyes rolled deliriously in his head, lit with the orange light of the distant bonfire. "*Not again!*"

"Shut him up!" hissed Orod. A pair of ax were pinning the mad one's arms while a third tried to clamp a hand over its jaw. Not that there was much point – with the sounds now echoing throughout the underground, sounds so terrible they frayed even orcish nerves, only they could hear his ramblings, and barely. Still, the panicked tones made it worse.

"Bites! Eats! Kills–"

The words muffled as the hand found purchase.

Orod turned his gaze back to the underground city. He had first seen it from higher up, from an overlook set near the top of an enormous column permeated with passageways, although then there had been nothing to see but an endless dark in the surrounding caverns. They came to it after traipsing through uncountable tunnels and stairways, the ex-slave's subterranean instincts serving as guide. Strange objects had littered their way; dim and fireless lamps, leading to rooms filled with devices, the machinery mercifully despoiled, but whose intricacy went far beyond any he'd seen in Tragar. Following the tunnels down through the column, the orcs had emerged from one of many broad portals at its base to find themselves on a bridge lined with yet more of the faint lamps, the air choked with ash and the city revealed by fire. Smoke lay heavy across much of its ruins, aglow with pulsating red.

And then there were the roars. Hundreds of them, erupting at once, coming from somewhere in the caverns, though the orcs saw no sign of their source. The collective sound shook their insides, echoed in their skulls. Mouth dry, Orod swallowed as a fresh burst of unspeakable braying reached his ears. The krudger had thought he'd known fear before now. He was wrong.

"This's one of the Bloodtusk's old mob!" grunted the orc with his hand over the maw. "Shum-brained nutters the lotta them!"

Bloodtusk…

The name brought vivid memory to the fore of Orod's mind. Tharg Bloodtusk, dying at Orod's feet. Laughing.

You are a shum-brain, slave.

The fire's heavy smoke was spreading rapidly, swallowing the settlement in swirling plumes. It was coming toward the bridge.

You think it was the humans that drove us from their lands?

In the distance, something stepped in front of the flames, taller than the buildings around it, casting an even greater silhouette into the smoke. The titanic form crashed blindly through the ruins, unleashing a bellow like thunder.

You've no idea! No clue what waits there!

There is a power, thought Orod desperately. *It was meant to be mine!*

It'll kill you!

Shouldering the others aside, Orod rounded on the mad orc. He grabbed him by the throat.

"What happened to the Bloodtusk's horde?! Speak!"

"No light!" coughed the orc. "Teeth! Bitin'!"

Orod stared into the babbling face, trying to draw on anger. But, perhaps for the first time in his life, there was none. There was only fear.

Their memories are short. They'll follow you because you promise victory. But you'll fail…

The krudger released his grip. Without a second's hesitation, the mad orc ran back toward the column.

...and when you do, you'll remember what I said here! You will remember!

Less than an hour ago, everything had made sense to Orod. His purpose had been clear. His destiny. Now, he understood nothing. Were Arlok with him, he might have had answers, but...

Orod's eyes narrowed as he watched the fleeing orc disappear into the column's lowermost chamber, his rambling long out of earshot. Something – not an answer, exactly, but something – seemed to have come almost within grasping distance of his thoughts. Something about the Godspeaker.

A *crack* of blackpowder. Close. The krudger spun to face the distant flames, scanning for the source of the familiar sound.

"There, Krudger! A fight!"

Orod looked. Across a chasm in the settlement floor, a dozen or so torches were set into a well of debris. They revealed carnage, a churn of violence in the mouth of a broken bridge arch. Humans, their backs to the cliff edge, were fighting a desperate battle against a swarm of multi-limbed creatures. They were putting up a hard resistance, bottling the enemy into the arch space. But they wouldn't be able to hold forever. They were losing.

A massive figure lurched forward from amongst the humans and into the nightmarish mass, sending them flying with every two-armed sweep of its weapon. Recognition surged. It was the ogre, the one he'd seen standing with the humans' lord. He had found them.

Orod's anger returned, swelling with such speed and intensity to utterly crush his fear.

"Those're the humans that challenged us!" he yelled, turning to look across his remaining ax. To stare down their fear. "Those things can't have them! *They are ours!*"

Anger flared along his words. He sensed it catching in their minds. Anger was like the orcs themselves – a fire. Even in the cold, it only took a spark to set tinder to flame.

The orcs' breaths plumed around them as they barked rage, banged their axe heads on shields and stone. Orod faced the wall of heavy smoke that was approaching them, sliding inexorably along the bridge.

"Kill them!" he commanded. "Kill everything!"

The orcs charged down the bridge. The smoke seemed to waver in the face of their fury, as throughout the caverns the unnatural roaring suddenly became pained.

All at once, the roars stopped dead.

*****

The shadow ones weren't the only things to vanish from the chamber. As the bruised light winked out, the swirls of mist dispersed from around Kolra's ankles, the alien flora withered to rot. The air ceased its nauseating sway. Only its smell lingered, cloying, shot-through with Abyssal blood.

Turning in a circle, Kolra spread his arms wide, a triumphant grin on his face as he watched the chamber dome ripple and spin, its ancient mechanisms grinding with sterile purpose. He began to laugh.

I win! My ascension comes!

"No!"

He brought his gaze around as the Basilean charged, watching her close through shuddering vision. Her spear glowed bright, her bloodied face contorting with righteous rage. Kolra's grin didn't waver.

The spearhead reached within mere inches of his exposed chest when a pair of *cracks* cut through the roar of chamber mechanisms. The weapon halted, straining, and then lurched back. Zenarei's whips were bound tightly around the Basilean's arms. With a shriek of delight, the succubus pulled hard, sending her snared victim to the floor. There was a clatter of metal on stone as Zexori kicked the Basilean's spear from her grasp, and then the sisters fell upon her, claws hunting gaps in the armor.

"Wait!" commanded Kolra.

They looked round, indignant. "But, my Lord—!"

"Do not question me!" he barked, grin morphing into a sneer. "Seize her! I will deal with that one myself!"

The sisters obeyed, their bare-toothed hisses lost amid the ongoing blare. Hauling the Basilean to her feet, they held her between them, arms locked behind her back.

Kolra looked to the portal. Already the space beneath its arch had begun to flicker as the arcane will probed across the planes, hunting for its goal. In place of flowing light, flames leapt in silent flares, each offering a glimpsed image as it built toward inferno. Yipposhix'Zal was sitting before the arch, watching its fire, gleeful expectation radiant upon his impish face.

The champion felt his entire being hum. The Abyss was near. It nourished him.

He moved to stand next to the warlock, and together they beheld the fleeting sight of steam clouds rising over broiling ocean. The portal plunged deeper, revealing an ashen plain, its once flaming sky reduced to smolder; deeper still, impossible labyrinths were set into a great pit, the halls echoing with the screams of the damned. A sulfur smell entered the chamber, sweeping aside any saccharine remnants. The dome walls were slowing, settling into their final arrangement, all the while the portal flames grew until they formed a towering conflagration that filled every part of its span. The images arrived faster: volcanic lakes, firing great forges; sprawling citadels, their legions warring without end. Fissures *cracked* open along the chamber floor, bright with the furious heat of the Abyss, warming the air until it swam once more.

Boom.

The walls stopped their motion, the last mechanisms slid into place – still the room continued to shake as the extra-planar energies morphed its stonework to basaltine slag. Shadows licked across them, cast from the fiery cracks below – the portal held only darkness, a mute inferno seeming to pull the meager light into its fathomless black.

He had found it. The Seventh Circle.

Standing tall, Kolra called into the dark.

"Wicked Ones of Pannithor! Mightiest Gods! It is I, your servant, Kolra! Hear me and know the works I have wrought! I beseech you, darkest masters, extend your prison across these lands, that your children may lay waste the mortal plane!"

The quakes redoubled, the immaterial essence of the Circles pouring forth. Laughing in triumph, Kolra looked round at the sisters, saw the ecstasy brimming upon their faces. The Basilean witch sagged between them as she looked on in horror.

"You should feel honored, mortal! You are witnessing the birth of a new age! Of a new god–"

"*Kolra…*"

The champion froze. His grin locked in a rictus.

No… it couldn't be…

"*Kolra… Kolra, Kolra, Kolra.*" The voice, harsh and deep, rolled through the gateway like a distant landslide, its tone rocking back and forth along a chiding inflection. "*Or do you prefer 'Arlok'?*"

Fear seized the champion's mind, pressed its cold grip along his entrails.

"Lord Anag'rha'su! How–? But I–!"

The Archfiend laughed. "*I have been waiting for you, Kolra. It was only a matter of time. Your game has amused me, but it ends here.*"

"It… I… It is not possible! You cannot speak from the Seventh Circle!"

This time the laughter came from inside the chamber itself. Uncomprehending, Kolra looked round at its source. Horror was gone from the Basilean's face, replaced by a derisive smirk.

"You failed, demon!" The Basilean coughed, spat blood, and resumed her smirk. "Worse than failed – you could never have succeeded! Nothing can subvert Domivar's justice! Your kind will never reach the prison of your foul masters! *It cannot be done!*"

"*The mortal is right. In all ways, your ambition has exceeded your grasp. This is not the Seventh Circle, Kolra. You have found only me.*"

The Sixth. A plane of myriad names, home to fiends, creatures second only to the Wicked Ones in power. Mere seconds ago, Kolra had thought himself on the verge of rising above all its denizens, of ruling the entire domain. Triumph had turned to ash.

"*It pains me to admit, but your achievement is of great worth. This will be the finest addition to my collection of gateways. Know that I will use it to spread my influence across the mortal plane and beyond, elevating my glory – pity that you will not be alive to witness it. No one steals from me without consequence.*"

As Anag'rha'su said this last, a pair of enormous, red hands pushed through the ebon flames of the portal, their claws gripping the arch on either side.

The succubus sisters shoved their prisoner aside before throwing themselves to the floor.

"Please, forgive us, Lord!"

"We were tricked! The champion lied to us!"

Anag'rha'su laughed again.

The impending threat to his life snapped Kolra from his shock. "Stop him, Yipposhix'Zal! I command you!"

The warlock looked at him, brow furrowed above his insane grin.

"Do it!" Panic surged through the champion's cry. "He's going to take it from you! The portal's power is yours as well as mine! *Push him back*!"

A leg came through the arch, cloven and huge. The ground around it burst to flame.

Yipposhix'Zal made his choice. Raising long fingers, the warlock squealed maniacally as he unleashed a storm of flaming bolts, choking the air with continuous *cracks*. They raked across the Archfiend's leg, scorched the flesh black. Anag'rha'su howled. One arm let go of the arch to lash out. Its long claws missed Kolra by a hair – Yipposhix'Zal was not so fortunate. The warlock vanished in a bloody mist, snuffing his magic instantly.

Anag'rha'su clamped both hands on the arch once more, pulling himself through. Kolra staggered back helplessly as the Archfiend's horns appeared, followed inevitably by a giant, leering face, rows of dagger-long teeth arrayed in a perpetual snarl.

"*There you are! You cannot escape me, Kolra, no matter–*"

"AAAAHHH–!"

The Basilean charged toward the portal, the recovered spear glowing brightly as she wound it over her shoulder. Surprise flared in Anag'rha'su's eyes. He made to swat at her, lifting a clawed arm high – the Basilean threw. The koliskos spearhead continued to emit pure white as it shot across the chamber; it flashed blindingly on impact.

Kolra blinked through the afterimage just in time to see Anag'rha'su recoil back into the portal, a silver shaft projecting from his chest.

"*NOOOO!*"

Something changed the moment the Basilean's weapon disappeared through the arch. The transformation of the chamber stopped, the heat of its fissures abruptly doused. In the portal, the black fires began to sputter and fail. The Archfiend held on, claws digging into the portalstone as he attempted to pull himself through.

"*I SHALL NOT BE DENIED!*"

"Wallow in your pit, demon! By the grace of the Shining Ones, I deny you!"

Anag'rha'su's final roar echoed around the chamber. His grasp slipped, the enormous hands vanishing as he was pulled back into the Sixth Circle.

Silence. Kolra held his breath for several seconds, remaining perfectly still. There was no longer any source of light in the chamber. Nevertheless, he could make out the lancet shape of the arch rising above him, the material darker than night.

Inert. The connection was severed. The portal was dead.

Slowly, Kolra released his breath.

Before he could so much as begin drawing another, an almighty *crack* burst through the darkness. He heard the grind of shifting rock, of stone breaking free from stone. There was an explosion to his left, immediately followed by the pain of a dozen shards cutting into his flank. The chamber was collapsing. And not just the chamber, he realized. The arch was toppling, broken along fault lines carved by the Archfiend's claws. He watched it fall, distantly aware of the sisters' screams.

With a tremendous *crash*, the arch shattered.

"Zexori?!" wailed Zenarei from the dark. "Speak to me! *Zexori*!"

Kolra was already hobbling into the antechamber, arms raised against the crumbling dome. He'd dropped his saber.

"I'm stuck! Lord Kolra, my love! *Help*–!" The rest was lost.

Coughing through clouds of dust, Kolra the Tormentor staggered along the cave passage, following its still-warm floor until he emerged beneath starry night. He did not look back.

*****

Xavire gasped, feeling as though he'd plunged into freezing water. The jolt of it leapt across his body, awaking pain, most notably in his neck. Pulling smoke-stung air through his teeth, he urged stillness to his muscles. Many seemed to have cramped against the hard ground.

Where…?

His vision was a blur, darkness hued by torchlight. He could see his breath float across it. It looked like fog.

Someone was next to him, laid shoulder-to-shoulder. Whoever it was let out a moan.

"Cauhin?!"

Xavire recognized the grindstone voice of Riuen and saw his fuzzy form hurriedly approach in the corner of his sight, a stream of Plains dialect issuing in reassuring tones. With sudden alarm, Xavire shut his eyes tight, trying to block out the sounds. He could remember… somewhere else. He had *been* somewhere else. Somewhere with Abyssals, the demons clashing with things yet more nightmarish. And Alea… she'd been there, too. Only, she was different…

Try as he might, the images refused his attempts to hold them. They slipped away to nothing.

"Xavire?"

He gave up.

"I'm here, Cauhin."

Grunting through the pain, Xavire pushed himself upright before instinctively fishing in his pouch for his glasses.

"Xavire! Alea, she…"

His hand found the familiar brass frame. Setting them in place, he looked round at Cauhin's furrowed features.

"…can you remember?" the youth finished, his expression defeated.

Xavire shook his head. He knew the question should surprise him. But it did not.

Because there is *something to remember*, he thought. *Isn't there?*

"Press harder, man! Quickly now, get it bound!"

Hearing Uslo's voice seemed to break the last thread between Xavire and his fading memories. All at once, he was struck by the scene around him. The Claws seemed to be wedged between two mounds of ruinous debris, facing into a single stone arch. And they'd been in a fight. At a glance, he counted near a dozen to have fallen, with more clutching wounds. He could see Nokrag using her wolf pelt to bind a puncture in her arm, her blunderbuss hanging at her side. Its serrated bayonet was coated in a dark and viscous substance, but other than that, there was no sign of any enemy, dead or alive. Xavire drew a shaky breath.

"General!"

"Xavire?! Here, take over." Uslo hurried toward him, scooping up his sword in the process. Xavire noticed the same viscosity dripping from its edge. The general crouched down, removing his helmet.

"Are you all right?" asked Uslo, continuing before Xavire could answer. "You collapsed all of a sudden! We couldn't wake you! Same for the lad, you were of a pair!" Cauhin stood up and clutched Riuen's cloak about his shoulders as the Plainsman pressed a waterskin to his lips.

Another memory swept across Xavire's mind, this one holding steady. They had just flooded the orcs, and he had been standing in the temple's square when…

Xavire's eyes went wide. He tried to stand. Uslo hooked an arm under him in support.

"Sir, this will sound mad, but the… the things from Cadalla, they're coming…"

But he saw Uslo was shaking his head.

"I know. We were fighting them only a minute ago. They had us, too, appalling creatures, and there were so many of them. Dozens at least, Xavire, maybe hundreds. But, well, out of nowhere they started wailing something awful, and then vanished!" Releasing him, Uslo ran forefinger and thumb along his mustache, watching Xavire's reaction. "That'll be just before you both woke up, I'd wager. Seems we'll have lots to talk about, you, the lad, and I. Why, I'm almost inclined to think–"

But whatever the inclination of his thinking, it would not be known; for at that moment, the ground began to hum beneath them. Uslo and Xavire stared at one another, listening to the patter rhythms of pebbles tumbling across the debris. Then the hum became vibration.

"Wha–?"

An almighty *crack* tore through the air. Xavire looked up into the darkness. It hadn't sounded like any thunder he'd ever known. He was suddenly aware that there was no wind. Not even the barest breeze.

"Uslo?"

"Hm?"

"Are we in Keatairn?"

"Not exactly."

"The cave is breaking!" boomed Nokrag, pointing toward the sky – or rather, Xavire realized, toward the cavern ceiling. There were more *cracks*, and he looked up in time to see a cluster of wagon-sized boulders loom from the dark. They disappeared behind the rubble piles and *crashed* thunderously against the ground. Though some distance away, Xavire felt the impacts shoot through him.

The horses bolted, screaming as they dashed under the arch and beyond.

"Leave them!" bellowed Uslo, fixing his helm in place. "Everyone, get under the arch!"

The ground was shaking now, tossing the debris together in an endless uproar of dead stone. Xavire saw Riuen lift Cauhin onto his back before practically bounding toward the archway; with an arm over Uslo's pauldron, Xavire followed. More rocks fell from the dark, their collisions felt more than heard amid the maelstrom. They reached the threshold, and it occurred to Xavire that sheltering under the remnant of a broken bridge might prove no better than standing in the open. Perhaps it was even worse. Regardless, for the time being, it was holding together.

Uslo released him, passing his weight to one of the Claws. Xavire looked back the way they'd come and saw for the first time the enormous column spanning the cavern's height. His mouth fell open. Veins of fire were spreading out along the top of the column and onto the ceiling surrounding it, sputtering and sparking as they warmed the rock to glow. He grabbed Uslo's arm, eyes never leaving the threads of light as he tried to direct the general's attention – but Xavire realized the general had seen something else. Something that had him hastily readying his sword.

"Orcs!" roared Nokrag.

By the molten glow above, Xavire saw them. The greenskins had scrambled to the top of one of the debris piles and were now pouring down its slope toward them, axes raised, battlecries lost in the quake's blare. Among them was one far larger than the rest, its arms and chest coiled with chains – Xavire recognized it instantly. It was the warlord, the one he'd seen on the surface. Somehow, it had survived the river's flood.

Xavire made to draw his sword but was shunted aside as Nokrag pushed to the fore, her blunderbuss leveled. The nearest orc disappeared in a bloody shrapnel mess.

"Shieldwall!" commanded Uslo. "Form in the archway!"

The Claws responded sluggishly, overwhelmed by the assault on their senses. Not even on the day of their fastest drill could they have formed up in time. The orcs were too close, their momentum too great.

As the man supporting Xavire began to pull him back, Xavire's eyes met those of his general. Torchlight flickered against the dusty red-bronze of his helm, pale skin shone through the cut of its visor. Uslo cast him a wink, and Xavire knew.

"No!" he cried, struggling to free himself. "General! Get back behind the line! *USLO*!"

Hefting his bastard sword in both hands, the Silver Cat turned and charged.

*****

As oblivious to the quaking cavern as to the strange light at his back, Orod bore down the slope, riding the shifting rubble toward his goal. The creatures were gone, the smoke dispersed – there was nothing to keep him from the cluster of humans. Nothing to prevent their slaughter. The humans seemed to panic at the sight of them, jostling uselessly beneath the broken bridge.

The ogre lurched forward. Its weapon barked fire, and Orod felt a warm mist against his face. In the next instant, four of his ax crashed into the hulking warrior, assailing it with teeth and blades. One notably wild-looking man rushed to its aid, an orcish weapon brandished in thick arms, while another figure ran past their brawl, large sword borne aloft. Orod felt a fresh surge of triumphant fury as he recognized the distinctive armor.

The humans' lord.

The lord had just enough time to sever the head of an ax before the krudger was on him. Leaping the final yards of debris, Orod raised his chained fists overhead, aiming to slam them down on the shoulders of his prey. With surprising speed, the human stepped out of the attack, sweeping the blade around for a waist-high hack. Orod made to block with his shackle bracer, only for the man to abandon the attack and move once more, the sword rising in an expansive arc before diving at the krudger's bare head. Orod crossed his forearms in its path, and there was an ear-splitting *shunk* of steel on iron. Pain flared. At least an inch of edge had found flesh, breaching the rusty coils to press against bone.

With a snarl of frustration, he grabbed for the blade with both hands, ignoring the pain as he attempted to lock it between chain links. To break it. But as soon as the orc set his grip, the lord pulled hard, drawing blood and sparks as the length *screeched* through. Orod let go. The human staggered with the sudden release. Not wasting a second, Orod whipped his arm out and launched a length of chain – it looped swiftly around the man's neck, catching under his bronze helm. The krudger yanked sharply. His prey lurched back toward him, barely maintaining footing, one hand desperately working to extricate his throat. Orod stepped forward, winding his fist back to strike.

There was a shout like breaking rock. Swinging his gaze round, Orod saw the wild human charging at him, orcish axe raised overhead. The krudger flung his arm out, knocking the clumsy hack aside before bringing his fist back around and into the man's face. He felt his neck *snap*, saw his body fall limply. Orod turned back to his prey and immediately felt a flash of panic. The lord had stepped forward, chain still at its throat, and was driving his blade for the now-exposed arm that held it. Too slow, Orod pulled back. The sword found his closed fist and bit deep. The chain fell slack.

Teeth grinding, the krudger clutched his hand, examining the yawning gash above his thumb. Everything – the chains, the skin, the blood – seemed to exist in a single hue, bathed in orange light from above. He looked up. Fire. The hills were burning, their heat pressing down from above. The power had never been below. It was never his.

A cold fury settled across his mind as Orod brought his gaze back to the lord. His prey had removed both chain and helmet, revealing pale flesh. It caught the light like the snow of the Howling Peaks. The sword was steady, raised in challenge.

Forcing his hand to close around the chain, Orod moved to meet his foe.

In that moment, the sky fell.

Orod heard a run of bone-jarring *cracks* directly overhead. Blazing rock hurtled toward them, its glow causing the shadows to sweep along the floor. With a sound so thunderous as to wipe away all others, it struck across the chasm's edge behind Orod. Shrapnel sprayed across him, denting plate or tearing flesh. The krudger barely had time to fall forward before the ground sank beneath him, lurching suddenly down before catching at a steep angle. Orod scrambled for purchase, the nails of his good hand digging through dirt. Debris from the nearby piles poured past, dragging his orcs into darkness. His legs went over – he caught a groove in the stone.

All of a sudden, the quaking stopped, the last of the falling debris crashed below. Orod could hear only his breaths, quick and ragged. They roared against the abrupt silence. No... not silence. The krudger could hear voices. He looked up the slope and saw that one other had held on.

The human lord lay spread-eagled against the cliff face, clinging desperately. His sword was gone. At the newly-formed edge beyond, Orod saw the faces of the other men, calling out to the lord in their flimsy tongue. The massive form of the ogre appeared among them. It began to lower a length of rope.

No, thought Orod, blood rising once more. *No!*

"NO!"

A jolt seemed to run through the lord as it swung its gaze down, expression hidden in shadow. The light above was fading.

"You won't escape me, human! Do you hear?! I will break you in the dark!" Orod began to free the shackles around his waist, ignoring the protest from his bleeding hand.

His prey barked something back before turning away, grabbing the rope with both hands. Orod launched his chain – with a *snap,* it coiled around the human's heel, catching tight.

Barking laughter, Orod heaved himself away from the drop, delighting in the lord's agonized cries.

"Not bad, human! You're stronger than I guessed! But how long can you hold out?" He pulled again, dragging his way three-feet at a time.

The humans above were shouting. Several threw stones. They bounced pitifully around the krudger. His laughter redoubled.

The ogre shouted something, cutting his laughter short. Somehow, the human tongue didn't sound so flimsy in its maw. Several humans stepped back, quickly replaced by–

Orod's blood froze. A huge crossbow pointed over the edge, held among several men. The one aiming at its fore wore something odd over his eyes and was as bearded as the hated masters.

"No!" The krudger stopped climbing, instead trying to pull the lord down to him. "No! *You're mine!*"

The bearded one gave a short yell. With an echoing *crack*, the crossbow spat its bolt. Orod saw the glint of its enormous head bear toward him – it struck the chain inches from his hands.

The links broke.

"NOOOOOOO!"

With rage thundering in his skull and the humans shrinking from sight, Orodren'val, whose name meant 'Doomed One,' fell into darkness.

*****

There was no mist in the valley. The clouds were thin. Like porous weaves teased by soft wind, they billowed above, offering scant resistance to the moonlight; if anything, they seemed to heighten its radiance, to take the silver glow and throw it far across the sky. Riverbed and flagstone shimmered below, each driving south from Keatairn's wall through the Ballamor Hills. Each empty of all but the dead.

Kolra felt weak. His joints were hard, creaking and popping with every hobbled step along the road. His skin, once a fiery crimson, now evoked ash, its surface wasted with countless fractures. The slash on his chest wept unattended, as did the shrapnel perforations in his side. His mouth was dry.

Too far. The champion was too far from the Abyss, had lost all possible connection to its life-sustaining power. For a while, the only remaining fire within him was an oath of vengeance, sworn to the Wicked Ones as he stumbled down the trail of stone steps, providing an obsession around which all other thoughts circled. Soon, even that had grown cold, and Kolra's mind dimmed as his blood continued to cool, eventually reduced to nothing more than the flagstone before him, the effort of the next step. He had known, once, that going south could not save him. Salvation was to the east. But he could no more cross the narrow range of hills than retrace the four hundred leagues that lay between here and Tragar. And so, bitter, stubborn, spent, he followed the old road.

There was a *whoom* of thrown metal – something coiled rapidly around Kolra's legs before biting into his calf. It pulled tight. Kolra fell.

Pain was sluggish, reaching awareness long after he'd crashed forward onto the flagstone. Kolra felt teeth dropping between broken lips as he rolled over, a spark of anger rousing his senses. The figure that stood over him was another shock entirely.

"Bolirm?" he croaked.

The orc's eyes widened in apparent surprise. One hand held the length of rope binding Kolra's legs, its slave-hook embedded in the demon's flesh, the other an axe. Blood stained Bolirm's hides, variously spattered from without or soaked through from hastily bound wounds. A dozen or so of the other ex-slaves stood around him. All were equally marred.

Kolra coughed with dry laughter. Somehow, these orcs had survived the humans' trap *and* the battle with shadow ones which evidently followed. Orod may have exhausted his usefulness, but there was no question Kolra had chosen well, that the krudger and his ilk were the toughest greenskins on the continent. Perhaps there was a chance for him to survive, as well.

"Bolirm... Krudger Bolirm..." Kolra drew a rasping breath, summoning the orcish tongue. "Listen to me carefully. My name is Kolra. I offer a pact. I can give you power... can make you the strongest orc in the world! The master of the greatest horde! All will know your name! In return, I need only for you to carry me east, take me back to Tragar... what do you say?"

"You're an Abyssal?"

"That's right!" He sat up haltingly, finally setting himself on protesting elbows. "Although not just any Abyssal – a Champion of the Fifth Circle! We do not make empty promises! Though I am weak now, if you carry me east, the Abyss will–"

"Arlok." It was not a question. Despite the darkness, Kolra understood the look on Bolirm's face, revealed by the moonlit sheens of furrowed features. Recognition. And fury.

"W-what?" Panic surged in Kolra's aching chest as the orc set one boot on his pelvis. "Stop! My name's not–!"

Kolra's world spun, swirls of silver and gray, lights racing across black. There was no pain. No anything. It might have been a relief, if not for the all consuming terror, the seared image of a battleaxe swooping toward him. His horns drummed on flagstone – the motion stopped.

"C'mon."

With cheek flat against road, Kolra felt as much as heard the *thumps* of orc boots passing, watched them appear around him and continue down the old road. Soon he could see the rest of them, their powerful shoulders, their stooped backs, their graceless strides. Darkness closed across his sight, stealing the world. Yet throughout those final seconds, the champion could still see the orcs, marching against the oblivion of his mind.

They did not look back.

16

...So concludes this diverting, if ultimately meaningless, aside.

Vespilo A., *On the Location and Identification of Primovantian Antiquity,* Appendix IX *'From the Gatekeepers' - The Mystery of Keatairn*

Xavire and Alea's mounts plodded side-by-side along the dirt road, having passed beyond Keatairn and its broken dam, finally reaching the graves. A simple monument had been erected at the center of the one-time grazing land, its earth remade to grant rest. They stopped.

"There's one thing I'm still not clear on," said Xavire. "Well, many things, in truth, but only one I wanted to ask about."

"And you've waited until now?"

"It seems I have."

"Then ask, by all means."

"In the chamber, the one with the gateway, and the... you know..."

"Abyssals."

"Right. Them. You said the gateway closed and the place began to fall apart – what happened next?"

"There isn't much to say. I escaped the way I came, below the chamber, and continued down until I reached the ruins."

"Where you found us."

"Yes."

He nodded. It was obvious, really. There wasn't much to say.

With reins in one hand, Xavire set his newly appropriated cap against the sun, taking a deep breath as he looked north along the valley. Though the calendar would doubtless mark winter as arrived, both the crisp air and the warm touch of the sunlight suggested a last gasp of autumnal temperance before the snows made their way south. Between the green and golden hues, the calm trickling of the river and streams, gentle slopes showed not the slightest hint of foreboding. Nor of memory. They were serene.

"So. Here we are again."

"Here we are again," agreed Xavire, turning his face to hers.

Alea was different. There was no escaping it. Her new robes, cobbled together from among the abandoned items of the town, couldn't hide her armor nearly so well as her last – although he supposed the fact he knew the armor was there played its part. Her face was bruised, lips scabbed. A vertical cut high on her left cheek was likely to scar, and the bags under her eyes told of scant sleep since the events of three days prior. And then there was the matter of her story, told only to Uslo, Cauhin, Sir Guilliver, and himself. A secret task, one where failure could prove unthinkable in consequence, burdened on the shoulders of a lone traveler. A huntress. The claimed ex-member of the Brotherhood was gone, and an agent of Shining Basilea revealed.

And yet, while the Claws recovered strength – dreamlessly in Xavire's case, much to his relief – Alea had worked without pause, tending the wounded with her skills, even while many looked on her Basilean garb with suspicion. More alone than ever, and despite her purpose being complete, she had nevertheless stayed until the southern men were fit to journey once more. For that, Xavire couldn't see her any other way. She was the same woman he'd come to know. Her hazel eyes, sharp and fierce, were the same.

"I expect you'll be getting a hero's welcome when you reach the Golden Horn," he said.

"Not likely."

"Why not? You fulfilled your task."

Alea leant forward, scratching behind the ears of her chestnut gelding, given to her by Uslo from among the leftover pole horses. "I did. But it is not the sort of task the Hegemon would wish generally known. Or known at all, in fact." She straightened up. "And besides, such a welcome… wouldn't be appropriate."

He followed her gaze. The graveyard's monument rose to head-height and was constructed from parts of the fencing which had once enclosed the field. It honored the names of more than those buried around it, for the creatures of the fog left little to bury, but Sergeant Eumenes was among the few so interned. With typical Sparthan grit, he'd kept his pikemen alive throughout the night, succumbing to his wounds on the morning of the next day. Not even Alea had been able to do anything for him.

Xavire turned back to find her looking at him, resignation plain on her oval face. "If anything, I expect my superiors will be inclined to censure me. I was entrusted with the Spear of Iustus, a weapon blessed centuries ago by Samacris, Mother of Phoenixes. Its loss will be keenly felt by my order."

"So don't return. Come with us."

Alea gave a small smile. "You mean join the Claws?"

"Well, yes. Not formally, perhaps. I doubt you'd have to put on the uniform."

She laughed. Then the resigned look returned. "Your comrades-in-arms won't be as forgiving, I think."

Xavire drew breath to respond, hesitated, and sighed through his nose. She wasn't wrong. "I suppose I can't blame them," he said finally.

"Nor should you. Nor can I. In any case, I wouldn't have accepted. We can't all run from our past, Xavire. There's always a reckoning. If mine is to be at the hands of my order, then I shall count myself fortunate." She closed her eyes, turning her face up into the sunlight.

Xavire looked across the rolling landscape. "Do you think they've gone far?" he asked.

"Waiting at the end of the valley, I expect. You know neither of them much liked being in Keatairn."

He nodded. "So you'll help the lad find his people before you go east."

"It's the least I can do."

"Nokrag can probably deliver him to them in one piece."

"Even so."

She opened her eyes, meeting his with a smile.

"You know," said Xavire, grinning awkwardly, "the lad said something to me as we bid our farewells. Something strange."

"Oh?"

Xavire nodded. "He said that when you told us what happened – with the gateway, with the Abyssals – he said he felt like he was there. Like he had *seen* pieces of what happened."

She raised an eyebrow. "How strange."

"Right. But that's not even the strangest thing. Because, you see, I knew *exactly* what he meant, because *I* felt it, too! It was as if I had watched it unfold!"

For a moment, Alea's smile broadened. Then it slowly fell away as her eyebrows drew together. She looked past him, head tilted in thought. "Very strange," she said finally.

"Do you think it means something?"

"I think..." Her eyes flicked back to his. "I think it means that I missed my calling."

"...Huh?"

"Clearly I possess the gifts of a bard." The smile was back.

Xavire stared at her dumbly. Then their laughter bubbled forth, perplexedly at first, quickly building to teary-eyed uproar, unconstrained even by the protests of bruised bodies. They stayed that way for near a minute, writhing in their saddles.

Disapproving, the horses shared a grunt.

*****

Above the east bank of the river Keata and in the shade of an adolescent poplar, Cauhin watched the parting of ways. Dust trailed Alea as she cantered up the dirt road on its far side; beyond, barely distinguishable against the town, Xavire was guiding his mount south toward its broken gate. Squinting after him, Cauhin found his hand resting on the sword at his belt, given to him that very morning. For the first of many times in the coming years of his life, the moment replayed in his mind.

"Go on. Take it."

Cauhin had shaken his head.

"I can't."

"So you'll learn."

"No, not that. I can't accept." He'd looked up, meeting the southerner's eyes through the strange lenses, glints of amber in wells of deep brown.

Xavire was smiling kindly.

"I helped trick you," said Cauhin. "Even after you saved my life at the pits. It's because of me you're out here. Because of me..." He'd looked away, eyes finding the distant graveyard and its monument.

Xavire followed his look. He said nothing for several moments. Quiet held them, disturbed only by the rumble of Nokrag and Dargent's nearby conversation.

"Listen to me, Cauhin," said Xavire finally. His expression was serious. "You did what you had to do. You saved yourself and your people. I mourn my men – my brothers – but we didn't come here for noble reasons. There's only one name carved on there who did. In any case, there'd be a lot more graves if you hadn't returned to warn us. Or none at all, for that matter."

Stepping forward, Xavire had passed the belted blade around Cauhin's waist and secured its buckle.

"Take it. Look after yourself. And if you find something you love, fight for it." Then Xavire had put his hand on Cauhin's shoulder, smiling sadly. "This world asks no less, I'm afraid."

The question that burned in Cauhin's mind had finally reached his lips. "Xavire… do you remember when Alea was–"

There was a *crunch* of vegetation, rousing Cauhin from the memory. He looked round. Nokrag was standing up, stretching copious muscle. The *pops* of her joints were like breaking timber.

"Here comes the witch," she yawned. Downriver, Alea was guiding her horse across a rickety farm bridge.

"Don't call her that," said Cauhin.

Nokrag shrugged, the hint of a smile on her lips. She began to gather her gear, slinging the twin weapons across her back. "So long as she doesn't slow me down."

"Any more than I do, you mean."

The ogre gave a low chortle. Cauhin smiled.

Alea drew up not long after, nodding to them both in greeting. She opened her mouth to speak.

"We go," said Nokrag bluntly, before striding away along the path.

Alea's eyebrows rose, but she nodded.

"It gets too narrow further up," said Cauhin. "For riding, I mean."

"Yes, I remember. May as well start walking now."

She dismounted and they set off after the ogre, Alea leading the horse behind her. For a while, they were silent, following the trail as it diverged from the river to head up across the arduous slopes of the Ballamor Hills. It wasn't until they reached the first crest that one of them spoke. Cauhin felt her hand on his shoulder.

"Is that Xavire's sword?"

"It is. He gave it to me." Cauhin had been holding the handle as he walked, the metal ball at its end warm from his thumb.

"I see. We are going to be traveling together for some time. I can teach you a little of its use, if you'd like?"

Cauhin kept his gaze locked on Nokrag, watching the ogre forge ahead along the next ridge. He wanted to be angry. For the lies, for the deaths, whether of Claws or Plainsmen. Anger would have made things simpler. But he couldn't. The Cauhin of three days ago could have felt so, but not now, and not just because of his own responsibility in matters. Something had happened in Keatairn, something he didn't fully understand. He felt as though he'd seen a world greater than himself. As though he'd glimpsed something as unthinkable as a floating city, and, unlike his disappointment at the sea, had found his wonder grow far beyond its previous bounds. Just the idea that Alea was part of that glimpsed world was enough – he no longer had room for selfish anger.

"I would," he said, turning to smile up at her. "Thank you, Lady Alea."

"Good." Alea hesitated. "I wanted to say that… that I was sorry to hear about Riuen."

"He was a good man. I owe him my life."

"You are not burdened with his death, Cauhin."

Cauhin shook his head. "Oh, I am. But don't worry. He carried me through the underground. It's the least I can do."

They set off along the descending trail.

"I think I've realized we're all burdened with something. We all have debts, and most of them we'll never be able to pay. We just have to do what we can, for who we can."

Alea said nothing, and Cauhin felt a twinge of self-consciousness. Glancing back, he saw the easterner was smiling. She looked amused. His face went hot.

"What?"

"You will be a wise elder, Cauhin, son of Hunlo."

"Pfft!"

"Come, slow humans!" called Nokrag. "Always you take such tiny steps!"

Cheeks burning on either side of a broad grin, Cauhin continued a steady descent. They were making good progress. He'd be back on the Plains before long.

*****

The Claws passed one more day and one more night among the Ballamor Hills. They journeyed back the way they'd come, taking the flagstone road south as far as it ran before following their own beaten track through thicket and dell. With fewer wagons in tow, they covered ground quickly, the remaining pole horses allowing one hundred and sixty-one men to take turns in the saddle. From the north, the cold winds spilled over them like a flood; and when they emerged mid-morning of the second day upon open plain, it was to behold the sky reflected in a sea of frosted grassland, shimmering like the corals of the Vieshan Gulf.

Uslo guided Volonto away from the men, a gloved hand shading his eyes as he looked across the panorama. The soft *crunch* of rime surrounded each of the palomino's steps, their rhythm like the creaking of a ship on the ocean swell, all while the air seemed to hint at some saline remnant, perhaps carried from the Straits of Von Terel across the wall of hills at his back. If Uslo were to have closed his eyes, he might almost have imagined himself on the waves once more, might almost have felt the familiar sway beneath him. He might have pictured Geneza rising over the waters and, for a moment, his heart might have lightened. But his eyes remained open, set upon the fiery clouds of the eastern horizon. His heart remained heavy.

The conflict between broken gods, which often seemed so distant in the West, had snared them. Without knowing it, they and the Plainsmen had been a shield in a hidden battle, ultimately aiding a victory of light over shadow and Abyssal fire. A weeping sore on the land had been stemmed, a still-worse wound averted. His men were the price. It was in all ways an incredible story, never to be told.

Pain gnawed dully at the joints in his leg. Lowering hand and gaze, Uslo massaged his knee. The orc warlord had truly done a number on it. Alea had helped it heal. He could walk straight, but he doubted he'd ever be rid of its reminder. Perhaps it was just as well.

And what of Keatairn and its treasures? In the end, it seemed that story had been the same as always. The bones of ages past were picked over by those who came after, their spoils claimed while their memory was left to rot. The Claws were simply the latest lot of scavengers, too late to the corpse. In a way Uslo knew to be selfish, he was glad they had been used by Alea. Though his intentions gave him no right, he was glad to have been part of something greater.

Uslo glanced back to look along the column of mounted men and wagons, the last of which were at that moment being rolled onto the plain. Howitzer and supplies aside, the Claws had managed to fill them with the few objects of value left in the abandoned town. They would trade along the way to Letharac in the east, where they would no doubt find a buyer for the cannon. Its auction would prove sufficient to restore their equipment and patch themselves for whatever came next.

Three figures approached on horseback from among the men. Uslo turned east once more and smiled as the jocular voice of one broke across the background hum.

"...a few dozen more, and the Claws could be a fully-mounted company! The cannon would more than cover it! What say you, Xavire? It'll be a challenge, but I believe I can teach you to handle a charging warhorse!"

"While I agree that riding beats walking any day of the week, I'll leave the charging to you, Sir Guilliver, just as I leave archery to the sergeant."

"With all due respect, sir," injected Peris smartly, "I think we could all stand to learn something from you there. Why, using an ogre crossbow to split a chain in the dark certainly qualifies–"

"Now look here! If I've said it once, I've said it a hundred times already – I was aiming for the orc's head!"

Uslo tightened his lips, mustache twitching as he held back a laugh. He wheeled Volonto around to meet the men. They sat up straight, expressions comported beneath their salute.

"At ease. What's the word, Xavire?"

"The last wagon is clear of the hills, sir. Ready to march on your command."

Uslo nodded, eyes turning to Sir Guilliver. "The adventurers?"

"Ready to venture forth, as always, General."

"And what about the rest of the men, Sergeant? How fares the mood?"

Peris hesitated. "Permission to speak freely, sir?"

"Of course."

"They're bruised. They took a beating without much to show. They… we lost brothers. I know you can't tell us anything more than you have about what happened here, and we believe you when you say it was important. But the fact is, with the mood as it is right now, we should be prepared for more than a few to resign once we reach Letharac."

Uslo nodded again, slower this time. He had sensed as much.

"But you have a recommendation, Sergeant."

"Yes, sir. We raise the standard."

"Unfortunately, I'm not sure that would be wise," said Xavire. "Lord Darvled's forces are likely on the lookout for us. The standard will be another sight to stick in the memory of anyone we pass."

"It's not without risk, sirs, I'll grant," said Peris, "but whatever that risk, I recommend it the same. I don't care if we are outlaws, we shouldn't be skulking our way east like them. We're the Claws. We should march with our heads high, Dargent's Claws on the Plain."

There was a moment of quiet.

"I agree with the sergeant," said Xavire, finally.

"As do I," said Sir Guilliver. His smile was broad.

Uslo ran thumb and forefinger across his mustache. Then he met their eyes one-by-one and marveled at how little he deserved the loyalty of such men. How he loved them for it.

"Raise the standard, Xavire."

And so it was that for the first time since crossing Darvled's Wall, the colors were set to soar, Silver Cat flying rampant on cardinal red. The sun continued its rise over a winter plain. The Claws marched on.

Epilogue

Orod lay in darkness, and the darkness lay across him. Body broken, his hold on the world had neither root nor form, suspended within fathomless black. There was no flickering promise of oblivion, no empty relief for his mind. Not this time. This time, there was only a crushing dark, one that seemed to press painfully on all sides, clenching him like a fist. The rattles of his breaths counted toward eternity. They assailed him.

Centuries in minutes, epochs in hours – a void. It appeared at great distance, small, skimming the brimful dark.

And it had a voice. Many voices.

...broke it... sealed it... huntress.... couldn't see... never escape...

Beneath a shadow mass, the drowning orc sensed his chance. He began to struggle, leveraging knotted rage against insensible walls. The darkness shook, ripples running out along its breadth. But the broken Orod was no match for its prison. It held him fast.

The void stopped, its chatter cut short. It considered him. Orod glared back, impotence and fury.

It moved closer.

Dreamer?

All at once, myriad sensations spilled through the orc's mind – Orod naked on the plain, his skin slick with blood, his name roared in a thousand throats. The burning hills before him. In violation were his dreams drawn forth, pulled hungrily into the void.

Power...

The void seemed to purr, coming still closer. Beyond the crush of darkness, Orod felt it reach toward him.

There is power... a powerful will... it can be ours...

It came within reach. Rage flaring in the dark, Orod leapt for it – oblivion snatched him in its claws.

Deep in the forgotten places beneath Ardovikia, the sound of rattling breaths died out, and a thing that was not Orod rose to its feet.

THE END

About the Author

Born in Aberdeen, 1989, James Dunbar grew up in Scotland's historic Royal Deeside, homeland of the ancient Picts whose ruins and stone circles can still be found among the straths, lochs, burns and glens. It was in this world of Druidic scenery that the young James first opened a worn copy of The Hobbit, and he has been an avid reader of fantasy ever since. He attended the University of Aberdeen, where he earned a Master of Arts First Class in Hispanic and Latin American Studies, as well as the Pamela Bacarisse Prize for his final thesis. His passion for learning languages has seen him live in Mexico and Italy, with decidedly mixed success. He contributed to the co-authored *Nature's Knight*, his first published work. *Claws on the Plain* is his first novel.